Oliver Heywood, J. Horsfall (Joseph Horsfall) Turner

The Rev. Oliver Heywood, B.A., 1630-1702

His Autobiography, Diaries, Anecdote and Event Books - Vol. III

Oliver Heywood, J. Horsfall (Joseph Horsfall) Turner

The Rev. Oliver Heywood, B.A., 1630-1702
His Autobiography, Diaries, Anecdote and Event Books - Vol. III

ISBN/EAN: 9783337121693

Printed in Europe, USA, Canada, Australia, Japan

Cover: Foto ©Raphael Reischuk / pixelio.de

More available books at **www.hansebooks.com**

THE

Rev. Oliver Heywood, B.A.,

1630—1702;

His Autobiography, Diaries, Anecdote
and Event Books;

ILLUSTRATING THE GENERAL AND FAMILY HISTORY OF YORKSHIRE
AND LANCASHIRE.

In Four (previously stated Three) Volumes,

with Illustrations.

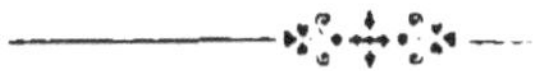

EDITED BY J. HORSFALL TURNER.

VOL. III.

Printed for the Editor.

BINGLEY:

T. HARRISON, PRINTER, BOOKBINDER, PUBLISHER, ETC., QUEEN STREET.
MDCCCLXXXIII.

To the Reader.

———⁘———

THIS Volume is respectfully inscribed to the many Admirers of the worthy Oliver Heywood, but especially to the comparatively few Subscribers to the publication of his MSS. It will be seen there is an alteration of the word *Three* on the Title-page, as, thanks to the generous owners of Mr. Heywood's original MSS., matter sufficient for a Fourth Volume is to hand. This consists of the Diary and Anecdotes of his last years. It would have been a graceful act to dedicate this Volume to the descendants of Nathaniel Heywood, but they have probably forgotten his relationship to good Oliver.

Idel, Bradford,

     Oct. 1883.

CONTENTS:

ILLUSTRATIONS:

₊ I thankfully acknowledge my obligations to S. Roberts, Esq., M.A.. F.R.S., for the loan of these MSS.; (*a*) concluded from Vol. I., (*b*) are completed in this Vol.; and to Mr. Adshead owner of MS. (*c*.)

July 18 89

These are to certify that Oliver Heywood of Northowram clark
county of york his own houce ni Northowram to assemble
cloth mater choyce of his own houce ni Northowram to assemble
ni for the service of god according as is allowed by a late Stot
of Parlt made in the first year of the reign of King
William and queen Mary entitled an Act for exempting
their Majestys dissenting subjects from certain penal laws

Oliver Heywood

Heywood's MSS.

Dr. Fawcett, when he wrote the "Life of O. Heywood," possessed only two volumes of Mr. Heywood's manuscripts. These became the property of the Rev. Dr. Raffles, of Liverpool, whose son, T. Stamford Raffles, Esq., Stipendiary Magistrate, now has them, as also the letter to Mr. Jolly, see facsimile in *Nonconformist Register*. The two volumes will be found printed in my Second Volume, pages 17—123, and the letter will be printed in the Fourth Volume.

Dr. Fawcett, who was the Baptist Minister at Hebden Bridge, contemplated at one time an enlarged edition, but advancing age induced him to encourage the Rev. Richard Slate, a Congregational Minister in Lancashire, to follow up the design. Mr. Slate had, as I gather from a memorandum in his own writing, twenty-two volumes, eighteen of which had been lent by Miss Heywood, of Mansfield, two by the Rev. Richard Astley, then of Halifax, one by the Rev. Dr. Fawcett, and the other by the Rev. Dr. Raffles. From these, and the Northowram Register, or rather extracts from it by the Rev. Dr. Ryland, Bristol, and the Heywood Genealogical Table compiled by the Rev. Joseph Hunter, Bath, Mr. Slate composed the well-known " Memoirs of the Rev. Oliver Heywood, B.A.," which, besides being published separately, forms the First Volume of the Rev. W. Vint's "Whole Works of the Rev. Oliver Heywood, B.A.," printed at Idle by John Vint, the Editor's son, in 1827.

Mr. Slate's List of MSS. is as follows :—

(*a*) A RELATION of the most considerable passages of his Life from infancy to nearly forty.

(*b*) SOLILOQUIES on various occurrences of his life and the state of his mind, from May 1653 to June 1682.

(*c*) COVENANTS occasional and annual, from Feb. 1673 to 1680.

(*d*) COVENANTS from June 1685 to February 1702.

(*e*) RETURNS OF PRAYER, from Jan. 1672 to 1677.

(*f*) Returns of Prayer, from 1682 to 1702.

(*g*) Self-Reflections, from November 1677 to 1700.

(*h*) Experiences with Reflections, Feb. 1680 to 1702.

(*i*) Diary, from its commencement in 1666 to 1673.

(*j*) Diary, from July 1677 to May 1680.

(*k*) Diary, from May 1682 to July 1686.

(*l*) Diary, from March 1695 to June 1699.

(*m*) Diary, from October 1699 to 1702, within five days of his decease.

(*n*) Particulars respecting Coley, collected by O. Heywood.

(*o*) Private Record of the Members of the Church at Northowram, with the Church Covenant, &c.

(*p*) The Heywood Family. Containing the Lives of Mr. Heywood's ancestors and pious relatives, written by himself. In this interesting Volume, the history of the Family is continued to the present day by surviving relatives.

Thus of the twenty-two volumes Mr. Slate received, he only describes thirteen; the remainder, I presume, were textual or other note books. The list seems to number sixteen but I find that (*a*) and (*i*) are in one book, (*d*) and (*f*) are in another book, and (*c*) and (*e*) form but a third. This volume [(*c*) and (*e*),] he obtained from Mr. Astley, as also (*p*); (*j*) he got from Dr. Fawcett; (*o*) from Dr. Raffles; the rest from Miss Heywood.

Some fragments of Mr. Heywood's writing passed from Mr. Slate to Mr. Adshead, now of Pendleton, and Mrs. Standen, Mr. Slate's daughter, has sent me such 'copy' as is preserved, which was used in her father's "Memoirs of Heywood."

The Rev. Joseph Hunter, Unitarian Minister, so far back as 1819, took extracts from these manuscripts, but did not publish his "Rise of the Old Dissent, exemplified in the Life of Oliver Heywood, one of the Founders of the Presbyterian Congregations in the County of York," until 1842. Mr.

Heywood's crabbed hand-writing, (which had been past Dr. Fawcett's powers of transcribing, as I have shown in another place, and which errors are copied by Mr. Slate,) finds in the accomplished antiquary accurate decipherment. Mr. Heywood wrote, he says, "in very diminutive volumes, in lines exceedingly close, and in penmanship small, but not indistinct." Notwithstanding this statement I have found few people able to read the Diaries which are in the smallest style of writing, but not so small as Charlotte Brontë's. Mr. Hunter occupies five pages of his " Preface " in describing these manuscripts. " The Diary commences with the 24th of March, 1666; a memorable day, being that on which he was driven from his home by the operation of one of the severe laws by which it was vainly hoped that the spirits of the Non-Conformists might be subdued." [The Five-Mile Act.]

It appears from Mr. Hunter's List of the DIARIES that between 1819 and the next half-dozen years, when Mr. Slate wrote, that a part of the last diary had been torn from its binding. The Diaries (*i*), (*j*), and (*k*) as given by Mr. Slate are so given by Mr. Hunter, but (*l*) and (*m*) are given by Mr. Hunter as one volume,—" March 1, 1695, to April 29, 1702, five days before his decease." On looking at volume (*m*), now before me, it seems certain that the first half of the book has been lost or torn out. Mr. Hunter gives several extracts from this lost portion, but Mr. Slate has very little, if anything, from it. Mr. Hunter's list next gives, A RELATION, (see (*a*) of Mr. Slate's List,) written in 1661, with notes written between 1661 and 1666, when the Diary commences. This " Relation " I have entitled " Autobiography," see Vol. I., 133—222. We have further in Mr. Hunter's List (besides 1—4, Diaries, 5, Relation) :—

(6) " Solemn Covenants, Temptations, Experiences, Returns of Prayer, Remarkable Providences." I think this will be the same as Mr. Slate's (*d*). It will be found in my Volumes I. and III. under the title EVENT BOOK.

(7) Solemn Covenants, with Reviews, year by year, of many of the later years of his life." This I take to be the same as printed in Vol. III., pp. 214—285.

(20) " Twenty ' Meditations upon the doleful Bartholo-

mew Day Act, and the effects thereof in silencing so many thousand Ministers in these three Nations'."

This volume I have not discovered, nor SOLILOQUIES, (b), which Mr. Slate quotes largely from, but which Mr. Hunter regrets he had not seen.

(9) "Biographical Accounts" of Mr. Heywood's Father, Mother, Brother, First Wife, Father-in-Law, Mother-in-Law. Of these, the lives of Mr. Angier and of Mr. Nathaniel Heywood were printed during his life. Of the less remarkable members of the family he has left a beautiful and affecting memorial, which opens with the words— 'When I was sitting in mine own house, on Lord's day night, Sept. 22, 1678, musing upon mine own death, and thinking on those thousands of blessed souls that have broken the ice, * * * * many of my godly relations that died in the Lord came fresh into my thoughts, and I at last resolved to make a catalogue of them'. These two volumes are now bound in one, and will be found printed in Vol. I., pp. 17—104, under the heading HEYWOOD FAMILY. Slate's List, (p).

(10) "A History of the Chapelry of Coley." I very much deplore the loss of this manuscript, and hope it may still be traced. It is the same as Mr. Slate's *Particulars respecting Coley.* (n)

(11) "A particular Account of his own Congregation at Northowram." This is either the same as Mr. Slate's *Private Record* (o) see my second volume, pp. 17—37, or a volume only known by extracts made by Mr. Hunter, which gives biographical notices of many Halifax families. (Hunter's MSS., Brit. Museum.)

(12) Account of the Ordinations of Ministers by himself and others." If this means a separate book, I have not met with it, but I think it refers to accounts in the same book as the Autobiography.

(13) "Account of the Meetings of Ministers in the West Riding from 1691, their commencement, to the time of his death." I have not seen this in any form.

(14) "A very copious Register of Births, Marriages and Deaths" for Yorkshire and Lancashire, a volume 'extremely

useful to persons engaged in genealogical inquiries.' This is the same as printed in Vol. II., pp. 129—236. Mr. Heywood has another volume which answers this description of Mr. Hunter's,—the *Coley, or Northowram, or Non-conformist Register.*

Mr. Dickenson, his successor at Northowram, continued this remarkable Register for forty years, and numerous entries are copied from Heywood's Private Register or 'Vellum Book,' as he called it, into this public Register. Thus, the *Non-conformist Register* and Vol. II., pp. 129—236, of the Diaries, should be read together.

(15) "Experiments with Reflections, and Objects and Observations." See (*h*) of Mr. Slate's List, and Vol. III., p. 303 of my edition. The second half will be printed in Vol. IV.

(16) Letters, see Thoresby's Correspondence, edited by Hunter.

Thoresby's Extracts from a lost volume of Mr. Heywood's, in the Birch MSS., British Museum.

Mr. Hunter obtained the MSS. from the same sources as Mr. Slate, except that Dr. Raffles had acquired Dr. Fawcett's portion of the Diary.

The manuscripts as I have received them are as follow :—

(1) The Non-conformist, or Northowram Register, which forms a volume of itself. Comparatively there is not much of Mr. Heywood's writing in this volume, but some one (Mr. Dickenson, I think,) has copied largely out of Mr. Heywood's private Vellum Book Register into it. This Register was continued by Mr. Dickenson for forty years.

In Vol. I. of the DIARIES, as printed by me, will be found

(2) Pedigree of the Heywood Family, from the time of Edward VI., with notices of the Rotherhams and Shaws, written by the Rev. Joseph Hunter, our celebrated South Yorkshire antiquary. [pp. 3—16.]

(3) Heywood Family, two volumes bound in one, in the

Rev. O. Heywood's writing, with notes by Messrs. Eliezer and Samuel Heywood. [17—104.]

(4)   Genealogy of Richard Heywood's family, a sheet by Rev. O. H. [105—9.]

(5)   Pedigrees of Heywood and Wylde by Joseph Hunter. [110—124.]

(6)   Genealogical Memoranda by Samuel Heywood, in fragments. [125—128.]

(7)   Nathaniel Heywood's Presentation to Ormskirk. [p. 129.]

(8)   Rev. O. Heywood's License to Preach, 1672 [p. 129.]

(9)   Poem. [130—1.]

(10)   Love Letter [131—2.]

(11)   Autobiography, with Memoranda, Anagram, and Observations. [133—222.]

(12)   Diary, 1666 to 1673, as printed pages 223 to 304, Vol. I., and Memoranda, as printed pages 17 to 103, Vol. III., and Library Catalogue, pages 123—8, Vol. II.

(13)   Event Book, as printed pages 305 to 362, Vol. I., and pages 103 to 213, Vol. III.

In Vol. II., in addition to six pages of Bibliography, are

(14)   Mr. Frankland's Scholars. [pp. 9—16.]

(15)   Northowram Members, and Memoranda in a later hand. [17—37].

(16)   Diary, 1677 to 1680. [38—123.]

(17)   "Vellum" Book, Notes to Northowram Register, and Memoranda. [129—236.]

"Rawson" Volume, 1678—82, a Series of Anecdotes and Events. [237—303.]

(19)   Scriptural Fast.   [304—350.]

In Volume III., in addition to this sketch on the MSS., are the conclusions of the two MS. books mentioned above, 11 and 12, and also

(20)   Solemn Covenants and Reflections. [214—302.]

[21]   Experiments with Reflections. [303—3.]   The other half of this MS. volume bears the title—Objects with Observations, and will form a part of Vol. IV.

(22)   Directions how to read the Bible in a year.

For Volume IV. I have ready " Objects with Observations," mentioned above. " Remarkable Returns of Prayer and the last volume of the Diaries, with several fragmentary sieces, letters, and notes.

I am still hoping to find the following, to me, lost volumes :—

(1) Diary, 1682—1686.

(2) Diary, 1695—1699.   'The portions of the Diary from Nov. 1673 to July 1677, May 1680 to May 1682, August 1686 to March 1695, are, I fear, irretrievably lost, as Mr. Hunter, in his day, made diligent inquiry.]

(3) Particulars respecting Coley.

(4) Soliloquies, known to Mr. Slate, but unseen by Mr. Hunter.

(5) Covenants, occasional and annual 1673—80.

(6) Twenty Meditations on Bartholomew Day Act.

(7) Private Record, partly transcribed by Mr. Hunter.

(8) Ordinations, if a separate book ever existed.

(9) Meetings of Ministers.

That others have been equally anxious for the preservation, if not the publication of these manuscripts, is apparent from the following copy of a letter from the Rev. Joseph Hunter addressed to Mr. James Everett, Market Place, Sheffield.

Bath, April 11th, 1825.

Dear Sir,

   I am ashamed that your letter of the 21 Feb. has remained so long unanswered. The truth has been that it lay under a heap of papers, and for a time escaped my recollection.

The Volumes which it appears Mr. Vicar [? Vint] has received from Mr. Slate are those which were for some time in my possession. I have no other M.S. of Mr. Heywoods. It is a curious question, which I am afraid no one can answer, how the intermediate volumes became seperated from the rest of the Diary, and into whose hands they fell. It would be more to the purpose if those who are interested in the life and labours of this most assidious Christian Minister to ascertain where they now are [if in existence], and I should be happy if it were in my power to afford Mr. Vint any assistance in his enquiries after them.

The Volume in the possession of Mr. Parsons is probably one which was once in the library of Thoresby, the historian of Leeds—See Duc. Leod. p 542, old Edition.

I rejoice to hear that your Second Volume is proceeding at the Press. Such works are truly valuable. They must be gratifying to readers of the present day, and what is more, useful and edifying to them : and they will relieve future enquirers from some embarrassment and uncertainty, when time has given to the subject of your pages something of historical interest and importance.

Believe me, dear Sir,

Very faithfully

JOSEPH HUNTER.

Mr. Roberts has the original MS. of *Youth's Monitor* which will be found in Mr. Vint's edition of the Works; also *Itinerarium Totius Sacra Scriptura* or some short notes collected out of the writings of Henry Bunting, Cambridge, written by Ol: Heywood and is to be found in his study in Trin. Coll. 1649. Another MS. of 41 pages, small quarto, dated May, 1649, is entitled " A Resolution of Certaine Questions and Cases of Conscience that these present times doe occasion.

1 Question. Whether when usurpers are in full possession, &c., &c." These are mainly political queries, and I question whether Mr. Heywood was anything more than the owner. This also belongs to Mr. Roberts.

The only fragment I possess of Mr. Heywood's writing, carefully treasured for several years, is the 1689 application for license. p. 8.

Memoranda.*

[*These notes are in the "Little Black Book with Two Clasps" from which the Diary, as printed in Vol. I., pages 223-304, is taken. The book bears the autograph signature of R. Astley, and, in Mr. Heywood's writing, "Ex libris Oliveri Heywood, cujus pretium apud Halifaxiam fuit. 9d. 1664." "I was admitted in trinity Coll. Camb. july 9, 1647."]

The Catalogue of Mr. Heywood's Books, as given in Vol. ii., p. 123, from the *Congregational Magazine*, was copied from this MS., but needs the following corrections:—

Marlorate on N. T.   -   -   -   li 01 00s. 00d
Prideaux fasciculus controv.   00 03   00
Venning's Mysteries
Weems.   *Mr. Harpur hath it.*
Burgerdicius
Gataker's Tetragram

After "Sharpius his symphonia,"—"*these of Mr. Johnsons books.*"

After "God's terrible voyce"—*bought of Mr. Smallwood.*

Bartlets practical christian.   00. 01. 08.

A ream of paper from Mr. Parkhurst cost 06s. 04d. feb. 12, 167¾

[Property.]			
Rothwel ground	04li	10s.	00
Scolecroft	02	06	08
Mason grounds	01	16	00
Leadbetter	00	10	04
Will Hulton	00	08	00
Abrah. Hulme	00	16	00

Membra radicalia	sunt	Jecur		Vitales	Venas
		cor	in quibus	naturales	per artas
		cerebrum	sunt spiritus	animales	nervos

Ep. for W.W.
To Christ I liv'd, in Christ I dye
And now live to eternity:
Earth was my short, this grave is my long home
Heaven is my best, blest, last and largest roome.

> Godly, grave, wise, knowing, and studious
> His soul, with God, his corps lodg homely thus
> Christ is the way, the walk is love,
> A rest is here, the rest above.

A few pages follow, of extracts from various classical and divinity authors, including Clark's " Lives."
One page gives a copy of

> The Warrant, by virtue wherof Mr. Hardcastle was taken at Shadwel with 24 more, he for preaching, they for hearing.

To al Bailiffs, Constables. [This will be found in Slates' *Life*.]

November 5, 1664

I am much afraid some remarkable Land-destroying judgment is ready to fall upon this my poore natiue country, whether it may be sword, famine or pestilence, I am not worthy to know, or al those, tho I am much afraid of the sword of a forreigne enemy, the grounds of my fear are these :

1 judgment is begun at the house of god ! who knows not the fearful desolations of many famous and flourishing congregations ! the sad silencing of many hundreds of precious ministers. Surely tho judgment begin there, yet it ends not there as Scripture and experience testify :

2 the ignorance and prophanes of many thrust into public work; the abominations of Hophni and phinehas are prognosticks of approaching judgmts : oh the swearing, drunkenes, uncleannes of those that bear the ark and vessels of the lord : who sees not ? oh the fruit of it !

3 the lords withdrawing from the ordinances : where any are dispensed according to institution, or by tollerable and sober conformists alas what good is done ? where are any souls converted ? how many edifyed ? wicked men are hardened, saints offended, troubled.

4 gods leaving governours in their councels, they act not wisely, their councels infatuated, young mens councel taken, people generally unsatisfyed exasperated, actings agt themselves as in Rehoboams case : undertaking warres on slight grounds, carnal confidence.

5 the national sins openly acted by governours: disowning the cause of god, casting off Christs interest and government: building again what was destroyed: covenant breaking, making snares for tender consciences: want of execution of justice punishing sin, incouraging piety, nay daunting it: for Manassehs sins was judah ruined:

6 the various strange inventions to squeeze money from subjects, pole-money, benevolences, sesments, subsidys, hearth-money, and now scarching for hearths, concealments, fines, to feed covetous humours of subjects, wch is the most horrible oppression that ever this nation groaned under, it makes wise men almost mad:

7 the woeful abuse of this present plenty, its conceited to proceed from the institution of prelacy, and ceremonye, and gods approbation thereof, as tho god were the patron of superstition: and accordingly its used, oh what riotting, rebelling, gluttony, drunkenes, abominable impudent beastly luxury, lechery, scarce heard of among heathen.

8 lamentable breaches, dissentions in familys, neighbourhood, congregations, civil, religious, oh what railings, barbarous revilings betwixt parents and children, fetching warrants, running for citations, miscalling, and cursing one another threatening with prisons, house of correction, bidding defiance one to another and al to heaven.

9 Sabbath-breaking, no Sermons in some places in afternoones, leaving loose people to liberty of recreations, or worldly occasions, sitting at home loytering, walking to see cattel, visit neighbours sit in ale houses togather, and good people doe not sanctify Sabbath as they ought, but if they stay at home they read historys, bookes, doe too much their pleasures on this holy day:

10 general security, settling ourselves as tho those things would last for ever, how many mind their trade inordinately, even professors run mad upon the world, are building, planting settling themselves, what abundance of mariages. I have heard of 16 couples publisht at a parish church on one day:—just so as in Noahs days:

11 Strait-hartednes in the best to publick good, al mind their owne, they heed not whether the church sink or swim, few are grieved for the afflictions of Joseph: contribute to the necessitys of Saints, exigencys of ministers, their old

ministrs are dead and forgotten in most places, and many of them, not one amongst ten will own them.

12 pride, vanity, expensive prodigality about themselves, nothing costly enough for their own backes, belleys, anything too much for chts poor ministers and members, theres more disciples for pastry, work for taylours, slaughtering of cattel than ever was known in the memory of man, 100 beasts killed in Halifax yesterday, infinit numbers besides in the country:

13 general complyance with the times, falling in with superstitious worship, willing walking after rulers command-mt, and this not so much out of conviction of lawfulnes, but carnal security, loathnes to be troubled, slavish fear, most wil doe any thing rather than suffer any thing, tho not satisfyed in what they doe:

14 Restraining of Season Spirit of prayer, tho we cannot according to law meet above 4 without great hazard, (wch people sit down wel content with) yet good people wil not meet in that number, when a meeting is appointed, we are fearfully disappointed, so that now we seem to be discouraged, and neglect private meetings:

15 Alas, the wonted spirit of prayer is gone, in most places in publick theres but an empty formality, and in private theres not such mighty wrestlings with god as I have seen in my time. Religion seems almost dead and gasping for breath most have lost their first loue, especially the spirit of prayer is gone: I see it, and feel it:

16 Some choyce and eminent persons are dead lately, both ministers and private christians, who are taken from the evil to come, these were banks and bulwarkes that kept off vengeance. oh what shall now become of us, when our Ramparts are gone, they that stood in the breach are removed, and these aliue let him alone that his wrath may break out:

17 Strange prodigyes have appeared these late years in the aire, earth, water, in al creatures, monstrous births, strange unheard of accidents, tho every thing in those bookes of prodigys be not to be believed, yet some things are most ceartainly true, wch are very strange, contrary to the course of nature, and betoken strange judgmts:

18 base effeminatenes of people yeelding to any thing for a little present ease, the wonted manliness, courage and

vigour of peoples spirits is taken away they are like Issachars
asse stooping under al burdens, yeeld to any termes: I
abhorre thoughts of rebellion, but tho the country be woe-
fully abused by fellow-subjects unheard of oppression, yet
none questions by what authority money is demanded, when
men are as women we are near ruine: Nah 3 13

19 the spite and spirit of hatred thats vented agt the
power of godlines and professors of it, the very name of
religion is become odious amongst some there is a persecut-
ing spirit abroad, they could wish the people of god rid out
of the world, and out of their way, that they may be quiet in
sinning: nor is this agt the non-conformists but theres as
great a malice agt pious conformists under the notion of
fanaticks and puritans, oh what fresh and fearful instances
have we:

20 tho none dare lay out themselves or part of their
estates by vindicating the liberty of the subjects yet there is
great speaking agt these unjust exactions, yea groundless
and sinful reproachings of the supreme magistrates, and
furious expressions of indignation against them, men are
mad in their rebellious speeches, and manifest so much
discontent and prejudice that most seem as tho they could
make the dutch welcome to bring down our present governours, and many are saying they think a forreigner cannot be
greater oppressor, tho alas theyl find it otherwise—

I look upon this dutch warre as very ominous, Lord have
mercy upon poore England—oh the dreadful pestilence in
London—8252 dye in a week this year 1665

London fired, almost consumed to ashes Sept. 1 1666.

this day, June 14 67 I have a strange experiment, I have
been 4 or 5 times dealing with that text in Heb 12 4 concerning suffering to blood, and I can make little of it, it
doth not prosper in my hands, but this day I have begun
with ps 65 5 about gods terrible answers to prayer, and I
am strongly assisted, wonderfully doe things come into my
mind in writing yt I never thought of, so that I have made
an unusual progress therein.

November 23 1669

Reasons why I frequently keep at home and preach upon
Lords days, tho not constantly—Not that I despise the

publick ordinances or cannot hear Sermons by conformists, but

1 Because god hath given me a call to preach, and in my ordination I solemnly promised before many witnesses to continue in my duty against all trouble and persecution, and I dare not play fast and loose with god and my conscience, but if men cast me out of publick, I ought to doe my work more privately—though I would study to doe it as prudently as the Lord helps me:

2 Because I had an observable call to preach at Coley, indeed god spake to me by strong hand, when he sent me hither, for by my good will I would not have come hither, and continued me here almost 20 yeares, he hath blessed my poor labours here, struck a speciall relation betwixt me and many of them which no power or force of man can dissolue—

3 Because there are some who cannot be satisfyed to hear in publick, though I have used several meanes for their satisfaction, and they will spend their time in private, and are in danger either to mispend time, or to be seduced to ways of errour, since Satan and his instrmts are busy to draw away unstable soules from the good ways of god.

4 Because the spiritual court (as they call it) did excommunicate me, after wch Doctor Hook sent to me to desire me to forbear coming to church and Nathan Whitley would have put me out of Coley chappel, after which I judged god called me to improve my time in private, which I had no thoughts of, till I was persecuted and driven out by mens violence—

5 Because god hath exceedingly satisfyed, quickened assisted my spirit in private, for severall yeares togather I spent the Sabbath with about 10 or 12 persons, and oh what a time of love was that! I never met with so much of gods presence in all my life, many a time have I thankt god for that occasion of with-drawing god did me good agt my will—

6 god hath made some use of me to doe good to others, he hath helpt me by this practice to lay out my poor talent for the good of soules, and hath not altogather withdrawn his blessing from my poor endeavours, and if I be an instrument to gain one soul to god I haue part of my

reward: this is my main study and design, tho dead to make soules liue.

7 There is great need of all god's harvest-men to be at work, for the harvest is great and labourers few. I say not but there may be honest preaching of some truths in some publick places, tho in too many theres mere quibling, and great deadnes little good done, prophanes much abounding, god calls all that can to put to an helping had in this great decay of religion :

8 God hath smiled upon us in his gracious providence, hitherto I have not been imprisoned, nor yet questioned, all designes agt my liberty have proved abortive, no weapon agt us hath prospered, some others that have done little have been more molested, but god hath secured us. This to former argumts is an incouraging one.—

On the Apocryphal post-scripts added to the Canonical epistles, by J. Kerby.*

May we the folly blame or the intents
of them who first set down these scribblements ?
So ful of lyes, and of unceartaintys
of noveltys and of absurditys
in writing this I doe not dread the pen
of simple readers or more learned men
who to their congregations read them all,
as if they were indeed canonicall
and when in pulpit they want proof wil cry,
tis in your bibles thus beleeve your eye.
I am but dul of sent yet I can smel
the reason which for shame they dare not tel
why these apocryphas are in request,
and which two of the fourteen please them best,
the placing of the post-scripts doth beguile
the simple people whilst the critics smile,
at the poor idiots, who think them all,
written with the epistles, and by paul,
Now let our learned Doctors tell us why
James, peter, John, and jude are passed by,
and none of the epistles except those,
which were of paul, and that wch some suppose
to have been also his were thus abus'd
by postscripts, and why still the same are us'd
is it because that the apostle paul   10]
labour'd more abundantly then them all, [1 cor 15 9
or is it because of the grudg wch Rome
owes pauls epistles, for writing her dome   2 thes 2 8
Now, Sir John Reader, when your lesson fals
in the last chapter of any of pauls
epistles and you find his last amen,
you have read far enough ; give over then,
and if your clark at the amen awake
the postscript for a respond let him take.
Such work agrees best with the parish clark,
for he and it were both hatcht in the dark :

* I suppose these were copied from the MS. of Mr. Kerby, of Wakefield.
The MS. is referred to by Mr. Heywood in his Diary.

But if Sir John wil read his mumpsimus
and one should ask him, Sir why doe you thus ?
possibly in the language of the beast,
he might plead for the postscript, scriptum est,
tis printed so in your books and in mine,
tis therefore without question divine :
if this suffice not (for all are not blind)
the common argument is yet behind ;
the church enjoyns it : her authority,
her wisdome, and infallibility,
may silence all our doubts ; the scarlet whore,
wil plead so much and may not we much more ?
What mean you by the church ? now fye on schisme ;
theres no such question in our catichisms :
Doe not you beleeue as the church beleeues ?
wil you not pin your faith upon lawn sleeues ?
cannot the church make lyes canonical
know you not her power theological ?
goe to your mother with her eyes discerne
the Reverend fathers ask, and of them learn :
from them receiue oracular replyes :
To your objections and inquirys
Rom: Why might not pauls inscription serue alone,
without adding a non-sensical one ?
did not paul know to wm he meant to write Rom 1 6
did he misse and the postscript hit the white ;
why to the Romans ; doe you think that paul
wrote them to one city or unto all ?   Ro 1 15
How could Cenchreas diaconesse attend   Ro 16 1 2
her needful businesse if paul did send
phœbe with his epistle far and wide
through all countrys where Romans did abide ?
paul to the pharisees for learning went Act 22 3: 5 34
and they knew wel what the word Romans meant [joh
Did not paul know wt the word Romans meant   11 47]
How then could he make it his argument ?
                              Act 16 37: 22 25
Before this letter paul wel knew its sense
and tryd it by double experience: Act 16 19 22: 38 39
It meaneth not the habitation
but the priviledges of a person :   Act 22 26-29 :—Act
                    23 27: 24 9 10 11 : 28 17 18 19 :

I will not post-scribe but subscribe to paul
and say that his epistle was to all :
Not to al at Rome, nor to all Romans
But to al the sts, brethren, christians : Rom 1 7 : Act
            28 14 11 26
at Rome, distinguisht by what ever stile
Roman or not Roman, jew or gentile :
1 Cor : First lookes, both before and behind,
  in both respects it stood not with pauls mind
  to cal this first : for one he cites before 1 cor 5 9
  and thereby shuts this firstnes out of doore :
  nor was a latter letter by paul meant
  when to come unto them was his intent : 1 cor 16 5
  to the Corinthians why ? I pray did paul
  write to the christians there or unto all ? 1 cor 5 11
  Corinth was large, the word Corinthians
  comprehendeth jews, heathens christians 1 cor 10 32
  besides the church there of the christians
  there was the idols temple of pagans : 1 cor 8 10
  and the jews synagogue, I beleeue paul Act 18 1 4
  wrote to the church of Corinth, not to all : 1 cor 1 1 2
  Achaia, fortunate, and Stephenas
  may in the crowd of uncertaintys passe :
  But why is Timothy joynd to th rest ? [10 11
  I thought paul understood the business best : 1 cor 16
  we must not leaue untaught the other lye
  written, the postscript says, from philippi
  it seems the post-scribler was dul of sight
  he could not see when he stood near the light,
  the door of Ephesus was opened wide
  and paul on that account did there abide 1 cor 16 8 9
  there also dwelt aquila and prisca : act 18 24 26
  from whom and the churches of Asia 2 tim 4 19
  paul sendeth salutations, but why
  no salutations from philippi,
  if paul wrote there, for there were christians
  at philippi, the macedonians   Phi 4 15 16
  chiefe or first city, and there were other Act 16 12
  churches of macedonia nearer
  to Corinth, and in them did loue abound 2 cor 8 1 4
  yet is there not one salutation found
  from them in this epistle therefore I

say it was written far from Philippi :
2 Cor   Neither is this to the Corinthians
but to the church at Corinth, and christians 2 cor 1 1
in al Achaia, we have found too other
therefore this latter is no second brother
for this comes after the last of the twain   1 cor 16 5 6
2 cor 1 15 16
and therefore must their junior remain :
the post-hast-scribe thought he had seen a passe
in this letter for Titus and Lucas :
gal   the post was blind before and now is lame
in all the letter he can find no name,
for a fit messenger five postscripts more
lye lame together I would know wherefore
unles the post-scribler were not inspired
or his invention were wel nigh tired
galatians, still novelty I see
the churches of galatia say we :   1 cor 16 1 : gal 1 2
Eph :   Ephesians, agen too wide tis thus
unto the Saints which are at Ephesus,   ·   Eph 1 1
for we must leave out both the Dianists   act 19 27 34
and the contradicting synagogists   Act 19 1 8 9
phil :   philippians say you, rather say I
al saints in cht jesus at philippi   phi 1 1
with the Bishops and deacons, we exclude
the city, magistrates, and multitude   act 16 12 9
col :   to the Colossians how wide you tosse
the letter sent to the saints at Colosse !   col 1 2
1 thes : why twice post to the thessalonians   2 th 22
2 thes : it was the church of the thessalonians   1 th 1 1
the post in writing at his wonted Rate
confounds the church-door with the city gate act 17 1 5
1 tim   was it the folly or the knavery,
of the first post in silence to passe by
the ordination of Timothy
under the hands of the presbitery   1 tim 4 14
2 tim   the second post crys, Room for prelacy
heres one from Rome to Bishop Timothy
ordained first of the Ephesian church
presbitery is now left in the lurch :
but prithee stay for al thy hast, and tel
did paul recant at Rome or did he wel,

    at miletus in telling the elders
    the Holy ghost made them overseers? act 20 17 18 28
Tit : Next from Nicapolis comes a letter
    written there by paul, ere he came thither tit 3 12
phil : wel guest at Rome, you shall find al the rest
    as plainly in the epistle exprest : philem 1 10 16 19
Heb : Lo, paul comes with and writes by timothy
    if he come tidings of his liberty,   Heb 13 23
    wel may the post script date from Italy
    its father is a lyar, it a ly   joh 8 44
    Gods word is pure, adde not thereto lest he pro 30 5 6
    reprove thee and a lyar found thou be

—::—

upon nominal excommunication.

The Apocriphal who stole the churches keys
and travels up and down to visit sees
as seers journey men he over-sees
and in purse real anathemas decrees

They say that I am excommunicate
for wch, o lord, thy name I celebrate
for thou hast blessed me with the worlds hate
and I rejoice in being separate :

The Bulla vera hath done what it can
to make an heathen and a publican
but in thy book my name is christian
and neighbours take me for an honest man

They tel me absolution may be had
for a few groats, I am not yet so mad
to be cast out to satan may be sad
to be cast out by satan I am glad :

I was born blind thy Son with sight me blest
in my poore measures I have thee confest
I am cast out but not from thy Sons brest
he sought me out and taught me where to rest

Selfe

I am a Riddle to my selfe, I find
my left hand saith that justice is unjust
my left hand saith why should a record.ly
why was not Argent staind wth sable oaths
I would be poring upon injurys
why was I taken on a Sabbath-day ?
why was I taken on that Sabbath-day ?
why was I taken coming forth from the church ?
why might I not the second sermon hear ?
why did the roaring bul rant it so high ?
you took on you to preach thats an offence,
you suffered others in your house to hear
why walkt you not with those yt are more wise
why kept you not within the limitation ?
why were you not to plead your own cause free ?
why would you not part with a little clay ?
was it not for a charitable use ?
why made you not a promise to forbear ?
why is your prison stricter then before ?
what wil you do in case of transportation ?
So let men curse for their curse thou wilt blesse
their hate to me, thy loue thou dost expresse
communion with thee is happines
I need no more & I shal haue no lesse :

—::—

Reflection.

two partys combating within my mind : Rom 7 23
my Right hand saith it may be & it must : Eccl 5 16
my Right hand saith my record is on high : job 16 16
Darknes fears light & yt light darknes loaths : joh 3 20
I should cast out the beams fro mine own eyes : luk 6 42
t'was Sabboth work men to thy charge did lay : luk 4 16
Satan knew wt I wrote & meant to say 1 the 2 18

fowls of the air were lying at the lurch mark 4 4
that I might pity those that have none near Heb 4 16
to make the jaile a goal-delivery 2 pet 2 8 :
with dispensation paul could not dispence, 1 cor 9 16
christ suffered more for such, & souls are dear act 20 28
because I saw not with my betters eyes : phi 3 15 16
inclosures suit not with commom salvation jud 8
my meaning was my cause should plead for me gen 30 33
because I durst not give my caus away job 27 6
faith knows not charity for an excuse : 1 cor 13 3
a promise not a prison I did fear ! Rev 2 10
because the judg is nearer to the door : Jam. 5 8
leave that to him that rules in every nation : 1 cor 10 13

—::—

No Bishop no king

Is this the motto of the mitred crew ?
a dream then novel prelacy more new,
Before this instant prelacy both kings
and kingdomes had their heaven-born flourishings
cannot an ordinance of god subsist
without such props as unholie Anti christ ?
are not the prelates creatures of the king,
doe creatures giue their maker his being ?
where gained the prelates that prerogatiue
to say to Royalty be thou alive ?
must the breath of our nostrils ceas unles
proud peter-lings vouchsafe the crown to bles ?
from prelates lungs this kingdon breath doth take
as sure as popish priests their maker make :
Ego et Rex meus cannot be done
into good English til the Royal sun
beg the reflection of a lunar ray
to shew the world the prophet of the day :
May not his Majesty draw forth the sword
until the Kirk masters giue out the word ?
Why should the brats of prelacy presume

a super-royal vertue to assume ?
in princes Diadems can no gold shine
but what is found in a prelatick mine ?
what beauty is in Rochets to adorn
the jewels wch in the Kings crowne are worn ?
Can no king send forth words in his own name
except the prelates imitate the same ?
or doth the wealth which by their courts they drain
return into the Royal mints again ?
Doe the Cathedral bellows cleanse the aire ?
and make the minds of Englishmen more fair ?
Is it the Learning or the piety
of prelates that scepters are upheld by ?
Doth a title or a solemnity
endue them above a presbitery ?
or doth experience prove them more devout
or studious when prefermt wheels about ?
Are they become more constant in preaching
to teach us how to fear god & the king ?
is there some secret Apocryphal charm
to put might into a prelatick arm ?
or doth the prelates sitting on a throne
by sympathy secure a firmer one ?
Doth his high climbing render him more nigh
and acceptable unto the most high ?
that the lifting of a prelates hand
should make a kingdome or a king to stand ?

      Vivat Rex Carolus secundus
      et in œternum Regnet :
      May Charles the 2d outline prelacy
      and reap the prayers of presbitery.

The church-porch :

Perirrhanterium*

Thou whose sweet youth and early hopes inhance
thy rate and price, and mark thee for a treasure
hearken unto a verser, who may chance,
Rhime thee to good, and make a bait of pleasure
    A verse may find him, who a sermon flys
    and turn delight into a sacrifice :

Beware of Lust, it doth pollute and foul
whom god in baptism washt with his own blood
it blots the lesson written in thy soul
the holy lines cannot be understood :
    How dare those eyes upon a bible look
    much lesse towards god whose lust is al their book

Wholly abstain or wed, thy bounteous lord
allows thee choyce of paths ; take no by-ways
but gladly welcome what he doth afford
not grudging that thy lust hath bounds or stays
    continence hath his joy, weigh both and so
    if rottenes hath more, let heaven goe :

If god had laid al common, ceartainly
man would have been th incloser : but since now
god hath impal'd us, on the contrary
man breaks the fence, and every ground will plough
    oh what were man, might he himself misplace
    sure to be crosse, he would shift feet & face :

If Reason move not gallants quit the Roome
(all in a shipwrack shift their several way)
let not a common ruine thee entomb
be not a beast in courtesy, but stay
    stay at the third cup, or forgoe the place
    wine above all things doth gods stamp deface

When thou dost tel anothers jest, therin
omit the oaths wch true wit cannot need
pick out of tales the mirth, but not the sin,
he pares his apple that would cleanly feed :
    play not away the vertue of that name
    wch is thy best stake when griefes make thee tame

---

* Are these also from Mr. Kerby's MS., or from some printed volume?
I have no copy of Herbert's Poems at hand.

Dare to be true, nothing can need a lye
a fault wch needs it most, grows too thereby
god gaue thy soul braue wings, put not those feathers
into a bed to sleep out al ill weathers:

O England ful of sin but most of sloth
spit out thy flegm and fil thy brest with glory
thy gentry bleats as if thy natiue cloth
transfusd a sheepishnes into thy story

   not that they alle are so, but that the most
   are gone to grasse and in the pasture lost
   for he that needs fiue hundred pound to liue
   is ful as poor as he that needs but fiue:

   But if thy son can make ten pounds his measure
   then al thou addest may be cald his treasure
   look on meat, think it dirt, then eat a bit
   and say withal, earth to earth I commit:
   make not thy sport, abuses, for the fly
   that feeds on dung is coloured thereby:
   al things are big with jest nothing yts plain
   but may be witty if thou hast the vein
   many affecting wit beyond their power
   haue got to be a dear fool for an hour:
   feed no man in his sins, for adulation
   doth make thee parcel-devil in damnation:
   fathers first enter bonds to natures ends
   and are her suretys ere they are a friends:
                a civil guest
   wil no more talk al then eat al the feast:
   truth dwels not in the clouds: the bow yts there
   doth often aim at, never hit the sphere:
   if truth be with thy friend, be with them both
   share in the conquest, and confesse a troth:
   who say, I care not, those I giue for lost,
   and to instruct them wil not quit the cost:
   let thy minds sweetnes haue his operation
   upon thy body cloaths and habitation:
   kneeling nere spoild silk stocking, quit thy state
   al equal are within the churches gate:
   who marks in church-time others symmetry
   makes al their beauty his deformity:

the worst speak something good, if al want sense
god takes a text, and preacheth patience :

Summe up at night what thou hast done by day
and in the morning what thou hast to doe
dresse and undresse thy soul, mark the decay
and growth of it, if with thy watch that too
    be down, then wind up both, since we shall be
    most surely judgd, make thy accounts agree :

in briefe acquit thee brauely : play the man
look not on pleasures, as they come but goe
defer not the least vertue, lifes poor span
make not an ell by trifling in thy woe :
    if thou doe il, the joy fades not the pain
    if wel the pain doth fade, the joy remains

ana $\cdot \begin{Bmatrix} \text{MARY} \\ \text{ARMY} \end{Bmatrix}$ gram

How wel her name an army doth present
in whom the lord of hosts doth pitch his tent

—::—

Redemption.

p 31

Having been tenant long to a rich lord
    not thriving, I resolved to be bold
    and make a suit unto him to afford
a new smal-rented lease and cancel th old

in heaven at his mannour I him sought
    they told me there that he was lately gone
    about some land wch he had dearly bought
long since on earth to take posession :

I streight returned and knowing his great birth
    sought him accordingly in great resorts
    in citys, theatres, gardens, parks and courts
at length I heard a ragged noise and mirth,
    of thieves and murderers, there I him espy'd
    who streight your suit is granted, sd & dyd

Easter.

I got me flowers to straw thy way
I got me boughs off many a tree
but thou wast up by break of day
and broughtst thy sweets along with thee

the sun arising in the East
tho he giue light and th' East perfume
if they should offer to contest
with thy arising, they presume

can there be any day but this
tho many suns to shine endeavour
we count three hundred, but we misse
ther is but one, and that one ever :

Ah my dear god ! tho I am clean forgot
let me not loue thee if I loue thee not   p 40

—::—

Prayer

p 43

prayer the churches banquet, angels age
   gods breath in man returning to his birth
   the soul in paraphrase, heart in pilgrimage
the christian plummet sounding heavn & earth

Engine agt th' almighty sinners towr
   reversed thunder, Christ-side-piercing spear
   the six-days world transposing in an hour
a kind of tune, wch al things hear and fear :

softnes and peace, and joy, and loue, and blisse
   exalted manna, gladnes of the best
   heaven in ordinary, man wel drest
the milky way the bird of paradise
church-bels beyond the stars heard, the soules bloud
the land of spices, something understood :

The ♄ communion

2
part

give me my captiue soul or take
   my body also thither
another lift like this wil make
   them both to be togather

before that sin turnd Flesh to stone
   and al our lump to leauen
a feruent sigh might wel haue blown
   our innocent earth to heauen

for sure, when Adam did not know
   to sin or sin to smother
he might to heauen from paradise goe
   as from one room to another:

thou hast restor'd us to this ease
   by this thy heauenly blood
wch I can goe to when I please
   and leaue th' earth to their food

—::—

Antiphon

cho   Let all the world in every corner sing my god and king
      vers   the heauens are not too high
          his praise may thither fly
          the earth is not too low
          his praises there may grow

cho   Let all the world in every corner sing my god and king
      vers   the church with psalmes must shout
          no door can keep them out
          but aboue al, the heart
          must bear the longest part

cho   Let all the world in every corner sing my god and king

The temper,

How should I praise thee, lord how should my Rhimes
    gladly ingraue thy loues in steel
    if what my soul doth feel sometimes
    my soul might ever feel

Altho there were some fourty heavens or more
    sometimes I peer above them all
    sometimes I hardly reach a score
    sometimes to hel I fall

O rack me not to such a vast extent
    those distances belong to thee
    the worlds too little for thy tent
    a graue too big for me :

Wilt thou mete armes with man that thou dost stretch
    a crumb of dust from heaven to hel
    wil great god measure with a wretch
    shal he thy stature spel :

O let me, when thy roof my soul hath hid,
    o let me roost and nestle there
    there of a sinner thou art rid,
    and I of hope and fear

yet take thy way, for sure thy way is best :
    stretch or contract me thy poor debter :
    this is but tuning of my breast
    to make the musick better :

Whether I fly with angels, fal with dust,
    thy hands made both and I am there :
    thy power and loue, my loue and trust
    make one place every where :

—::—

Grace

    my stock lyes dead and no increase
    doth my dul husbandry improue :
    oh let thy graces without cease
    drop from aboue :

if stil the sun should hide his face
thy house would but a dungeon proue,
thy works nights captiues : oh let grace
      drop from aboue :

the dew doth every morning fall
and shall the dew outstrip thy doue
the dew for wch grasse cannot cal
      drop from aboue :

Death is stil working like a mole,
and digs my graue at each remoue
let grace work too and on my soul
      drop from aboue :

sin is stil hammering my heart
unto a hardnes void of loue :
let suppling grace to crosse his art
      drop from aboue :

o come ! for thou dost know the way
or if to me thou wilt not moue
Remoue me where I need not say
      drop from aboue :

—::—

The church-floore

Mark you the floor ! that square and speckled stone
      wch looks so firm and strong
            is patience :

and th' other black and graue, wherwth each one
      is checkered al along,
            humility :

the gentle rising wch on either hand
      leads to the quire aboue
            is confidence

But the sweet cement wch in one sare band
      ties the whole frame is loue
            and charity :

Hither some times sin steals, and stains
the marbles neat and curious veines ;

But al is cleansed when the marble weeps
  sometimes death puffing at the doore
  blows al the dust about the floore :
But while he thinks to spoil the room he sweeps
  Blest be the architect, whose art
  could build so strong in a weak heart :

—::—

The Quiddity

  my god a verse is not a crown
  no point of honour or gay suit
  no hawk or banquet or renown
  nor a good sword nor yet a lute

  it cannot vault or dance or play
  it never was in france or spain
  nor can it entertain the day
  with my great stable or demain :

  it is no office, art, or news,
  nor the exchange or busy hall :
  but it is that wch while I use
  I am with thee, and most take all :

—::—

Humility

I saw the virtues sitting hand in hand
in several ranks upon an azure throne
where al the beasts and fowls by their command
presented tokens of submission :
humility who sate the lowest there
          to execute their call
when by the beasts the presents tendered were
          gaue them about to all :
the angry lion did present his paw
wch by consent was given to mansuetude
the fearful hare her ears, wch by their law
humility did reach to fortitude
the jeolous turkey brought his coral-chain
          that went to temperance,
on justice was bestowed the foxes brain
          kild in the way by chance :

at length the crow bringing the peacocks-plume
(for he would not) as they beheld the grace
of that braue gift each one began to fume,
and challenge it as proper to his place;
til they fel out: wch when the beasts espied
     they leapt upon the throne
and if the fox liv'd to rule their side,
     they had depos'd each one

Humility who held the plume, at this
did weep so fast, that the tears trickling down
spoild al the train: then saying here it is
for wch ye wrangle, made them turn their frown
against the beasts, so jointly bandying
     they drive them soon away
and then amerc'd them double gifts to bring
     at the next session-day:

—::—

The world

Loue built a stately house, where fortune came
and spinning fanceys, she was heard to say,
that her fine cobwebs did support the frame
whereas they were supported by the same
but wisdome quickly swept them al away:

there pleasure came, who liking not the fashion
began to make balcones, teraces,
til she had weakened al by alteration
but reverend laws and many a proclamation
reformed al at length with menaces:

then entred sin, and with that sycamore
whose leaf first sheltered man from draught & dew
working and winding slily evermore
the inward walls and sommers cleft and tore
but grace shor'd these, and cut that as it grew:

then sin combin'd with death in a firm band
to rase the building to the very floore:
which they effected none could them withstand
but love and grace took glory by the hand
and built a braver pallace then before:

Justice

I cannot skil of these thy ways
Lord thou didst make me, yet thou woundest me:
Lord thou dost wound me, yet thou dost relieve me:
Lord thou relievest, yet I dye by thee:
Lord thou dost kil me, yet thou dost reprieve me
But when I mark my life and praise,
thy justice me most fitly pays

for I doe praise thee yet I praise thee not:
my prayers mean thee, yet my prayers stray:
I would doe wel, yet sin the hand hath got:
my soul doth loue thee yet it loues delay:
I cannot skil of these my ways

—::—

Charms and knots

Who read a chapter when they rise,
shal nere be troubled with il eyes:

a poor mans rod when thou dost ride,
is both a weapon and a guide:

who shuts his hand hath lost his gold:
who opens it hath it twice told:

who goes to bed and doth not pray,
maketh too nights to every day:

who by aspersions throw a stone,
at th head of others, hit their own:

who looks on ground with humble eyes,
finds himself there and seeks to rise:

when th hair is sweet through pride or lust
the powder doth forget the dust:

take one from ten, and what remains
ten stil if sermons goe for gains:

in shallow waters heaven doth show:
but who drinks on, to hel may goe:

𝕳𝕠𝕞𝕖

Come lord, my head doth burn, my heart is sick
    while thou dost ever, ever stay
thy long deferrings wound me to the quick,
    my spirit gaspeth night and day
        o shew thy selfe to me,
        or take me up to thee :

How canst thou stay, considering the pace
    the blood did make weh thou didst wast ?
when I behold it trickling down thy face
    I never saw thing make such hast :
        o shew &c

When man was lost, thy pity looks about,
    to see what help in th earth or sky :
but ther was none : at least no help without,
    the help did in thy bosome lye
        o shew &c

Here lay thy son : and must he leaue that rest
    that hive of sweetnes, to remove
thraldome from those who would not at a feast
    leaue one poor apple for thy loue ?
        o shew &c

He did, he came, oh my redeemer dear,
    after al this canst thou be strange ?
so many years baptiz'd and not appear ?
    as if thy loue could fail or change :
        o shew &c

yet if thou stayest stil why must I stay ?
    my god what is this world to me ?
this world of woe : hence al ye clouds, away
    away, I must get up and see :
        o shew &c

what is this weary world, this meat and drink
    that chains us by the teeth so fast
what is this woman-kind which I can wink
    into a blacknes and distast ?
        o shew &c

with one small sigh thou gavst me th' other day
  I blasted al the joys about me,
and scouling on them as they pin'd away
  now come again, said I, and flout me.
     o shew &c

nothing but drought and dearth, but brush & brake
  which way soere I look I see,
some may dream merrily but when they wake
  they dresse themselves, & come to thee
     o shew &c

we talk of harvests, ther are no such things
  but when we leaue our corn and hay
there is no fruitful year but that wch brings
  the last and lov'd tho dreadful day
     o shew &c

oh loose this frame, this knot of man unty,
  that my free soul may use her wing,
which is now pinion'd with mortality,
  as an intangled hampered thing
     o shew &c

what haue I left that I should stay and grone ?
  the most of me to heaven is fled
my thoughts and joys are al packt up and gone,
  and for their old acquaintance plead.
     o shew &c

come dearest lord, passe not this holy season
  my flesh and bones and joynts doe pray
and even my verse, wh by the rhime & reason
  the word is stay, sais, ever, come
     o shew thy self to me
     or take me up to thee:

—::—

Jesu

Jesu is in my heart, his sacred name
is deeply carved there ; but th other week
a great affliction broke the little frame,
even al to peeces ; wch I went to seek:

and first I found the corner, where was I
after wher ES, and next wher U was graved
when I had got these parcels, instantly
I sate me down to spel them, and perceived
that to my broken heart he was I ease you
and to my whole IESU

—::—

Loue-joy

As on a window late I cast mine eye,
I saw a vine drop grapes with I and C
anneal'd on every bunch,--one standing by
askt what it meant: I (who am never loth
to spend my judgment) said it seemd to me
to be the body and the letters both
of Joy and Charity: Sir, you haue not mist
the man replyd: it figures JESUS CHRIST

—::—

Probidence see p 109 to 114

sometimes thou dost divide thy gifts to man,
sometimes unite: the indian nut alone
is cloathing, meat, and trencher, drink & can
boat, cable, sail and needle al in one
    al good

—::—

To the king

Great Charles who ful of mercy wouldst command
in peace and pleasure this thy native land,
at least take pity of thy tottering throne
shook by the faults of others not thy own
let not thy life and crown togather end
destroy'd by a false brother and a friend
obserue the dangers that appear so near
wch all your subjects doe each minute fear,
a drop of poyson and a papists knife,
ends all the joys of England with youre life,
brother its true by nature should be kind,
but to a zealous and ambitious mind,

> bribd by a crown on earth for one aboue
> theres no more friendship tendernes and loue,
> so in all ages what examples ever,
> of monarch murdered by th' impatient heir
> hard fate of princes who wil nere beleeue
> til stroak be struck wch they can ne're retrieue
>
> this was put into the kings
> private closet at the keyhole
> about Nov 29 1673 :

—::—

Rules of practice I desire to charge upon my own base heart in the course of my life.

1 Be serious (whether short or long) in all religious excercises: doe thy best in the best works: trifle not in any thing, much lesse in the dutys of religion:

2 Haue speciall regard to thy thoughts: what thou art afraid to doe before men, be afraid to think before god: study thy heart most: eye that pure eye that discerns heart-workings:

3 let thy heart be composed in all states: be set aside by nothing: oh for an holy state of soul that it may be under the power of nothing beneath itself! nothing can be worth the losse of a quick spirit:

4 Be catholic both in principles and practices: neither confine thy loue to a party, nor thy obedience to one or more dutys: partiality is a note of hypocricy: universality of sincerity:

5 Be content with witnesses above and within: doe thy beste workes invisibly to men: doe dutys without outward incouragents—yea agt discouragents—be better god-wards then man-wards:

6 crosse speciall lust with peculiar grace and watch, make best fence where hedg is lowest, and where great counsels bend agt thy inclination: crosse that sin that opposeth thy soules peace and safty:

7 Study self-denyal, its the highest and hardest lesson of a christian: whatever excellencys thou hast they are cyphers without this: if thou have little this will be instead of all:

8 Conceiue of things now as thou wilt judg, of wn at death and judgment: or wn trouble and sicknes or sad accidents befall: the best way of happines is not to multiply honours, riches, but cure thy conceit of these things—

9 get thy will mastered unto gods: learn to doe gods will or thoult not bear it: bear the yoke of commands or thoult not bear the yoke of thy crosse, let nothing displease that pleaseth god, nor any thing please thee that displeaseth him—propria voluntas deum quantum in ipsa exiunt—

10 pray most for those that hate thee worst: they need it most: let these coales of loue fall on their heads—and on heartes, oh for conversion: god is a god of vengeance, meddle not with his prerogatiue the wronged side is the safer side.

Then follow twelve pages of an index of Sermon-notes in twenty books. In book 1, the texts are Pro. 19 20, 2 Cor. 4 18, Ezra 8 21, John 4 35, Isai. 26 20, Heb. 1 14, Eph. 1 3, Luk. 2 11, Ezra 6 14, and Heb. 4 18.

Another Bundle of notes [eighteen books.] These seven last bookes were my first days labours.

[Total number of] Texts 826
Little notes, fiue bundles. [Total 119]
Books of my sermons of another sort, 16 books
Ditto 9 books
Ditto 7 books [Total about 120 texts]

—::—

Psal 122

1   I did rejoice that day
    when they to me did say
    unto the house of god let us
    togather take our way:

2   the feet of all our train
    now shortly shal remain
    in ful resorts within thy courts
    o thou jerusalem:

3   Ierusalems buildings are
    like to a city faire
    in form exact and al compact
    togather every where

4 the tribes to that place came
     the tribes of god by name
to th' oracle of Israel
     gods praises to proclaim :

5 For at Jerusalem
     are set the thrones for them
the judgmt thrones, those royal ones
     of Davids diadem :

6 pray earnestly with me
     Jerusalems peace to see,
o salem such shall prosper much
     as bear true loue to thee

7 Let al tranquillity
     be in thy wals said I
also in these thy pallaces
     as much prosperity :

8 now for my brethren here
     and my companions deare
even for their sake this prayer I make
     peace be within thee there :

9 And for the neighbour-hood
     of sion where hath stood,
the blest abode of our great god
     Ile always seek thy good :

—::—

Psal 124

1 If that it had not been the lord
     who tooke our part this day
and but that he did help afford
     may Israel now say

2 had not the lord been on our side
     when enemys rose so thick

3 then in their wrath & swelling pride
     they had devourd us quick

4 the waters had ore-whelmd us then
     the stream without controll

5   and waters of imperious men
      had gone quite ore our soul

6   blessed be god who gave us not
      into their teeth a prey
as birds from snares of fowlers got
      our soules escapt away

the snare is broke that held the game
      so safely we evade
our help is in Jehovahs name
      that earth and heaven made

—::—

Psal 125

Al those that trust in god
      shal be as sion hill
that cannot be removd away
      but standeth steadfast still:
And as Jerusalem
      the mountains strong & high
like bulwarks compassing about
      doth guard and fortify:

so doth the mighty lord
      about the people stand
saving them now and evermore
      with his most mighty hand:
the sharp afflicting rod
      of wicked cruel foes
shal not for ever on the lot
      of righteous men repose

left fainting in their minds
      when endles griefs them presse
weary and hopeless they put forth
      their hands to wickednes
doe good unto thy saints,
      and blessings Lord, impart
unto the good thine Israelites
      that are upwright in heart:

But such as turn aside
   and loue to go astray
led by their loose and wandring lusts
   in their own crooked way
these in the fearful paths
   of judgment god shal guide
with wicked workers but his peace
   on Israel shal abide :

—::—

𝔓sal 126

When Sions sad captivity
   the lord again did bring
like to a dream it did appear
   and as a feigned thing :
then was our mouth with laughter fild
   right joyful was our tongue
and of this wonder thus they spake
   the heathen folke among :

great things the lord hath done for them :
   great things we doe confesse
the lord for us hath done, which call
   for joy and thankfulnes
Bring our captivity again
   to joy our sorrow turn
as flowing streams doe change the ground
   wch parching heat did burn

those that in tears and sorrows deep
   their seed doe sadly sow
at harvest they their corn with joy
   shal gladly reap and mow :
they caryed forth their precious seed
   and going they did mourn
but bringing home their sheaues with joy
   they gladly shal returne :

Ps 14

But who shall giue thy people health
  and when wilt thou fulfill
thy promise made to Israel
  from out of Sion hill.
Even when thou shalt restore again
  such as were captiue led
then Jacob shal therein rejoice
  and Israel shal be glad:

—::—

Psal 127

1 Except the lord doe build the house
  man buildeth but in vain
and man in building doth but lose
  his labour and his pain

2 Except the lords alseeing eye
  the city safely keep,
in vain the watchmans waking eye
  doth hold itselfe from sleep:

3 To rise up early is but vain,
  and vain late watchings are,
vain is it pensiuely to eat
  the bread of griefe and care:

4 for the beloved of the lord
  are by his loue so blest,
that unto them he freely giues
  most quiet sleep and rest:

5 Loe children are an heritage,
  which doth from god descend,
and the wombs fruit is his reward
  gods bounty doth it send:

6 and look what strength sharp arrows are,
  in hands of men of power,
such strength are children blest with grace
  amid this youthful flower:

7 and blessed is the man that hath
his quiver ful of those
for they undaunted in the gate
shal speak unto their foes:

—::—

Mr. Parkhurst sent me 8 dozen of books of Sure mercy's—
feb. 17 167½   100 books bindg

John Kershaw	...	1	Mr Sotwel	...	1
Jonathan Priestley	...	1	Susan Longbottom	...	1
James Oates	...	1	Mr Joh Lister	...	1
Mr Hodgson	...	1	Mtris Cheater	...	1
Micael Broadly	...	1	Nath: Crosland	...	1
Thomas Liedg	...	1	Will Cordingly	...	1
Joshua Walker	...	1	Joh Smiths wife	...	1
Mary Walker	...	1	Rich Cook	...	1
Alice Holt	...	1	Jerem Woral	...	1
Jeron Jaggar	...	1	Sam: Ellison	...	1
Margt Rushworth	...	1	John Bland	...	1
Mic Booths wife	...	1	Dority Bolton	...	1
James Brook'sb.	...	1	Mary Robinson	...	1
Mr Jolly	...	1	Anthony gill	...	1
Will Clay	...	1	James Smith	...	1
phœbe Firth	...	1	Sam: Holdworth	...	1
grace Butler	...	1	Hanna Hardger	...	1
Martha Hanson	...	1	Sarah Walker	...	1
Dinah Tetlaw	...	1	Tim: Kershaw	...	1
Sarah Langly	...	1	Judith field	...	
Rich: Appleyard	...	1	Mr Middlebrough	...	1
Susan Dean	...	1	Mr Milner p	...	1
Mr Watkinson	...	1	Ellis Bury	...	1
James Dickson	...	1	George Stanford	...	1
Will Heawood	...	1	Sam: Wilkinson	...	1
John Hide	...	1	Elias Hinchbal	...	1
John Kirk	...	1	Mr Moxon	...	1
Mtris Kerby	...	1	Mr Hickson	...	1
Mary potter	...	1	Mr Paul Thirsby	...	1
Nat: Bottomly	...	1	Mr John Thursby	...	1
Will Robuck	...	1	Mr W Milner L	...	1
Mr Cotton	...	1	Mr R Spencer	...	1

Mr Tim Smith	1	Mtris Sharp	...
Mark Freeman	1	Mtris Bagnal	...
John Cumming	1	Will Hodgson	...
Jeffery Beck	1	Robt Ramsden	...
Jane Milner	1	Susan Appleyard	...
Sam : Boys	1	Daniel Parker	...
John Heywood	1	John Broksbank	...
Eliezer Heywood	1	Will Walker W	...
Martha Bairstow	1	Anthony Lea	...
Mtris Dawson	1	Anne Priestley	...
phœbe Stancliff	1		

guilded b

Lady Hewly York	1	Sister Crompton	...
Lady Watson	1	Lady Standley	...
Mr Wiltans daght	1	My wife	...
Mtris Thorp	1	Madam Dymmocks	...
Mtris Ardington	1	Mr Dineley	...
Mother Angier	1	Mr John Oates	...
Sister Hulton	1	Bridget mellin	...

Received another dozen of books of sure mercys
march 30 1672—

Mr Foster Wadsworth	1	John Cordingly	..
Mr R Wilson	1	Thomas Ellison	...
Mr Root	1	Abrah : Walker	...
Mr Horton S	1	Mercy Brown	...
Mtris Robinson S	1	John Stephenson	...
Mr gregory	1		

2 Dozen into Lanc April 12 1672—

Father Angier	1	Cozen M Holt	...
Mtris Hall	1	Brother Heywood	...
Mr Burtons	1	Mtis Ashurst	...
Mr Hopwood	1	Cozn Robt : Cretchlaw	
Aunt Russel	1	Coz : James Crompton	
Brother Okey	1	Cozen Rich : Heywood	
Broth : goodwin	1	Sistre Dorat	...
Father Heywood	1	Uncle Pet Winstanley	
Sister Hanna C	1	Elizab : Haslam	...
Sistre Estre W :	1	Mat : Hallows	...
Sistre Alice B.	1	Robert Milnes	...
Cozen H Crompton	1		

Received 12 books from Mr Parkhurst of Sure mercys may 4 1672

Robert Swain	...	1	Mtris Noble	...	1
James Mitchel	...	1	Joshua Soynier	...	1
Jerom Baxter	...	1	Joh : Butterworth	...	1
his Sister	...	1	Cozen Edm Hilb	...	1
Tim Mellin	...	1	Robt Bins wif	...	1
Josiah Stansfield	...	1	Lidia Murfot	...	1

Received 2 Dozen of Books of Sure mercys of Mr Parkhurst Aug 17 72

Uncle Angier	...	1	J B. for a woman	...	1
W : Butler	...	1	Micael Broadly	...	1
Tho : Dawson	...	1	Mr Ch : Fairfax	...	1
Mr Foster	...	1	Mtris Malevery	...	1
John green	...	1	Rich : Keghley	...	1
Richard Mason	...	1	Mtris Murgatrod	...	1
John Stot	...	1	Eden Ellis	...	1
Anne Northend	...	1	John Roberts	...	1
Simeon Robinson	...	1	Mtris Malevery	...	1
Baitings woman	...	1	Mtris pagett	...	1

Received 6 books of Closet prayer Dec 13 73

Tho : Atkinson	...	1	Cozen Crompton	...	1
Arthur Lee	...	1	Will Walkers wif	...	1

he gaue me 59 I bought 100 for £10   Mr Parkhurst sent me 140 Bookes of Baptismal bonds octob 10 1687

12 better bound then ordinary in calues leath : guilt—

My wife	...	1	Lady Hewly	...	1
Lady Duckinfield	...	1	Lady Ascough	...	1
Sister Hilton	...	1	Morton Lambert	...	1
Ms Taylor	...	1	Madam Baildon	...	1
Ms Westby	...	1	Mrs Whitaker	...	1

of Books sent to Manchester

ordinary ones	...	10	To my sons	...	4
To Bolton	...	12	To York	...	10
To Leeds	...	4			

10 given at London   franc Bently 28 ordinary ones

John Stots wife	...	1	Tho Leach	...	1
Jer Baxter jun	...	1	Micael Broadly	...	1
Jonath priestly jun	...	1	Josh Walker	...	1
Josh Wrights wife	...	1	Mr J Brooksbank	...	1
Margaret Rushworth		1	Ralph Higson	...	1
William Ellis	...	1	Jon Priestly sen	...	1
Susan Tillotson	...	1	Sarah Spencer	...	1
John Robinson	...	1	Ms Langley	...	1
Susanna Butler	...	1	Mtris Frankland	...	1
Roger Stocks	...	1	Jonathan Sonier	...	1
Jonas Northend	...	1	Mary Bentley	...	1
William Clay	...	1	Mr John Kirk	...	1
John Holdworth	...	1	Mr Rich Harrison	...	1
John Hartly	...	1	Ms Kerby	...	1
Joseph Haliday	...	1	Ms Naylor	...	1
Martin Longbottom	...	1	Mr Jolly	...	1
Anne Northend	...	1	Mary Burnel	...	1
John Milnes	...	1	John Hey	...	1
Jer Baxter sen	...	1	Rich : Mitchel	...	1
Mr Dawson	...	1	Ms Cotton sen	...	1
Isaac Longbothon	...	1	Hanna Robuck	...	1
Joshua Sonier	...	1	Hanna Holden	...	1
Antony Lea	...	1	Ester Ray	...	1
Sam : Holdworth	...	1	Ms Gill	...	1
Tho : Longbothon	...	1	Mr Wadsworth	...	1
John Armitage	...	1	Mr Ab Dawson	...	1
Willm Naylor	...	1	Martha Green	...	1
Robt Ramsden	...	1	Martha Lister	...	1
James Tetlaw	...	1	Tim Poulard	...	1
Mary Roberts	...	1	Mr Scolfield	...	1
Timothy Holt	...	1	Mr Hallows	...	1
John Broadly	...	1	Mr Ogden	...	1
Judith Hoyl	...	1	Mr Pendlebury	...	1
Antony gil	...	1	Robt Miln	...	1
John Learoyd	...	1	Charles Hamar	...	1

I had 12 back from franc Bently other 16 from franc Bently

Nov 20 87 Mr Parkhurst gave me 12 more Nov 5 1687

Received on Jan 28 168⅞ 12 bookes more for wch I payd
him 01-00-00

given Sarah Walker...	1	James Cash ...	1
Ms Cotton junior ...	1	John Hanson ...	1
Ms Gill of okes ...	1	Mr Hotham ...	1
Mr Gunter ...	1	Rowland Mitchel ...	1
Mr Hen Priestly ...	1	Abr Scots wife ...	1
Ester Stead ...	1	Mr Dinely sen ...	1
Ms Elizab Rhodes ...	1	Josiah Stansfield ...	1
Mr John Lister ...	1	Ms Drake Bradf ...	1
Mr Lockwood ...	1	Mary Murgatroyd ...	1
Mr Whitehurst ...	1	James Dixon son ...	1
Mr Rich ...	1	paid for ...	2
Sarah Brook ...	1	Isaac Balm ...	1
James Holsted ...	1	Tho : Ledgard ...	1
John Butterworth ...	1	Judith Scarborogh ...	1
Martha Wardman ...	1	John Bland ...	1
Mr Wakefield ...	1	Henry Naylor ...	1
Mr Sargeant jun ...	1	Rebecca Kershaw ...	1
Mary Walker ...	1	Mr Buxtons of Bilbrugh	1
Daniel Walker ...	1	Mtris Spencer Leeds	1

Received of Mr Parkhurst 24 books of Baptismal bonds
March 31 1688   paid for them £2

Mr Gledhil ...	1	Ms Sharp Horton ...	1
Thomas Gill ...	1	Ms Waller York ...	
Mr Cock Kendal ...	1	Mr Taylor York ...	
Samuel Brigs ...	1	Tho Hague Marsh ...	
John Hardaker ...	1	Ms Thorp ...	1
Cozen Eliz Warren ...	1		

John Armitage had 6 books   paid me 11 sh—
Abraham Broadly had 2 books
John Armitage had 4 more—

Received of Mr Parkhurst 200 books of meetnes for heaven
April 1 1690   paid 7 li 10 sh

My wife ...	1	Ms Middlebrough ...	1
Susan Tillotson ...	1	Mr Broadly ...	1
Phœbe King ...	1	Tho Longbothom ...	1
Sister Ester ...	1	Rebecca Kershey ...	1
Cozen J. Lomax ...	1	Willm Clay ...	1

Jonathan Priestly sen		Richard Mitchel ...	1
Mr Ratcliff Scollfield		Ms Frankland ...	1
Peter Rothwell ...	1	Thomas Hodgson ...	1
Willm Whitehead ...	1	Mtris Dinely ...	1
Sister Colburn ...	1	Nephew S Angier ...	1
Sister Hilton ...	1	Richard Kighly ...	1
Cozen S Angier ...	1	Mtris Drake ...	1
Mtris Lambert ...	1	Mtris Freeman ...	1
Ms Kershaw ...	1	Mr Thorsby ...	1
John Hey ...	1	Mrs Whitaker ...	1
William Lupton ...	1	Mr Lockwood ...	1
Mr Dawson ...	1	John Armitage ...	1
Martha Bins ...	1	Ms Naylor ...	1
Sarah Hardaker ...	1		

distributed at London

Mr Streaton ...	1	Mrs Westby ...	1
Mr Denham ...	1	My son ...	1
Mr Longbothom ...	1	Ms Taylor ...	1
Cozen Hilton ...	1	John Walkers wife ...	1
Brother Crompton ...	1	Mr Oates Chickenly...	1
Sir Tho Rookby ...	1		—
Mr Westby ...	1		40

Dame Kirk ...	1	Anne Blakbrough ...	1
Ms Eliz Rhodes ...	1	Jeremiah Baxter sen	1
Mr Gill ...	1	Mary Lister do Br ...	1
John Butterworth ...	1	Antony Lea ...	1
Josh Squire jun ...	1	James Halsted ...	1
Mtris Langly Pe ...	1	Susan Saxton ...	1
Mtris Hough ...	1	James Oates Wyk ...	1
Timothy Holt ...	1	Elizab Weeder Wbsy	1
Mr Brooksbank ...	1	Willm Wadsworth ...	1
James Brooksbank ...	1		—
Tho Naylor Wakf ...	1		60

Ralph Higson ...	1	Margaret Rushworth	1
Tho Horrocks Bolton	1	Isaac Longbottom ...	1
Robt Miln Ratchd ...	1	Sarah Spencer ...	1
Mtris Sharp ...	1	Grace Ramsden ...	1
Cozen Ruth Davis ...	1	Ms Kirby ...	1
Old John Marsden ...	1	James Hailsworth ...	1

Mr Hutton	1	Sister Heywood	1
Ms Smith T	1	John Stot	1
Ms Hallows	1	James Cash	1
Ms Shackston	1	Mary Northend	1
Sam Holdworth	1		—
Mary Broadly	1		80
Joshu Stocks	1	Ms Cotton jun	1
Mtris Cotton sen	1	Roger Stocks	1
Cozen Tho Worsnam	1	Susan Butler	1
Sister M Angier	1	Joshua Sonier sen	1
Lady Duckenfield	1	Martin Longbothom	1
Nathaniel Tetley	1	John Hartley	1
Jonas Foster	1	Henry Naylor	1
Anne Northend	1	Rachel Gill	1
John Holdworths	1	Mtris Priestly	1
John Milnes	1	Justice Farrand	1
Mary Bently	1	Phœbe Midgly	1
Mother Heywood	1	Isabel Cook	1
Ms Drake of York	1	Willm Naylor	1
Mr Hotham York	1	Martha Greaves	1
Josiah Stansfield sen	1	Timothy Bancroft	1
Cozen J Crompton	1	Martha Wardman	1
Ralph Holt	1	Mtris Rookby	1
Katharin Ledgard	1	Mary Paulard	1
Antony Gill	1	Jeremiah Dickenson	1
Mtris Smith Leeds	1	Mary Bradley	1
Jonas Tillotson	1	Hanna Robuck	1
Richard Morley	1	Isaac Balm jun	1
Ms Horton	1	John Stot jun	1
John Beamount	1	Robt Ramsden Park	1
Jonathan Priestly jun	1	Mr Smith Minist	1
Tho : Farrand Bradf	1	Maid at Benj Waughs	1
Joshua Walker Bingly	1	Joseph Wooler	1
Mr Tho Leach	1	Stephen Hall	1
Joshua Wright	1	Joseph Wood	1
John Learoyd	1	Hanna Holden	1
Jerem Baxter jun	1	Rebecca Marsden	1
Judith Hoyl	1	William Hurd	1
Mrs Rich jun	1	turn 21 leaues	
Ms Shaw	1		

What a Nonconformist can swear and what he cannot,

REFERRING TO THE ACT OF PARL. EXCLUDING MINISTERS OUT OF CORPORATIONS, UPON THEIR REFUSING AN OATH, EXECUTED MARCH 24 166⅞ BY DR R: WYLDE

1 I fear an oath before I swear, to take it,
   and wel I may for its the oath of god,
   I fear an oath, when I haue sworn, to break it
   and wel I may for vengeance hath a rod :

2 Yet I may swear and must, sometimes its due,
   both to my heavenly and my earthly king,
   if I assert, it must be just and true,
   and if I promise I must doe the thing :

3 I am no quaker, not at all to swear
   nor papist to swear East & mean the West
   but Ime a protestant and wil declare
   what I cannot and what I can protest

4 I never will endeavour alteration,
   of monarchy nor of that Royal name,
   wch god hath chosen to command this nation
   but will maintain his person, crown and fame.

5 What he commands if conscience say not nay
   (for conscience is a greater king than he)
   for conscience sake not fear I will obey
   and if not actiue, passiue I will be :

6 Ile pray that all his subjects may agree,
   and never more be crumbled into parts,
   I will endeavour that his majesty
   may not be king of clubs but king of hearts.

7 The civil government I will obey,
   but for church-policy I swear I doubt it
   and if my bible want Apocrypha
   I hope my book may be compleat without it

8 the Royal oak I swear I will defend
   but for the Ivy wch doth hug it so,
   Ile swear it is a thiefe & not a friend
   & about steeples fitter is to grow :

9   I dare not swear church-governmt is right
    as it should be, but this I dare to swear
    if they will put me tot that Bishops might
    doe better and be better than they are

10 Nor will I swear for all that they are worth,
    that Bishopricks shal stand & Doomes-day see,
    yet I will swear the gospel holdeth forth
    Christ with his ministers till then will be :

11 That Peter was a prelate they averre
    but Ile not swear it when als said & done
    But I dare swear, and hope I shal not erre,
    he preacht an hundred sermons for their one :

12 Saint Peter was a fisher and catcht men
    and they have nets and in them catch men too
    but Ile not swear they are alike for them
    he catcht and savd but they catch & undoe

13 I dare not swear that courts Ecclesiastick
    doe in their laws make just and gentle votes
    But this Ile swear that Burton, prin & Bastwick
    were once ear-witnesses* of harsher notes

14 Arch-deacons, Deans, & chapters are braue men
    by Canon but not scripture, and to this
    if I be calld Ile swear & swear agen
    that in my bible no such chapter is :

15 Ile not condemn those presbiterians who
    refused Bishopricks that might haue had um
    But Mistres Calamy Ile swear doth doe
    as if she were a spiritual madam

16 For holy vests I dare not take an oath
    what linnen most canonical may be
    some are for Lawn, some Holland, some Scotch cloath
    and hemp for some is fitter than all three :

17 Paul had a cloak & books & parchments too
    but that he wore a { surplice / cassock } Ile not swear
    nor that his parchments did his orders shew
    or in his book there was a common-prayer

[*These men had their ears cut off.]

18   I owe assistance to the king by oath,
     and if he please to put the prelates down
     (as who can tel what may be) Ide be loath
     to see Tom Beckets miter push the crown :

19   And yet church-governours I doe allow
     and am contented Bishops be the men
     and that I speak in earnest, here I vow
     where we haue one I wish we may haue ten

20   In fine the civil power I shall obey
     and seek the peace & welfare of the nations
     if this wont doe I know not what to say
     But farewel London, farewel corporations :

—::—

1   When one with three times six doe meet
         to reckon for the year
     the bloody English colours shal
         on the French coasts appear

2   When sol in Cancer enters first
         upon that very day
     the ensignes of these mighty foes
         shal in the field display

3   Twelue noble lords that day shall fal
         with thousands by their side
     and then the fates end and begin
         the French and English pride

4   three battles more ere Christmas end
         the lillys fight and loose
     then peace ensues wch puts an end
         unto the subjects woes

5   Then high and mighty look about
         your wooden and stone wall
     shal not defend you but shall then
         begin to sink & fall

6   plagues, pannicks, swords, prodigious sights
     those troubles shall forerun
     and fiue and fifty years shall end
     ere this hauo wel begun

* this was copied by a gentleman of quality out of a book had ten yeares before the time, and the gentleman who writ the original his hand very wel known in Montgomery-shire:

     Anno cui Tria sex
     obruetur Rex
     Dispergetur grex
     evertetur lex

Dic mihi fatalis regem quera denotat annus?
     LVDoVICVM:

Dic quis grex? et quis sit dispersurus eum hostis?
     ReX AngLIœ, HoLLanDVM

Sed quœso, quœ lex tunc evertetur et a quo?
     NepanDa a WestphaLIœ
     DVCe BernarDo

J.P. in a conference with Mr W upon a speciall occasion, concerning my preaching and his attendance—for vindication propounded these 4 Qu—debated May 4 1677

1 Whether the obligation betwixt a minister and his people was not great, and whether the act of uniformity be sufficient to disanull it? it was answ— Neg—

2 Whether non-observation of liturgy and ceremonys, when theres harmony in doctrin and the main of worship be sufficient to brand dissenters wth schisme? its Ans neg—

3 Whether the place or stone-walls or timber, or rather the people met together to celebrate gods ordinances did giue the denomination of a church. it was Ans people

4 Whether it was not fit that husband and wife that pray together in family, secret should not also worship god togather in publick ordinances? it was Ans yes—

these things were propounded by J. P. to Mr W a conformable minister, in order to his marrying Ms M N who is a religious woman but had been bred up in conformity and was somthing shy in joyning with us, but upon a thorough debate upon these questions was abundantly satisfyed, Mr

* The above six verses.

W saying theres was a singular case, and there was few
such instances in the country of one so freely chosen 24
yeares agoe by the people and hath stuck so close to his
people, they to him in all these 14 yeares stormes.

—::—

Upon the Death of Mr Calamy

Not known to the author of a long time after:
By Dr R W:

And must our deaths be silenc'd too ? I guesse
tis some dumb devil hath posest the presse,
Calamy dead without a publication
tis great injustice to our English nation :
for had the prophets funeral been known
it must haue had an universal groan
Afflicted London would then haue been found
in the same year to be both burnd and drownd
and those who found no waues their flames to quench
would yet haue wept a showr his herse to drench :
Methinkes the man who stuffs the weekly sheet
with fine new nothings what hard names did meet
the Empresse how her petticoat was lac'd
and how her laqueys liverys were fac'd
whats her chiefe womans name, what dons doe bring
Almonds and figs to Spains great little king ;
is much concerned if the popes toe but akes,
when he breaks wind or when a purge he takes
he who can grauely advertise and tel,
Where Lochier and Rowland pippin dwell,
where a black box or a green bag was lost
and who was knighted tho not what it cost
Methinks he might haue thought it worth the while
tho not to tell us who the state beguile
or what new conquest Engl. hath acquired
nor that poor trifle who the city fired
tho not how popery exalts its head
and priests and Jesuites their poison spread
yet in swollen characters he might let fly,
the presbiterians haue lost an eye :

Had Crack   s fiddle been in tune (but he
is now a silenc'd man as well as we)
he had struck up loud musick and had playd
a jig for joy that Calamy was laid:
he would haue told how many coaches went
how many Lords and ladys did lament
what handkerchiefs were sent and in them gold
to wipe the widows eyes he would haue told,
all had come out and we beholden all
to him for the oreflowing of his gall:
but why doe I thus rant without a cause,
is not concealment policy whose laws
my silly peevish muse doth ill t oppose,
for publick losses no man should disclose,
and such was this, a greater loss by far
one man of god than twenty men of warre:
it was a king who when a prophet dy'd
wept over him and father, father, cry'd
oh if thy life and ministry be done,
my chariots and horsemens strength is gone,
I must speak sober words for well I know
if saints in heaven doe hear us here below
a lye tho in his praise would make him frowne
and chide me when with Jesus he comes downe
to judge the world   this little little he
this silly, sickly, silenced Calamy
Aldermanburgs curate and no more,
tho he a mighty miter might haue wore,
could haue vy'd interest in god and man
with the most pompous metropolitan
how haue we known him captivate a throng
and make a sermon twenty thousand strong
and the black mouths his loyalty did charge
how strong his tug was at the royal barge,
to hale it home, great George can wel attest
then when pure prelacy lay dead in its nest,
for if a collect could not fetch him home
Charles must stay out that interest was mum:
Nor did ambition of a miter make
him serue the crown it was for conscience sake
unbribed loyalty his highest reach
was to be Master Calamy and preach,

he blest the king who Bp did him name,
and I blesse him who did refuse the same,
oh had our Reverend Clergy been as free
to serue their prince without reward as he
they might have had lesse wealth with greater loue
envy like winds indangers things aboue,
worth not advancement doth beget esteem
the highest weather-cock the least doth seem,
if you would know of what disease he dyd
his griefe was chronical it is replyd
for had he opened been by surgeons art
they had found London burning in his heart
how many messengers of death did he
receive with christian magnanimity.
the stone, gout, dropsy, ills which did arise
from griefes and studys not from luxurys.
the megrim too which still strikes at the head
these he stood under and scarce staggered,
might he but work tho loaded with these chaines
he prayd and preacht and sung away his paines,
then by a fatal bill he was struck dead,
and tho that blow he nere recovered
(for he remained speechless to his close)
yet did he breath and breath out prayers for those
from whom he had that wound, he livd to hear
an hundred thousand buryed in one year :
in his dear city, over which he wept
and many fasts to keep off judgments kept
yet he livd stout heart he liv'd to be
deprivd, driven out, he liv'd to see
wars blazing stars, torches which heaven nere burns
but to light kings or kingdoms to their urnes :
he livd to see the glory of our ile
London consumed in its funerall pile :
he livd to see the lesser day of dome
London the priests burnt sacrifice to Rome,
that blow he could not stand but with that fire
as with a burning feaver did expire,
thus dy'd this saint of whom it may be said
he dy'd a martyr tho he dy'd in s bed,
so father Eli in the sacred page
sate quivering for fear as much as age,

longing to know yet loath to ask the news
how it fared with th army of the jews
Israel flys that struck his palsy head,
the next blow stunned him your sons are dead
when the third stroak came the ark is lost
his heart was wounded and his life it cost
    thus fel the father and we wel doe know
    he feard our ark was going long ago :

—::—

The Epitaph.

Here a poore minister of cht doth lye
who did indeed a bishopric deny
when his lord comes, then then the world shal see
such humble ones the rising men shal be,
how many saints whom he had sent before,
shouted to see him enter heavens doore
there his blest soul beholds the face of god
while we below groan out our Icabod
under his burned church his body lyes
but shal itselfe a glorious temple rise
may his kind flock when a new church they make
call it St. Edmundsbury for his sake,

Anno 1667

[Mr. Heywood lent so many books that he had to keep a list. Amongst the borrowers were Mr. Bentley, Mr. Dawson, Capt. Hodgson (who dipped into "God's terrible voyce," "Quenching the Spirit," Clark's "Martyrology," &c.), Mr. David Noble, Mr. Frankland, Dinah Tetlow, Jer. Baxter, John Kershaw, Richard Robinson. Phœbe Firth, Grace Butler, Mr. Furnace, Mr. Williams, John Stancliffe, Mr. Dighton, Brother Heywood, Mr. Waddington, Mr. Lee, Sarah Northend, Michael Broadley, Jonathan Priestley (who borrowed "Theatre of God's Judgments" a book dipped into now to see the practical turn of our puritan forefathers.)]

Mr. . . . . . I conceiue that its either the time of the slaying of the witnesses or of E destruction : for this is a special

E

remarkable passage scarce paraleld by any history : he con-
ceiues that the burial of them is their banishment, according
to Ezek 37 12 I wil cause you to come out of your graues,
and bring you into the land of Israel, *i e* redeem you from a
banished state : now tho there be an act for banishment yet
he thinks people wil not be forward to informe, witnes, and
put on to the execution of it, nay rather oppose it, and not
suffer their dead bodys to be put into graues, but onely
triumph over them Rev 11 9 10 :

Mr P at H delivered these assertions—1 that as man made
the first defection from God so he must first return unto
God : 2 if thou fal away from gods electing loue, yet redeeming loue wil take hold of thee : 3 that threatenings are a
stronger motiue to us to draw near to god than mercy : 4
that god never executes judgmts but it is to doe good to the
persons under them

—::—

My book of Heart-treasure thus disposed of

there came to my hands in Yorkshire 60 for 5li			John Simpson		
William Robuck	...	6	John Simpson	...	1
William Brig	...	1	John Kirshaw	...	1
Robert Ramsden	...	1	Martha Hanson	...	1
Capt. Hodgson	...	1	Dinah Tetlaw	...	1
Alice Holt	...	1	James Smith	...	2
Mary Rhodes	...	1	Martha Bairstowe	...	1
Jonathan Priestley	...	1	Will Robuck	...	6
Elizab. Sagar	...	1	Mr Dawson	...	1
Joshua Walker	...	1	James Brooksbank	...	1
Mtris Furnace	...	1	Anthony Lea	...	1
James Smith	...	1	Margaret Rushworth		1
Grace Kitchin	...	1	Joshua Soynier	...	1
Henry Smith	...	1	Eliz. Pierson	...	1
Mary Walker	...	1	James Brooksbank	...	1
Mary Kirk	...	1	Joseph Jackson	...	3
Mr Bentley	...	1	Rich Robinson	...	1
Sarah Langly	...	1	Phœbe Firth	. .	1
Tim : Hodgson	...	1	John Ramsden	...	1
John Brerely	...	1	James Mitchel	...	1
Mtris Horton	...	1	Mr Horton	...	1
John Appleyard	...	1	John Heywood	...	1
			Lady Stan		

those that came into Lanca-shire, 60	
My father Hey: ...	1
Sister Hanna ...	3
John Massey ...	1
Will Crompton ...	1
Ralph Friscoe ...	1
Edmund Hill ...	1
Mathew Hollis ...	1
Sister Alice ...	1
Mr Crompton ...	1
Brother Crompton ...	1
Mr Strangeways ...	1
Will Tong ...	1
Brother Okey ...	1
Sister Donne ...	1
Mtris Ambrose ...	1
Unkle Francis ...	1
Cosin Rebecca ...	1
Robert Roscoe ...	1
Brother Heywood ...	1
Mtris Ashurst ...	1
Mary Roscoe ...	1
John Roscoe ...	1
Richard Heywood ...	1
Brother Heywood ...	2
Couzen Hanna ...	2
Sister Hanna ...	1
Brother Whiteh: ...	1
Sister Hulton ...	1
Caleb Broadhead ...	8
little Will Whiteh. ...	1
James Pilkinton ...	1
Couzen Seddon ...	1
Aunt Crompton ...	1
Father Angier ...	1
Mtris Ardern ...	1
Mrs Howarth ...	1
Mr Buxtons ...	1
Aunt Russel ...	1
Aunt Hulton ...	1
Mr Hopwood ...	1

Brother Heywood ...	2
Lady Stanly ...	1

Another Dozen came Christmas 166⁷⁄₈

Alice Holt ...	1
Mary Kendall ...	1
John Kershaw ...	1
Jerem Watson ...	2
Mr Moxon ...	1
Mr Sharp ...	1
Math: Bottonly ...	1
Sam Ellison ...	1
Mtris Rawden ..	1
Mtris Ardington ...	1
Rich: Cook ...	1
George Stanford ...	1
Mtris Rose Lamning	1

Two dozen more

Robert Atkinson ...	1
John Scot ...	1
Ester Baraclough ...	1
Anthony Lea ...	1
Jonathan Priestley ...	2
Micael Boys ...	1
Elizab. Roberts ...	1
Eden Brooksbank ...	1
George Town ...	1
Mr Sale ...	1
Ellis Bury ...	1
Sam Wilkinson ...	1
Sam. Ellison ...	2
Edw: Wildman ...	1
Mtris Walker ...	1
Nath: Bottomley ...	6
Abrah: Walker ...	1
Martha Wardman ...	1
Jerem: Jagger ...	1
Ms Aukland ...	1
Mr Thorp ...	1

28 Books more Feb 20
1667/8

Mr Cotton	...	1
Lady Hoyle	...	1
Mr Kitchin	...	1
Rich : Sharp	...	1
Thom : Beck	...	1
Jeffery Beck	...	2
James Smith	...	2
Will Gelderd	...	1
Martha Brig	...	1
Jerem : Bairstow	...	1
Martha Smith	...	1
Joseph Kitchin	...	1
Sam : Craven	...	2
Martha Hodgson	...	1
Jeffery Beck	...	2
Mtris Robinson	...	1
Elizabeth Haslam	...	1
Mary Dickinson	...	1
Ms Crosley	...	1
Phœbe Lister	...	1
Will Hodgson	...	1
Ms Kerby	...	1
Ms Kitchin	...	1
Mr Cholmley	...	1

———

My sons had one Dozen of
14 to the dozen

———

James Smith disposed of 11 :

Jerem Bairstow	...	1
John Kershaw	...	1
Judith Field	...	1

———

28 bookes more come
july 18 68 :

John Wilkinson	...	1
Robert Hickson	...	1
Aunt Rathband	...	1

Warley people	...	2
Eden Brooksb	...	2
James Smith	...	2
Jane Milner	...	1
Cousin Angier	...	1
Anne Garside	...	1
Lady Rhodes	...	1
Henry Jackson	...	1
Eliezer Hodgson	...	6
Anne Priestley	...	1
Jer : Watson	...	1
Hanna Hardger	...	1
Jer Jaggar	...	1
Warley man	...	1
Another woman	...	1
Warley woman	...	1

these another dozen—uiz

James Brooksb	...	1
Jeffrey Beck	...	1
Mr. Dincley	...	1
Sist Hanna	...	1
Jer Jaggar	...	1

———

Received of Mr. Parkhurst
13 books of Heart treasure
jan 5 69-70—

James Smith Hort	...	1
John Nickol	...	1
J Scolfield	..	1
Lidia of Boltons	...	1
James Smith	...	2
Mary Wilton	...	1
Eden Brooksbank	...	2
Mtris Marshal	...	1

———

Received of Mr. Parkhurst
13 books of Heart treasure
Feb 12 1670-1 cost 20s

Eden Brooksbank	...	1
John Hagues wife	...	1
Mtris Earnshaw	...	1

John Wilkinson	...	1	Elizabeth Lee	...	1
Rich : Armitage	...	1	Bridget Mellin	...	1
James Smith for Y	...	1	Jerem Walker	...	1
Will Cook of Rip	...	1	Eliezer Heywood	...	1
Mary Northend	...	1	John Brooksbank	...	1

—::—

My Book of Closet prayer thus disposed of—there came into
Lanc : 12. unto Yorksh : 8 dozen.

Mr Richardson	...	1	Mtris Sharp	...	1
Betty Riddlesden	...	1	Joseph Bentley	...	1
My wife	...	1	Th : Langsters lad	...	1
John Heywood	...	1	John Kershaw	...	1
Eliezer Heywood	...	1	Jeffrey Beck	...	1
Martha Bairstow	...	1	Mtris Spencer	...	1
Rich : Cook	...	1	Ms Sarah Kitchin	...	1
Will Butler	...	1	John Gill	...	1
Hanna Hardger	...	1	Mr Moxon	...	1
Tho : Harrison	...	1	Mr Milner	...	1
Mtris Hodgson	...	1	Robt Hickson	...	1
James Smith	...	6	Tim Smith	...	1
John Wilkinson	...	1	Mr John Thursby	...	1
James Oates	...	1	Mr Paul Thursby	...	1
Joshua Wright	...	1	John Hopkinson	...	1
Marg : Rushworth	...	1	Jane Milner	...	1
Mary Walker	...	1	Robert Coulen	...	1
Rich Robinson	...	1	John Cummin	...	1
James Brookbank	...	1	Sicily Skelton	...	1
Martha Hanson	...	1	Mark Freeman	...	1
Rose Watson	...	1	Dorithy Bolton	...	1
Warley woman	...	1	Elizabeth Lee	...	1
Will Clay	...	1	James Smith	...	4
Phœbe Firth	...	1	Ellis Bury	...	1
James Mitchel	...	1	James Breafit	...	1
Alice Holt	...	1	William Farrar	...	1
Thomas Langster	...	1	Mary Rhodes	...	1
Isaac Balme	...	1	Mr Kitchen	...	1
Mtris Milner	...	1	Susan Northend	...	1
Mr Dawson	...	1	Eden Brooksb	...	1

Mr Smith of G	...	1	Th : Beck ...	1
Abrah : Dawson	...	1	Mr Dinely ...	1
John Scur H H	...	1	Mtris Ardington ...	1
Mr Root jun	...	1	Br Goodwin ...	1
Sarah Langley	...	1	Nat Crompton ...	1
James Dickson	...	1	Sist Hanna ...	1
John Hide	...	1	Jane Allison ...	1
Ms Kerby	...	1	Phœbe Lister ...	1
Mary Potter	...	1	Mathew Hollis ...	1
Nath. Bottonley	...	1	Edmund Hill ...	1
Will Robuck	...	1	Sist : M Angier ...	1
Andrew Watson	...	1	Phœbe Stanclif ...	1
Tho : Ledger	...	1	Lady Hewet ...	1
Elk. Brooksbank	...	1	Elizab. Haslam ...	1
Sam : Ellison	...	1	Lady Rodes ...	1
W. Wrigglesworth	...	1		

—::—

12 in Lancash			Josiah Oates ...	1
My father Heywood	...	1	James Dixon ...	1
Brother Heywood	...	1	Estre Hoyle ...	1
Broth. Okey	...	1	Marg : Rushworth ...	2
Broth. Whiteh [ead]		1	Mary Kirk ...	1
Broth. Bradly	...	1	James Smith ...	1
Broth. T Crompt	...	1	Sam : Hardger ...	1
B L Crompton	...	1	Sam : Wilkinson ...	1
Brother Hulton	...	1	Lidias mother ...	1
Ms Buxtons	...	1	Mary Learoyd ...	1
Mary Holt	...	1	John Burroughs ...	1
Lady Stanley	...	1	Ms Jackson ...	1
Ms Ashurst	...	1	Jer Jaggar ...	1
Coz : Anna Crompton		1	Grace Bunny ...	1
			Ab. Walker ...	1
44 Books sent by Mr Park-			Mr Haliday ...	1
hurst Aug 28 of Closet			Hanna Watson ...	1
prayer—			Mtris Cudworth ...	1
Marg : Hodgson	...	1	John Crowther ...	1
John Bland	...	1	Aunt Russel ...	1
Coz : Bullen	...	1	Father Angier ...	1
Sistre Donne	...	1	Aunt Crowther ...	1

Ms Ardern	1	Mr Wadington	1
Ms Gr: Hide	1	Tho: Atkinson	1
Ja: Smith	1	Mat: Boys	1
Rich Hargreaves	1	Ms Thursby	1
Janit Douglasse	1	Ms Thompson	1
James Smith	1	James Smith	2
John Apleby	1	El. Hinchball	1
Nath: Heaton	1	Sa. Wilkinson	1
Sam: Holdworth	1	John Brown	1
Sam: Smith	1	Mr Sotwel	1
Aunt Darcy	1	Mr Rich	1
Lady Watson	1	Mr Wadsworth	1
Mtris Rose Lamning	1	Est Baraclough	1
Susan Longbottom	1	Dame Woodhead	1
John Bury	1	James Dixon	3
Jerem Kershaw	1	Will: Dickinson	1
Mr Crompton	1	Mr Thursby	3
Lady Hewly	1	Ms Dison	1
Mr J Lister	1	John Simpson	1
Mr Holdsworth	1	Joh Burrough	1
Mary Tomlinson	1	Pris: Walker	1
		James Taylor	1
Bought at Manchest		Jo. Priestley	1
Cozen Mary Knight	1	Mary Rhodes	1
Judith Heawood	1	Joh Robinson	1
Aunt Hulton	1	Micael Smith	2
		George Horsman	1
Ordered to be bought at		Edith Hickson	1
Bolton octob 19		Ruth Holdw.	1
Brother Whitehead	1	John Bury	1
Uncle Winstandly	1	Martha Robinson	1
Uncle John Heywood	1		
Cozen Rebecca Croth	1	Received of Mr Parkhurst	
Brother Angier	1	26 books of Closet prayer,	
		Jan 5 1669-70	
Received 44 Books of Mr		John Cordingley	1
Parkhurst Closet prayer		Mtris Crossley	1
Decem 4 69		Huthersfild woman	1
Ja: Brooksbank	1	Sarah Parker	1
Gra Butler	1	Ms Middeborough	1
M Wardman	1	Jerem Bairstow	1
Ms Bagnal	1	Ester Glover L.	1

Mr Marsden	...	1	J Scolfield	...	1
Mtris Thorp	...	1	Ab Naylour	...	1
Mtris Malivery	...	1	Estre Baraclough	...	1
Wid. Armitage	...	1	Eden Brooksbank	...	1
A Butterworth	...	1			
Cozen J. Crompton	...	1	Received of Mr Parkhurst		
John Roberts	...	1	13 books of Closet prayer,		
Sister Ester Whit	...	1	Aug 27 70		
Ms Robinson	...	1	Eden Broosbank	...	1
Ms Furnace	...	1	Warley woman	...	1
Warley woman	...	1	Will Wilton wif	...	1
Mr Holdsworth	...	2	Joh Soltenstal	...	1
John Nichols wife	...	1	Honley man	...	1
Robert Ramsden	...	1	Susan Appleyard	...	1
Jam : Smith for Maid		1	Tim Holt	...	1
Jer Jos : Fields Maid		1			
Tho : Langster	...	1	Received of Mr Parkhurst		
Robt Baraclough wife		1	3 dozen of bookes of		
Mr Braithwait	...	1	Closet pr : Aug 26 1671		
			2d Edition*		
Received of Mr Parkhurst			James Smith	...	1
12 books of Closet prayer,			Isaac Smith	...	1
Feb 12 69-70			Elizab : Cummin	...	1
John Watson	...	1	Josiah Stansfield	...	2
John Marsden	...	1	Mtris Paget	...	1
Cozen Critchlaw	...	1	Katerin Fern	...	1
Jane France	...	1	Mtris Baily	...	1
John Smith wife	...	1	Hen Wrigly	...	1
Jer Worrel wife	...	1	Mtris Drake	...	1
Rich Wilsons wife	...	1	Mtris Jolly	...	1
John Brearcliff	...	1	Mtris Hickson	...	1
Rich Armitage	...	1	Sim Ellison	...	2
Mr Foster	...	1	Sam Holdworth	...	1
John Rhodes	...	1	James Smith	...	1
			Sam : Ellison	...	2
Received 13 books of Closet			Mtris Root	...	1
prayer from Mr Parkhurst			Mts Walker	...	1
june 1 1670			Tim Mellen	...	1
Thom : Brook	...	6	Robt Swain	...	1
James Cordingley	...	1	Eden Brooksb	...	1

* [There were thus three editions, 1669, 1671, and 1700. The second edition I supposed was the first. See Vol. 2, p. 4.]

Sam Holdworth	...	1	Jonathan Priestley	...	1
John Heywood	...	1	John Brooksbank	...	1
Eliezer Heyw.	...	1	Jeremiah Baxter	...	1
Margaret Denton	...	1	James Tetlaw	...	1
Sister M. Angier	...	1	Mr Dawson	...	1
Annie Carington	...	1	John Stancliff	...	1
A woman	...	1	Mr Jolly	...	1
Matthew Clay	...	1	Mr Wadington	...	1
Joh Burkhead	...	2	John Kershaw	...	1
Ellen Drake	...	1	Josiah Stansfield	...	1
			Martha Slater	...	1

Received of Mr Parkhurst 4 books of Cl pr May 21 73

Anthony Lea	...	1
Timothy Holt	...	1
Sam : Holdworth	...	1
James Oates	...	1

Judith Cockcroft	...	1
Jerem Baxter	...	1
Sarah Walker	...	1
Anne Bolton	...	1

Received of Mr Parkhurst 6 of Closet prayer, Feb 28 1681-2

Mtris Dawson	...	1
John Dickon	...	1
Martha Greenwood	...	1

Received of Mr Parkh 2 dozen of Prot Catich june 28 73

—::—

[𝔐r. 𝔎irby's 𝔓oem.]

Joshua joyeth in his Saviours name
beleevd on, preacht in suffering for the same,
Mary did wisely chose the better part
Susanna of her own to cht impart
Elizabeth religiously did liue
Phœbe unto many succour giue
Camdena of my foundresse minded me
Welcome expresseth what a child should be
Gods-gift his fathers name doth bear & spread
twin is the living monumt of the dead :

To my family

In prison I a wife & children found	mat 9 29
Mariage with womb & brest blessings is crownd	hos 9 10
God gaue me one god giue to him his son	gal 4 19
God gaue me more, the same to them be done,	
Striue to be better as you elder are	tit 2 4
Expect not to liue long to live with care	Eph 5
Prevent sin or it wil you circumvent	heb 12 1
Covet first not to sin next to repent	2 cor 12
Wel think wel speak wel doe, come at cht cal	2 th 18 21
Tho you set out last yet outrun them al	1 cor 13 8

—::—

A prisoners verdict

An Army Rampant first me prisoner made
A Rampant Kirk now taketh up their trade
fallen is that army and that Kirk must fall
the temple will consume that Cathedrall (Ezek 43 8)
the stones haue been removd in wch was found
the leprosy, the house was scraped round :
new stones are laid al is new plaistered
yet still the fretting leprosy doth spread
the Harlots marks cannot be purgd wth nitre
nor can Melchisedek brook Aarons mitre

—::—

To my fellow prisoners at Wakefield in the house of——

C annot the prisons meet, the prisoners may
O pen from both to heaven there a way
R eligious meetings make our bodys part
R eligious meeting makes us of one heart
E xcept the saints communion be denyed
C orrection and castle, are defyed
T o you I send my heart, you are my joy
I n gods way keep and nought shal you annoy
O f family and busines god takes care
N o want of us at home while god is there

BartheLoMeVs fLet qVIa DesIs presbyter AngLe
ADVentV Leeta est SanCta MarIa tVo
MDLLLVVII 1662
MDCLVVVI 1666

Th ApostLe Moanes for EngLanDs WItnes sLaIn
The VIrgIn gLaDLy SpIes hIM LIVe agaIn
MDLLLVVII 1662
MDLLLVVIIIIII 1666

—::—

Another Bundle of Books opened wherein I think is
100 of Meetness for Heaven Apr. 20, 1692.

Mr. D. Noble,	Ann Hinchb,	Mary Oldfield,
Jonathan Rig,	Mr. Waterhouse,	Tho Bradbury,
Mtris Haugh,	Martha Robinson,	Ab. Walker,
Rich. Armitage,	Joseph Brear,	Josiah Stansfeld
Ms Lambert,	Steven Bradshaw,	Mr fenton,
Abr. Firth,	Rich. Pilkington	Simeon Robinson
Joyce Milner,	Sam Wilkinson	Mr. Thorp, 3
daughter Elizab.,	John Bothumley,	John Walker,
Grace Grub,	John Ryleys wife,	Rich. Boys wife,
Jos. fornesse,	Wm. Northen,	M. Booth,
Tho. Dobson,	Abr. Whitwham.	John Oxly,
Eliz. Milner,	Debora Bradley,	John Simpson,
James Swyft,	Will Sharp,	Esther Brigg,
James Cash,	Cozen O. Mosely,	Joshua Crompton

—::—

More Bookes of meetnes for heaven given by me		47 Mr W Handen ...	1
		48 Phœbe Renier ...	1
38 My Lady Moseley	1	49 Joseph Hollins ...	1
39 Cozen Russel MS	1	50 Mr Jon Wright ...	1
40 Ester Hunt, Worsly	1	51 Thomas Hague M	1
41 Sarah Northend ...	1	52 Joseph Lister All'erton]1	
42 James Barret ...	1	53 Mathew Heywood	1
43 Thomas Gill ...	1	54 Sinteon Robinson	1
44 Samuel Swain Revy	1	55 Ms Sale Pudsey ...	1
45 Gyles Shaw Sadd	1	56 Willm Fenton ...	1
46 Andrew Watson ...	1	57 Samuel Bradly ...	1

58	John Bradly	...	1	Francis Becket	...	1
59	Joseph Ianson	...	1	Ms Sale	...	1
60	John Farrar	...	1	Mr Stead	...	1
61	Mr Thorp bought		2	Mtris Stanhup	...	1
62	Ms Ivison	...	1	Mary Ingham	...	1
63	Tho Atkinson	...	1	Hanna Pannel	...	1
64	Mr Hardwick	...	1	Humphrey Stead	...	1
65	Ms Rimer	...	1	Dr Cotton	...	1
66	Ms Rhodes	...	1	Mtris Holdworth	...	1
67	Mr Priestly	...	1	Mr John Ash	...	1
68	Mr Whitworth	...	1	Obadiah Dawson	...	1
69	Mrs Serjeant	...	1	W. Stocks	...	1
70	Dr Hall Kipping	...	1	John Bland	...	1
71	One in Lane	...	1	James Jagger	...	1
72	One at home	...	1	Alice Greenhough	...	1
73	Nat Holdens man		1	Eliz Wardman	...	1
74	Sarah Brook	...	1	Thomas Bauden	...	1
75	Joseph Heywood		1	Mr Nic Donnel	...	1
76	John Scot Alverth		1	Joshua Stansfield	...	1
77	Esther Scotcroft	...	1	John Wood	...	1
78	Joshua Rodes	...	1	Lidia Hodgson	...	1
79	Horton woman	...	1	Mr Tho Lambert	...	1
80	Joseph Moor	...	1	Cozen Davis	...	1
				John Hitchin	...	1
	Another Bundle			Martha Greenwood	...	1
	John Foster	...	1	Willm Garths wife	...	1
	Mr Thorp	...	3	Tim Dighton	...	1
	Mr Sagar sen	...	1	Mr David Hartly	...	1
	Mr Jolly sen	...	1	Mr Foxcroft	...	1
	Mr Jolly jun	...	1			

—::—

Mr Douglas* the Scotch minister who was the great instrument in crowning King charles 2d (it is some other,* theres a mistake in the person yet I haue not learned the name) is now banished, and was very poore in Holland he came to an English merchant and intreated some reliefe, he perceived by his speech of what country he was and askt him why he did not goe to his countrymen, he told him he was ashamed to own them being in that low condition. he gave him a shilling, and told him he had no publick moneys in his hands since he was now out of the office wherein he was the year before. As he was walking in the streets he met one of his countrymen who lookt intently upon him, askt him his name, and at last brought him to the rest of the merchants, who chid him for not making himself known to them. they bought hansome rayment for him, set him to preach, and he is now in the Duke of Brandenburgs country and the city where he resides, hath disputed with the lutheran Doctors & is too good for them, young scholars desired to come to his chamber, where he reads lectures to them, discourseth with y^m and doth abundance of good. the Drs were vexed and complained to the Duke, who discoursed with him, was abundantly satisfyed and gaue him free liberty to preach in publick and tis said he is to preach in his chappel : who knows but he may be sent thither for some good :

there is a great number of scotch ministers banished beyond seas, many which are in Holland. the councel in Scotland, sent to the states, expostulating with them for entertaining them, whom they are pleased to call the scum of the country. they write largely back again to them, with confident denyals to turn them out of the country, telling them withal that if these be the scum of the country al the rest are angels :

Mr James Wood professor of the University of St Andrews in Scotland lying upon his death-bed, was visited by Dr Sharp Archbishop of that Diocese, he urged him to declare his thoughts about discipline, whether he preferred Episcopacy or presbitery. he desired him to forbear such discourse and told him he had other matters more weighty to think of. he went away and gaue it out that Mr Wood had declared for episcopacy, several ministers heard of it and sent three of their company to Mr Wood yet living, he gaue them the like answer that he had no list to disclose of those things, they urged him because of the bishops report, he bade them write the declaration, and he would subscribe it, wch was done, and they set downe their hands to it as witnesses thereof. the bishop hearing of it was very angry and cited them to appear at his court, where they were accused as slanderers in belying the Bishop, they answered negatiuely, but affirmed that he had belyed Mr Wood, they produced the declaration and were willing to depose upon oath if they

were lawfully called to it that that was Mr Woods own hand
and those his words, whereby he declared for presbitery.
the court was ashamed, and made nothing of it, tho before
the matter was tryed some of them had cast downe their
half-crowne and departed, and would not be present at the
tryal of the case.

Too church-wardens about Faukingham in Lincolnshire
were excommunicated by Sr Edward Lake chancellor of
Lincolne for refusing to take the church-wardens oath, they
went to one Col. King a Lawyer for councell, he advised
them to sue him in the kings bench, and he would plead for
them, the chancellor heard of his councel and in displeasure
he excommunicated Mr King saying Ile teach him how he
meddles with my proceedings.   King gets a writ to summon
him to the kings bench, and at last found a sturdy fellow to
serve it upon him—in the suit the court cast the chancellor
in 200li damages, then the Ch. would haue agreed with the
church-wardens but they refused because they had been
abused by him, but tryed it, and recovered other 200li for
themselues, wch provoked the chancellor to complain of the
court saying never man was so abused for doing his duty.
wt sth the judg doe you attach me of injustice, be silent or
you shall be laid fast by the heeles—Dr Uly was preacher in
Essex, and in the beginning of the long parl. he was accused
before a committee of much superstition, they produced and
laid upon a table before them a curious surplice, with a
crosse and glorious workmanship on the brest. it was
inquired of the church-wardens who put them on to make
it, they said Dr Uly, who at last confessed it, that he made
it after a pattern in the church-window, and wept much
saying, tis true indeed I have been too too zealous for the
ceremonys wch are the trash and trumpery of the church,
and ever since I read the book for sports on the sabbath, I
have found the power of godlines decaying in me,—but since
the kings return home, he returned to his vomit of superstition, and worse he had yt living in Essex and Stepney,
and was halfe a year before he preacht a sermon at the one,
but since and not long since he dyed a professed papist as
it is reported :

September 2d 1664 : there was a correction at Halifax,
multitudes were cited to appear there, after some prayers in
the church, they called over the citations, amongst the rest

one man of fashion answered to his name. they told him
he was cited for not coming to the sacrament, for hearing a
non-conformist preach and for contributing to him : to the
first he said he would say nothing at present, to the other
too he desired to see his accusers and witnesses : they said
nothing to him but dismist him requiring his attendance in
the afternoon : After dinner they sate in the checker
chamber at Mr Hansons, where was only the proctor to
recciue money, and while they were busy in that work that
side of the chamber floore shrunk, and fel down, and many
fel through into the cellar below, the proctor and his son
both fel down, one upon another, there was no great hurt
done, onely there was a woman hurt, and some bear spilt,
and the table frame was quite broken to peces, the prejudice
the house hath suffered amounts to about 40s : An happy
omen of their future fall : it was a strong wel-built roome,
and the other side of the chamber did not shrink at all : the
timber had not a crack nor decay in it, and the roome hath
been formerly thronged ful at a sessions and never shrunk,
they haue allowd the house 20s for the losse : it was the first
time that spiritual court hath been kept at Halifax in the
memory of man : I hope it may be the last :

Mr Walbank preacher at Cothurn, preaching upon that
text a good name is better than precious oyntment, sd it
was better to make shipwrack of a good conscience than to
lose a good name, and gaue this reason for it, because in the
former we had to deal with god who is merciful, and easily
reconciled, but men are unreasonable and wil not be won :
he affirmed another time that a christian is to liue upon
inherent righteousnes : being drinking with one of his brother-
hood of his own coat, when the reckoning came to be paid,
the other puld out some halfe-crowns, thou art very rich
sth he, thou shalt be called much-worth, he tooke some
liquor in his hand & threw it in his face, saying the words
of institution in baptisme, in the name of the trinity calling
him much-worth there were too church-wardens present,
that constantly affirme it :

When B Bancroft was a student in the University his
chamber-fellow rising one morning to write letters, and he
lying stil he perceived that as he slept he changed cheer,
and his countenance spoke him much affected with joy, &
after that with griefe. When he awakt he asked him what

he ailed, he replyed I have had the strangest dreams that
ever I had, I haue been dreaming sth he that I was made
Doctor and afterwards Bishop and at last Archbishop of
Canterbury, and then I dyed and went to hel : When al was
come to passe upon his death-bed he remembered his dream,
and not before, and was much affrighted he was a great
persecutor of good ministers, and silenced very many : especially Mr Midgley of Rochdale, whom he not only silenced
from his work, but degraded from his office : who dyed in
Halifax :

I am told this day by an ancient man that is 86 yeares of
age that al the ministers that haue been at Coley this 70
yeares and upwards came out of Lancashire, he reckoned
them up, Mr Nicols, (who was the first preaching minister
there was, after one Sir Adam a Reader) Mr Gibson, Mr
Marsden, Mr Hierst, Mr Denton, Mr Lathum, Mr Cudworth,
Mr Cleton, and my selfe, who am the last and least of these
famous predecessors into whose labours I haue entered, and
haue laboured about 12 years in this part of the vineyard,
but haue been cast out of my publick work, because of my
unprofitableness, now this too yeares and upwards : O when
wil the lord return ?   this is Septemb 7 1664 :

Colonel Holland of Denton in Lanc. dying left an estate
of 800 per annum, his yonger brother being almost 60 yeares
of age heired his lands had never been marryed, found out a
suitable gentle-woman, one Ms Britland, the mariage-day
was appointed, al things settled and concluded in the mean-
time he fel sick and dyed, and was buryed upon the day that
was prefixed for mariage-solemnities.   the Minister preacht
upon the same text at the funerals that was appointed for
the nuptials—onely changing the words, Mat 25 6 : there
was a cry made—for, behold the bridegroome cometh :
there was lately a great meeting of papists in Ireland, of the
nobility, gentry, & their clergy a legate was come from Rome
to giue orders, &c several received orders to be priests—it
was so publick and notoriously known that it fel under the
cognisance and censure of the councel, and they sent out a
favourable indulgent proclamation, shewing the offensiuenes
of it and desiring them to doe so no more, so that the popish
party are very high and seem to be much animated and
incouraged :

Sir Francis Wortlys great grandfather being a man of a great estate was owner of a towne near unto him, onely there were some freeholders in it, with whom he wrangled and sued untill he had beggared them and cast them out of their inheritance, and so the town was wholly his, wch he pulled quite downe and laid the buildings and town-fields even as a common, wherein his main design was to keep deer, and made a lodge to wch he came at the time of the year and lay there taking great delight to hear the deere bell, but it came to passe that before he dyed he belled like a deer and was destracted, some rubbish there may be seen of the town, it is upon a great moore betwixt Peniston & Sheffield in Yorkshire :

there is a high bridg near peniston over wch a woman riding in a high wind, the wind blew both her and the horse off the bridg, the water was something high, and there were fishers below who tooke them out and neither she nor the horse had any hurt, tho she was with child, she had brought forth 19 children, and was at that time with child of the 20th.

As king Charles the 2d was riding through the streets in a coach he spyed a man that he took more than ordinary notice of, setting his eyes upon him, and drew him to aside, asking him saying haue not I seen you somewhere? yes my liedge, sd he, he asked him where, he replyed at Worcester fight but sd the king I remember you by some remarkable circumstance, what is it? at last he told him that when the battel was lost, and al was in an uproar, and his majesty bade them al shift for themselves, he sd to the king, farewel until 60, wch the king calling to mind proceeded in discourse with him, saying if thou canst tel that, thou canst tel more, what dost thou study by the state of things now? he was loath to say anything when the king urged him, he sd, your mtys dominions are now ful of bishops, but before 66 I wil undertake to keep them all for a gray groate :

At Eccles in Lanc there was to be a bear bait, a yong man there living was zealous for it, & would haue it at his house for gain, & sel ale at that time. Mr Joanes lately minister there urged him to forbear with many argumts, & told him he would repent of it, he made light of his councel, went to Manchester on Saturday cryed in the streets a bear, a bear, would haue given the bel-man a groat to cry it, Mr

Jones went to him agen told him al his predecessors in that place had declaimed agt it his father that was minister before him, had sd if there be a rogue in the country heel be there, told him of a man slain there on that occasion, but he was wilful, the day came, & the sport was over, people gone, al peace, but that night a drunken man comes, takes occasion to wrangle with him, and gaue him such a blow as he thinkes he shal feel while he liues, he is yet aliue but scarce likely to recover, Mr Joanes hath endeavoured to convince him, and he begins to soften tho at first he did not see he was in any fault, the lord doe him saving good by it :

there is strange storys of several german prophets the book Mr Geering a worcester-shire minister hath translated, being asisted by a neighbour that was born in Germany and was committed to the tuition of Joh. Comenius, betwixt whom & this man passe many letters. the book was strangely preserved, one prophesying that the castle where Comenius was should be destroyed, the people fled out of the town at the enemys approach, the castle was fired, abundance of writings burnt, yet they had liberty to search the rubbish for what they could find. Comenius found the book of prophets & prophecys amongst the rubbish not consumed, in wch there is very strange passages :—   get the book :

Christina a ministers daughter in Bohemia was committed to the tuition of Comenius, she had an apoplexy by wch means her one side was struck dead, she foretold the day of her death several persons waited on her upon that day ministers and matrons, she sensibly declined, took solemn leaue of them, then departed, too stayed with her to look out linnens for the dead, Comenius went out last, he heard a great cry in the roome, turned back and saw the virgin revived, he was affrighted and said in the name of god whats the matter she answered I am aliue, he said are thy hands and feet sound, she replied, sound, adding that god had returned her into the land of the living and had more work for her to doe here, but sd she trouble me no more to-night, for to morrow I wil write down al that god hath spoken to me, wch she did—

while she was lying so very sick languishing and drawing near her end, came several persons to visit her, ministers and others, amongst the rest one Tichicus a minister of the city, who gaue her good exhortations, when he went away

she said this good man little knows that he must dye before
me, but I haue been with god & haue seen several going to
him, and named many in that city, who indeed al dyed
shortly after and that minister tho he was a strong lusty
man, dyed before her, Comenius asked her if she saw him
amongst them, she sd no, and she asked the reason, it was
answered he must stay a while for he had more work to doe:
her father was much displeased and judged it to be a de-
lusion wch exceedingly grieved her, and when he heard her
humble acknowledgmts and wonders wrought about her was
convinced, and charged her not to adde or diminish of the
lords mind, she told him she could not for when she writ
she knew not what she was to write, and if she had a mind
she could not altar a syllable :

the year before the king was restored, a man came to
Harborough lodged at night in an inne and when he was to
goe away in the morning he told his host & hostesse that
upon that day twelue-moneth King Charles should come in
to Engl and it proved accordingly, now lately he came to
the same house, asked the man of the house if he remembered him, he ans no, then he told him what he had sd to
him at that time, and he called him and his speeches to
mind as being much famed and talkt of through the town,
he added that that day too years would be a day of great
rejoicing through England, and then took his horse and rid
away :

there is one Mr Holcroft minister nonconformist a ladys
son in Cambridg-shire, who is proceeded agt according to
the late act for conventicles and the stat 85th of El. he was
clapt up in the castle of Cambridge, and was brought out to
be tryed for his life, and in the issue was condemned, his
punishment is either to take the oath of abjuration of the
kingdome, never to return, or be hanged. Some friends
haue begged a reprieue for a season that he may haue time
to consider of it, he thinks he ought to refuse that oath,
except they wil giue him leaue to goe whither he please out
of the kingdome, but if theyl transport him, & sel him for a
slaue it wil be worse then death :

At Burnsall in Craven was a grievous feaver amongst very
many, a man and his wife were both sick the woman rose
out of her bed and came to her husbands bed side in her
smock, and said, its now ten a clock, its time for me to be

gone, and so went out and was never found nor heard of since, wch is almost three weekes agoe:

A man near Draighton being sick in bed in his sleep he dreamed that he saw his father in law (who dyed some days before) coming to him with sword & armour, charging him to get up and fight telling him they must goe to a great battel, and within a short space that young man also dyed:

a dog pulled out the throat of a gentlemans mare that was worth 30li, the gentleman begged that he might be devoured by a lion, he was cast into the den, the lion seemed to scorn him but the dog receiving an hint from his master set on him, and he roaring, the dog pulled out his tongue, and presently after the lion dropt down and dyed: this was (as tis said) the queens lion, an old one, the dog is kept to have a conflict with another lion:

a gentleman told me one Mr G M that he having occasion to dig for stones to build a house he found a place in the middle of a field where there was a strange conglomeration of stones and earth, the field is in Bury parish in Lanc it lyes high and hath a fair prospect, the whole field hath a little swarfe with grasse at the top but stoney under like a causey and could never be plowed, but about the middle of it for about a rood of ground compasse in digging they found a strange incredible glueing and clottering of stones and earth so that they stuck so close togather that they could not part them and this was for about halfe a yard deep they conjecture that that is a place where the heathens in ancient times offered their sacrifices, and that the blood of the beasts runing down might soake into the earth, and congeal the dust and stones and earth to such incredible hardnes:

One Richard Wood a man of an exceeding vitious flagitious life, being an ancient man, and having buryed his wife who was a papist he hath lately lived at Lostock with Mr Anderton a papist, on friday being the 14th of this instant October he came home, having been abroad about his masters busines, and swore he had got his death, he ate his supper, went into his chamber, called for his master, bade them bring him a cup of sack, but before they came to him again he was dead in his chaire: 1664: he blasphemed fearfully a little before he dyed:

Jane Thompson was borne in Craven, whose brother dying the land fel to her, she was maryed to Mr Whitley of

Sinder-hils, who with her consent sold her land, spent abundance, run a wild tho short race, hastening his death by excesse, dyed young, left a son, which dyed shortly after: then there was at least a pretence of mariage betwixt Mr Ed. Firth and this yong wanton widow, tho tis sd they were never marryed, & himselfe profest so on his death-bed, but they lived togather as man & wife: this second husband was blind a considerable time before his death, and she abused him several times, as is notoriously known, especially by her too much familiarity with this man who was her last husband, her second husband lay long sick and was exceedingly afflicted in spirit, dealt seriously with his reputed wife, admonishing her to repent and reform her ways, adding, that it may be death would not giue her the like warning that it had given him: she sometimes jestingly spoke of his expressions, but made a scorn of them: Wel, this gentleman dyed and left her with child, and tho he had a great estate yet he cut her off with scarce 20l a year and left the child some smal thing to bring it up to a certain age, if it lived, but it dyed, and she was quickly marryed to Mr Will Greenwood an attorney born in Skipton but being settled in the house with her: she buryed her husband, was delivered of a child and buryed it, and was marryed to this husband in lesse than 8 weekes space:

She came and lived where her first husband dyed, who had left her a joynture of about 60li per an. and they sold for her life what Mr Firth left her, and made it away, they did not agree, being jealous of each other, the truth is she was notoriously addicted to wantones, she was a swinish drunkard, and took delight to see others drunk, she usually sent a great jugge to the alehouse several times in the day onely for herselfe, specially if she had been drunk the night before she was so habituated therin that she could eat nothing, but drink ale altogather, her stinking pride, her horrible swearing & cursing were too wel known by al that knew her:

As her life was abominable so her death was remarkable, she had not been wel about a fourtnight, and had taken physick being something better, she would goe with her husband up to J M, an alehouse about halfe a mile off, to lighten her and chear up her spirits with ale and company, and tho formerly she had cursed herselfe and bade the Devil

break her neck if ever she rid upon that mare wch her
husband had bought without her consent yet now she would
needs ride upon her, tho much dissuaded from it, yet she sd
if she was not the devil she would ride her, the mare caryed
her very quietly thither, and having spent some time there,
the man of the house set her on horse back and led the mare
a good space, as soone as ever he let goe, the beast fel a
capering and running straight from homewards, the bridle
and crupper brake, and she came downe, the spectators
thought she light upon her feet, but her arme was broken,
and a hole was made in it wch bled profusely, and another
under her arme hole she was taken up by her husband,
and fainted into a swoone several times, when she was
sensible she cryed out o death, death, what shal I doe with
death, yet when she was a little recruited she went the
greatest part of the way home on foot, when her arm was
set she felt little pain, tho several bones stuck out visibly,
that were broken, this was on the thursday night, on the
friday she talkt merrily and drunk heartily, and often sent
her husband from her upon some excuse that she might get
more ale, her body swelled excessiuely and she was stretched
out in length incredibly while she was living, her wounds
kept constantly running, so that its strange to think what
issued from her, and she stunk so that some were sick with
being near her : Upon the friday night an honest neighbour
watcht with her, who put her in mind of her approaching
death, but she seemed to be offended with her, onely saying
I am a miserable wretch, and put off those matters with
other discourse, she was not at al sensible, nor did she
desire any minister to come to her, tho she had partakt of
the sacrament at Halifax a little before, she continued in
that trade of excessiue drinking til she dyed, so that its
verily beleeved by some that she dyed drunk, for she had
drunk six meribauk pots ful of ale that day she dyed wch
was before 11 a clock on saturday being june 18 1664 : that
night the coroner came to view her, and the jury found the
beast that cast her accessory to her death, her husband took
on most sadly and cryed out that he was undone, having
lost all the estate and being in debt : her body was swelled
to an incredible quantity it was as big as three ordinary
womens, her face was as blew as a painted blew wal, out of
her nose and mouth constantly streamed something like

drink, about her neck where she was wont to wear her neck-
lace a great wreath of flesh stood higher than the rest, that
had several freckled, coloured spots upon it, her eyes were
exceeding great as tho they would have started out, but that
wch was most strange, her body was not swelled proportionably, for tho her higher parts & thighs were monstrous great,
yet her legs and feet were of their ordinary bulk, and as
pure white and neat as ever were living gentlewomans, yea
tho her better arme that was not hurt was swelled aboue
the elbow as thick as a mans thigh, yet below it was as it
was wont to be : the corpse smelt very strong, the stench
was more loathsome then any carion, so that none could
endure to be in the roome, the women went to her husband
and told him she must be buryed yt night, for she could not
be kept both by reason of the stench and they feared the
bursting of the body, abundance of corrupt matter still issu-
ing out, he bade them burn frankincense and odoures in the
roome, but tho it was ful of smoak yet the steam of the
corps overcame that perfume : yea al the house stunk of the
dead body, and every roome, they again intreated Mr Greenwood to come see her and giue his judgment whether she
could be kept til munday, they wiped her face he kissed her,
and immediately as he turned his back too drops of blood
came out of her nostrils, out of either nostril one drop of
pure red blood, and then came other corrupt matter as
before : they concluded to bury her that night, and tho they
had bespoken an huge great coffin, very wide and too yards
long yet the body did but lean in it on one side, and as
much as a lusty womans body was out, the lid would not
come down, but they bound it about with cords, and eight
men carryed her with much difficulty to Coley chappel, wch
is not a bow shoot from the house, and she was buryed on
the sabboth day morning, by that time it was light enough
to see to read common-prayers at the graue, much earth was
laid by that could not goe into the graue : and the funerals was celebrated at Halifax upon munday where there was
a sermon, & drinking according to the usual manner :

    there is a boy about too miles from Tadcaster that is not
fiue years of age, whose stature is aboue an elle high, his
thigh is three quarters about, his face is like a mans, with
much haire upon it, he hath capacity for imployment as a
man, and eats as much as another ordinary man, as is able

to cary the third part of a ful horse-load of any thing: this Nov 1 1664: many people goe to see him, a gentleman offered his father 40li to let him take up his son to London, & keep him wel, & deliver him safely to him agen, but he refused:

A company of gentlemen (among them this Mr Greenwood before mentioned) were drinking at John Rushworths, after they had drunk healths in the parlour, went out of doores drunk health with their feet upon their hats then went up to the fold head, upon the lane side and kneeled there in a row with hats off and drunk healths, and sent for a horse to kneel with them but he refused:

Divine providence hath graciously stept in to rescue the fore-mentioned, Mr Hole-croft that was condemned, either to death or banishment, for an instrument to that purpose being brought to the king to be sealed by him, and he having the pen in his hand and the paper before him, ready to subscribe it, a nobleman stept in (who some think was the Earl of Manchester) and said, Sr it is blood, I entreat your majesty to consider what you doe, and with such like words stopt the subscription, and prevented the execution, and he is escaped that danger, blessed be god:

one told me this day that there was a company of great gentlemen came to visit an ancient gentlewoman near (one Mtris Thornel of Tootil) where they discoursed very prophanely, one said I matter not for the bible any more then another booke, I read more in other authors then in it, sd she why doe you not look upon it as the word of god, no sth he, I read it, and look upon it but as another history: Another affirmed that theres no hel, being asked what becomes of the wicked after death, or some such like question, he replyed, why if there be any its nothing but the want of gods presence, partly hinting that he could doe wel enough without that:

upon thursday last wch was Decemb 18 1664 there hath been seen a comet or blazing-star in the air, under the one a clock sun, it seemes many times bigger than an ordinary star, and hath a long taile westwards, 3 yeards long, say some, others say more, many haue seen it by times aboue a fortnight togather, it appeares usually in a very clear morning, betwixt 4 a clock and 6 before day—its formidable sometimes:

Mr Rostorn of Lum and Mr Tho Bradshaw walkt out and after they had drunk a cup of ale returned home, going in the night by a pit side Mr Rostorn (being troubled with the falling sicknes) fel in, Mr Bradshaw leapt after him to take him out, because he could swim, but they were both drowned, Mr R swam at top, but Mr B could not be found, a woman bad them cast a white loafe in, & they doing so it would not be removed from over the place where he was so they tooke him up, and they were buryed togather, a sad family it was, my brother being eye witnes thereof:

Roger Topping an ancient christian was taken with a palsy riding by the way, fel off his horse and dyed shortly after, was buryed at Holland Decemb ult 1664

on munday morning after Jan 2 Mtris Meadowcroft of Breakmit dyed suddenly of an impost: a gracious woman—

A woman that used to be drunk was frozen to death in a ditch this week, she was one Smiths wife upon Cleton height,

A man about Ealand went to the Colepit on munday last, fel to drinking and as he came home at night being top-heavy fel down a shore and brake his neck & burst his body lamentably:

a woman being with child & near her time, was turned out of the town where she had lived, viz Rastrick, & going towards Ealand was delivered in the town-field, in cold frost & snow, the child dyed, the woman is distracted, it was base-begotten

Joshua Nicol of Southourum having a child about 2 years of age, that fel into a pan ful of hot water, the hinder parts were grievously scalded whereof it dyed within 24 houres:

a man at Soyland came drunk home, abused his wife, cast the child upon the fire and when his wife went to take it off, he threw her downe trampled upon her, she cryed fearfully out til a neighbour came from the next house, & took him off, he had got hold of the hot barrs, and was wofully burnt, tho yet aliue, yet he is in danger al these happened very near us since the first of jan. and this day is jan 17 1664

this moneth also was a trumpet heard in the aire about Howarth and Stanbury by several familys that were called out to hear the sound it terrifyed a caryers horses, it sounded long and went on as if it went towards Lanc: it seemed musical, and sounded like an Howboy as they say that heard it.

Mr Lyddel a scotch-minister having a wife and six children conformed to maintain them, then lost a loving people for greater maintenance in Glasco where he buryed fiue of his children in a year and received not too pence profit, went to the Bp to complain, who promised him reliefe upon recovery But the Bp dyed and immediately after Mr Liddal buryed his wife, and he is become a reproach in the country, and hath none to maintain but himselfe and one child—

Yesterday being jan 17 6⁷ Mr Jeremiah Bentley of Elland being in good health, eat his breakfast, put on his boots to goe to a dinner at Halifax, about ten a clock lost speech, and dyed the same day—he was a middle-aged man, very witty, thriving in the world, and tis said he hath left an estate worth wel towards twenty thousand pound—he lay about the space of foure houres drawing away, that they could scarce tel, whether he was aliue or no—he had bought a wood that cost him ten thousand pounds, he built very stately malt-houses at Halifax, had taken a lease of the 4 mills, of the too hals, and intended to pull them down and build them up new, with shops under and dwelling houses aboue, and to make great alterations in the corne-market, but in that day did all his thoughts perish—

there was a man at Bealdon about the same time being a young man that fel down dead very suddenly as he was feeding a spaniel that he kept, and ailed nothing before :

this Christmas Sr John Armitage kept open house at Christmas, & being captain of a troop, he had too trumpett-ers, one whereof was a little low man but exceeding fat, and there was a woman of equal stature, & fatnes at Kirkleys that was a dame to some of their children, now it was the great delight of the lady A & others in their mirth to set this fat couple a dancing, wch they did, and they strove so long wch should continue longer that the woman fel down & was caryed to bed, & dyed within too days, & the man went home & he also dyed within a few days after that :—

there is also intelligence from Cambridg that 30 schollars were drowned as the [y] were sliding on the yce on the river

and there are 11 young men drowned at York on the river ouse, in this moneth of january 1664

the reports of these too last are various, some say 13 in the former & too in the latter—

But this is ceartain, Jeremiah Walton of Halifax white-smith being a lusty man, & in sound health drinking a shot at 7 or 8 a clock on Friday last, (being Feb 4 166⅔) was laid out & dead before ten a clock, yea his next neighbour sd he was wel and dead within a quarter of an houre he was but a vain man, yet he had erected a tombe for himselfe & his former wife in the church yard at Halifax, and had writ his decease upon the stone, except the day of the moneth,—

On thursday night march 2 166⅔ some company came to my house, and as they came they saw a strange flaming northwards, one said it was just like that streaming that she saw about 20 yeares ago, immediately before the Scotch-wars, & she never saw any except that, we al went out to look at it, it was a dark night, something stormy, and in the north we saw a bright place wch was constantly light, but sometimes far brighter, and bowed always, far and wide in the aire, it was so bright sometimes that one might haue seen anything clearly on the ground, it shone in at windows, and was in my apprehension very formidable to behold—the lord sanctify such strange sights—
it hath been seen again the night after in the west.

there is also a strange noyse in the aire heard of many in these parts this winter, called Gabriel-Ratches by this country-people, the noyse is as if a great number of whelps were barking and howling, and tis observed that if any see them the persons that see them dye shortly after, they are never heard but before a great death or dearth.

there is another noyse heard in the aire, wch here they call night-whisslers, wch make a whizzing, or whistling in the aire, as if it were a piece of timber thats caryed with violence through the aire, and some say they haue seen it but very many haue heard it, tho it be rarely heard, and presage something more than ordinary, yet several haue heard this also this winter—tho I never heard either of them:

There is an extraordinary hand of god out agt us in the unseasonablenes of the weather, this day being march 10 there is a most fearful tempest (especially this night) of snowing and driuing, such as scarce hath been remembered at this time of the year, ther hath fallen much snow this week, and it hath frozen hard so that people cannot plow, they are wont to be forward in seeding by this time & little is plowed as yet, there hath been very little intermissione of

frost since Christmas and fodder grows very scant: the lord
sanctify these tokens of his displeasure: how soon can our
god turn our abused plenty into deserted penury:

Upon the Revolution of affaires in the nation, and at the
kings coming in, there was excessive joy and among the
testimonys therof that of making bonefires was more than
ordinarily visible and extravagant, so that in great townes
there was an intollerable wast made of coales, and now
there hath been exceeding scarcity of sea-coal in great towns
that haue been supplyed from New-castle, especially London,
Hul & York, by reason that the Hollanders lye upon the
sea-coast and hinder passage, insomuch as coal is at 5li a
chauldron, and very difficult to be gotten, and this sharp
winter many poore people have been in great danger of
perishing by cold: the lord is holy in al his ways and
righteous in al his workes:

this morning march 29 (65) there was a considerable snow
when we rose, and it hath continued snowing the greatest
part of the fore noon

On Easter day and a good part of a moneth after there
hath appeared every morning when clear another blazing
star in the north-east wch some say is more glorious than
the other

Mr Banister of Bank in Lanc being at a horse-race in
Cheshire at Sr Philip Egertons with the earle of Derby &
most of the gentlemen in the country, fel out with a Manks-
man, they gaue challenge for a duel, Mr Banister was run
through and buryed at Croston April 10 1665

One Mather a drunken priest (who they say had too
places) who was to preach at Ormes church march 19 in the
present vicars roome, who was sick threatened the week before to haue my dear brother (late minister there) excommunicate, & railed on him in his ale very loud, on thursday
after in the evening (march 14 as I think) having drunk too
days in Prescot, fel off his horse within a mile of that town
and was taken up dead:

one Mr Moore a Darbishire minister told me that 5 men
being fishing one night saw a great ball of fire (as they
thought) goe through the aire with a horrible noise, and
incredible brightnes so that they could see a pin in the
bottome of the water,—many others saw it in other counties
at the same time.

Mr Sharp told me yesterday that at a place near Hul in a church in the open congregation three drops of blood light upon the apron of a young maid about 16 yeares of age one Mr Clarks daughter (an ancient nonconforming minister) wch while some were wondering at and thought her nose bled, they perceived other three drops descending.

a Scotch-minister told me, that those three men that were the great instruments to place Bishops in Scotland are either snatcht away or are quite out of favour or in a very low condition, viz the earl of Glencarn, and Middleton, and one Fletcher, wch too latter are very low and almost next to beggery, the meeting appointed the 1 of may is put off—blessed be god.

Mr Oddey a nonconforming minister (prisoner in Cambridg Castle for preaching) told me of a minister that had conformed, a good man yet after his subscription was sore troubled in conscience, and could not be at peace til he had renounced what he had done, before the Bp. and afterwards made a public recantation, and when he was turned out of his living fell to preaching in houses, barnes, fields and where he could, multitudes of people flock to hear him, and he not fearing prisons or any dangers preached in order to conversion and abundance of soules were wrought upon (as its hoped) savingly, and being at London he follows the same course, and hath the like successe.

Mr Ball that made the Catich. having many schollars in his house, had one who since is one Captain Jackson to whom he said, (clapping him on the head) thou wilt be among them in 66 wch wil be a dreadful day in England: Seeing him an actiue spark, he said thou wilt be busy amongst them in 66—this Mr Jackson of Darbishire told my father Angier lately.

At Bolton in Lanc: upon the Day of thanksgiving for the victory over the Dutch july 4 65 there was some men that after they had been drinking would needs haue colours, drum and weapons, and goe up and down the town in a hostile manner. Russel the drummer refused to let them haue the drum, but going from home they came forcibly into his house and took it, abusing his daughter shamefully: a watchmaker that was born at London, had lived in Ireland, but at that time lived in the town was standing in a doore, & sd Ile break a jest upon them, aimed at them with his

shafte as though he would shoot them, they run furiously
upon him, and run him to the heart with the shaft where-
upon the colours were, another slasht him fearfully with a
sword, a third shot him, and another dasht out his brains,
and they kept beating him when he was dead—they were
five that did this, and were al taken presently and put in the
dungeon, and are now at Lancaster, one is Mr Wil Bray who
was parish clark at Bolton, another his servant another
John Ward who vapered that he had killed the Philistine,
and the turk—the fanatick another one Dickson a baker, it
was a monstrous prodigious, barbarous murder—

Yet at the Assizes at Lancaster they are al quit, several
persons about Bolton suborning witnesses to forswear themselves, and retract what they had sworn before the Coroner
and jury, & justices before so that the thing was strangely
audaciously huddled up. I pray god it be not laid to the
charge of Bolton—

On lords day Octob 29 one Nathan Sharp near Coley went
out from his family, he told his wife he would goe to one
Ramsden of Rastrick who had owed him 10li and had paid
him in 8li he said he would get corne for the rest, he went
to no church nor chappel that day but continued at the ale
house drinking both fore-noon & after and that Ramsden &
he fel out concerning the delivering in of the corne, and
there was some brabling betwixt him and some other persons, being got into drink, & going out upon some occasion,
the people of the ale-house refused to let him come in, he
made homewards but as tis thought, fel off the bridg and
was drowned, much seeking was made for him almost a
fortnight, & at last yesterday being novemb 11 he was found
near the bridg, and was buryed this day nov 12 1665—an
observable hand of god for breaking the Sabboth. he had
not been ordinarily a drunkard, but an exceeding sparing
man—& painful mason :

Mr Will Bray formerly parish clark of Bolton after the
forementioned murder and freedome being at home went to
old Mr Bradshaw of Bradshaw, who lay a dying, & being
very ancient, forgetting passages, desired Mr Bray to sing
the 88 psalm at his funeral, which being upon Saturday feb
3 166⅔ this Mr Bray pulled him away that was in the place
and gaue out the psalme, but could neither find nor read

one line, and thus he bungled for a quarter of an hour togather, the people were astonished, the other man William
Mooris came into the place, led a psalme, sung a verse himselfe, none of the people following, Bray pluckt the book out
of his hand, but could not read a word, and run away out of
the church—a remarkable hand of god upon a wilful
murderer, as was apparent—

that same night was the common prayer book at Bolton,
cut and slasht to pieces, and that which was left of it,
hanged upon a stake in the water near Bolton Bridge—

one Henry Foster going on thursday with some wild
company to bring a schollar upon his way towds Cambridg,
they drunk togather excessinely at several places in their
return to Wakefield where he lived, several strange healths
they drunk, he got home, but wandered about the next day
as though he was not his owne man, & grew worse, being
distracted, and never sensible while he lived, he dyed upon
the friday after, being march 2 1661. I was with him when
he dyed he was a notable witty man, and an adversory to
conformity, had much knowledg, a lover of good people this
opens the mouths of many. Mr Kerby was closing his
prayer as he drew his last breath :

One Thomas Hanson at Thomas Walshaws house in Silk-
stone parish, had been a loose man, yet had born & bolstered
up himselfe with conceits of free-grace, now is in lamentable
despair, sth god cannot pardon his sins, his time is past,
was not willing I should pray with him, he sd it was to no
purpose, uttered many sad despairing expressions to me, I
spent some time with him, but to little purpose, Satan hath
got great hold of him, hath many times brought him near
upon the brink of making himselfe away. I perceiue some
mixture of melancholy, he is aboue three-score yeares of
age.—

A yong man in Halifax newly out of his prentiship
(Anthony Rookeby apprentice with Mr Shrigly) his father
had given him an horse & purposed to give him 300li to set
up, he and another young man riding madly out of town, he
fell and never spoke more, but lived some few days in ex-
treme pain :

Another young man of a good estate living at Hunslet-
Carre near Leeds, riding to his own wedding fel off his horse
& dyed the morning after, he had been very wild—

Mr Sawry coming from his brother at York the water being out was drowned at Skipton being carryed tho dead to be buryed in his own country. Some men were drowned with the tide upon the sands beyond Lancaster, & corpes also were taken away:

Methinkes this day of our scattering (march 24 6⅔) is a liuely embleme of our state, and I could not but think of it as I travelled from mine own home to sojourne, for all day it hath been terrible stormes of hail & snow, sent on with a violent wind, yet hath cleared presently, and after a short intermission of beautiful sunshine suddenly overcast and darkening & snowing fast, yet now from 4 a clock til night very clear: just such is the life of a christian, but of this we may say nubecula est, cito transitura, and its but a storme against the wall, and the end of a godly man is peace.

Sr William Adams at Pomfret sessions, gaue a strict charge concerning papists, sabboth-breaking, and of conventicles he sd you are to take notice of them that meet togather & pray, contrary to the word of god—expressing himself very moderately, and concerning Mr Dinely & others incited for a conventicle, they were wonderfully cleared. Mr Wadington their accuser was drunk and came up to the justices bench, who bade take him away. the Bailiffe was a going to take him to prison, he accused them of 200 conventicles they bade him proue one, but he could not, his witnesses failed, his man sd his master sent him to watch & there came fiue or six persons out of Mr Dineleys house, but he knew not what they did there, the bench & jury cleared them, none contradicted, but Sr John Armitage but he was quickly taken off by the chairman, Wadington grumbled much and cryed, alas poore king, that his friends are no more regarded, & sd if that took not effect he would serue the king no more. Blessed be god for bringing off this leading cast in this case—Wadington dyed soon after

Mr Hartley preacher at Idle took occasion to speak freely of the sins of Engl. from the story of Manasseh and sd, haue they not silenced all our best ministers, & thrust in dumb dogs that cannot or wil not preach ? & now turned them out of their houses what shal become of us ? &c thus he proceeded though he be a conformist: Dr Laighton Bishop of Galloway in Scotland, being summoned to an assembly, &

challenged by the other Bishops for suffering non-conformists to preach, he vindicated them, they threatened him but he voluntarily degraded himselfe, saying he would be Bp. no longer if such as those might not preach: He is bishop still.

Sir Francis Wortley dyed very lately, having no child by his Lady, he having turned her off many yeares agoe, but hath left his estate (wch is 3 or 4 thousand a year) to the Earl of Manchesters second son if he wil change his name to Wortley, and marry a bastard that Sr Francis had by a common whore in London, he hath left him a large treasury to defend it against all claimers, tis likely that estate wil be prodigally scattered as it was penuriously scraped:

the publick liberty of ordinances is maintained at Peniston now near 4 years after our black Bartholomew day: the providence is the more remarkable, considering that Sr Francis Wortley in the warre time kept that church as a garrison for the king, tho he did him no good, but from thence roved up & down the country robbing, & vexing many honest people,—and now the good people from all parts flock thither and there are sweetly refreshed with the bread of life in publick, when a spiritual famine is through the land—

One John Pickles being urged, & threatened to the sacrament, yet resolved to keep the sitting gesture but the church-warden bad him kneel, & got hold of him to bend his knees, & did bow him, shortly after that church-warden had his knee broken, wch could never be set streight, but he goeth still bowing & bending his knee & wil doe, while he liues this was in the parish of Kirk-heaton:

on june 19 1666 we had news that my Lady Barwicks eldest son & heir togather with his man were drowned in Wharfe water as they were washing their horses, he had often spoke against the fanaticks, his mother (being a good woman) had admonisht him, a little before that she having spoken to him, & he taking it ill, she resolved to speake no more to him about it—

Roger Hallowels son in farnworth after his worke going out to bath him, saturday night jun 23 light in a whirlepit and was drowned:

two young men at Manchester the same night I saw their graues on munday while they were a-filling in the church-yard at Manchester, the one was a butchers son, one

Shelmenden, onely son, very wild, had once got a rope about his fathers neck to hang him, sd he would never mend til he saw his mothers hart blood—his mother dissuaded him from bathing him, he sd he would goe if his head kept on, they got into a place they call Bolton-wheel, the other venturing too far to saue him was drowned with him, he was to haue marryed his sister within too or three days.

John Stoppart yongest son to widdow Stoppart as she her selfe told us the story yesterday sadly dyed with griefe, this yong man was ready to be marryed to a yong woman, whom he intirely loved, upon the munday night he was with her on the thuesday night she dyed very suddenly, he was sent for after she was dead he sate by her corpse exceeding sad, after the funeral he came home, told his mother he thought his heart was dead, she laid her hand on it, felt it not moue, and within a day or too he dyed, and was buryed that day sennight that his sweet-heart was, as I remember he lived at Redich hall where I was yesterd to see his afflicted mother—june 27 1666

At the very time when the king came in 1660 at Chorley there was a stately may-pole erected, upon wch was set a crown, and a crosse, with a coat of armes, & adorned with braue garlands, at certain times every year they met there & had hired a piper to play on Sundays and holy-days had very lately drest it, but upon thuesday july 1666 there was terrible thunder, & the thunder bolt split it to shivers, & caryed the ornaments no body knows whither, & broke it to the very bottom tho set too yards within the ground this is a certain truth : I lookt at the place——

on thursday Aug 2 1666 there came the Bailif of Rastrick & his wife riding by Coley, & drunk a while at Jack Hansons, the woman said it was late but they would ride the faster, but they had not rid a mile, in shelfe lane the woman fel off and broke her neck, never spoke word, was taken up dead, being a fat hostesse :

on july 21 1661 near Sheffield by the river Dun was seen a great army of white souldiers upon the earth, after them went another great multitude of horsemen all in white with white horses, after appearance near an houre they all vanished away asserted by many credible persons. Mr Bloome formerly minister at Addercliffe near Sheffield where the sight was seen having examined some neighbours & living in the town told me of it, and from credible persons

Mr Ferman hearing it had rained blood sent to know the truth of it, & a man newly come in out of the field was wet with blood :

the famous city of London begun to be burnt septemb 2 being lords day morning about 2 a clock it continued till thursday—and burnt the exchangeBlackwel-hal—86 churches & parishes—oh the desolation it hath made 1666 :

in the same moneth was seen a strange prodigy near us, Grace Butler my near neighbour that saw it told me of it, togather with several of James Brookesbankes family, it was too stars fighting, they struck violently one at the other, and fetcht compasses and returned, striking, striving with great violence, a cloud covered them from sight, but when that vanished they saw them again, thus they continued almost an houre, the one they see every night in the same place, but the other they see not.

One Micael . . . . . about 5 weekes agoe who lived at Aurdsley went out upon the lords day with a fowling peece to shoot birds, as he was accustomed (for he seldome or never came to church) but missing the game and seeing people goe to church & being unwilling to be taken notice of, hid his peece in a bog bottome, went home, returned when people were gone, was taking out his peece by the small end it went off, shot him through the head, and killed him, he was found with one eye shut & other open as he wont to shoot—

there was one Samuel Mitchel drinking in Halifax, April 11 1667 at Mr Wades, there came a man and woman to Mr Wade desiring him to tel them where to find something they had lost, for they took him for a conjuror, he said he could not tel but he had an Egiptian in the house that could, they together came to Sam Mitchel, he blubbered that no body could tel what he sd, Wade was his interpreter, and gaue them instructions about the lost thing, they were satisfyed and gaue him three shillings for his paines, they drunk that merrily, but upon munday after this Mitchel dyed and was buryed upon wednesday, and a thousand to one he had dyed at a whores house that he frequented for having been at one, and called to see another she not being within he came home and dyed presently after. he threatened his wife (as

tis said) the day before he dyed that if she went not to wak.
and swore that the inventory was lesse of her former
husbands goods he would kill her—but god took him away:

In Cheshire not far from Maxfield a woman killed too of
her children, the third run to his father in the barn, who
coming in met his wife in the doore, who sd I haue saved
thee two shillings and if the other had stayed I had saved
thee three, meaning she would have killed that lad, for fear
of paying the pole-money for them, wch at that time was
imposed.

Near Barnet Castle in the north a man was plowing
lately the boy that driues the plow angered him, he took up
the plowstaff and knockt him down, there the boy lay, he
stird him but found him dead, seeing that he set up three
great shricks the wife in the house hearing it, run out in
hast left the child in the cradle, when she came again a soo
had got into the house, had eaten part of the child, seeing
that she came to a river near by and drowned herselfe, the
man was conveyed to prison for murder—

A woman murdered at Wakefield, suspected for bewitching
Nathan Dodgson, he hath been wel since she was killed at
this instant Aug 16 and she was killed june 19 : three men
were hanged for it at York this last assizes circumstance remarkable—

Mr Savil of Marley having sold his land and living a
sharking wandering life, came to an alehouse near Ealand
called Nutters oth coat sate downe in a chaire, dyed immediately of an impostume as is thought, jan 8 166$\frac{7}{8}$

several other sudden deaths lately—

One Thomas Hollins near bradford was found dead in the
way home on friday morning jan 24 166$\frac{7}{8}$ his face was frozen
up in a little rivulet which could not possibly drown him, it
was judged a palsey struck him, having had two fits of it
formerly. a wary wise man for the world.

March 6 166$\frac{7}{8}$. Dr Creaton preacht before the king, on
those words, master shew us a sign from heaven, thence
took occasion to affirm—that the last plague and fire were
signes from heaven agt the rebellious city, that had exceeded
the sins of manasseh, for he filled the streets of Jerusalem
onely with blood of subjects, but this city *i e* London with
the blood of king & nobles, and therfore was destroyed immediately from heaven, tho some would haue the world

beleeve otherwise that men did it, which discourse he would haue concluded with a text out of the psalmes but was not able to name or find it, nor to proceed to his next head agt indulgence, but in the middle of his sermon was glad to come Down this is affirmed to be a truth:

Micael Empsal of norwood-green boasted what braue sport he would haue at pace with fighting his cocks, which he had purposely prepared, but he fel sick, dyed and was buryed on Easter day march 22 166⅞

Mr Will greenwood hath been ranting abroad, and at last is come to liue at Halifax, and met with Mr Mathew Whitleys daughter who would needs haue had him, but friends parted them, he went to bring her upon the way towards Wiltshire—

as he returned homeward lighting vapouringly off his horse he broke his leg, which was set there but corrupted, and grew to a gangrene so that his leg must be cut off, it was broken july 22 it was cut off july 29 1668—he sd when it was cut off you haue spoiled my dancing the report was he was dead but yet he liues the lord awaken him: now dead & buryed aug 5

Joseph   wife of Marley was coming to Halifax church—last lords day Aug 2 and fel down in the way and was caryed home dead, an hansome yong woman—

Precious Lady Hoyle hauing been 8 yeares under desertion and in melancholy gaue them a sign by lifting up her hands that god was returned, and then dyed, was buryed at Sandal july 24 68: thursday night Octob 15 68 was James Duhurst of Newhav, found dead huddling by the church gate at Ratchedale his armes over the gate, they found no wound oncly his arme hurt with a glasse he had broken being very drunk, tis thought he bled to death, not being able to help himselfe he was lately turned papist, but indeed an atheist being an exceeding vile person, arrived at a great height of wickednes specially in disobedience to his parents whom he had grosly abused:

Novemb 5 68 some 14 persons were going over the boate to Normanton statutes, the boatman was drunk, an unruly horse was in the boat and overturned it ten were drowned, and four got out with great difficulty—

George Howroyds son found dead on Saturday night Nov 7 68 on Norland moore going from Halifax within evening, tis thought he and another rid a race and his horse cast him, and broke his neck—

Mr . . . . a minister riding over wharfe on lords day morning another behind him, their horse stuck and they fell, the minister drowned the other got hold of the horse, escaped : Nov 1

A son of Mr Sandels vicar of Coverley was crusht to death under the church-doore on Lords day at night Nov 30 68, the doore being lift off the hinges by some ringers—

this day *i e* Decemb 17 68 Timothy Kirby of Halifax is buryed, he dyed on saturday a strange person, a little before he dyed he would haue them brew two load of malt that he might drink an health to the devil, that he might use him wel, when he went to him, he often kneeled downe to curse his wife, and wisht that god would harden his heart as Pharaoh's that he might curse her, he sd they hoped to be rid of him but he wisht he might come again to   them —prodigious things—Dr Hook hath a list of 35 yong women with child of bastards in Halifax this year—

a man found dead in a colepit yesterday fel down in night feb 15 69—near Ambry—

Mr John Smith of Gildersam having an unruly bull his man came to him and told him he must not come near him desired him to sell or feed him he ans. the bull is quiet enough he went to him the bull got him on his hornes and killed him, on thursday, july 8 69 he was buryed on Saturday a good man, rich, and very useful—Abel Whitaker in Ratchdale parish had an onley child a son, upon whom his heart was set, going with him into the field, with cart, got his head through the spokes, wn they moved the cart, lift him up and crusht his head betwixt cart & wheel—he dyed that night— july 9 69 I went to see them on sabbath day night, found a sad family, prayed with them—lord set in—

3 men stifled in a draw-well at Huthersfield with Damp jun 1 1670—going into it one after another—in Mr Hursts well son dead—

R firth Bailiffe in Halifax dying in terrour told James Reiner dost thou not see the room full of Divels, theyl fetch me, and thoult follow me within three days, who was then wel, but dyed within three days, june 1671 :   Thos : Benson of Wakefield riding from Pomfret his horse fell and broke his neck   Aug 28 1671—

So far communion we may haue with a church as to acknowledg it to be a true church, and haue communion with it in
some dutys, yet not haue communion with it in at ordinances, in those cases 1 if this church shal so mingle
any ordinance, as I cannot joyn with it without con-
tracting guilt upon me, as not seeing gods wil in it:
2 if a church shall require me to yeeld in my judgment, and
require me to subscribe to such things as I cannot satisfy
my conscience in, 3 when they shal not suffer me to doe the
duty that god requires of me—I should contract guilt: yet
there are cases wherein tho I haue communion yet I may
not joyn therewith as a constant member when I cannot
haue al ordinances with them. 2 when a doore is opened to
injoy ordinances with more power and purity—supposing
the man to be free not tyed—and remoue dwelling: Bur on
hosea p 162 163—

—::—

Experiences.[*]

1 In this journey to Heckenwick Jan 23 167$\frac{1}{2}$ I haue had
2 experiments, 1 I had set myself seriously to study upon a
text mal 2 16 about a treacherous spirit, yet could make
little of it, and yet found my heart strongly pressed to preach
upon it, wch I did, and matter came flowing in upon me
abundantly extempore as fast as I could deliver it, sometimes god will work by unpremeditated conceptions for
he stirred up wonderful attentions, and affections: wch
makes me think of 1 cor 1 25 : 23 4 : 2 cor 12 9 10 : 2 I
found some content in my own spirit, for I did that work
gratis and had no reward from men as sometimes I haue
this puts me upon self-denying acts, wherin I find most
comfort, hoping god may blesse it the more—1 cor 9 15- to
24 : 2 cor 11 9-12 :
2 Jan 28 7$\frac{1}{2}$ I preacht at Micael Gargreaues, a funeral
sermon for Josh : Farrand shop-keeper at Bradford, buryed
there Jan 13—to whom god had done good by my ministry
tho altogether unknown to me he had received good by a
sermon I preacht on that text Job 22 21, and left with his

* Conclusion of the *Event Book*, commenced at page 305, Vol. I.

wife that I should preach on it again at little Horton,—he
also got good by a sermon on the almost christian I preacht
at pudsey chappel—gaue good grounds of hope to the people
of Horton of a saving work, tho I never knew him, yet
theres hope he is in heaven, blessed be god—I am persuaded
theres good done to souls that we know not off—blessed be
god—

3 Jan 31 at a day of thanksgiving for our liberty in ordinances, I did not find my heart so affected as sometimes,
yet the night before and that morning I did feel some kindly
workings: betwixt the time of our appointing it and observing it, god gaue in a considerable mercy to a neigh-bour
woman of some importance concerning the world, D B wch
indeed was an apparent answer of many prayers, inclining
the hearts of some great persons to her, beyond expectation
blessed be god:

4 Feb 7 I had a call to goe baptise a child at Bramley,
and another at Cottingley, John Hall was in the way to the
latter, wth whom I had a mind to consult about my sons
shoulder, I was very doubtfull whether way to take, tossed
the case, commending it to god, resolved for Bramley, set
forward, at Boltons, leading my horse I had a grievous fall
on my back, yet was not hurt, but it put me a considering
whether I was in my way: I rid forward, upon Wibsey
Slack my horse got his foot fast in an hole, being a hard
frost, gaue two great plucks, wresting his body to get it out,
the second time he fell down and part of my body under
him, I got up, felt no hurt, I had thought my horses leg had
been broken, tryed, he was not at all hurt: getting on again
I begun more vehemently to suspect whether I was in my
way, I thought of Balaams forwardnes to goe even when
providence crossed him: but withall I did consider, that
providence is not our rule, some times gods way is beset
with difficultys—I went on, got quickly thither where friends
were expecting me I did my work, went to Cottingley after,
came home next day, my sons shoulder mends, and all is
right through mercy: blessed be god: pro 16 3: ps 87 5:
23: psal 35 10: psal 112 5 6:

5 Feb 13 7½ being invited to the funerall of Rich: Hoyles
child, after sermon &c I had an inclination to visit Mr Sam:
Mitchel lying near death of a dropsy: I had an hint from
Capt: Hodgson that he would be glad to see me—I went,

and was made gladly welcome, tho they be persons of
another strain : I discoursed long with him, he told me one
thing had much troubled him, that he had heard me say in
publick in Halifax about woe be to them that are not assured
of their salvation before they dye I told him I never spoke
such a word, I was confident, yet withall I told him I was
glad if that his mistake caused him to search his heart more
narrowly concerning his state—I did not percciue that sensiblenes I could haue desired : my heart was something
straitened more than ordinarily in prayer at that time—I
often feel in my own spirit some hints and tokens of the
Lords designs in particular cases : ps 10 17 : Jer 7 16 :

6 This morning Feb 13 reading 2 Chron 17 of Gods
promise to Davids house I was very much affected especially
having last night an account of some hopes of my purchasing of an house to liue in here at Colcy the one helped the
other in my meditations, so that my heart was very much
quickened, melted—I desired to doe as David, fell down on
my knees again, god helped my heart sweetly in prayer : and
god dealt graciously with my soul blessed be his name, he
can and sometimes doth make small occasions to produce
great affections : especially the sense of kindnes is wonderfull melting : 1 chron 29 14—judg 13 23 :

7 Being at Leeds at John Cummings Feb 14 7½ in the
morning I read part of 119 psalm, and ere I was aware my
soul was wonderfully transported, and melted, and then I
fell upon my knees and the Lord helped me a considerable
season, yet preaching and praying immediately after at ten
of clock at Jane Milners my heart was wonderfully shut up,
dead, distracted,—I fear there was too high expectations of
some there present from wt they had had the night before,
and it may be god punished them in me, his will be done,
grace is free : god is arbitrary in communications suspensions—psal 84 6 : 1 cor 15 10 :

8 Upon a solemne day of fasting and prayer at Bramhop,
Febr 15 167½ I found that tho I continued aboue an hour
togather in prayer and was wonderfully carryed out in expressions, that things flowed into my mind freely, and words
were poured out strangely, yet to my grief I may speak it
my heart was little affected nor carryed out to god in the
duty, but to the outward part of the duty, words and phrases,

how easily may others be cheated with seeming life and devotion in speakers, for I was conscious to myself of that wch
none present would haue suspected,—did I not sett up idols
in mine heart! oh what a treacherous spirit in so great pre-
tences to run a whoring from god: I feel what that meanes
too sadly—Isai 29 13: oh that yt word may not be made
good upon me Ezek 14 3 4 5: others may lift me up but the
Lord humbles me in my own eyes, for I know more of my
self than others doe—

9 Being to goe to Bramley Feb 29 7½ to keep a fast upon
the account of Mr Middebroughs eldest son a dying, I designed to preach upon that text about self-humiliation 1 pet
5 7: but though I had had the sermon in my hands and read
of it not two days before, yet I could not find it tho I spent
much time in seeking it, but was forced to take another
sermon from Jer 17 16 about appeal to god, and god inlarged me wonderfully therein affected several heartes, made
it a good day, gods thoughts are not as ours Isai 55 8 9:
thus haue I been crossed severall times in my purposes upon
that account, wch brings into my thoughts pro 19 21:

10 on thursday March 5 the day after my purchase of
house and land in Northouram, I was called to keep a
private fast at Mr Sharps in little Horton, much of the day
was spent before I could get my hand to the work, worldly
thoughts much prevailing, but after while Joseph Lister was
at prayer my heart was wonderfully melted, and kept in a
wonderfull sweet frame, and as he is a very choyce christian,
so god graciously helpt him: and in the close of the day god
dealt well with my heart, and so inlarged me, that he made
the world stink in my account, and raised my heart to an
high rate of heavenly things—at last god made it a good
day: oh blessed be his name:

11 On Munday April 1 being sent for to visit Benjamin
Boys wife being sick at Halifax I went after dinner, discoursed, prayed with her some women in the room were
much affected, god graciously helped, and having visited
more friends I returned home, as I came just at Halifax
bank top, amongst a company of knobby stones my horse
stumbled, fell down violently my leg and thigh were under
him, got up again, felt no hurt at all, blessed be god, it was
a wonderful preservation, afterwards I reflected upon what I
was thinking of when I fell, and I had been thinking of the

great companys that came from Halifax to Coley the day
before, and pleasing myself with imagining what a great
assembly I should haue if god graunt liberty in the chappel—
and methought that was a seasonable correction of my pride:
and did me good in after-meditation, and gaue me occasion
to think on pro 16 18: blessed be god for his gracious con-
futation of my pride, and withall the preservation of my
body:

12 On thursday morning being April 4, after I was risen
to set myself to prepare my heart for that days work, being
a fast, I struggled a good while but found my heart dul,
dead distracted I could doe no good with it, thought after
family prayer, breakfast—to return to it again, but was prevented by the time, but god assisted by heart wonderfully in
the work of the day, especially in prayer. I see god will
sometimes be found in preparation, and not in the ordinances prepared for, sometimes he will manifest his grace
in ordinances, not in the preparation, grace is free—yea I
am persuaded god accepts of purpose of further preparation,
tho he deny opportunity as he did of David in the busines of
building him an house 2 Sam 6 8—

13 This time two yeares when the act against conventicles came out, so severely seconded with penaltys, I remember I said that I was persuaded that none would suffer by it,
at least that an 100li in fines would not be paid in all
England, but I was mistaken, for many suffered deeply, yea
god was pleased to punish my folly and security by loosing
a 10li fine myself: and now at this time when the kings
declaration for liberty cm out, I had a conceit, that I should
haue the first licence in this country, but herein I see also
my pride and vain confidence crossed: though I hear of few
that haue got licences, and I hear mine is procured and
coming down, wch I much wonder at, since I haue not as
yet sent up a petition, as others doe but I perceiue I haue
friends in the great city, and this day may 4th it came to
my hands—signed with the kings hand-writing, and his
seal, fairly writ on two papers, the one for my liberty in my
own house, the other for my liberty in any licenced place,
and accordingly this day I haue made use of it, and preacht
from Rom 3 8. to a numerous company in Coley hall wch is
the last day I am likely to be there, blessed be god for this
mercy—

14 The same day being Lords day morning going pretty timely to my horse, and having been in the chamber, and coming down stairs both my feet slipt from under me, almost at the top, I fell clear down to the ground betwixt the raile and staires, but was not in the least manner hurt, only tore some of my cloaths, blessed be my good god, this was may 5 1672—it may be god will bring me into some difficultys, yet I trust he will preserve me, under this indulgence, I bless god my heart was sweetly inlarged in the ordinances of this blessed sabboth :

15 I was almost 3 weekes at home, and had no call abroad to any place, I was wont to goe to, but god hath cut out work for me in a new place, for upon whitsun-thuesday, may 28 72 I was called to preach at John Butterworths house in Warley, where a great multitude of people were got togather. I hired the house for preaching in a twelue-mouth for 5sh—god helped my heart, quickened peoples affections, gaue me some incouragemt that god hath some work in that barren place, yea there is several of that neighbourhood that haue come to hear me in mine owne house aboue a year, and haue set up religious dutys and meetings togather, so that there is good hopes of mercy for them, blessed be god, oh that god would doe good there : that day I hear the minister of Luddenden was there, and came incognito, was much affected, wept much, they say he is a very weake man, oh for some work upon his heart !

16 upon thursday June 13 72 upon a solemne invitation I went to Jonas Fosters house in Howarth parish, where I was never before in all my life, a very ignorant place, where there was never good preaching, multitudes of people flockt to hear me, some were affected, god helped my heart graciously in praying and preaching about four houres to-gather, it was strange preaching amongst them, who knows what work god may haue on some hearts ? oh that some soul might be awakened ! both these were upon n ral occasions :

17 the day before that, june 12 72 on wednesday we had the solemne ordinance of the Lords Supper, and tho my heart was out of order in preparatory work, yet in the exercises of that day I was exceedingly melted and carryed out to god : oh it was a sweet day : god united our spirits so that after that we unanimously made a solemne profession

of our faith, and entred an ingagement to be the Lords there
the Lords people renewed their owning of me to be their
pastour, and I solemnly owned them in that relation, to
discharge all ministerial dutys to them: oh that we could
perform what we promise,—2 cor 8 5: Isai 44 5: tho we doe
a like work, yet not upon the same grounds with our congregational brethren: and upon some restrictions and limit-
ations:

18 Upon Thuesday june 18 72 there was a solemne
meeting appointed at my house betwixt our brethren of the
congregational persuasion and us, accordingly there came
several of Mr Roots church, expressing their desires to joyn
in communion with us in all ordinances, we declared
plainly the state of both societys, our present actings and
the principles upon which we acted, and tho our principles
were different, yet we concurred in our actings for the main,
and both partys were willing to overlook any matters of
difference, and upon further debate. and enumerating our
members they fully acquiesced in my fidelity as to admission,
were willing to take them as they stood without demanding
any further satisfaction concerning them and we also owned
theirs and were willing to entertain them to all ordinances,
and a speciall season was appointed for communicating
togather in the Lords supper, both partys went away
abundantly satisfyed—this is the strange work of god, mens
spirits are strangely altered, Capt: Hodgson earnestly pro-
moted this work,—blessed be god: Zeph 3 9: Jer 50 5:
Phi 3 15:

19 Of late I doe still find for some yeares past that god
hath given good successe to all things that I haue taken in
hand, there hath been a continual series and course of
divine providences for outward comfort and supply, if I
haue undertaken journeys god hath preserved and prospered
me, if I haue fallen he hath secured me from hurts, if I
haue followed my studys at home god hath graciously
directed and assisted, if I haue made any bargains god hath
inclined persons to favor me, if I haue wanted help (as I
haue wanted much in repairing my house) god hath sent in
abundant help on free cost, god hath blessed me with
supplys in my estate strangely, and far beyond expectations,
he hath wonderfully advanced my credit amongst all sorts:
if I haue had an hand in any agreemts the work hath been

strangely effected : god hath disposed mercifully of my
children, and they come on exceedingly in learning in their
new schoole at Morley : in all things I haue injoyed what
my heart can desire for outward things I haue a sweet loving
wife, peace in my family, so that in most things of the world
I cannot say this is amisse, or that I would haue mended :
wch sometimes puts me in mind of gods promises to godly
soules, job 22 28, psal 1 3 : 1 tim 4 8 : but then I consider
again that even wicked men may prosper in outward things
job 21 8-13 : psal 23 3 12 : Jer 12 1 2 : mal 3 15 : so that I
can make no grounded guesse at my state from outward
providences, Eccl 9 1 2 3 : I may haue all these with a
curse, I had need look upon what termes these come, be
jeolous lest I be put off with these things, or lest my heart
be stollen away with these matters, god excercised me with
a low condition previously and I have met with crosse providences, now with comfortable, surely god hath some end
in it, it may be its for tryal, to see how I shall carry, oh
that I may not now mis-carry by carnal confidence or
security—

20 On Lords day jun 30 72 I preaching at home, at noon
Dr Hook came by my house, and he went to preach at the
chappel in the afternoone and he overtooke or met abundance of people in his way, he spoke to very many of them,
some he bad turn back to the chappel and serue god, others
he told they would soon be weary in coming hither, others
he told they would be disappointed, a number of people togather he asked if they were going to a play or a wedding,
some, (tho few) he affrighted to goe to the chappel, being in
a most fearful rage : when he light at John Hansons (or
before I am not certain) he sent his man with a note, who
heard me all the afternoon, and at night delivered it to me
from his master, desiring me to let him haue a sight of my
licence, I writ an answer to him—immediately after one
Martha Fletcher living in Holdworth came to me being in
great trouble of conscience—an hopeful sign of god, wch
puts me in mind of 1 cor 16 9 : J. C was in a great rage agt
our meetings, and said, what stark mad fooles were we, that
we could not have bought the house if we had given it to the
beggars to live in, but that such abundance of naughts must
meet there, but he said, if any of them come upon my land
Ile sue them.   N C his uncle sd last night amongst a great

company at John Hansons, we dare not come thither (meaning to my house) for fear of witches: relating it seems to a story, that a maid at Anthony Waterhouses met one B Jaggars wife one sabboth-day night when she had been here and that then she got power over her, and. after this lasse was distempered and strangely taken, and cryed out that she saw such a woman B J wife in her fits, and was sore tormented and dyed within a fourtnight, this is the common rumour the truth I am not certainly informed of, but its possible such a thing may fall out in judgment to wicked men, hardening them:

21 I am again put upon self-denying work, on july 5 72 I went to To Ap: formerly a great professer, my intimate companion, one that was wont to sit down with us at Lords supper, but hath quite disowned us and joyned with men of another spirit, since these times came in, but besides that hath grown deboist in drunkennes and grosse enormitys, I went to him, found him making hay in the field, tooke him away, we walked about an houre in another field, I dealt plainly with him, told him of all his faults that I had heard of, dealing so unhansomely with his own mother, in that he excused himselfe that I had much adoe to fasten anything on him, and in the busines of drunkenes he extenuated it sd it was not his practice but for that I told him some particular circumstances that he could not deny, I could produce evident proof & at last with much adoe he fell under it, but not satisfactory sensiblenes or kindly confession, but said he had been much abroad by reason of suits in law and other occasions, that were now over, and he hoped he should be better, desired me to pray for him, that he might be sensible of sin and of his corrupt heart, but yet for all this I am not satisfyed that his soul is thoroughly humbled, or that the work of repentance in him is kindly:

22 On Saturday july 6 72 I went upon a call to Ratchdale, to spend the Sabbath in their new meeting house, the first sabboth I was from home since I had my licence which was aboue 9 weekes, and tho it was a very rainy day, yet I had no rain, and multitudes of people flockt to that place the Lord graciously assisted me, and tho I had left my own place destitute, giving warning of my absence the sabboth before, and took much paines, yet I had not one peny given me, blessed be god, it may be god will recompence it another

way, in soules good, which is infinitely better, I am not
without hopes of it, for old Roger Whitworth told me on
munday that he saw more tears shed, and more affections
stirred those two last lords days, wn Mr Pike and I preacht,
than he had seen of 12 yeares before, and heard groanes,
sighs—god helpt in pursuing that great convicting work
both in praying and preaching, oh for a blessed issue:

23 July 9 72 being in my house, upon some slight occasion, my wife gaue out some peevish discontented words, I
durst not speak for fear of grieving her but withdrew myself
into my study, and oh what a melting season was it! god
sweetly helped my heart in meditation and secret prayer,
I had not such a sweet presence of god, of a long time, then
god helped me to see it was not in house, estate or relations,
or anything below to giue content, he helped me to pray for
the church, king, my congregation, wife, children, all my
relations, and mine own soule, sweetly for about an hour
togather—blessed be his name:

24 Another thing there is which tho but small hath some
influence to help my devotion, many times, tis this, the
cushion on wch I sit at my study, on wch I kneel at prayer
hath the two first letters of my first wiues first name, E A
wch I usually see when going to prayer alone, and it much
quickens my heart not only considering how much shes
prayed alone and now is praising god in heavn, but also
reflecting upon her inlarged prayers for me, wch are upon
the file still: yea and also her sweet persuading of me to
the duty of sweet prayer. wch I often think of its not to tell
how little a thing, if god set in. will stirre up great affections,
even the crowing of a cock shall excite repentance in Peter,
Mat 26 74 75:

25 this day being saturday july 13 1672—I set my self to
secret close work of preparation for the solemne ordinance of
the Lords supper to morrow, and oh wt a sweet season haue
I met with in reading some scriptures in self examination.
meditation prayer, god hath abased me exceedingly in mine
own eyes, prostrated me upon the ground, confounded me
for sin, lifted me up by his grace, helped me in prayer, and
supplication for my self both as to my personal capacity and
ministerial. especially considering the many christians of
several persuasions that god hath made me pastour of, united
togather and this is the first time of our communion.—god

helped me exceedingly to plead with him for converting work, and for soules of adversarys, oh what a melting season it was! it may be a pledge of more, now I haue solemnly renewed my covenant with god, the lord grant me more strength to keep it.—

26 Accordingly on Lords day we had that sweet and solemne ordinance, at night after the rest of people were gone, and tho I cannot but say god helped me in preaching and prayer all day yet I found not such a presence of god in that sealing ordinance as sometimes I haue found—what the reason may be I know not, but desire to inquire, whether the Lord saw that I trusted too much in my preparations, or whether I had too vain, proud, self-conceited thoughts of the numerous increase of our society and union of another church to us, or whether others might not haue too high expectations from me, wch god would disappoint,—fain would I know that I may be humbled, haue sin pardoned it is true god helped me with suitable and abundant expressions, I cannot deny it, but I alone was too conscious to myself of vain distracting thoughts, of inward straitnes, of want of those warm affections my soul hath sometimes met with in that ordinance : The Lords will be done, only as tis sin in me tis matter of humiliation—

27 At Slawait Mr Dawson and I preacht an exercise Aug 14 1672 He preacht first, very well, I followed, but could neither pray nor preach as I was wont, I had a weighty subject about the difficulty of salvation from 1 Pet 4 18— but it would not off, I stroue, and sweat about it but it would not doe, yet towards the latter end of my sermon I found some inlargemt. Mr Dawson and I were discoursing as we came home of such things, I told him how I perceived the Lords withdrawings, he told me he was abundantly satisfyed with my sermon, and it was a profitable discourse to him : god I see doth not see as man sees, but can make use of that most that we judge meanest, and layeth aside that wch we judge best—I haue seen it the Lords will be done, its welcome—

28 upon Friday Aug 23 72 at a private fast before the sacrament I was wonderfully assisted with a great measure of inlargemt a flood of teares, wherein god wonderfully helped me—But on Saturday I was much shut up, yet upon

Lords day night at that sealing ordinance, my spirit was sweetly carryed out god-wards, blessed be god—he is a free agent—

29 Lords day being Sept 2 72 preaching in my meeting-house there was a multitude of people in the forenoon, god sweetly helped my heart in prayer—but in the afternoon the multitude increased, to such a number as in Mark 2 2: many were out of doores, it fell a great shower, they were sore wet, yet stuck at the windows, the roomes were excessiuely crowded they trod one upon another yet for all that abundance went away and could not hear, so that we want room exceedingly—wch puts me in mind of those wels that Isaacs servants digged, Gen 26 20 21 22, there hath been Eseck for men haue striven with us, now Sitnah for they hate us, when they cannot hurt us, oh for Rehoboth! Isai 49 19 30—

30 on lords day at Cockey Sept 29 1672 called micaels day, I preaching there all day in the afternoone my heart was strangely inlarged in the duty of thankfulnes so that I cannot remember my spirit was so affected or drawn out in publick this many yeares, god helped to expressions in an enumeration of my own mercys al along from my childhood to that day, and upon other accounts, oh with what meltings of hearts, and inlargemts did the Lord assist me to pour out my soul to god! that afternoon about 4 a clock at Bury was that strange hurry that drewe all the people out of church wch relation I refer to another place,—Exod 15 11 : psal 65 5 : I must confesse my heart was wonderfully carryed out to god in a day of fasting and prayer the munday before Sept 23 at Brother Hultons in March : where Mr Newcom, Mr Finch, Mr Eaton and I kept a day upon the account of John Hultons wife who hath been long upon the rack of torturing pain—oh for a return of these prayers !

31 At Mr Bailys house at Morley I was two nights upon occasion of an exercise I preacht with Mr Jolly, and tho I was not put upon family-prayer, yet upon thursday octob 17 72 J B being to marry M B desired I would goe to prayer on their behalf, we withdrew ourselues into the chamber, some 8 or 10 of us, and oh how was my heart drawn out upon that account togather with the family affaires, publick, personal &c as it was upon thuesday at Joseph Wrights where some few of us met togather to pray for his son

Jonathan : and I found also abundant meltings in my spirit at Capt : Hodgsons on friday at a day of solemne humiliation : oh what a frame did my heart keep in !

32 That Friday night being octob 18 72 having the oppertunity of my sons being with me, and gates shut our house solitary I resolved to spend some time in family work, as I had preacht the week before from Zech 12 11 and accordingly we set our selues to it I spoke something of family concernmts that might affect our hearts, and my son Eliezer begun, prayed sweetly, sensibly, tho but short, wept much, did well, but John was both a good while, and prayed to my admiration, pleading with god, and using such expostulations as I wondered at, togather with liuely affections, many teares, then Martha, then my wife, and then myself—oh wt a heart-melting evening was it ! Blessed be god for the gift and spirit of prayer : oh thats worth a world—

33 tho I had found so much inlargents in prayer at Mr Bailys yet the same day calling at Atherton to pray with a woman my heart was wonderfully distracted, shut up that I could get no quickenings, and suddenly after in my family, god withdrew, and on oct 23 wednesday after going beyond Ovenden to see a sick woman, tho I judged her case miserable yet could not get my heart into any good frame in prayer, altho the same day I preaching at J B in Warley, god graciously helped in prayer, and preaching I see grace is free, and the assistances, withdrawings therof are arbitrary, the wind bloweth where and when it listeth joh 6 8— I feel it many a time haue I had this experiment in times near togather—

34 On munday octob 28 1672 Mr Dawson and I went into Lanc : the day after, being thuesday according to appointment we kept a private fast upon an extraordinary occasion, in my cozen Eatons study in Deans-gate in Manchester, it was for ordaining and setting apart to the work of the ministry three young men, viz Mr Joseph Dawson, Mr Samuel Angier, Mr John Jolly, Cozen Eaton begun the day in prayer, then Mr Finch prayed, then my self went to prayer wherein my heart was exceedingly affected confessing ministerial sins, and begging mercy for those persons, our selues, children devoted to god, then my father Angier requested Mr Dawson to make a confession of his faith, wch he did and asked him the wonted questions, then prayed

over him by imposition of hands, Mr Newcom did the like
to my Cozen Angier, Mr Eaton to Mr Jolly: then Mr Newcom spoke to that scripture 1 tim 4 12: then gaue them a
solemne charge, then prayed, and so pronounced the blessing, it was a sweet, solemne day, an hopefull budding of
Aarons rod, after a sharp winter: blessed be the Lord:

85 I having an invitation to preach an excercise at Heck-
enwike with Mr Holdsworth in his meeting-place there, rose
timely that morning being Novemb 14 1672 and set upon
my journey but in Lightcliffe street, my horse got his foot
fast in a hole in the causy, and came downe, and threw me
into abundance of mire and clay so that I was all tumbled
and rolled in dirt, yet blessed be god without hurt I went to
an alehouse and got myself and horse washt and rubd and
scrapt, my face being all clay and filth, and so set on my
journey, Mr Holdsworth was begun, whom god graciously
assisted, but tho my heart was helped in prayer, yet in
preaching I thought I was scarce in my ordinary frame, but
god is not limited to our inlargements,—oh that I could
learn the mind of god in that fall, whether the Lord saw
some pride, vanity, vain glory in me, and would stain the
pride of my glory by letting me fall into the dirt, or whether
it was disciplinary to teach me some lessons, or preparatory
for some mercy 2 things I know 1 that the devil aimed by
my fall to prevent my doing good, but god by his angel kept
me, 2 that that mire was not so ill filthy as the mire of sin.

86 upon thursday Nov 19 72 upon a call I travelled to
one Rich: Wilkinsons near Kighly where I preacht, and tho
it be a barren place for religion yet there was a great number
assembled and oh how was my heart wonderfully drawne
out in prayer for the conversion of some soul! and many
there were strangely affected, who knows wt good may be
done in that ignorant prophane place! when I was preaching, one that heard me all on a sudden cryed out a fl——
for him, what dost thou sit prating there! and opened the
door and run away, and we saw him not again, I inquired
after who he was, they told me it was one West of Kighley,
who was a great professor in the Antinomian way, then a
quaker marryed two wives at one time but now is fallen off
to drunkennes and horrible debauchery,—two great Antinomians heard me that day, oh what god would work by his

grace: I was much drawne out in preaching about unseen
things—

37 at night lodging at Joshua Walkers in Bingley, there
came to me a man called John Wright, who hath not heard
a minister preach scarce this ten yeares, we fell into discourse about ordinances, he said he was well satisfyed without because he liues (as he sth) in the injoyment of god,
and god hath promised that his people shall be all taught of
god, and therefore need no teaching by man,—&c the Lord
did wonderfully help me in opening some scriptures speaking
home to his case, answering his cavils, insomuch that he
was silenced, and said as I said, when I convinced him that
if he was unconverted ordinances were means of conversion,
if converted ordinances were as necessary for edification, he
confessed he was not without sin,—yet I had much adoe to
bring him off, having spent 4 or 5 houres in discourse with
till I was weary could not prevail with him for a promise
but putt-offs, I perceiue he is an halfe-witted man—

38 This day Nov 27 1672 we haue been keeping a day of
solemne thankfulnes to god in my house, wherein my heart
hath been extraordinarily carryed out in that sweet work,
recounting gods mercys that concerned soul, body, state
relations, and found an unusual presence of god especially
upon my remembrance of the strange way how god brought
me to this place, as by strong hand, my mean condition at
first coming, and the good god hath done in me, to me, by
me, not withstanding all my troubles, but principally for
restoring to me and the rest of his ministers this publick
liberty, wch was the chief busines of the day :—blessed be
god for occasion of blessing him, and an heart to and help
in blessing the name of my good god : Hallelujah :

39 This day Decemb 4 72 being at Bingley having preacht
yesterday upon the subject of self-denyal at old Mr Farrands
house, I found my spirit dull, tho a little quickened towards
the close of the day, but this morning before I went out of
my chamber falling down on my knees my spirit was in a
melting frame, and at a solemne day of thankfulnes at Will
Hurds my heart was much inlarged, blessed be god—.

40 yesterday Dec 5 I was at a private day at Halifax with
Mr Bentley, Mr Dawson &c they spent the day profitably, I
being to conclude began to be a little warmed, but for want
of time cut short—but this day, both in the morning in

closet-prayer, and in a solemne day of prayer in my house
my heart was exceedingly affected for about an hour and
half togather, oh what a melting season was it! I take it as
a token for good, and a pledg of further mercy upon Lords
day following abroad—

41 Decemb 8 I preacht at Allethorp in a malt-kilne, ordered for a conuenient meeting-place where there was many
hundreds of hearers, my heart was affected in prayer in the
evening, and in preaching I had some presence of god tho
not in such measure as I desired, what the issue shall be,
god knows—but on thuesday in afternoon at Mr Kerbys in
a solemne work of prayer among a room-full. I stroue a
pretty while and it would not doe, at last god helped my
spirit, especially for the chief concernmt of that meeting,
wch was for Mr Rich: Wilson, who lyes a dying, who hath
been a rich old useful townsman, yet not accounted a professor of stricter sort—Lord answer—I came away, left Mr
Kerby and Mr Root to carry on that work—blessed be god—

42 On thursday following Decemb 12 72 at Mr Dawsons
my heart was much inlarged, in prayer and god was
graciously seen in that meeting, also Dec 16 at Will Clays
at a day of solemne thankfulnes I met with some measure
of assistance, and god was graciously present in our assembly, as also the day before viz Lords day in publick ordinances—and at Jonathan Priestlys new house wch we
dedicated with a solemne day of thankfulnes, Decemb 20 72
preacht on psal 56 and god helped—I cannot but obserue
gods gracious providence to giue us occasion of thankfulnes
and such opportunitys also as we haue not had the like of
many yeares, we haue   in so many several places in a
short time viz at Eden Brooksbanks No 18: in my house
Nov 27: at Will Hurds Dec 14: at Will Clays Dec 16, at
Jonathan Priestleys Dec 20: all near togather blessed be
god that puts it into his peoples hearts to pay their vows, it
may be its in order to further mercy—ps 76 11 12: 71 14:
paying for old as a presage of coming for new—

43 Lords day Decemb 22 72 we had the Lords Supper, it
was a sweet and refreshing ordinance although neither the
night before nor in the morning in preparatory dutys was
my heart affected as I desired, yet several times in the foregoing week my heart was put into a tollerable good frame, I
see god is a free agent, and he is gracious in his approaches,

and righteous in his withdrawings—it was a blessed cove-
nant-renewing—

44 Upon new-yeares day Jan 1 7¾ I had a call to preach
at Idle-chappel god wonderfully helped in handling a suitable subject of making all things new Rev 21 5—people
were much affected, there was a numerous assembly,—tho
upon the wednesday before (called Christmas day) preaching
upon that subject at home, I found myself much straitened,
Lord shew me thy mind in all this,—however I take this
publick opportunity this first day in the new year for a presage of more mercy all the following year—

45 On Jan 2 7½ I joyned with Mr Richardson at an excercise at Lassel-hall, abundance of people came, when Mr R
was preaching Sr John Kays sergeant came, and thrust
through the crowd, made inquiry whether he had a licence
to preach there, Mr R smartly answered wt haue you to doe
with that? the man withdrew Mr Richardson went on, I
confesse at first it something affrighted me, and I thought
with my self if he come again wn I am in preaching it will
put me quite out,—well he finished, I succeeded, and when
I had prayed and was preaching, he came again, demanded
if we had licence, Mr Rich: ans: sharply saying what
authority haue you to inquire, he ans: his master sent him,'
who is your master sd he, he ans: Sr John Kay, and he
commanded us both in the kings name to goe along with
him to his master, Mr R ans: we would not goe without a
warrant, he told him he had a warrant, we desired to see it,
he shewed it us, I read it, wherein both our right names
were, when I saw that I gaue him mild words and desired
him to stay awhile till we had done our work and then we
would obey him, wcl sth he I shall wait your leisure, he
stood by, I went on with my sermon, and god graciously
helped aboue fear, it was quite gone, and god helpt memory,
and elocution, and affection,—when we had done our work
we went along with that man and two of Sr Johns livery-
men, came to Woodsome that Clark (I suppose he was) was
churlish, and snappish, told me he thought we had not made
such particular reflections as we did, I askt him in wht?
sth he, I took good notice of your words, I bade him speak
truth and I cared not what he said: we went into the hall,
wherein many waiting-men were playing at cards at the
table, we waited a pretty while, at last, Sr John came, who

askt us if we had any licences, saying his majesty hath
graciously incouraged conformists, and indulged others of
his subjects that pretend conscience in not conforming, but
his princely clemency had been abused, in many places,
therefore, sth he, he hath sent us expresse order to inquire
into persons licences, we told him we had there a licence
for the place, but licences for our persons were at our
homes, he demanded a sight of that we had, we produced it,
he read it, said so far he was satisfyed, but required a sight
of the other, we desired time to produce them, he gaue us
time till saturday, and then sending them by another should
serue, I haue sent mine this day by John Robuck, and Arthur
Lee wil let Sr John see it to-morrow,—thus gods gracious
providence hath wrought for us, so that with confidence we
may look upon authority having authority for what we doe,
—blessed be god—   I cannot but observe how spight-
ful the devil is agt preaching, when he will not hinder but
promote keeping open house, feasting, dancing, revelling,—
there I saw a great number of gentlemen, (among whom was
Mr Tho : Horton) musitians, master of misrule, or Lord of
misrule as they call him &c—

46 I went from home on munday morning Jan 13 upon a
cal to preach at Mr James Disons house at Westwood near
Slaughwait, when I came thither the people were going down
to the chappel, and so had concluded and ordered, that there
I should preach for the license for his house was not come,
I was a little startled at having been so lately before that
great man that is Lord of Slaughwait,—but I must either
preach there or no where so I continued, and there was a
great congregation, god helped my heart, affections, voyce,
for I was very hoarse through a cold—after sermon Mr Jo :
Earnshaw told me I was expected the day following at lidget
aboue 5 miles further, I had not thought of it, or look upon
it as a conclusion, tho Mr Lockwood had a word about it at
Lassel-hall, but fear of a disappointment I went, there was
a great assembly, much affection, great hopes of good, god
graciously helped me that day—blessed be god. I haue this
experiment, that upon committing affairs to god, he orders
them unexpectedly to the beste : on thursday I preacht at
home, had a large auditory, god graciously assisting in speaking to young people—my cold continuing—

47 according to my doctrine to put young people upon private meetings I appointed some to come to my house upon thuesday night, wch they did, I put four of them upon prayer whom I never heard before, I discovered a very serious sensible spirit, good gifts, I was much affected with their hopefulnes for future usefulnes, blessed be god, we propounded a question, designing conference every fortnight, the lord assisting,—

48 the day after being wednesday we had a private fast at Capt Hodgsons, my body being discomposed by reason of cold, and hoarsenes I found not such outward inlargemt nor yet on thursday Jan 23 as I could desire, yet perceived some affectionate meltings in my congregation in Warley—blessed be god—let god come in wt he pleaseth

49 having promised to preach at Lassel-hall, Jan 30 $7\frac{3}{4}$ and being pressed in spirit to goe, I had a great disadvantage in several cases to grapple with, my own bodily infirmity of a sad cold, in a stopping, cough, hoarsenes, but that was not all, J B apothecary and other friends had set my wife on to dissuade me from going, her dear affection to me, and mine to her wrought strangely with me she intreated me in the night, I would not yield, she kept urging me with teares all morning at last I told her if she would not giue me free leaue, I would not goe, tho my heart was set upon it, thus we debated till almost nine a clock, at last she yielded, I went yet met with some discouragemts before gone a quarter of a mile from my house,—came thither about 11 a clock, Mr R was begun, people had long lookt for me, god helped beyond my expectation in body & hart in preaching praying much affection stirred, two gentlemen, that had been great opposors, came purposely to the latter sermon to hear me, Mr Longly of Dalton and Mr Beamount sate under the window because they could not get in for presse of people, at night I lodged at John Norths house, the house was filled with people in the night, I expounded a chapter and god wonderfully helpt,—who knows what may be done in that ignorant prophane place ? I returned home on friday morning better in health than when I went from home,—I found that promise made good to me in this journey psal 37 5 : pro 3 5 6 : 16 3 : it was satisfaction to all, the waving it would haue been a sad disappointment and of bad consequence in all likelihood :

50 At Mr Sharpes house in little Horton Feb 12 7⅔ we
had a solemne day of fasting and prayer upon special occasions, his mariage, afflictions on several members, of the
family &c George Ward stood up, desired us to pray for the
seed of the faithfull, spake affectionately, fell a weeping,
could speak no more, sate down, it was a good day, my
heart was exceedingly affected in prayer—upon several
accounts—chiefly that about children—

51 Yesterday, being Feb 24 7⅓ I was left and led on to a
rash inconsiderate act, for being at Halifax at the funeral of
Ben : Baites son, &c having dispatcht much busines in town,
as buying me a cloak hat &c just as I was ready to come
home, Micael Boys (at whose house I set up my horse) came
up town told me that A G a constant hearer of mine desired
me to baptize a Kinswoman's child, I gaue him no answ :
but told him I would follow him, wn I came thither, women
were ready with the child, I askt for the father they told me
he was a quaker and was unwilling it should be baptized, I
desired them to get some one else to doe it, they urged me
to it, I condescended, did it but it hath cost me a restles
night, wakening by two of clock, pondering things in my
mind aggravating matters, so that it kept me waking the rest
of the night this morning my mind was disquieted, lest it
proue a reproach to my ministry, and disparagement to my
profession and my brethren, 1 bec : I had not sent for the
father of the child first to talk with him, 2 bec : I did it in
an ale-house, 3 bec : I fear the mother and grandmother are
(I fear) not serious christians, 4 bec : of the relation, the
child baptized being Mr Gills great-grandchild, who is Dr
Hookes curate who (as I urged) might haue done it, and the
Dr will know of it and upbraid us with such acts : 5 bec : I
did not giue such serious exhortations as I ought, 6 this M B
brother of that stamp hath two children unbaptized, the
mother having been twice with me, I had told her I would
speak with her husband first, but acted contrary now,—7 its
a doubtful case to act in about such persons children, I haue
found reluctancy in my own spirit, yet would goe on, being
too flexible to yield to peoples importunity : But for this act
thus circumstantiated god hath cast me down in mine own
eyes this morning, laid me low, tooke this occasion to awake
conscience, and soften my heart, in prayer, and hath helped
me to plead with him for pardon power for future, favour for

church ministers securing the credit of the gospel notwithstanding this and all other occasions—blessed be god—ended well—

52 I preached at Lassel-hall with Mr Richardson—Feb 27 7¾—had a comfortable assistance, god inlarged my mouth much both in praying and preaching—but the day after being friday at a private fast in my house preparatory to the Lords Supper amongst aboue 40 persons, communicants, my heart was so drawn out for near 2 houres togather, as of late it seldom hath been, oh, what a warm spirit was there! in the behalf of the people (as wel as my own) in prayer I declared a profession of a solemne covenant wch we entered with god that day, and hope to haue it sealed on Lords day, and I hope most of them sd Amen to it, and subscribed it, god helped in laying some professors sins in confession, begging pardon, pleading for posterity, congregations, nation, in an unusual manner, I hope he hath some signall mercys in store for us—blessed be god—

53 On Thuesday March 4 I went upon a call, to Bingley, preacht at Joshua Walkers house being licenced, there was a considerable company god sweetly helped my heart both in praying and preaching on these words Act 16 30 wt must I doe to be saved, wherin God helped me in many things extemporarily wch I knew were proper the auditory, being either prophane or Antinomians, or generally both, much of god was in that excercise, wt the fruit will be god knows, whether conversion or hardening, however god hath helped me to leave my testimony there in good sound earnest, and people were wonderfull attentive, some I saw much affected, god almighty grant a blessed effect, John Foster a choyce christian came to me after sermon, and sd Sr you have brought strange things to our eares to day, I answered they are not strange to you, he replyed, no, but to that assembly they were, people are set on talking of them—tis thought some rich persons there were offended, I blesse god I am at a point with my self what people think of me so they may feel it wholsome good—

54 this day being March 15 7¾ (that day last year that his majestys declaration set us at liberty, and just 43 yeares this day that I was baptized) I retired into my best chamber, and there I fell upon my face and god graciously met and

melted my heart—my soul mourned for breaking my baptismal covenant, entered a solemne covenant to be the Lords, found my heart willing through grace that as I was at first baptized with water, that day, with a suffering imprisonment that day at Leedes about 2 yeares agoe, and this day was in a sort baptized with teares, so now here after to be baptized with blood, if god call me to it, oh for strengthening grace, by vertue of Chts death and resurrection, in wch I haue been buryed, and risen again by spiritual Baptism of fire!—For wch mercy my soul was thankful in some measure,—and pleaded for that mercy for the soules of my children—blessed be god grace is free—1 Cor 15 10 :

55 March 24 7¾ I tooke a journey into Lancash to visit my ancient weake and dying father, providence disposed mercifully of my journey to doe good, I overtook the messenger that came for me J R let him ride had a full opportunity, and through grace liberty of spirit to talk with him about soul affaires, askt him of his condition, draue things home,—as I returned I met with one John Ward a poor ignorant man, how I posed and pressed home some things on him, both upon Blackstone-edg, I haue often travelled that roade but never had such an opportunity and heart to help soules in heavens road, they were very tractable, with others god also helped me to discourse freely and god helped my heart with my own dear father but seldome have I found such melting of soule as I experienced when I was at prayer that morning I took my leaue of him, in pleading for him, and acknowledging gods goodnes to him hitherto and commending him into the hands of god who was the instrumt of my being in the world, and had prayed for me before I could pray for my selfe, he was 77 yeares of age about Micaelmas last—I think of Josephs coming to his father Jacob, Gen. 48—

56 April 7 73 my wife and I, and my two sons set out upon a journey into Lanc : Mr. Dawson with us, it was a sad day of rain and storm, yet towards night it pleased god to clear up the weather, Thuesday Mr. Dawson and I preacht at the meeting-place at Ratchdale, and tho it pleased god graciously to assist in preaching, yet I cannot tell that ever my heart was so drawn out in publick prayer, and abundance of teares and heart-melting matter and expressions scarce in all my life, oh it was a warm season, blessed be god, a token for good—

57 having preacht at Lassel-hall April 24 I lodged at Mr
Longleys of Dolton, where three of a family under the roof
where I lodged lay out till near midnight, drinking, I knew
some of them had been out most of the night before, Mr
Pickles came into the house where I was, but I saw he was
not capable of being spoken to, so I forbore, in the morning
I got up early, fell down on my knees, god helped my heart
sweetly in prayer, and in the family, and at Jon : Priestlys
in prayer for 3 sick children and at Hanna Hardgers, who
lay a dying as was judged, god melted my heart in prayer
oh it was a sweet day, I lookt my almanack and there its
called St Marks day April 25 the day of my first marriage
18 yeares agoe, but its memorable most for these sweet
evidences of my spiritual marriage to Jesus Cht—Hallelujah—

58 on thursday May 1 73 preaching at home having had
but a little time that forenoon for my study god wonderfully
drew out my heart and tongue in extemporary practical
pertinent matter for about 2 houres togather, I did wonder
at it, but god was seen in it, having been necessarily detained
from my studys by gods work abroad : but upon friday at
Mr Dawsons house May 2 upon a day of fasting and prayer
for his wife that she may be safely delivered in child-bearing,
god helped me patly to inlarge upon that subject, and to
plead for her, and oh how sweetly did god carry out my heart
in many passionate groanes and tears ! the company was
much affected, blessed be my good god for that sweet day—

59 I preacht upon May 6 73 at Mr Hortons meeting-place,
and upon a call went the day after to visit one Samuel
Crowthers wife, beyond Barsland towards Dean-head, I found
her distempered with Splen &c but principally melancholy,
tis ten yeares since she begun, I spoke much to her, but I
fear to little purpose, yet upon that occasion* many neighbours and others, a considerable congregation came togather,
to whom I preacht, prayed with them, it was an uncouth
work in that ignorant place yet god did much affect the
hearts and eyes of many of them, who knows wt good may
be done in that place ! grace is free—he can make a new
plantation in the wilderness—Amen

60 May 9 being friday we had a fast at my house in preparation for the Lords supper on Lords day, Oh what a
wonderful strange presence of god was with us ! seldom

hath been heart drawn out after that manner—oh what a
flood of teares! surely it was a Bethel, it was (as I remember) the first fast we kept in the meeting-house this
summer at least, and it was well-warmed and wel watered,
blessed be god for this token for good, grace is wonderfull
free to poor sinners :

61 My sons being to go abroad to learning next week I
took them with me to 3 private days this week one was at
Halifax May 14, at home May 15, the last at Mr. Dawsons
May 16 : but Thursday at home was such a day as we have
seldome had, I purposely appointed it to seek god on their
behalf and god wonderfully helped all his servants to plead
for them, about the middle of the day I called them both
forth, before the company askt them several questions, as wt
calling they chose, with teares they both answered, the
ministry, I askt them for what end, they might suffer persecution, must not dream of honour therein and to liue like
gentlemen &c they told me their only end was to glorify god,
and win soules, I markt Johns words he said he desired to
doe god more service than any of his anncestours, I askt
them what they desired Mr Dawson and the rest of gods
servants might pray to god for on their behalf—they spoke
openly both of them, Eliezer spake first in that that god
would give them grace, and gifts, forgive the sins of their
childhood, and losse of time, would make them studious,
keep them from temptation, and sinfull company,—Johns
answer was much-what of that nature, they both wept
exceedingly, teares dropt down apace, the whole company
wept, and then I gaue them up solemnly to god in his work,
—they that went to prayer read also a scripture, W B read
1 Sam 1 of dedicating Samuel to god, Mr Dawson read Gen.
28 of Isaac sending away his son Jacob—R R read pro 3
about getting, prizing wisdom, Mr. Hodgson read the latter
end of Gen 48 from 8 to end and when he came to these
words v 16 the angel wch redeemed me from all evil blesse
the lads, teares stopt him, he made a pause in weeping, we
all wept,—the scripture I read and expounded briefly was 1
Chron 28—of Solomons charge by David about building the
temple—but in prayer god helped all, but god wrought
strangely in my heart, oh wt a flood of teares, what pleadings
with god! I can scarce remember the like, blessed be
god, its a token for good at night after the young mens

conference, I set my two sons a praying, Eliezer begun and wept and prayed very feelingly, but John exceeded, both in strong scriptural expostulations, and sobbing and weeping that sometimes he could hardly speak, and such an evening of such a day I seldome haue had in al my life, I watch to hear what the Lord wil speak to all these, surely he will speak peace, but oh that I and mine might not return to folly, on friday may 16 1673 Mr Dawson had appointed a day of thanksgiving, the day after this sweet fast, Mr Bentley and he and I kept the day with many more, and god graciously helped our hearts, tho I had not such strange motions of affections as the day before, yet I look upon this as a pledge and presage of occasions of thankfulnes to god in future times, yea a kind of antedating and anticipating a day of rejoycing in the mercys begged of god the day before, and as we held the ordinance of baptisme, so they named the child Eliezer, god is my help, after my younger sons name, hitherto god hath helped, blessed be god for all this EBENEZER:

62 on thuesday june 3 at Mr Hortons meeting place and on thursday jun 5 at John Butterworths I found my heart in an extraordinary melting frame in prayer, especially in pleading with god for conversion of sinners, teares dropt abundantly from mine eyes and expostulations from my lips, beyond the usual frame, and accordingly god graciously helped me in preaching, upon two worthy subjects, who knows but some good may be done upon some hearts, many were affected,—blessed be the name of my god:

63 on munday June 9 I spent some time in praying and preaching in the house of one Edmund Taylour in Norland, on the thuesday we had an excercise in Rushworth-hall near Bingley, in both places god did wonderfully help my heart, and many others, so that I saw many teares dropt down from many eyes, both ignort. prophane places blessed be god, and tho in this latter week my affections were not so melting yet my expressions were more fluent, and at Josh Walkers I was much carryed out in many expostulations for a work of conversion : yet that night I was left to myself in some con-templative sins, wherin I was sensible of guilt—the lord make me more watchfull, and pardon thought-sins :

64 On Thursday June 12 73 the same week, we spent some part of the day in my house in prayer it was our

fourtnight-day conference, but we turned it into prayer (the young-mens day and work) and blessed be god, it was a good day, an hopefull beginning among yong professors, the persons that usually meet at conference are these, William Clay, Anthony Lea, James Tetley, John Kershaw, jun: Samuel Nickoll, Samuel Holdworth, Timothy Holt, John Rhodes, Samuel Drake, John Hanson, James Oates, James Bland, John Gill, Timothy Crowther, &c these are our yong store, besides the old stock, they meet every fourtnight begin and end with prayer, conferre upon a subject,—this time was spent in prayer aboute six houres, god helped very graciously, they all prayed sweetly and sensibly for my sons, my heart was much affected, oh what mercy was there in this yong mens day, blessed be god for the budding of Aarons rod:

65 On Wednesday june 18 and Friday june 20, 73 the former time at Hanna Hardgers, the latter at Jonathan Priestleys—in days of prayer my heart was sweetly and graciously affected and assisted, but on saturday night june 21 in my closet work of prayer, my heart was wonderfully shut up—and I could not get it into any frame, I guess the reason, I fear I grieved quenched the spirit, for having a resolution to goe to prayer I barred the door, wch wn it was done, something came into my mind to write, and I did not then pray but put it off till after family-prayer and supper and then god was withdrawn—Lord humble my heart, and teach me more diligence,—

66 on Thursday at Quarrel-hill in Sowerby, and on Wednesday (july 1 and 2) at Slead within half a mile of Padium in Lanc: my heart was wonderfully drawn out both in praying and preaching, especially in the latter place, where I preacht a lecture among Mr Jollys people, a godly people, concerning a token for good, ps 86 ult god helped wonderfully, people were much affected,—especially in pleading for conversion god inlarged much,—yet that night I had some dark thoughts wch damped my spirit, july 2—73—Lord how ill can we bear any smiles from god—when shall my soul be set at liberty ?

67 On munday july 7 78 I went to the funeral of Mary Boys the wife of John Boys of Mixenden a very choyce, humble, tenderhearted christian as any I know in all this country, with whom I had been not long before, and who

had manifested many experiments to me, her funerall this day was solemnly carryed on, god directed the Clark to sing a suitable psalme, viz psal 50 from v 3 to v 7: Mr Wilkinson prayed honestly, and preached profitably upon the text she left him viz 1 Tim 1 15 : especially the last words of whom I am chiefe,—did commend her for severall things, but fell very far short of speaking her great worth—when they laid her body to the graue, saying we commit her body to the graue, in sure and certain hope of an happy resurrection, my heart tendered, and was wonderfully melted, I withdrew from amongst the people god helped with some meditations, many wept, I thought of my good mother—and haue seldom been so much affected as at this funerall—triumphing soul—

68 July 8 73 I went to Joshua Walkers at Rushworth hall near Bingley to preach, Mr Whitehurst preacht the former, his text was lam 3 14 about saints experiences, but he had not one word in all his sermon reaching to the unconverted, my spirit was sore troubled, knowing the state of that people, being a numerous mixt assembly, I intended the subject of a token for good, but hearing his discourse changed my thoughts, treated of self-deceit from Sam 1 22. god did wonderfully assist, blessed be god, who knoweth wt good may be done! many were affected—the morning after riding over the moores to Bramhup (tho it was a terrible rain yet) my heart was affected much in meditation, self-reflection, and covenanting with god, tho I found not such assistances at Bramhup either in prayer or sacramt as sometimes, yet god helped my tongue with competent elocution :—the morning after at Ardington god helped with good words, both in expounding a chapter and prayer suitable to the gentlewomens conditions : blessed be god :

69 July 29 73 I rode in my course to preach at Mr Hortons place at Sowerby, but having strained my self more than ordinarily upon Lords [day] to speak that all might hear, there being a very numerous assembly at my house, my head was much out of order on munday, and thuesday morning, so that I was in no good posture for preaching, told them I should be short, but wn I was at work my head mended, I continued till two a clock, god wonderfully helped, melted my heart, and I doe not remember I saw such weeping while I was preaching this many yeares, it was a good word

god helped me—and blessed be god in sustaining my spirit
in delivering it affectionately : jam 1 22

70 But the day after being wednesday july 30 73 having
a call to preach in Mr. Bentleys house and room (in his
absence) at Halifax I found not my heart so affected either
in praying or preaching as ordinarily I haue—I partly guesse
the reason partly because I made too much confident account
of my preparations for that work, partly because people
might have too great expectations from me, there being a
great assembly—gods will be done tis to my credit so his
work may be done—

71 Aug 10 being at York, Mr Ward hauing the supper I
resolved to sit downe, he gaue me the right hand of fellow-
ship, sate me at his right hand : delivered it first to me, my
heart was not in such a melting frame this many yeares in
that ordinance, god came in abundantly, satisfyed my heart
of his loue in cht helped me in meditation, and self-resigna-
tion to god, I found it indeed a sealing ordinance, blessed,
blessed be god,—but the next lords day at home, Aug 17 73
my heart was not so sweetly touched, and seldome is when
myself administereth it, gods will be done : he is infinitly
wise—

72 I was most of the week at home the last week in
August, and tho god was pleased to leave me to my self on
thuesday in committing a sin, yet that day and wednesday,
and thursday the Lord graciously helped my heart in renewing my repentance, and covenants oh wt heart-melting
seasons had I ! and I hope he was pleased to accept of me,
for upon friday Aug 29 73 at Mr Hortons meeting-place,
god helped me both in praying and preaching, and was also
pleased to give me the seal of the covenant, god sweetly
helping my heart in dispensing and receiving the supper
amongst Mr Roots members—

73 On thuesday at Lidget I was helped (Sept 2 73) god
graciously inlarged my heart both in praying and preaching,
and it was a good day but upon friday Sept 5 at John Halls
of Kipping preaching with Mr Whitehurst I was much
straitened and confounded in preaching (tho the Lord
melted my heart in praying) it may be because I was much
straitened in time or rather to confute my carnal confidence,
for I must confesse I was self-conceited having preacht with
him formerly at Bingly and conceiving my self much aboue

him, now god set me far below him for god wonderfully helped Mr. Whitehurst both in praying and preaching, he had a very profitable discourse about not knowing the time of visitation, and tho god withdrew from me for wise ends yet I heartily desired god would blesse his labours for the good of sinners, tho I am likely to be of little use—

74 On saturday Sept 6 73 I set my selfe seriously to consider wt text to preach on the day following at Lassel-hall, I pitcht on lant 8 9 went on in that resolution, set my self to spend some time in prayer that afternoon and indeed god did graciously help my heart in meditation and prayer for nigh two houres, but especially pleading for the conversion of soules, oh wt a warm heart had I! well, I went on Lordsday morning to Lassel-hall, had the notes of that text in my book, expounded that chapter, sang the psalm, still not thinking of any other subject, but towards the latter end of the psal : singing a strong notion came prevailingly into my mind to take another text, I lookt among my sermons, found one discourse upon phi 3 9 of being found in cht, I closed with it, put the notes into my bible, preacht upon it, was wonderfully inlarged, there was a mighty congregation, much attention, affection, I have some secret persuasions that god will doe some good upon some soules by that days work, I haue not met with such a providence in all my life :

75 On Sept 9 73 being thuesday I rid out to the heights within this township of Northorum, to see three persons aged and weak, near their death Timothy Sutliues wife aged 84, Jeremiah Bairstow aged 84, and John Smith aged 76 in all 244 ; two of them I found something ignorant, whose condition I doubted, and laboured with them for their soules good, but alas I find I can doe but little good, yet it did a little affect my heart when I considered that those were my ancient hearers, and how I was a taking my last farewel of them, being all likely to dye, and know not what condition their soules are, but alas I find it wonderfull difficult to speak convincingly, and to answer their carnal evasions : John Smith (one of Mr Colliers converts and an ancient member of Mr Roots church, who also sate down with us) I found in a good plight very comfortable, and I hope safe— dyed Sept 11 :

76 Having kept up a monethly meeting in Warley aboue a year now it grows towards an end, providence strangely

concurring, 1 Mr Horton having set up a weekly lecture at his meeting-place its judged by some that they are too near togather to be both in one week, tho I know it that not 4 persons that goe to the one, doe or would goe to the other but my dear brother Bentley sets himself agt it saying people will be tyred out with preaching, and it giues offence to adversarys, and with these arguings so far prevailed that the lecture at Quarrel-hill was totally intermitted bec : of my preaching in Warley, which much troubled me, and ingaged me to suspend this lecture in Warley, especially considering 2 that tho at my first preaching there, there was mighty flocking, yet now theres but a very few, and those such as I have hopes have got good by the word, wch are willing to travel,—so preaching thuesday Sept 16 73 I gaue no notice of any more meeting, and gaue some hints of ceasing in my prayer god helpt me wonderfully in that excercise, some good women flockt about me after, lamented my withdraw-ing, gods will be done—its agt my desire—I observed a providence that never happened to me before that I re-member, while I was very earnest and affectionate in my former prayer my nose fell a bleeding, and bled much into my handkerchief—wt the meaning of that is god alone knowes :

77 On wednesday Sept 24 73 Mr Jolly and I preacht an excercise at my place, in my own house, and god helped us both very graciously in our work, there was a numerous assembly, but I heare since that Mr Bentley is much offended that we pitcht upon his lecture day, And I must confesse I thought upon it before, but Mr Jolly had been often pre-vented in his coming to us, and writ to me before-hand, pitching upon that day, and the week before I went to Mr Bentley told him how it was, and I was sorry it was so cast he said little then to it, but desired me to bring Mr Jolly and my congregation to his house, wch I told him I could not doe because he would but come that evening, wch he did and it was full 11 a clock wn he came,—some of Mr Bentleys house came to us after, yet he frets and tels people that I pitcht upon that day on purpose that so I might crosse him —this troubles me—

78 on munday Octob 13 73 we had a private fast at John Stancliffs house, but it was not such a good day to me as ordinarily I haue had : I begun the day, and my heart begun

to be affected, but afterwards in the same duty I struggled
and tugged, but found much deadnes, distraction, and could
not get the work forward, wch wn I perceived I cut short:
the Lord humble me for it, and shew me the cause, he is
infinitly wise and righteous:

79 friday octob 24 at a private fast in my house god
graciously helpt—and several other times in secret—the day
after,—being alone, and munday being alone, oh wt melting
seasons had I in my study: and on wednesday octob 28, in
Warley god wonderfully helped both in praying and preaching—Blessed be my god:

80 I cannot but take notice and exceedingly admire gods
providence that wn one door is shut up, god opens another
for service and imployment: by an observable call I was
brought to one Mrs Brookes at New-house, to keep a fast
upon a special occasion, Nov 18 73 and indeed I haue very
seldome found such inlargemts and meltings of spirit, it
may be god hath some design of good in that very ignorant
place, the old woman was carnal, I fear, her daughters civil,
Mr Gill the young gentleman that marryed the one keeps a
Kennel of hounds, yet much affected, al of them very thankfull, gratifyed me—oh wt a mercy if god would work!—

81 this day having been at Quarry-hill preaching as I
came home I called of Mr Bentley, where I found John
Brearcliffe, who amongst other discourse told me Dr. Hook
threatened to get a writ agt me for making a marriage this
week—I came home went to my study, set my self to pray,
god did sweetly help my heart to mourn for sin if I had
done any thing inconsiderately, to deprecate gods displeasure
intreat reconciliation with him tho men be implacable—oh
god hears Nov 28 1673:

82 Nov 29 1673 Micael Broadly of Bingley being all night
with me told me that he had been a professor of religion
many years, but myself came to preach an excercise at
Bingley church almost 20 yeares agoe upon that text 2 cor
4 4 if our gospel be hid its hid to them that are lost, his
heart was so rivetted at that sermon that he thought the
word was spoke to none but him, saw himself lost, yet kept
councell laments he opened not his case to me, I never knew
of it til this night—blessed be god for this mercy to him—
he is a gracious man:

83 my own father having had much trouble, hath been in hopes and frustrated, at this time my Cozen Nath: Hulton (whom he was the very instrument to raise) being come from Lancash undertakes to agree with creditors, they want me, send a special messenger. then I was ingaged in necessary busines, could not goe, he sends another message by letter, but it reacht me not till the time was expired, I had also a letter from cozen Hulton,—this night another letter from my father Heywood, urging me to come, yet not giving an account for wt end, but the time is past this day, while I was poring upon it and perplext, comes a letter from my father and mother Angier, both mentioning my coming over into Lanc the one saying it was no matter of my coming, they might have drawn me to some inconvenience, the other, pray take heed wt you doe considering wt you haue done, and wt you haue to doe wth wt god hath lent you, these things jumping togather this evening Decmb 2, 73: I take them as remarkable providences prohibiting my going, having I think discharged my duty to my father in doing more for him than all the relations he hath, both in pay and trouble, having taken the burden of travel and care for him long togather myself, and can make account of aboue 200 li that he hath had of mine, my sons now costing dear—

84 on Lords day Decemb 14 73 my wife had a letter out of Lanc: that that week my sister Hanna Crompton was dead and buryed, tis a sad losse, her husband dying but a little before, she was my own eldest sister, about 50 yeares of age, a precious saint of god, very like my mother, whom I haue heard say, that she never had cause to question Hannas conversion, after god had wrought upon her, I question not but her soul is lodged safe in Abrahams bosom: in the same letter we had the news that my own father was taken by the Bailiffs yet was released the next day, blessed be god—I doubted it, wn Cozen Hulton agreed with some not with all:

85 on friday feb 27 we had a fast in my house, preparatory to the Lords supper, but alas my heart was not so affected as sometimes it was wont to be especially on behalf of the nation I was much straitened, the day after tidings was brought me of the Parlts adjourning when they were in a hopefull way of doing much good in the nation—I feared bad news, and felt it in my spirit—the Lord sanctify it—

86 on march 24 74 I came to Leeds, went to Tim: Smiths shop, there found Jane Milner who was overjoyed to see me, pleased her self with hopes of having me the day after at Milne hill, where I preacht but she was prevented, for just as she was ready to come to the meeting-place, her horse fell and put her into a great fright, tho no hurt was done, blessed be god yet she lookt upon it as a sad providence to prevent her of that opportunity: god had an hand in it:

87 April 5 1674 having preacht in the morning and coming out of the meeting-place at noon as my custom is to refresh my self in the parlour I met with a note lying upon the table, I tooke it up and read it, in these words, One that hath made some profession of religion, but now finds that they never had their heart truely broken for their sin, and hath great cause to fear that the Lord will no longer striue with her, desires your prayers that the Lord would meet her in his ordinance, and let her find that her conscience is truely awakened by convicting grace: this note I tooke notice of, and though I did not read it publickly, yet prayed for her particularly, and god helped my heart in sweet and suitable pleas for her soule, my heart was mueh affected therein, and so were others hearts as I sensibly perceived by their groanes,—god made it a blessed note though from an unknown hand: blessed be god:

88 April 10 1674 my wife, maid, children, and whole family being gone abroad, and my selfe left alone in the house about 3 a clock in the afternoon I set my self to the work of self-examination prayer, in my best chamber, spent two houres till 5 in that work, and god sweetly helped my heart, oh it was a sweet season, having kept the day before in publick fast, and being to prepare for the ordinances of the ensuing sabboth and the Lords supper, god drew out my heart in repentance, faith, renewing covenant, pleading for the church, my relations, congregation, conversion of soules, —some advantage to those dutys did the consideration of my dear mothers flight to heaven out of that very roome adde to my spirit, blessed be god for that sweet season:

89 April 19 being lords day another note was presented to me to this effect, Sr this is the humble suit of one afflicted in conscience, under sad apprehensions of gods displeasure with many grievous temptations, that you would be pleased to remember them in your prayers to god, not only publick

but private—this note my servant had given her but forgot
to give it me till night—and I blesse god for these cases—

90 having preacht at Alverthorp April 26 74 and at Mr
Kerbys house in Wakefield, April 28—many flockt to hear
me, god having been gracious to me in inlarging my heart
and mouth and being to preach an excercise at Alverthorp
on wednesday Apr 29 much people flockt togather having (as
I imagine) high expectations, but were disappointed as I
may conceiue, for god did much with-draw from me so that
I found not his presence as at other times, let god haue
glory and me haue shame,—oh that this might doe me and
his people some good!

91 On Lords day may 10 74 several came to me with
troubled spirits, complaints, one from Horton called Martha
Thacker, two daughters of James Smith, one Samuel Bairstow,—on munday I having been to see Daniel Dison at
Crosland, returning back, upon the moor, a young man went
before me wn I made up to him he fell down on his knees
lift up his hands and eyes to me cryed out, good sir tel
me what I shall doe to get rid of my sins I bade him rise
up, wch he did, I thought he had been melancholy, but upon
further discourse with him I found it proceeded from the
grievous agony and great bitternes of spirit for sin, oh how
he wept and wrung his hands! he walkt a mile with me as
I rode, I discoursed with him, found him very sensible yet
confused in his troubles, his name is John Chadwick, he
liues with this Daniel Dison, had heard me the day before,
—blessed be god for these strivings of conviction, who
knows but these are pangs—

92 Susanna Northend my old neighbour a good woman of
about 80 yeares of age, having formerly liued in Northourun,
wn she had a house of her owne was more forward for good
dutys than most in these parts, at whose house we had
many private days, hath been under great afflictions by the
death of all her children, the sad miscarriage of most of
them, the horrid wickednes of her grandson, lately dead in
prison had sold all, brought them into straits, she was glad
to agree with Mr Thurstan upon his own termes, being a
potent man, the poor widows quitted all upon a sum of
money, sold all for two yeares, but last week, immediately
after she fell ill, dyed on Lords day may 24 74—very seasonably for her, for had that money been spent her life would
have been uncomfortable—

93 May 31 74 being Lords day Mr Josh : Witton being a non-conformist minister living in York formerly parson of Thornhil, tho he had not preacht being rich, yet had been of great use, for his poore brethrens supply, that day went to church twice, came home, was pretty well, eat his supper, went to prayer, so to bed, and was dead before the morning, buryed June 3 1674 : tis a sad blow the lord sanctify this and other sad strokes, wch bode much evil to the nation :— just so good Mr Jones of Eccles walkt out was tollerably wel tho he had been distempered went to bed at 9 a clock was dead before twelve—may 2 74—

94 June 13 74 being saturday night, Mr Claiton of Rotheram, an eminent minister in this county dyed suddenly, he had been to see Mr Burbeck at Sheffield on thursday, walkt abroad on friday saturday, several friends came to visit him that evening, with whom as he was discoursing in his own house, he fell a coughing, vomiting blood, cryed out god be mercifull to me, I am gone, and dyed immediately—

95 these two days viz munday and thuesday June 22 and 23, 1674 I haue been at two as solemne funerals as ever I was in all my life, the former day, Mr. Baylys wife, at Morley, who had been down in a consumption 10 weekes, the latter Joshua Stansfields wife who dyed in child-birth June 21 and the child with her, whom I saw laid in one coffin, the child in her arms, as tho it were asleep, an affecting sight, sad for relations, Lord sanctify it to all—

96 I went from home June 27 returned July 1 1674 in wch journey I haue this experiment that god hath put me on some self-denying acts, for tho I preacht at Alverthorp al day on Lords day took pains at a meeting on munday to reconcile the neighbours, preacht and baptized a child at Mr. Kerbys on thuesday, yet returning on wednesday I had not one penny given me in this journey, tho I spent some money and gaue, this is a smal piece of self-denyal, yet it may be introductory to more, god wil teach me both how to want and abound, or possibly I was too selfish in leaving mine own people, tho it went hard with me, Lord forgive sin, teach me good lessons—

97 this day being friday july 3 1674 hath been a solemne day on account of Marthas removal, my old servant who hath lived with me about 16 yeares, hath been exceedingly

faithful and careful of me and mine, afflicted with me in al my afflictions, and shared with me in all conditions, now at last she is marryed to a good man, James Tetley, I loved her as a child, my bowels yearned for her, she was ful of heavines at parting my heart was much affected in secret prayer but in the family affections run over into passion, in reading Gen 24 of Abrahams faithful servant, and Rebeccas parting from home, very pat to the purpose, commenting on them, and in prayer—in wch I spent near an houre god wonderfully working—especially considering that there is not one now in my family but my self that was in it wn it was first erected and if I goe it will be no family—

98 July 30 74 Mr Richardson and I preacht an excercise at Lady Rodes chappel, I begun concerning the root of the matter, he went on from col 1 20 of fruitfulnes in every good work, god ordered our subjects as if we had purposely cast them into this mold, helped both, blessed be his name —it was a good day—

99 as I was riding towards Lassel-hall about 9 a clock in the morning from Lidget near Farnley aboue Woodson, being an high hill, having a lovely prospect all over the country, the sun shining gloriously I had some meditations of the glory of the world, thinking of Satans taking cht into an exceedingly high mountain, but behold upon my winking all vanisht away into blacknes, wch helped my meditations, that all that glory was but a lump of vanity.

100 I called of S D talkt seriously my heart to her about marrying J B she took it very ill, resolved to hear me no more, the Lords day after went to Illing.[th] there heard one that she also fled from—the Lords day after went by my house to hear Mr. W : but missed of him he not being there, then went to W— in afternoon to Mr D place, came to Halif. at night, so being crossed and weary of wandering, came this day again to hear to me,—faithful dealing may anger at present, but brings friendship afterwards, oh for an upright heart!

101 I preacht at Alverthorp, Sept 20 74 3 Bailiffs came in the forenoon, yet say it is not to take names,—in the afternoon many came, amongst whome was a wild young schollar one Ratliff, he hearkened diligently, yet on munday night he helpt down liquor with his companions by sporting with my sermon the subject was chts preciousnes to believers

he canted as he pretended like me—repeating saying (wch I spake not) is not this a precious cht that can make your rags precious : his companions were one Pindar born in Wakefield, Boys.............in Leeds, Ledgers son of Bradford, all Oxford scholars—but very prophane, sitting in the chair of the scornful—father forgiue them—

102 On Lords day octob 4 1674 having preacht all day at home shortly after I had done John Stevensons men came into my croft to their tenters, tooke their peeces off, made hast and cast them over the wall, yet I saw them, my heart was full of it, yet I rested that night, but in the morning when they came to tenter other pecces, I went to John askt him why they took peeces of the tenters on the Lords day, he said they had occasion I told him of the sin of it in breaking of the sabboth repeated the 4th comt, argued the case with him, he made poor allegations of looking to cattel, that hundreds did so &c I told him I lived by rule not by example,—told him plainly the sabboth should not be broken where I had anything to doe, required him to take away his tenters—he sd they would forbear—

103 when I was at prayers in my family on thuesday morning Oct 20 74 three people cryed at the gates for almes, I heard them my heart was much affected I gaue god praise that I was not in that condition, going about to beg my bread from door to door—

104 on saturday morning octob 24 in family prayer we read the passage of Samuels entertaining David 1 Sam 16 and it much affected my heart in my study that god should chuse him—so even the least in my fathers house for his great work

105 on Lords day morning in the meeting-place after my first prayer—I said the Lords prayer, mist it in the last petition—but god made me amends by inlarging my heart in my prayer before sermon—oh wt meltings !

106 The most heart-melting day and work that ever I can remember was Feb 14 1675 the Lords day—the weeke before we received the Kings order to call in his licences and it was judged we should cease as to that publick way of preaching openly to all—I took my solemne farewel upon that Lords day—preaching on Rev 2 4 5 of removing the candlestick, and in the close dismissed that meeting—gave

my reasons—some advice, then—god caused abundant affection—floods of teares such as I never had experience of in
all my life in publick—promising my best assistance to them
all in private—and oh that god would set the stamp of his
grace and spirit upon their words affections—who knows
what good may be done by that closing sermon—however
those affections are a token for good—and presage the
Lords gracious return—

107 Tho I took my leaue Feb 14 1675—with much
affection, many tears,—yet god was pleased to remember us,
I observed what others did, who generally kept on their
work in meetings I was troubled at my cessation, within 2
days I fell to preaching again, many flockt to ordinances,
god graciously helpt, there was no danger, not a dog moving
his tongue against us, and thus we haue continued in as
full assemblys as formerly all the summer, thus far of the
winter til this day wch is Decemb 12 1675—in wch time
many ministers haue been at Coley, but settled not, the
last minister a scotchman dyed, was buryed Dec 9 75—since
which the heads of the chapelry of Coley haue been consulting to giue me a call to preach in publick and say things
will not be right till I be brought to it again, what god will
doe in these matters I know not—

108 Saturday Dec 18 1675 going to prayer in my study
in the morning, god sweetly melting my heart in my pleadings ere I was aware, and far beyond my expectation, haue-
ing not so solemnly set my self to the duty as sometimes, I
was earnestly desiring of the Lord restoration to publick
work, suddenly objections stopt me saying how can this be,
since Dr Hook is so great an adversary, and the heads of my
congregation complying with the times and loath to anger
him, and as suddenly a thought was suggested into my mind,
that the day before I was standing by a workman that I had
and in a difficult peece of work he usually said to me Master
how must we doe this? I told him I know not, but he being
a very correct workman, had witty contrivances that I
wondered at, and so brought about that speedily and easily
wch to me seemed impossible before, this was a wonderfull
support and incouragement to my weak faith, that though
poor weak man be puzzled, yet the infinit wise god is not
non-plust, but can bring to passe things both for matter,
manner and season far beyond our conceptions—according

to Zech 8 6 : gathering heart from this consideration god helped me to wrestle with some faith and tears for this mercy, and particularly to plead for Dr Hook, that god would hnmble his heart, pardon his sin, make use of him for the good of sinners,—and methought in the close of the duty my heart was wonderfully quieted and satisfyed that let god doe what he pleaseth with me whether he restored me to the vacant chappel or upheld my liberty in my own house, so that he would make use of me in either, I should blesse his name :

109 Dec 28 1675 I flitted my bookes and goods out of my lower study beyond the parlour into my new-made study in the meeting-place chamber, which is made convenient for me, and is better for my bookes which were almost spoyled in the other moyst room, coming into it at night after my preaching and conference that day, I fell down on my face, god helpt me a good part of an houre to confesse my sins in all the other places where I had been, to give him praise for the sweet incomes I had in my fathers house, at Cambridge, Landimer, Godley, this house, Norwood-green, Coley-hall and in my lower study since my return hither, all wch places I may call Peniel for I haue seen gods face, in these places— pleading now that I may come with a new heart spend more time with god,—find more of his grace oh it was a sweet heart-melting evening, Oh that god would hear my groanes, accept my vows—be with me still—

110 As I came home from Leeds, munday Jan 10 76 just by Newel upon a knotty caucey, having some sad and solemne thoughts about my sons, my horse fell all along threw me in the mire, that I was lamentably dirtyed, but I blesse god I was not hurt, wch was a rich mercy for my leg was under the horse, I rid home, still feel no hurt, blessed be god, Lord for a thankfull heart !

111 on friday Jan 21 1676 hauing a call to goe to a meeting at Cromwel-bottom, Captain Hodgson's, I went, when I came thither I found some persons I knew not, Mr Hodgson told me they were some young men, that were my hearers, hopefull for religion, and that they had set up a monethly meeting, wch they us'd to spend in prayer, but since I was come they desired me to spend some time in some discourse, I begd a blessing on the work, Mr Hodgson prayed, then Nathan Baxter therin god much affected my heart in his affectionate requests for me and my sons, after that I took a

text viz Zach 4 6 intended only a few words extempore upon
it, but hauing a little begun, raised a doctrine god cast into
my thoughts abundance of matter suitable to the text and
company, far far beyond my expectation, I spent about an
hour in that work comfortably to my self, and I hope profitably to the company, then concluded with prayer wherin god
wonderfully melted and inlarged my heart, I haue seldom
had experiments of things so suitably suggested to my
thoughts, or of so much liberty of speech, blessed be my
Lord for it, oh that it may doe their hearts good, who knows
but it may!—

112 The like experiment I had at John Cordinglys near
high-town, Feb 20 75 where Mr Dawson Mr Holdsworth and
I kept a fast, I was to close, it was a day set apart with
reference to the danger of the losse of ordinances, disturbed
in two meeting-places in that parish the two sabboths immediately preceding I thought to hint a few notes from 1 Sam
4 13—and god suggested matter for aboue an houres discourse profitably, wherewith many were much affected, but
in prayer I was straitened in affection more than usually—
god is wise, I am vile—

113 on tuesday Feb 29 75 I designed to spend some considerable time by my self in heart-searching, humbling my
soul, secret prayer but visiting some in the afternoon, not
well, I was hindered till 5 a clock, then went to my study
read a psalm viz 71 with wch my heart was wonderfully
affected, then fell on my face, confessed my sins with aggravations, poured out my soul to god for pardon, wherin god
wonderfully helpt with a flood of tears, then I pleaded for
conversion of soules, then for my children wherein my
affections exceeded, and while I was pleading for them in
the bitternes of my soule, that scripture in that psalm I had
been newly reading psalm 71 14 but I will hope continually
and will yet praise thee more and more—especially the last
clause wch supported my spirit wonderfully, oh that it may
be verifyed! and thus god helpt me aboue an hour in my
wrestlings with god, and likewise a considerable time in
family-prayer that night with strong crys and teares, to
plead for poor silenced ministers, blessed be god:

114 On wednesday march 1 75 having a call to John
Brooksbanks of Ealand at a private fast for his wife near
child-bearing, himself, Mr Dawson, Nathan Baxter, Capt

Hodgson having been at prayer, they put me to conclude, Mr Dawsons case was also presented, being to appear before a magistrate this week for preaching. I took a texte, thought to speak a few words upon Gen 22 14—but god did so giue an abundance of matter extemporary, that I continued the discourse aboue an hour, I hope very pertinently and profitably—

115 the day after march 2 at Robt Bins being called to preach amongst a considerable number of people, having put into my book two sermons on two several texts Deut 32 29 and job 23 10 I was not satisfyed with the matter I had in either of them, lifting up my heart to god for direction, he suggested another scripture to my mind, that [I] never had preach[d] upon, viz job 23 27 and god helped on a sudden with matter upon that text that lasted aboue an houre and half discoursed very profitably to my admiration, both for matter and method, and apt proofs, so that I cannot tell I could haue framed a more profitable discourse in a days solemne studying—

116 The day after that march 3 being at Jerem : Baxters at a fast, Jonathan Priestly went to prayer, prayed for Mr. Dawson and many others : but prayed not one word for me or my sons which others did,—I took a conciet that he had taken offence at me and that god had shut me out of good peoples prayers—wch did so work with me that wn I prayed it exceedingly tended to the melting and breaking of my heart—oh what a duty was that !

117 In my journey into Westmorland upon wednesday April 5 1676, having baited at Ingleton about a mile beyond in a stony lane my horse blundered amongst the stones, and came down and I under him side-ways, but was not hurt, I rose up, went forward, lapt the bridle fast about my hand to hold him fast, but by that time I had rid another mile down a little hill in a very stony lane he stumbled again, fell on his nose, kickt me clean over his neck, there I lay got up, was not hurt, blessed be the keeper of Israel, another fall I had in that journey by a stone lying hollow, and my horse falling in Northourum township, as I went from home, I was discouraged about my old horse, yet god wonderfully preserved me from hurt, he kept all my bones not one of them is broken, let god alone haue all the glory in his gracious providence, not my prudence in self-preservation—

118 Before I was to take that journeying I had great
need of money to take with me, and about a fortnight before
had not above 8ˡⁱ and knew not by what meanes to get up
what I needed, which was a considerable summe, having
more then ordinary occasion, well, god saw my necessity,
being at that time to receive my wages, I gaue my people
but a modest hint of my necessitys, and behold their bounty,
I had brought in almost 8li—wch was double to what I used
to receive so that togather with that and other helps I had,
I was able to discharge my sons quarterage to Mr Frankland
wch was 6 li to pay my sons debts wch they had contracted
wch was near 8 li - to leaue 20 sh in Mr Franklands hands
on their behalf, and to bear my charges in my journey, (wch
was but smal bec I lodged with friends) and brought almost
10 sh home with me —and borrowed not a farthing its matter of wonder to me—

119 On saturday Apr 29 76 I resolved for study upon the
text that Hanna Hardger had left me (being buryed the day
before) and imagined I could quickly furnish myself with
sermons on it, having found a funeral sermon I preacht at
Bradford 18 yeares agoe, the text was psal 119 75 I set
about it, studyed hard, but could get little forward as I
desired, I prayed with my wife, went to't again, still it
would not doe, I was confused, sweat at it, god let me see
what I was, tho the day before at a meeting god helpt me to
frame an extemporary discourse of an houre long at Mr
Burkheads, wth some wit, and I too much pleased and ap-
plauded my self in it, for wch god blasted my present studys,
yet lord-day morning god helped my heart in prayer, and
did make those sermons very profitable and suitable beyond
expectation blessed be his name—

120 on Tuesday morning being something afflicted in
some unpleasing discourse with my wife about my going to
J T with whom hath been some difference, I spake my mind
very freely to her, dealt plainly with her in admonition, lest
malice lodge in her heart and satan get advantage—she was
troubled it was grief to me, I went to my study wept before
the Lord on my face, pleading for her soul, before night she
was much composed, in a good frame,—all having on occas-
sion left the house I betook my self into the best chamber,
and about an houre god wonderfully melted my heart in
thankfulnes, and repeating his kindnesses, this was a sweet

day—it was may 2 1676, wednesday was the private fast at
Ja Tetleys but my head akt violently, I was very sick that
day vomited, yet was better but had a sufficient apology for
not going—

121 Being at Leeds on may 28 76 at Mr Elk Hicksons
having to preach that day being Lords day I rose early, read
my chapters, in course one was 1 chron 17 and I set myself
to comment upon it, and oh what meltings of heart had I
from verse to verse about gods promise to David and his
seed, and then in prayer, pleading with god, I haue not often
found my heart in such a frame, and it was the more kindly
because love melted me, then was I helped to believe for my
children, oh the wonderfull morning—a good preparatory to
the solemne ordinances of that day, wch god graciously
helpt me to manage—

122 on munday morning 1 rose at Leeds by 4 a clock, but
my head akt very bitterly, it was ill that forenoon, at noon
I ate a little but it made me desperately sick, I went to the
backside, vomited all up—got on horsback, was something
better, was to haue been at day of thanksgiving at Isaac
Balmes, did goe came to the latter part of the work, god
helpt Mr Sharp in prayer, I expounded 1 cor 12 13 about
baptism—profitably, yet extempore for a full hour, baptized
the child, prayed, god helpt my heart and head, was perfectly cured then had a stomach to eat, came home, o wonder
of mercy! preaching and praying hath helpt my soul and
body, both at once—

123 I am pressed in spirit to take notice of the fruit of
my poor labours and the return of prayers, wch is best
evidenced by observing the increase of visible professours,
private meetings and forwardnes therin, and there are 4
sorts of meetings amongst my constant hearers at home, 1
our stated fast amongst the members of our society, every
Friday before the sacramt at my house, and monethly for
the nation: 2 theres W: Butler, Will Hurd, Tho Gill, John
Nickol, Jer Watson haue kept a meeting every fortnight for
prayer at some of their houses by turnes—3 my young men
for conference monethly, and at other times and places
meeting for prayer upon particular cals and occasions, such
as S Holdworth T Holt, S Nickol, J. Oates, J Kershaw jun
R Smith J Gill, J Learoyd &c 4 there is a society set and
kept up in Southourum keeping monethly a day of prayer,

Capt: Hodgson J Firth J Brooksbank N Barker W Maud,
and some young men my hearers that come from Rastrick,
Tootill, Brighouse all these carry on very hopefully—
and since my going to Jo Butterworths in Warly theres 3
meetings set up there. 1 one every fortnight at J Butterworths, or at James Wadingtons or at Tho: Bentlys by
Harewood wel—2 another every moneth at Nathan Bates
house in Norland, where some christians of my hearers in
Norland and Steneland meet, and haue done about a year,
—3 and now lately since I begun to preach at Sam: Hop-
kinsons another meeting of christians is set up about
Soyland at Tim Stansfields &c and I am informed they are
wonderfull forward and affectionate, many come, they weep
sore, a good sign, oh for sincerity, theres good hopes, great
reformations, many strong convictions, who knows what
good may be done by these—Blessed be the name of my god
—this is July 20 1676
These meetings are a token for good to England

124 In the year 1662 and 1663 I had a call to preach
frequently at Motteram church in Cheshire, and tho the
Uniformity act was in force yet the preacher then there Mr
Hopkins suffered it and in the year 1676 July 7 I had a
letter from my father Angier with these words, You shall
now understand that it was gods provision, (viz 17 sh - 3d
sent me) sent in to you by two motteram-men (Robt Turner
de brook—ue) as a thankfull remembrance of your preaching
amongst them long agoe, and an incouragement in your
masters work—I lookt upon it as strange and seasonable, yt
a reward should come for work done 13 yeares agoe, wch
could not have come in a fitter time bec of my charges for
my sons education, god lays in and lays out seasonably—oh
that sermon then may also haue a resurrection—

125 I haue had a call 3 times already this summer into
Craven, and have found very great incouragemt that god
hath a people there, whom he intends to doe good to, 1 bec
they are willing to attend ordinances, and 2 every time I
goe the number is increasing 3 god stirs up some affections
under the word 4 I haue found my heart more than ordinarily inlarged in pleading for their conversion when
amongst them, especially this time being Aug 10 76—5 it is
an ignorant place and hath had no good preaching of many
generations, and now theres stirring who knows wt may be

done,--there are some serious gracious christians among them, wch occasioned my going, with whom I haue had sweet communion in fast-days Lords-supper,—oh wt two refreshing days had we togather in those ordinances! 7 god hath by his gracious providence settled a godly zealous minister, Mr Hough at Thornton, a man of parts and piety, very industrious in doing good every way, tho much envyed by some lazy scandalous preachers—I was much affected with the zealous, experimental importunate prayers and groanes of two conformable ministers in that day of our fast, viz Mr Hough and Mr Lund, very choyce, holy, moderate man—

126 on wednesday morning Aug 16 76 I was to goe to John Armitages in Burton parish to preach, that morning it was much rain, as I was going in my own fold I got a sad fall fell all along upon the stones, yet was not hurt, on this side Brighouse, leading my horse down an hill, upon a slippery stone, both my feet shot from under me, I was not much hurt, but much dirtyed, yet I found my shoulder aking after, and my body was jumbled that day, but am no worse blessed be my god—

127 on friday Sept 8 76 I had a call to John Butterworths to keep a private fast with those young converts on that side and it was a marvellous sweet day, all of them prayd far beyond my expectation, John Butterworth prayed solidly and tenderly, Thomas Bently prayed zealously and importunatly, James Wadington prayed understandingly and affectionately, Micael Stead (a blind man) prayed pertinently and savourily, John Simpson prayed wonderfully rationally and experimentally, my heart was melted with many teares at the prayers of the first and last, and I concluded with thankfulnes to see such forwardnes and oh how my heart was inlarged! it was a day far beyond my expectation, yea to my admiration,—other two should haue been imployd Nathan Bates and James Hosfield—but there was not time, there was abouc 60 persons, much affection,—when I went first thither wch was 4 yeares agoe there was not a praying family in that township but one, one John Wilkinson, who when he prayed, wild people gathered about his house, mockt abused him, called him witch he dying left his desire that I might preach his funeral sermon on Joh 14 2 wch I did, at J Butterworths, and ...   ... still wch hath had this effect—blessed be god—

128 I haue been of late more called to and imployed in the duty of thankfulnes then of a long time before, having kept 7 or 8 days of thanksgiving within these few weeks in one place or other upon various accounts, viz july 4 Aug 28, Aug 30: Sept 2: Sept 15: Sept 18, Sept 20: Sept 27: this last was in a publick manner upon a publick account of our liberty till this year 1676—god helpt our hearts very sweetly in this work of thankfulnes in all times, blessed be god that hath helpt us to pay our vows, and now we are waiting what the next dispensation shall be: let god doe with us as seemes good in his eyes:

129 On tuesday Octob 3 1676, in the morning I found my body dull, having risen early, and my heart as dull, but I know not how, ere I was aware, my soul became as the chariots of ... ... oh wt a frame was my soul got into un-expectedly, god lifted up my heart in prayer and especially in praise with abundant meltings sometimes prostrate for an houre togather, and at noone with my wife, oh how my heart was inlarged,—and towards night again in my closet for the church, and then in my family, beyond my usual manner in all my prayers my heart was much carryed out for my poor lads, I haue seldom had such a day, I knew not what was the meaning of it, I could not get off, but took delight in my work, but upon thursday night I received letters from my two sons, intimating that they were to set upon their journey for Scotland that very day, being tues-day much incouragement in their letters then I understood the reason of these timely impressions—blessed be god —

130 on thursday Nov 9 76 I stayd at home, and most of that week, being busy about preparing my book of loue-token for the presse, and god in some measure helpt my heart, about 3 a clock Benjamin Butterworth comes to my house, told me abundance of people were met at his brother John Butterworths in Warly in expectation of my preaching there that day, many stayed till near one a clock, went away disappointed, it struck me to the heart wn I heard it, for there was some mistake either in him or me, for I never thought of any such thing, the mention of it was aboue a fourtnight before, none put me in mind—I understood not that appointment, I was much troubled, went into my study, and oh what an houres improuemt of that providence did god help me to in meditation and prayer! pleading for my

own soul, labours, those that were disappointed, other congregations, my sons—blessed be god for that sweet season, —that evening god graciously helpt in the young men's conference to speak to them, pray for them, blessed be my god, that frustration hath done good:

131 Dec 13 1676 in the evening in my study I set myself seriously to plead with god for the successe of my labours I being to preach the day following at Sowerby and 2 for my sons in Scotland, and it was a warm melting evening, towards the close of my prayer for my lads, I know not how, my heart was drawn out in a particular faith for the conversion, and salvation of my two sons, tho I might have some discouragemts in the mean time—the event will declare it—

132 On Jan 1 167⅞ preaching at John Butterworths in Warly as I was preaching there was suddenly a pash of a chamber-floore down into the room where we were, part of it, women cryed out, the case was this—wn JB came to that house there was a hole he put a stone into it, plaistered it under, being very throng that day below, some went into that false-floore, one man treads on this stone being but weakly supported, it fell brought plaistering off, yet hurt no body though they stood very thick below, and the stone was about 12 or 14 pound weight blessed be god for this gracious providence, and multitudes more—

133 This year I was put to more then ordinary charges about my sons, being abroad in Westmorland Scotland, they haue cost me aboue 60 li—and god hath sent in proportionably for upon accounts summed up of my receits, in all I have received 78 li—2sh—11d—wch is a far larger sum then any I received yearly before, blessed be my god, that so wonderfully provides and stirs up friends for me wherof 28 li —9sh—10d I had of mine owne hearers at home, and 49 li —13sh—01d of my friends abroad, oh admirable providence! god supplys fast as I need—

133 on wednesday we had a fast, thursday I preacht at Sowrby, friday Jan 12 7⅞ we were to haue a private fast in my house in preparation for Sacramt, I had little time to make ready a sermon, wt time I had I spent in puzzling about a text in Luke 15 23 could make little of it;—wn at work, 1 cor 11 20 was cast into my thoughts god helpt me to frame an hours discourse, extempore, pertinently wch after I committed to writing—

134 on Tuesday Jan 16 7⅞ I set forward towards Craven (according to appointmt) riding because the weather and way was dangerous I desired my friends to meet me at Kighly I came thither, no body came, I was in great doubt wt to doe, yet thought to goe on, rode two miles to Steeton hill, disputed still, weighing reasons on all hands, stopt in the way, went sometimes forward, back again, was in great suspense a long time, it was a perplexing case trouble and excercise, I lookt up to god for direction, satisfaction, at last god satisfyed me to turn back, I went to Josh: Walkers was kindly entertained, preacht that night to a full assembly. and the night after at Micael Broadlys, visited Thos Leeches family, prayed with them, was of some use, got safe back home on thursday, on wch day it fell a great snow, wch would haue rendered my coming out of Craven difficult, blessed be god for thus ordering my affaires to the best god is infinitly gracious—after I understood that my coming into Craven at that time would not haue been seasonable they not having my letter till wednesday—Mtris Lambert not being at leisure her husband coming home that day, at that day fortnight J Hey came for me I preacht, had a full assembly, aboue 60 more then ever I saw before in that place —god wonderfully inlarged—R Mitchel brought me home— blessed be god for thus ordering matters to the best—

135 the like suspense I was in upon Feb 12 167⅞ about going into Lanc: for I promised to goe, designing gathering some rents as my main business, yet intending to preach at Ratchdal on munday night, but upon saturday it fell a considerable snow, my wife was unwilling I should venture over Blackstone edg my maid on Saturday told John Stot that it was doubtfull whether I came, my friends advised me not to goe I promised my wife that morning that if it snowed I would stay at home about 9 a clock it snowed again, upon wch I settled myself in a resolution to stay at home, studyed till noon, then the sun shone, it was fair, one came and dined with us, told us it was good travelling, upon wch I got myself ready, set forward after one a clock, yet had some discouragemts 1 my wife was troubled at my going, 2 I was much straitened at parting in prayer, 3 at the end of my croft my horse stumbled to his knees wch my wife observed, called me againe I went on still, and 4 found bad way in the Hough—there I debated with myself, turned back, to my

inner satisfaction, visited M : Clay sick, was helped to pray with him, god wonderfully inlarged my heart in family-duty, —the week following I went, and it proved much better for 1 Mtris Lambert, and others came out of Craven, next saturday, spent the Sabboth with me, designing a journey into Lan : I went with them, very oppertunely—2 it was seasonable weather, I had a comfortable journey, 3 I found my own father sick, begun that week, came as if I had been called—where god melted my heart—4 I was not expected at Ratchdal, performed my preaching work before the week following—got home safely—blessed be my god—

136 As I went into Lanc : near Ratchdale being market day, meeting loaden horses in a strait place my horse climbing by a bank cast me off behind—not hurt—

—::—

Returnes of prayer.

Upon Munday March 18 167½ I had a cal to keep a fast at one John Smiths house near grt Horton in Bradford-dale, god wonderfully helpt my heart both in preaching and prayer, but especially in prayer for the church, and particularly for poor ministers, that after almost ten years silence their mouths might be opened, indeed it hath long been my earnest request, but then more inlargedly : and behold a sudden return, upon thuesday towards night, too messengers came, the one from Halifax, the other from Leeds, to bring me the joyful tidings of the Kings proclamation of liberty to non-conformists, to preach in publick places : I confesse it was welcom tidings, and at first incredible, but having heard the partial relation, togather with the reasons and grounds asserted, I was bound to credit it, and rejoyce in gods mercy : the Lord conforme it and suit us to it : that scripture came into my thoughts upon the news Ezra 7 27 28 : and with reference to the return of prayer, that is very pat and proper, Isai 65 24 : this day march 20 we had appointed for a solemne fast, and god casts in this mercy beforehand to melt our hearts and incourage us in our waiting on him, and truly it was a melting day, god wonderfully drew out my heart, and I hope will giue further returnes—only I observed one providence that after I had received the news my teeth fell of aking and kept me waking most of that night : that I rose out of my bed—wch intimated to me that though I may haue the mercy of publick liberty, yet I might meet with some lesser troubles herewth as toothach tho not ... ... yet, might proue afflictions— and discompose my rest—the will of the Lord be done—

2 Hanna Hardger a truely gracious woman, one of my first converts, aboue 20 yeares agoe. having been consumptive and wearing away many yeares, of late hath exceedingly decayed, had a grievous cough, her flesh was worn quite off her, her spirits spent, so that there was no hopes of life, I called to see her as I went abroad June 3—72, made account she would not liue a day, she had made her will, disposed of what she had, discovered several experiences to me, her breath seemed to stop—the lord helped me to pray for her, principally for her safe passage to heauen, for I lookt upon her as gone, only I desired her life if god saw good, for I knew all things were possible with him : and behold a considerable recovery, this is july 1 and she hath been at my house two lords days togather, is much better then she was several moneths before, its almost a miracle, I wondered to see it, and methought the sight of her suggested grounds of hope that god makes her an emblem of our resurrection, either that god will restore us to a full injoyment of publick ordinances, or that there shal be a restauration of the work of conversion, which is far better : I look and long for both : psal 88 10 11 : Isai 88 12—22 : Ezek 37 3—11 12 :

3 The servants of god through the nation and particularly in this congregation haue a long time been begging an union and accommodation among the Lords people—particularly it hath been my prayer to god for this poor congregation, that we might be united togather in christian communion, and many yeares agoe we had many meetings for that end and still broke—but now at last the congregational men amongst us have desired to sit down with us at the Lords supper, we had a conference and agreed upon it, and now accordingly july 14 1672 we injoyed that distinguishing ordinance togather, being Lords day evening, were about 60 communicants of our and their members, sweet harmony, some comfortable presence of god, and good satisfaction,— blessed be god for this rich mercy : he is a god hearing prayer, performing promises :

4 We kept a private fast at Capt Hodgsons on wednesday Jan 22 on the behalf of his daughter Hanna, whom they judged to be far gone in a dangerous consumption, and god heard prayer quickly, for he desired us to return thanks for her gracious recovery that day sennight at my house, Jan 29, and upon Lords day she came to my meeting-place—the like fast we had for her sister Rachel, and god hath almost miraculusly spared her life, that she also was with us in the publick ordinances,—blessed be god :

5 The Parlt beginning to sit Feb 4 167⅔—there were many there of our adversarys and great fears of gods people lest they should disanull the kings declaration for our indulgence god helpt us many times in prayer, on wednesday Feb 5 my wife and I keeping house, my maid being gone abroad we some time in prayer—that very day the king made a speech to the parlt tels them of the good effect of it vindicates it from the liberty of papists thereby, tels them he shal take very ill to receive contradictions in wt he hath done, he tels them plainly he is resolved to stand to his declaration,—on munday we spent some time in prayer at Jerem : Watsons, and god sweetly helped and melted my heart about publick affairs, on thuesday I preacht publickly and that night was this declaration brought me, on wednesday we had a private day at Mr Sharpes, this quickened our prayers, but on friday wh had appointed a solemne day of fasting and prayer principally upon that account of publick affaires at JB—and in the mean time we haue this mercy cast in to animate our spirits incourage in duty—blessed be our good god—we spent it sweetly...... yet on the day after, saturday we received news from Parlt that they had voted this indulgence illegall, the other party being over voted by 60 votes, agt it—

6 Yesterday march 6 we had a further account of the controversy betwixt the king and parlmt concerning his prerogatiue in dispensing with the penaltys of Ecclesiastical laws, the kings Answer to them wherin still he seems peremptory in adhering to the declaration for liberty, and theire reply, which he sth is a matter of consequence, and will require some time to consider of—thus theres Naphthalim, *i e* great strugglings :—gods servants giue themselves to prayer, our adversarys ply the oares, seek to undermine us, what the effect will be god knows, hitherto god hath helped—

Our adversarys are high and wrath agt us—tho I pitty their soules, yet I like our cause and case no worse,—on Wednesday March 5 Mr Bentley preacht his lecture at his house, put it off from ten to one, because of the Uncles sermon at church, yet Dr Hook was waiting to see people come out, J B and several others going up toun from Mr Bentleys, and there stood a company of ranters in a shop— and fell a railing at them in most unworthy scurrilous language, up aloud, called them hypocrites, sd they would goe to Conventicles and they would do so and so—speaking reproachfully and then bid them goe and cursing them in an horrible manner, wheras they spoke not a word to them, but passed along the street peacebly : and indeed its no wonder that prophane wretches dare revile out of shops, wn Dr Hook shamefully rates at us out of the pulpit for several days togather, comparing the non-conformists (by name) to papists in a many things principally in putting the late King to death, &c Hear o our god for we are despised,—Neh 4 4 : psal 123 3 4 : I hope we may say in this case as David of Shimei 2 Sam 16 12 it may be that the Lord will look on mine affliction and that the Lord will requite good for his cursing this day—

7 Yesterday April 3 73 I had intelligence that god hath owned his ministers and people and heard prayer in the face of the nation, particularly that though the Parlt haue been long puzzling about our liberty and were resolved at least to alter it, and settle it some other way according to law, wch we should haue been glad of had the terms been tolerable, but they could not accord and haue therefore left it to his majestys pleasure to doe as he sees occasion, wch is that he hath stickled so much for, but withall they haue passed a severe bill agt the papists, wch we take as a rich mercy also, since togather with our liberty they also haue thrust in to the increase of popery—god hath vindi- cated his servants uprightnes hitherto agt extremes on both sides—god is wiser then we and orders things mercifully by his gracious providence, blessed, blessed be god—Eben-ezer :

8 god set his servants awork to pray in this tickle junc- ture, the parlt so much agt us, the king gratifying them in plucking off the seale, upon which adversary begin to threaten executing penaltys, and some good ministers about Manchester haue given over their work, most being in a

mase what to doe, but the king hath called the judges to
consult with them in the case, they put him in mind of his
promise to his parlt not to draw the practice into a president
yet tell him all offices depend upon him, and he may shew
his displeasure agt the justices severity by discommission-
ating them, accordingly he hath done, for one Mr Hicks a
non-conformist minister being disturbed and fined, he rid
up to the king, who graunted an order to restoring his goods
again, and also for taking away the justices commissions
from them that did it—and upon this the ministers are
fallen to their work again—blessed be god, all is to the
best—

9 May 2d 73 we kept a private fast at Mr Dawsons house
for his wife, to beg mercy for her in childbearing god wonderfully helped my heart, —on that day sennight, may 9 we had
a private day at my house preparatory to the Lords supper,
Mr Dawson came told us his wife had the midwife, was not
well, went to prayer, left us, went home, and—within an
hour after his wife was deliuered safely of a fine son, he sent
me a note wch came to me before we parted. and we gaue
god thanks for that mercy: blessed be god for this quick
return, who would not pray to this god, and keep in this
profitable trade oh that I could resolve with David, to call
upon god as long as long as I liue psal 116 2 :

10 May 15 73 we kept a private fast for our young men
that were going abroad to learning, and god graciously
helped us to plead with him for mercy in our journey, and
god mercifully heard prayers, we went on munday morning
may 19 (just that day 26 yeares that I set out from my
fathers house towards Cambridg) were carryed safely to
Manchestr : first night, to Trentam the second, to Mr Hick-
mans the third, on thursday came back to Stafford, on
friday to Manchester, with safety tho it was a long journey
we riding 170 miles in fiue days time—accomplisht our designs, blessed be god we had rich mercy in our journey—

11 June 14 73 my wife and I were thinking of a journey
to York, there were severall reasons that might induce us to
take that season, and some that contradicted, I was long in
æquilibrio, doubted much what course to take, went to god
in prayer, as I haue done many a time, according to wt I
find pro 3 6, and presently I found a strong inclination to

stay at home, and in a little time my thoughts were established that way, according to Pro 16 3 the day after (being Lords day) I had a letter from Kirkheaton desiring me come to come thither, wch I could not haue denyed, on munday another weighty business fell in, from wch I could not haue been absent, and besides, two oppertunitys of prayer in mine oune congregation, tho I knew of neither before my resolution, but besides all that the weather changed and it was a week of abundance of excessive rain, as hath not ordinarily been known at that of the year, so that if we had gone our journey had been uncomfortable, and it may be we had been stopt with waters,—thus god ordered us as psal 37 23 : about the same time I was exceedingly dissatisfyed about the choyce of a text, committed it to god by prayer after many counterworkings—god decided me to that in Hos 14 8 last part—

12 on Munday June 23 1673 some friends were with me from about Woodkirk upon a speciall occasion, and John Koppindal told me before them all, and sd he was ingaged to declare it for my incouragemt, that most of the persons that had been admitted into Mr Marshalls church of late yeares, delivering their experiences haue confessed that their first work was by my ministry, where they haue had occasion to hear me in this sad and silencing time, and indeed I confesse god drew me out to preach abroad at Hunslet, Bramley, Farsly, Pudsey, Morley, Idle,—in publick, and multitudes of people flockt and were affected, in such a time wn none did or durst adventure upon that necessary work of preaching the gospell, and in private houses in multitudes of places, and he was pleased to draw out my heart wonderfully in those times, and I now hear of some fruit, I hope there is more, yet not discovered, blessed, blessed be my god for this hint of return of prayer—

13 A sweet and signal return of prayer I haue seen and heard this day, wch is Mr Samuel Baily of Allerton in Bradford parish, a solid, gracious, useful, peaceable, tender-hearted christian, as any I haue known, I haue been with him at many a sweet day of prayer, and a few days before he dyed we were at a private fast togather in Ovenden-wood, and oh how melting and affectionate was his heart for his children, a son and daughter both here this day, the daughter is marryed to John Brooksbank of Ealand a godly

man, the son preacht with me this day, prayed admirably wel, preacht a sweet solid experimental sermon concerning chts withdrawing from soules from Cant 3 1 : handled it exceeding profitably, and awakeningly to sinners,—I succeeded, and my heart was much melted, and in the beginning of prayer god helped my expressions and affections in breaking forth into gods praises, for his infinit mercy in returning an answer to prayer wch had influence upon my following discourse, and animated my hopes for my children —this was midsummer day june 24 1673—in my house—

14 july 7 73 I called of Dinah Tetley who hath been a woman of a troubled spirit, about her condition, and hath often laid her case over before us, complaining grievously of unbelief, temptations, darknes but this day she hath got satisfaction, partly by reading some scriptures she told me of, partly by my sermon about fruitfulnes the day before, and now she expressed her satisfaction to me, and sd I am persuaded I must goe to heaven at last. this I look upon as a signall return of those redobled importunate prayers wch the society put up for her: at the same time Mary Rhodes expressed her abundant satisfaction with my answering their object about fruitfulnes—R Cook and some others, blessed be god that the word doth good to them that walke uprightly—if others haue not benefit—

15 july 14 73 we had a private fast at John Kershaws, god extraordinarily helped our hearts in prayer upon many accounts, particularly about the season of the weather, it having been immoderate rain for a moneth togather, not aboue four days in that moneth fair, which was a great obstruction to the fruits of the earth, yet abundance of hurt is done in all parts by strange and almost unheard of floods, behold while we were praying that afternoon god cleared up the heavens, tho it had been excessiue rain the day before and that day in the forenoon, and was two exceeding fair days, viz thuesday and wednesday and the weather seems to be settled.—the day after viz thuesday, we had a day of thanksgiving at Capt : Hodgsons, there god helped in part to pay our vows. as upon other accounts so on this as to the weather, blessed be god, it calls to my mind the passage of Elias and the two witnesses, Jam 5 17 18 : and Rev 11 6 : not that we can compare ourselues with those worthys, but may take notice to gods glory and our comfort of the power

of prayer and gods gracious owning of such pittifull poor
persons and prayers as we bring: and to be a token for god
in this day of wicked mens threatening to cut short our
liberty, wch we haue so long injoyed—both from Assizes and
Sessions this week:

16 We haue now received three letters from my sons this
being july 31 73—in all wch they expresse a great deal of
satisfaction in the place where they are set a learned and
loving tutour, that takes a loue to them peculiarly, abundant
provisions, pretty chamber, sweet companions,—but aboue
all they both expresse abundance of sensiblenes and serious.
in matters of religion, complain of corruption, fears of
hypocrisy, desires of truth and grace, and begging prayers
in these cases—wch seemes to breath a gracious spirit, and
buddings of gods grace in their soules, as an earnest and
first-fruits of a future larger harvest,—blessed, blessed be
our god, for this beginning of returnes of prayer:

17 My York journey had been long deferred, Mr Ward
and I having proposed an exchange could not jump in one,
as to time, winter drew on, my friends at York long expected
me, I was disappointed last year, I had no visible busines
before me the first week in August (wch was rare) where-
upon I considered of it, commended it to god in prayer, god
satisfyed my heart to goe, I resolved upon it, gaue notice to
my people of my absence, god found me out work at Leeds,
York Lords supper with Mr Wood, wch was wonderfull
refreshing we had nice weather, tho it had been and was
after much rain. kind entertainment, many loving friends,
provided Mr Whitehurst for my place in my absence,
brought us safely home, blessed be god—every thing fell
right as I could desire, I accomplisht my journey just as I
purposed:—oh wt mercy! came home this day being Aug
14 1673:

18 upon munday Sept 29 73 I set upon my journey for
Lancashire, and committed my self and concernments to the
Lords providence and tho it had been sad rainy weather
before, yet we had very little rain in the journey, most of
that week being fair, we were mercifully preserved in all our
ways, on thuesday I preacht at Ratchdale—an excercise,
had the day to my selfe, Mr Bentley failing to come, spent
an hour in prayer 3 in preaching god wonderfully helping,
the day after god heard pleadings about weather, it was an

exceeding fair sun-shine day,—on wch he brought us home,
the like he had done after Sept 19 73 having then a private
fast for weather, immediately several fair days followed—
Blessed be god—

19 It is now aboue thirteen weeks since we had a letter
from my two sons abroad, expecting every week a letter for
a long time togather but were still disappointed, so that our
hearts were ready to fail, hopes deferred made the heart
sick, this quickened prayer, and pleading with god, many
and many a time particularly my heart was much drawn
out last night both in family-prayer and in my study on this
account and behold a speedy return, this day being—Octob
31 73 preaching at Quarrel-hil in my course, John Simpson
brought me a letter from Mr Baron, wch came to Manchester
from my sons dated oct 7 this moneth, wch signifieth not
only health of body, and progress in learning but good incouragement about their soules for a work of grace : blessed,
oh blessed be the name of my god for this mercy : I had
almost given over expecting, and my heart was got to a free
submissiue frame with much adoe, whether they were aliue
or dead, having given them up into the hands of my good
god, whose they are :

20 on Friday Nov 23 73 we had been keeping a fast at
Capt : Hodgsons, and my heart had been wonderfully drawn
out both for church and many particular concerns, especially
my children. others also had prayed for them, and that
night, before I went to bed a letter came from my son
Eliezer intimating that he had a great fall from the top of
the stairs to the bottom had hurt his back, could not goe
streight of two or three days, but was now well : I obserue
also that that week I was much carryed out in service for
my god, and god lookt to my child at that distance in that
danger :

21 of late I haue found a wonderful return of prayer from
god in soul-affaires, in helping my heart agt those corruptions to wch I haue been inclined, and that haue cost
me many deep sighs, groanes, teares, feares, and for mortifying wherof I haue besought the Lord many a time. of late
I am much helped—this is Dec 9 73 :

22 My servant-maid Martha Bairstow was sent abroad
into service and hardship wn but 10 yeares of age, hath
lived with me 15 yeares, her relations much disowned her,

her father made his will, left her much lesse then any of the other, but a 3d part to such as had least, he dyed, was buryed Decemb 1 73, yet much questioned whether she could get that, her relations were churlish,—yet this day Decemb 10 73 they haue divided the goods, mony, her share is near 20li—and though she feared wrangling, yet matters were very lovingly carryed this day, tho formerly they haue often sent her home weeping, now she is much satisfyed with that little (to wt she had before) and this I oune as a return of prayer, to compose spirits tho she be put off with losses :

23 this day Dec 18 73 Mr Dawson and I keeping a publick fast in my meeting place and tho I was straitened in time as to preaching yet I took time and was exceedingly inlarged in my spirit in prayer, and I haue seldome found my heart in such a frame in prayer,—at night J B sent me this weeks publick news wch was that the poles had got the victory over the turks killed 30 000 men, 3 bashaws [Pashas], taken 2 prisoners—very rich spoiles—&c that french haue left Utrecht, Campen, Swoll, Daventer,—and other towns, wch are now under their old masters the estates of Holland,— next summer (sth the intelligencer) if our sins hinder not I hope it will bid fair to the destruction both of Turk and Pope : Dec 10 73 : Amen :

24 Dec 27 73 I had a strange experiment, it was this, I had been studying and toyling hard that day, being satur- day for my Lords-day work, having been imployed most of the week, much of my time I spent in studying upon a text agt the papists, but had not got a quarter of a sermon all that day, was called off towards night upon special busines— night came, we went to supper, prayers, my spirit was restles, god graciously helped my heart in family-prayer, after that I went to my study, still unsatisfyed, it was past six a clock, I had thoughts of beginning upon a new text, laid that aside, instantly god suggested a prosecution of a text I had had the thursday before, mat 22 12 and he was speechles, and that in a new method, new matter, gaue in 30 pleas that great pretenders may haue here, wch will not bear weight at the great day, wch was my forenoons work, and other things I hope profitable for afternoon—I cannot tell that god ever helpt me with such convincing suitable matter all day, Yet all that I said that day was what god helpt me to at almost

7 a clock the night before : it was strange to me, if I had studyed all the week, I could not haue got fitter matter, adored be his name, god will doe as he pleaseth, many were affected, who knoweth what good is done, Lord help me to trust god, pray more, tho I study less. Bene orasse est bene studuisse :

25 On Friday jan.30 7¾ at a private day in my house god wonderfully melted, inlarged my heart in prayer, particularly about sending for my sons home, I had been at great unceartaintys all the week, my thoughts much perplext, argts swayed strangely both ways, sometimes I was for it, sometimes agt it, after that day my heart was much quieted, in hopes of god clearing up his will to me—behold on saturday night, the very night after god abundantly satisfyed my heart, by one letter from my father Angier—whose freedom I questioned in this affair, had another from Mr Frankland, who is willing to entertain them, who (I am satisfyed) is both able and faithfull: their grandfather also is willing, especially upon further inquiry of my cozen John Angier, who hath given him satisfaction of some things amisse there : oh how gracious is god herin !—

26 on wednesday Feb 11 74 we had a solemne publick national fast wherin god did wonderfully draw out my heart in preaching and praying especially for the nation, particularly for peace with the united provinces, and disappointment of popish projects, in the former god heard speedily, for on Lords day following Feb 15 news came by several letters that theres a peace concluded betwixt us and the states of Holland, I take this as a pledge of more blessed be god—

27 god had helped me both to preach and pray for peace at Alverthorp meeting-place, on Lords day jun 28 1674, and on munday the inhabitants met about choyce of a minister, and tho in the beginning the storms of unruly passions grew very high amongst them, yet towards the close their spirits were so sweetly calmed, that they all condescended to one thing, agreed lovingly and parted good friends—

28 July 29 1674, Mr Kerby, Mr Richardson Mr Wright and my self, spent part of a day in prayer at Mr Cottons at Denbigh, on the behalf of our 5 sons with Mr Frankland who is much threatened and opposed in his work both of teaching and preaching, oh how sweetly did god help our hearts wednesday following Aug 5 I had a letter from my

son Eliezer, wch brings a return of prayer, for the justices
condescended that he should stay quietly till the next quarter
sessions, viz at Micaelmas then he might take an house 5
miles from Kendal, but doe not prosecute at present—
blessed be god for this reprieue—

29 Aug 21 74 betwixt 4 and 5 a clock afternoon I set
myself to meditate and pray, cast myself down on my face,
found sweet inlargemts, oh it was a good season, amongst
the rest, I prayed earnestly for my wife, that god would
make her more forward in religion, particularly quicken her
to discourse with me about good things, to wch I had found
her backward, that night, as soon as lying down in bed she
freely opened her soules case, communicated experiences—
blessed be god—

30 we had the case of Leeds much upon our hearts to god
in prayer, because its most considerable place in these parts,
and god hath graciously brought them off, indeed wonderfully, after some shocks, one Abrah Haliway and John
Rawson (inconsiderable Bailiffs) informed agt aboue 50
persons being at mill-hill may 24 and june 7 1674 : but
were baffled, indited of perjury, bil found at Leeds sessions
and York assizes, warrants out for them, still they are
nibling at their heel, had prevailed with the mayor to send
6 officers to the meeting-place who came Aug 16 Mr Tod
was preaching, the constable said the mayor charged them
to desist that work in that place, Mr Tod boldly replyed, are
not you christians, and surely you will not be worse to us
than heathens were to Paul who had liberty to preach the
gospell in heathen Rome—they went away—

We hearing that the Archbishop was at Leeds were afraid
of some combination agt them, we earnestly prayed for them
Aug 24 being Bartholomew day—the day after we had
account of their full liberty still, even that Lords day the
Bp was at Leeds—blessed be god—

31 I had designed a journey to Leeds &c but was unre-
solved, on munday night Octob 26 74 I set my self to pray,
in the morning god cleared up my way by stopping my way
for travelling for it was a terrible wind, and excessiue rain—
so I stayed all week at home, went not out of town, scarce
out of my ground and oh it was a sweet week, my soul
injoyed god in duty most of that time—I was helped in my
study, reading, had a good opportunity to lay in as I haue
had many to lay out, blessed be god—

32 I was with Mr Ralph Ardern when in Lanc : who was wonderfull melancholy, lay in his bed till 4 a clock in the afternoon, he got up when I was there, I discoursed with him, prayed with him god sweetly helped my heart, his wife saw he was better, after that he fell to mending is perfectly wel goeth to chappel, about his busines, they haue kept a day of thanksgiving for him, blessed be god for this sweet return—1674

33 Dec 30 74 being at a fast at Captain Hodgsons, Phœbe Stancliff called me out in the midst of our work told me her daughter Sarah, was struck into exceeding terrour of conscience, by a sermon I preached about readines for death the lords day but one before, from mat 24 44--I went to see her the day after, found her in great troubles of conscience, hopeful for a sound work, under hideous temptations, her spirits wasted, body weakened, but pretty kindly workings, blessed be god :

34 I found an observable experimt, on Tuesday being march 2 1674 wch was this, I went to Jonathan Priestleys, visited that afflicted family in wch the feaver hath laid on 5—I found Phœbe Jonathans wife very weak took no notice of any body, Jonathan desired me to goe to prayer, wch I did, and god did wonderfully affect my heart, and their hearts there, but one thing I observed, that though I prayed for her life, yet not in many words, nor with that faith and fervour I desired, tho I confesse I loved her dearly, being a precious good woman and exceeding useful in her place, to her husband and 6 children, to the society and neighbourhood and church, yet my heart was much shut up, but wn I prayed for pardon of her sin, acceptance with god, a good passage into heaven, and submission of her husband to gods will, I found much freedom of spirit, and inlargemt,—so I left her, he desiring me to get some friends togather to spend some time in prayer for her the day following, wn I came home, told my wife how she was, she thought it not good to deferre till the day after, I sent that night, her brother R Hoyl and some more came, but before we begun the duty tidings came that she was departed, I spent some time then in prayer for him her sad husband, the children the church, and our preparation for death, and god helped my heart sweetly in that duty—

30 [Error in numbering only.] on saturday evening octob 24 74 I had put out my candle and wept in prayer upon my face and knees, pleading especially for the conversion of some soul, god sweetly inlarged my heart—instantly after I heard of one............in Burstal parish a young man, accompanying another to hear me, savingly wrought upon, hath carnal relations yet rich, he gets alone and weeps wn they are tipling longs to liue near us—could wish to be turned out of doores that he might be free for god Oh wt a remarkable mercy is this!

On thursday evening being at prayer in my study lying all along, sweetly inlarged, as I was pleading with the Lord for my two sons, being Decemb 17 74 my wife called me off my work when I came into the house Jer: Watson brought me a letter from my son Eli—which had good tidings in it, much to my satisfaction, amongst the rest these 2 things— 1 our tutour according to your desire in your letter, puts us upon meeting togather to pray, every sabboth day night after he hath done preaching, we meet in our chamber, and the young men are very willing 2 every saturday we chuse 12 or 13 divinity questions out of Amesius and dispute ym pro and con before him on munday morning: blessed be god for this answer of prayer: Ebenezer hitherto god hath helpt—

32 being abroad at Wakefield Edw: Ezzat came to me to Mr Boys⁸, told me what his son had writ concerning our lads tutour that he was grown remisse and careles of them, I was much troubled, prayed, when I came home Jan 14 75 I found a letter from Mr Frankland, who seems to complain of discouragements in his work from friends as wel as opposition from enemys, saying if I may but approue myself to god, and doe service that may be acceptable to his servants, I desire no more—appealing to god in his endeavours that he hath not willingly omitted any thing within the sphear of his power wch he judged might haue a proper tendency to the advantage of those committed to his charge,—he also commends both my sons, for their sober deportment, and industry in their studys—commends my elder son John he sth his capacity may equallize if not exceed most of his yeares, &c blessed be god for any answer of prayer in this particular—

33 Though theres threatenings on all hands, as to our liberty, and though tis sd 400 persons are summoned to appear at Pomfret Sessions this week upon an inditement graunted on an act in 33 of Eliz : for not coming to church, and tho I had (in a sort) taken my leave of publick work Feb 14 75 (and most days since), I did preach in my meeting-place, had 400 hearers—much what as great an assembly as formerly injoyed the Lords supper, without any molestation blessed be my good god, I was afraid of it, god helpt me to pray for liberty, he graunted it upon answer of prayer, blessed be my god—

34 I set forward my journey to my sons in Westmorland Apr 14 came to them Apr 16 found them well, spent Lords day with them Apr 18—(that day in the year on wch they were both born, the one 18 the other 19 years agoe) was exceedingly melted and carryed out in prayer and praise, had a considerable auditory it was a good day, munday I heard their logick disputes, saw their proficiency to my great satisfaction, as to humane learning, Lords day night I went to my sons chamber-door, heard them at prayer togather, Mr Frankland and his wife gaue them a good character, Will Scill and others told me I should haue, and had now as much comfort of them as a man could haue of children, all this is good, a great mercy for wch I desire to be thankfull, yet to rejoyce with trembling, especially considering that wn I talk with them about soul-concernmts I find not that satisfaction from them in conference as I could desire, it may proceed from their modesty however I desire to make this use of it, that god keepes me in suspense as to full returne of prayer that my heart may be quickened in the work—

35 God hath been pleased to excercise his people here in Yorkshire and Lanc : all this spring with a very scorching drought, so that in March, April, May, there was scarce any rain grasse withered corn languished, cattel begun to pine, people to repine and murmure,—god helpt his people to pray in several fast days where I was, and at last graciously heard the cry of his peoples prayers, and sent a plentiful raine wch begun about May 24 75 wch continued a month in some settled rain, showers, and hot sun-gleames, wch **did** wonderfully change the face of the earth, so that now grasse

and corn spring abundantly, and there is great hopes of
plenty, blessed be our good god :

36 on thursday June 24 75 Hanna Hardger was taken
with an extraordinary stopping and was very near death,—
on Friday she sent to haue her case recommended to god,
being also in some troubles as to her spirit, though a good
woman,—god helpt us affectionately in prayer to god for
her,—presently he healed both her soul and body, so that
she tels me this day she hopes she must goe to heaven, and
her body is much recruited—

37 this day in the morning, being july 17 75 I was a little
troubled about my wife, because I feared she was not so
forward and diligent in religious dutys as I could desire—
therefore I prayed that god would quicken her heart—and
was resolving to speak to her, but in the afternoon, she and
I spent some time togather in prayer, and oh what a flood
of teares was there, wt warmth of heart had she in pouring
out her soul, so that I was abundantly satisfyed in her
gracious growing frame :

38 july 19 1675 came John Stancliffe to me to communi-
cate a remarkable return of our prayers on behalf of his
son James, apprentice at London, upon whose heart god
hath wrought a remarkable and I hope saving change, he
shewed me a large and experimental letter of his state,
teares, temptations, desires, the instrumt by whom this work
was wrought was Mr Doolittle, an eminent city-minister to
whom he hath opened his case, and he hath given him his
advice,—blessed be god for this mercy for wch we prayed
both at his first going up, and in the sad sicknes he had
there, his good mother and grandmother also laid up many
prayers—I take this as an incouragemt as to my sons—

39 July 22 75 my wife was exceedingly troubled in spirit
for some reports that Martha (my old servant) had spread
abroad concerning her and was restles in spirit, wept much,
in the afternoon we went down to Jon : Priestleys, sent for
Martha and Margaret Rushworth, went into the chamber I
begun to speak of the busines, my wife went on, related
wt she heard of Marthas talking some things she excused,
some she confessed, and twice did earnestly beg forgiuenes
of her, she did forgiue her, they were lovingly reconciled, I
closed with prayer, god wonderfully melted all our hearts, it
was a sweet oppertunity blessed be god, at the same time

Margaret R and Martha Tetley were reconciled, and are loving, blessed be my good god :

40 After my sons were come home, on Lords day at night, Aug 1 75 after repetition and supper I put them both on prayer, Eliezer prayd wel, wept, was affected, was methodical, but John exceeded, both in warm affections, expostulations and experimental discourses, we all wept sore, and truely it was an heart-melting season, I thought there was the liuely springings of the spirit of adoption, oh how freely did he confesse sin, giue up himself to god, by covenant, plead for acceptance into gods vineyard, with desires to be a minister to convert sinners, with many tears groanes beg sincerity of grace, a discovery of hypocrisy—it was a surprising amazing duty, I did not expect such a thing, it was admirable in mine eyes,—how earnestly did he desire to be put into the room of Mr Bentley, whose funerals we celebrate this day. blessed be god—

41 this day Aug 30 75 I hear an incouraging word, that little Sarah Marshal was admitted member at Woodkirk a moneth agoe, and she related her condition before the church, and particularly mentioned me as an instrumt of her good, this summer they were at my house, she and her sister, and she mentioned some experimts or convictions both in the forenoon, and afternoon work blessed be god good may be done that we know not of—

42 this morning Sept 2 75 in my closet prayer, I was sweetly carryed out to god for my two sons, especially for Eliezer (of whom I had lesse hopes or incouragemts when with me) and the very same day I went to Halifax, and there met with a letter from him particularly wherin he giues me a good hopeful account of his state godwards, expressing how god had helpt him since he saw my face, with grounds of thankfulnes,—propounding a grand case of consc: whether a person may be converted, and not distinctly know time, place, instrumts of conversion, with many very sensible expressions : blessed be my god :

43 octob 7 1675 in the morning upon an occasion, my heart was very sad, I went to prayer alone, god helpt,—presently after, Jonathan Priestly came to my house took me out, told me my son John was come to priestly-green, the night before, wanted money, I was much astonisht, got ready went down, but he being afraid to see me, was gone,

tho by the chappel I saw him, but knew him not, for he had
a periwig on, tho he saw and knew me but would not own
me, I got an horse, and overtook him at Ab : Holts, he told
me his busines was to borrow 3 li to pay for bookes that T
Cotton and he had bought, I took him to Sim : Robinsons
that day, wch we spent in prayer he prayed, I kept him two
nights, he wept sore, and was much ashamed of his folly,
went back on friday—I hope it will doe him good—

44 this morning being octob 18 1675 was as sad a morning as ordinarily I haue had, my wife was sorely afflicted,
and expressed sad things to me, so that I was in the bitternes of my spirit much perplexed upon some base unworthy
reports abroad, god helpt me in morning prayer sweetly by
the bed-side, in secret prayer by my self, in family prayer,
and in prayer togather before dinner (wch this day we
revived after long neglect) and after dinner we went to Mr
R the person concerned in this report, who cleared the
busines much to my wiues present satisfaction,—the same
evening Mr Boys writ me a letter that then came to my
house that his dear wife (my good friend for wm we lately
had a day of prayer at Wakefield) is delivered of a fine
daughter, and is in a comfortable plight blessed be god, her
former weaknes makes it more admirable, she was delivered
on Saturday morning wch was octob 16 1675, wt shal I
render to god for these mercys!—god did help me this night,
viz oct 18 in family prayer inlargedly to declare his mercys
and blesse him :

45 Octob 28 75 came Sam Drake, brought me a paper
that I should pay some money for my sons, I was troubled,
fell down on my knees god sweetly helped my heart in
prayer, I was a little composed, yet troubled exceedingly
that I had not had a letter from them since John had his
wild vagary home, I went to Halifax, at last met with two
letters from them, indeed melting affectionate, penitent
letters, such as melted my heart into many teares in the
reading, and receit John did abundantly aggravate his fault
and folly informed me in the very truth of things as I hope,
confessing his rashnes, inconsideratenes in ingaging in other
mens busines, for he borrowed this 3 li for Mr Th : Cotton
who laid it out in bookes, and could not haue it, because his
mother and brother were in Wales, promiseth seriously to
undertake no busines for future without my consent and

councel, both of them expresse with what teares and workings of heart they read my letter—blessed be god Oh that it
might be a sincere work—

46 Nov 5 after I had preacht at home upon a call I went
to Wakefield to visit my dear friend Mtris Boys, who was
judged a dying woman tho safely delivered in childbed, I
found her better Mr Kerby came, went to prayer, prayed
sweetly she at that time fell ill, into a very sore fit, all
thought she had been drawing away, could perceiue no
breath, or motion, I went to prayer, stroue with my dead
heart in that duty, had little heart yet before I had done she
recovered, yet was not sensible of a good season after, but
got a good nights rest, I left her in the morning in a tollerable frame, she eating more then she had at once this 13
weekes, blessed be god, oh what a rich and quick return of
a poor dull prayer! blessed be god—

47 Mr Boys her dear husband in his letter to me (dated
at 10 a clock on lords day night octob 31 1675) coming to
my house at 6 a clock the morning after, but found me not
at home hath these feeling passages in it wch I look upon to
be a return of my weak prayer Her ilnes is violent, yet her
lips drop fatnes and sweetnes, to all by-standers, she is full
of heavenly councel to all her visitors especially relations, is
full of comfort as she can hold, hath her experiences stored
up by her, and brings them out abundantly her evidences
for heaven very full and clear she hath this day spoken fully
to all her relations and given them all abundant satisfaction
about her fitnes for and assurance of glory amongst other
her discourses she is pleased very much to make use of your
name, and acknowledg god hath made you an instrumt of
this comfort and peace and joy, she now hath at the seeming
approach of death—so desires my coming—blessed be god
that hath thus tuned this poor instrumt for the good of his
hand-maid—

48 Upon Tuesday Nov 25 1675 having been to visit sick
persons at Norwood-green, returning home I called at J
Tetleys, had some talk with Martha, at my return home,
my wife askt me if I called there, I sd yes, she had solemly
declared agt it, was troubled, I gaue her my reasons, and
busines, she was the more offended, I could not satisfy her,
but was much disquieted all night wept and sighed sadly,
wch was a mighty burden to my spirit, the more I said the

more she was troubled, I went into my study poured out my
soul before god, that night, and in the morning, was wonderfully helped both times with a penitent soul, prostrate body,
I spake in the bitternes of my spirit,—and behold before
night her spirit was calmed, she was loving to me, breaches
healed, and we haue had sweet comunion togather since both
in civils and spiritual dutys, and I hope god hath done her
good by it, I feel the advantage, blessed be my god, for this
signal hearing prayer—

49 Upon munday Dec 6 75 hauing been abroad to see
some sick persons at my return home I found a note from
J Brooksbank signifying that his brother Bayly was dead,
desiring me to preach his funeral on wednesday, I was much
affected with his losse, I had to preach both tuesday and
thursday, was not satisfyed what text to take any of these
days, the places were distant, Bingley, Morlay, Sowerby, I
knew not how to dispatch all, for I was loath to disappoint
any of these places, I got on my knees, god affected my
heart sweetly with that heavy blow, stirred up a spirit of
prayer for direction. I rolled my matters upon him, he
graciously helpt me to perform all my workes in all those
distant places, to my abundant satisfaction, blessed be god—

50 On munday being Jan 10 1676 there was a meeting of
the tounsmen at Will Crofts to pay Capt Lister Lord Hali-
faxes chief rents, at wch time Ed: Slater had prepared a
paper and presented it to the inhabitants, expressing their
desires that I might preach at the chappel, he desired such
as were present to subscribe it wch they did very freely, viz
Nathan Crowther, James Brig, John Best, John Appleyard,
Tim Starky, Joseph Crowther,—and others that haue
neither heard nor owned me for almost two seven yeares
this is wonderful, and a beginning of return of prayer, whatever be the issue of it, they now propose they will either
haue me or none at the chappel, if I must not preach it
shall be vacant—this is strange, all things considered, that
they should thus own a poor despised persecuted minister,
thats cast out as a vessel wherin is no pleasure, that their
cause at last begins to reflourish, phi 4 10: Blessed be god:

51 On friday Jan 14 and saturday Jan 15 upon some bad
tidings concerning my sons, I was exceedingly discomposed,
went to prayer wherin god wonderfully helpt my heart, yet
was not satisfyed, hoping to hear from them on saturday,

on friday night I had very sad and dismal apprehensions
concerning them, fearing lest they should haue fallen into
some grosse sin, upon some reports I heard of their being
out one night these fears increased, and were the more
strengthened because they seized on my spirit when upon
my face in earnest prayer, saturday night came, still I heard
nothing, my jealousy increased, I had bitter agony that
night as ever I had in all my life, begged of god to quiet my
spirit, he did so, I slept quietly, followed my work com-
posedly on Lords day—

52 Upon wednesday Dec 29 1675 we had a private day at
my house upon the account of M Rushworth, whose eldest
son John being hopeful and civil, was got ingaged by
promise to goe to be servant with Mr Lacy in Halifax she
was much afflicted with feares of it, on many accounts, she
could not dissuade him, he was hired would goe, there was
no remedy, she foresaw his undoing if he went, she set
friends on him to persuade, but he was inflexible, she desired
our prayers in the case, god helped wonderfully that day, I
was seldom so inlarged in company for nigh 2 houres, behold a sudden answer, the saturday after he changed of his
own accord, would not goe tho under great temptations, Mr
Mitchel (their son) promising to give him 5 pound they
knew not of, but he turned. came home, set close to his
calling, blessed be god, this, his mother acquaints me with
this day, being Jan 18 1676 : this is an incouragemt to me
for my poor lads—

53 My heart was exceedingly cast down upon the account
of my sons jan 14 15—1676 and had formidable imaginations
concerning such miscarriages as I thought would cost them
their liues by the hands of justice, as a publick scandall for
some capital offence, I told the Lord if he would consult the
honour of his name and credit of religion in that case I was
better content with what might be only an affliction to myself, herin god answered me for Jan 27 76 Mr Frankland
writ me something a sad account of them, that John had
run 8 li into debt, which I must pay, but herin my prayer
is answered, but withall that he is exceedingly penitent,
weeps much before him and alone—blessed be god—oh for a
draw of sincerity !

54 On Feb 15 1675 at night came a letter from Wakefield
desiring my company at Alverthorp, but I could not goe, not

hauing given my people notice of my abseuce, on wednesday
Mr Dawson sent to me desiring me to change with him, I
designed to accommodate this busines by sending to Wakefield to intreat them to get provision for Mr Dawsons place,
and he would preach in mine, and there desiring them to
send me word on friday, no letter came, that perplext me,
for I hoped they expected me, Mr Dawson and I agreed, for
him to supply mine, and I to goe supply his if none else
came, I rode on Saturday Feb 19 to High: town, there
heard of an adjourmt from Wakefield, by letter, but withall
they advised me to turn again bec of danger in Mr Dawsons
place, warrants out—I did so, yet was unsatisfyed turned
backward and forwards, several times on Hardger moor, yet
came home, upon Lightliff hill-top met Mr Boys who told
me I was confidently expected at Alverthorp, still I was
more perplexed, yet came home, my family was affrighted at
my going, went down to Mr Dawson—who was willing to
goe to his own place, but the worst was I was unprepared
for home, tossed my papers, could not sleep, was disquieted
in bed, lay waking, at 2 a clock got up, went into my study,
fell on my face and prayed, god satisfyed me with a suitable
subject on Isai 50 11 proper to wt I was driving on about
the hearts deceit, preacht at Idle, but not at home, god
brought a multitude of people, helped my heart wonderfully
all day oh how mercifully did god dispose! half of that
people could not haue heard Mr Dawson—god made it a
sweet day to me—

55 I did according to purpose and promise take a journey
into Westmorland to see my sons April 3 1676—and though
I had no good news of them, they hauing wasted me a great
deal of money I knew not how—but suspected the worst, yet
when I came thither, I was comforted in all my bitter
agonys of affliction I had had for them, 1 in that things
were not so bad as I imagined, they not hauing made such
outrage as I feared, theyr expences hauing been occasioned
by Johns intangling himself in borrowing 6 li for Tho:
Cotton, to pay for bookes he had bought, and so shifting
from one to another, wch drew him to needles expences and
unsuitable company—2 yet withall I hope god hath troubled
their hearts and given them repentance, the grounds of hope
I haue of the sincerity of repentance, are 1 their owning and
aggravating of their sin and guiltines, before god and man,

2 their affectionate weeping and many teares when I talkt
with them about their miscarriage, 3 their melting and
frequent prayers, I put them both on to duty, and found
them in a good frame, John said that sometimes when he is
upon his knees before god, he cares not if he never rise off
them, his heart is so inlarged, 4 their reformation, for
hitherto, through grace their lines haue been conformable,
and they are much ashamed of themselues and it tendeth
much to their humiliation, it may be god suffered them thus
to fall—(as he left Hezekiah 2 chron 82 88) to try them that
they might know what was in their heart: free grace takes
strange methods to doe good, and sometimes god workes by
contrarys,—oh that the work might be saving!—however
thus far god hath heard prayer—

56 On Thursday in the afternoon, May 4 76 I had about
10 young men with me, which haue kept up meetings for
conference and prayer about 8 yeares: this time we had
appointed to spend in prayers Sam: Nickol, Jer: Watson,
Joh: Kershaw Jon: Priestley Jam Oates John Gill, Tim
Holt, Sam Holdworth went to prayer, god graciously helpt
them with the gift, and I hope with the grace and spirit of
prayer they all prayed affectionately for me and my sons
and also did solemnly blesse god for my labours and the
good god had done by me to their hearts, thanking god that
ever they saw my face—oh what mercy is this in return of
prayer—

57 On wednesday may 81 76 I spent some time in prayer
for my sons, god sweetly drew out my heart, with importunate pleadings, and then in meditation, writing down my
workings of soul in my book of soliloquys, and it was a good
day, the cause of my bitter trouble was some reports I had
heard of my son John the day before wch discouraged me,
the day after viz June 1 I received a large and ingenious
letter from my son Eliezer, very savoury and experimentall
withall intimating that his studys are more facile and
successefull then formerly, blessed be my god for this return
of prayer—

58 on Lords day morning June 4 76 there came a young
man to me, born at Pudsey but liuing with Mr Sharp at
Horton, who did acquaint me that god had awakened his
conscience by a sermon that I preacht at Idle a year or two
agoe upon new yeares day, upon Rev 21 5 he had been then

much affected but discovered it to none liuing, made use of
James Smith to acquaint me, I called him into the chamber
discoursed with him, found him in bitter troubles under
legal terrours many temptations of Satan, in a hopeful way
of god, blessed be god—Lord carry on—

59 on tuesday June 27 76 I went to visit Joshua Soynier,
being very sick, his wife lying lame by him, wept much for
fear of him, his pain and sicknes were violent wn I came in,
yet he opened his sweet experiences to me, I discoursed a
good while, went to prayer wherin god did marvellously melt
my heart, in desiring his life we designed the day following
to spend time in prayer with him, and did so, but god gaue
us in occasions of thankfulnes for from the time I was with
him he mended sensibly, had a good night, was able to sit
up with us, gaue us an account of his state and matters to
be prayed for, yea prayed with us, is in a hopefull way of
recovery, blessed be god: this was according to that promise
Isai 65 24 :

60 July 4 1676 we kept a solemne day of fasting and
prayer, mixt with praise and thankfulnes, upon the account
of James Stancliff son to John Stancliff of Hagstocks, 3 or 4
things we had often begged for him, at solemne days in that
house and god had answered in all, 1 a convenient and
comfortable settlement, and in that they are abundantly
satisfyed, 2 recovery out of two dangerous fits of sicknes,
wherein he was brought very low, but god raised him
strangely, 3 converting grace, wherin god mercifully appeared by Mr Doolittels ministry, convincing his conscience,
humbling his heart, and carrying on his work to a wonderfull
height, so that he is lively to an extraordinary height of
grace, comfort, 4 he was tempt in amongst the Anabaptists
by occasion of his nurse, in the family that attended him in
his sicknes, was much staggered almost gone he consulted
with Mr Nat : Vincent and writ to us, we to him, at last got
satisfaction, is joyned with Mr Nat Vincents society—blessed
be god—is now with us :

61 Mr Richardson and Mr Hawden, two of Mrs Kerbys
daughters went to meet Chr: Richardson Gods-gift Kerby,
and my two sons at Rich: Mitchel at Marton-scar in Craven,
Sept 12 76 according to appointment they came, we saw one
anothers faces with joy, I and my sons lodged at John Heys
they all lodged at Rich Mitchels, on wednesday Sept 13 they

went back, took their yong men to Kighly, so sent them back to Marton Scar, at night,—but I and my sons hauing the oppertunity of privacy in a retired chamber, none to distress us, spent some time in prayer in the forenoon, god marvellously helpt them both in groaning, weeping, pleading, my heart was much melted, and satisfyed, the rest of the time we discoursed, then John Hey came to us, we dined, company came to us in the afternoon, bec I was to preach, but till our company was all come I put in John Hey to pray and my two sons again, god wonderfully helpt them in that duty, the company was affected—but oh what a presence of god was there when I was at prayer! I haue seldome felt or seen such workings in my self and others— blessed, blessed be my god, on thursday morning I parted with my sons with great satisfaction, they are for a journey to Edinburgh in Scotland, to take degrees, before I saw them I was doubtful about their going, now I am better satisfyed, seeing their hopefulnes

62 on Sept 18 1676 we kept a day of solemne thankfulnes to god, at James Tetlys for his wiues mercy in child-bearing, Martha my old maid, and tho Satan had been busy to set distance, yet god inclined my wife to goe, and was wel composed blessed be god, it was a mercy I had oft prayed for, almost despaired of,—had so wearyed her, and her spirit was so imbittered—it was a good day—

63 on wednesday oct 25 I was at Robt Ramsdens at a private fast, god sweetly melted my heart especially for my sons—I came home my young men had conference, before we had done my sons horse and letters came to signify their health and comfortable settlemt in Edinburgh in Scotland, in a godly Non-conformist ministers house, wise, good tutor blessed be god—quick answer—

also another letter from them on Lords day night, wherin I understand still more mercy good incouragmt—tho charges great—

64 On Thursday night Dec 7 1676 I set myself to pray, two things I begged earnestly in my study alone, 1 the successe of my labours in the ministerial work, 2 grace for my sons, and god wonderfully melted my heart,—and amongst the rest of my petitions I begged an heart quieted with gods dispose, and faith to commit matters to him, and was helped that evening more then ever: I was afraid to goe to bed,

hauing lyen much waking, exceedingly tossed about my sons
many nights before, went to bed, slept quietly all that night
without distraction, had not such a comfortable night of
many nights before Blessed be god, in the morning I fell
down on my knees in my study, gaue god praise, and my
Lord wonderfully melted my soule in the family immediately
after, we read in course the 59 ch of Isaiah, and in family
prayer, god graciously drew out my heart in thankfulnes to
god for making such a covenant with me and my soul, as in
ver 21—and god helped me to plead it, and to trust my Lord
in making it good,—1 take this composednes of spirit to be
a sweet signal return of prayer : blessed be my god—

65 Dec 20) 76 I desired some friends to come to my house
and joyn with me in prayer to god principally and particularly for my sons, and the young men with them, Oh what a
melting day was it! the night before (with submission to
gods will) this token for good, that if the Lord had mercy in
store for my sons, he would shew it by inlarging his servants
hearts that day, and this he did abundantly I haue seldom
been at such a day, wt a flood of teares was there, especially
when Mr Dawson and Jonathan Priestly prayd, my heart
hath been seldom so affected in joyning—and behold a
sudden answer, that night J Tetley brought me a letter (a
very sweet satisfactory letter from my son John, that was
good news from a far country, signifying their health, happines, taking away some of my feares, blessed be god, it was
long lookt for hauing had no letter for about a moneth
before,—at the same time came to my hands 50sh as a token
from Mr St [retton] of publick money, wch was a seasonable
supply, being I am to pay 10li- for my sons this week Oh wt
it is to liue by faith !—blessed be god—my soul distrust god
no more he out-bids faith hope—

66 Jan 24 167: according to appointmt I took a journey
to John Hardakers of Rawden-hall to preach there, there
was a full assembly, just as I was beginning R Tenant giues
me a letter from Mr Dinely of Bramhup, and withall tells
me of a report generally spread in the country yt my two
sons were both drowned in Scotland, it troubled me a little
then but having other work before me, god put it out of my
mind, and helpt me to pray and preach as if I had heard no
such thing, but towards the latter end of my sermon it
struck cold to my heart, overpowered me, and I was ready

to faint under astonishing apprehensions of it, immediatly
I went into the parlour inquired of J B, J S- and others wt
they heard of it, J Smith told me, Mr Whitaker had told it
Sam: Wilkinsons sons, and it was repeated 3 weekes togather, I dispatcht a messenger and letter to Mr Whitaker,
to inquire the grounds of that report, but he being not at
home I received no satisfaction, I remained in astonishmt
could not weep—but put it off by discourse with Josiah
Collier (82 yeares of age) Mr Collier of Bradfords brother,
a great antinomian and preacher) wn I went to bed, god
kindly melted my heart in secret prayer, I was much helpt
to say, the will of the Lord be done, and to hold my peace
with Aaron in a like case, oh how sweet was it to be at gods
feet! I thought I could sleep and be satisfyed, but imaginations of my heart kept me waking most part of the night,
oh how wearisom was it, god helpt in the morning-duty, all
the way home my heart was full, in great suspense betwixt
hopes and fears, I feared hauing had no letter for a moneth
before, from them. I dispatcht a letter to Mtris Kerby to
know of her wt she heard from her son with them. I found
some sweet meltings of heart in meditation when I came to
my own gates a boy called to me and told me of a letter
from my sons, coming into my house I found and read it,
found that all was well with them, Blessed, blessed be my
god, who prevented my feares, outbid my hopes, that letter
was dated at Edinb Jan 18 came to Halifax Jan 23 167?

67 on tuesday Feb 6 167: I was further satisfyed not only
in their health, but by two letters from my two sons, dated
at 2 days distance I was much satisfyed. 1 of their frugality,
giuing me an exact account of their money. 2 of their degree,
upon my writing the prince and regent are willing to giue
them their laureation, 3 of their studiousnes and sobriety,
avoiding vaine company—4 of their piety, they both writing
strongly and experimentally—blessed, blessed be my god for
this return of prayer, begun to be manifested—

68 this day being March 29 1676 I was at Mr Hodgsons,
whose wife told me of a letter from her son Eliezer (who is
tabled in the same house with my sons,) I askt whether he
writ of my lads, yes sth she, he writes that they carry very
well, and are likely to be instruments of good in the church,
and comfort to all their friends—blessed be god for this
returne of prayer—

L

69 April 18 1677, the same day on wch both my sons
were born, in the morning I set my self solemnly to closet
prayer, and spent about an hour in it much of wch time I
was wonderfully helpt to travel in birth again for my sons
soules, oh what a melting season was it! surely god was
with me, at noon god graciously helpt me in prayer with my
wife, in the afternoon we had a meeting at Thos: Gills there
god strangely drew out my heart in praying, weeping, oh
what inlargmts—at 5 a clock went home to my young mens
conference—god helpt—and behold god sent my sons home
out of Scotland, safe and sound, that night, very hopefull,
blessed be god, tis not in vain to pray and wait—god is
good—

70 On Friday April 20 1677 being the friday following
god sent my dear and only brother Nath: Heywood, with
his wife and two sons to my house, oh what a comfort was
it to haue these 3 couples of Heywoods to meet togather,
who are a rising generation all very hopefull, my brothers
elder son Nath went on Apr 24 towards Natland to be
trained up a schollar, my sons went with him, his second
son Richard is to goe to London to be apprentice my brother
stayd with us aboue a week viz till April 30, preacht two
Lords days for me very affectionatly, powerfully—blessed be
god, this was a prayd-for mercy, god hath heard oh what a
good god haue I! god brought my sons safely home on
Saturday night, they carry soberly and studiously, blessed
be my god—

71 On Wednesday May 2 1677 as soon as I had parted
with my brother, in the morning I called my sons into a
little parlour set them to pray, they and I togather Eliezer
begun, oh how affectionatly did he pour out his soul with
many teares! how ingeniously did he confesse miscarriages
and how importunatly did he beg mercy! surely it was a
melting season, John was no less affectionate and longer
then he: it extorted from me teares of joy, I concluded, god
drew out my heart wonderfully, blessed, blessed be my god,
he hath done for me great things, hath magnifyed his mercy
to me hitherto, I shall blesse his name for ever and ever—

𝔐emorials of 𝔐ercy.

this day Feb. 2, 167½ I sent my two sons to the smith to get my horse shod and tho he was smooth as they went and was a great frost, the way slippery, and three boys rid on him thither, yet they went safely but as they two rid home he boggled and started and then began a running, they both slipt off, Eliezer riding before fell on John and his shoulder is something hurt, blessed be god that tis no worse, god preserveth us—psal. 9. 11 : ps. 121. 8.

this morning following I sent my son John up to J.R. a bone setter who found his shoulder out of joynt and he hath put it in again : herein is mercy also that it was not broken, Psal 34. 20, blessed be god that help was so near, and that god hath made it so helpfull and effectuall

December 15 1672 Martha Bairstow my old servant going down into the cellar to draw a cup of bear for my sons, at the top of the staires both her feet slipt from under her and fell with head forwards to the bottom. I knew nothing that night but in the morning she complained of her shoulder, could not well stirre her arme, I sent her to John Rushworth who was not at home, we feared it had been out, but it was not, the pain ceased and she mended apace blessed be god.

Decemb 26 72 Mr Root and I preacht an excercise in Warley, multitudes of people were in and about the house so that they could not come near the doores and windows, many stood out in the wet and rain all day—when Mr. Root was at prayer near two a clock there was a great noyse and hurry in the chamber by reason of some persons that were sick presently upon that there was a crack wch many thought to be the timber so that there was confusion the noyse ceased some people amazed but we perceived it was only a board that had an hole in it and a rotten side so all was appeased, he proceeded and finished safely—blessed be god.

I was travelling towards Lanc [ashire] to preach an excercise near Padium, having preached at Quarry-hill that day viz. July 1, 73, and I walkt down an huge hill from Sowerby to Tillyholm bridg, it was very hot, I sweat, was weary with walking, would get on horsback (itt was W. Clays horse) I leapt up but fell over on the other side, fell down, I wondered how my foot got out of the stirrup wch was put in in

mounting for I found the stirrup on the horse-back, I fell on
my side, but blessed be god was not hurt at all. I walkt
down then to the bottom having a steep hill to goe down
after that in wch my horse might well have fallen to my
greater prejudice, god is wiser then man, a lesser danger
may prevent a greater. the same journey Will. Cellar shewed
me the very place where Thomas Hammond, a godly ancient
christian was killed on a lords day at night having been to
hear Mr. Jolly, returning home to his sons house about 3 or
4 yeares agoe just under Pendle-hill, at a brook, his horse
did stumble, he fell forward over his horses head, never
spake word after that, tho he lived till about 8 a clock in the
morning : why might not this have been my case !

July 8 as I was travelling to Bingley over the heights my
horse had got a stone into his foot, I light to take it out, my
horse having a sore neck with greasing for the scab, paused
with me, came down upon me yet blessed be god no worse.

In December 1671 at Christmas there was three fresh red
roses sprung up in Dinah Tetleys garden though it was frost
and snow. Mary Rhodes went in the mornings still put off
the snow warmed them with her hand.   Dinah sent me the
biggest, she presaged a spring of the gospel therefrom,
imagined those 3 roses to be 3 yeares of liberty wch came
to passe for March 15 following the Kings declaration for
liberty commenced, lasted just 3 yeares there was a knop of
a 4th but withered, came to no perfection, yet this 4th year
we have liberty by indulgence from heaven.

Anno Domini 1671, Capt Hodgsons lease for Coley hall
was expired, at Candlem. feb 2 7½ and he made account to
remove, and for that end hath inquired and travelled all the
country over to take a farm, we being in the same condition
as likely to remove, god bore me up in hopes of his providing
an house in convenient time, I never stirred my foot about
it, only my wife made some inquiry whether Bridget Mellen
removed or no, she came to hear of it, sent to talk with my
maid, told her she would goe. Jonathan Priestley went to
Benjamin Boys the owner of it, desired him to let it me, he
told him he would sell it, he ans. he could help him to a
chapman, and in the issue they bargained, and he bought
the house, barn, crofts—upon my account and upon Monday
March 4, 167½ I paid for it, according to bargain 100 marks
or 67 - 13 - 4, and haue it assured to me and mine as

strongly as the law could make it. there are severall observable providences interwoven with this affair and transaction.

1 This is the first house that ever I kept house in upon
my first marriage, there my two sons tooke their first breath,
and in that house my precious mother tooke her last,
mounting thence to heaven, there I injoyed much mercy,
some affliction, I prefer it aboue all the houses in the
country to liue in.*

2 It comes clear and free on all hands, and all are content, none contradicting. B. B. that had it as part of his
wiues portion being a tradesman, puts it into a stock into
content only these aunt Bridget Mellen wants something to
remove from him, they are upon terms, she is or seems to
be wel pleased that I haue it.

3 it comes seasonably, just upon necessity of removal, in
the nick of time, when we were under disputes what course
to take, yea it came immediatly after we had paid our vows
to god for our libertys and priviledges in this place, sense of
mercy is acceptable to god, obtaines further mercy—

4 God hath strangely sent me in mony to doe it with, wn
I was turned out of publick work I was aboue 30li in debt,
wn I was turned out of my house at Norwood green I got
out, but till within this 4 yeares I never had 20li at once of
mine own in all my life, lately god hath sent me in severall
presents from many persons I never thought of, I wondered
wt his meaning was in it now I understand, he designed I
should make this purchase and stockt me for it, so that I
borrowed but 5li to make it up of wt I had of my own, my
wiues, childrens, my wiues portion being intire still.

5 my manner of leaving that house was strange in that
day the states governmt being up and the year before the
rising in Lanc. and Cheshire, I was suspected, apprehended
prosecuted as a plotter, disaffected to the state, two young
men rash and heady prevailed with this weak woman my
landlady B.M. to remove me, hauing raised my rent twice
before, so I was turned out anno 1660 in hopes to get me
from the chappel but god found me an house and the one of
these yong men M D. broke his thigh shortly after and dyed
sadly as to outward man, tho I hope wel as to soul. J.L. the
other hath sold his own and wiues land aboue 50li a year—
haunts alehouses dayly and is fallen from all good society
and excercises tho he made a glorious profession. B.M. had

* See *Frontispiece*, Vol. I.

the house stood empty severall years after, hath buryed her
husband and 4 children, some of long lingring and running
diseases, hath sold the house, her eldest son is in want and
very bad and I am restored to it again in point of title as
mine owne.

6 its strange that god should provide my settlement for
me, or mine and in this place at Coley where my heart is
more then any place in the world besides, hauing continued
aboue 21 yeares amongst them, and its scituate among my
old neighbours, yea god blessed my publick and private
labours when I lived in that house more then all the time
besides, either before or since, who knows what work he
hath for me to doe there, however I shall not be at the
courtesy of ill willed landlords. wn men curse god blesseth,
wn men resist god assists, when men withdraw god affords
supply, the worse men are the better god is. I know it and
could relate many experiments of it

7 that wch is more then all the rest I take it as a presage
and pledg of future mercy and settlement in the church and
nation that evening at my return home I appointed my son
to read that chapter of Jeremiahs purchase, or Chap. 32,
wherein me thinks there are several particulars paralel to
my case (1) the King of Babilons army then besieged Jerusalem v. 2. the Anti-cht. of Rome, mistical Babilon is at
this day, if ever, compassing the camp of hosts and beloved
city, plotting mischiefe, setting the French and us upon the
Dutch to root out the protestant interest as will appear: (2)
Jeremiah was a prisoner, shut up in the courts of the prison,
and that as a punishment for preaching and to hinder him
from preaching and tho we are not all prisoners, yet thats the
standing legal punishmt of our preaching at this day and we
are shut out from discharge of our office. (3) Hanameel came
to Jerem. in prison saying buy my field I pray thee thats in
Anathoth, so J.P. [Jonathan Priestley] came again and again
saying buy the house and land. urging me to it, if I would not
he would have bought it for himselfe, and since it was sold
several have been to haue bought it, not knowing of it before, so that god in his providence hid it from others, discovered it strangly to me, and made the right of inheritance
mine. (4) the prophet was to buy it for himself, i.e. it may
be for himself to liue in when in a persecuted condition, for
in this captivity the Levites were fled every one to his field

Neh. 13. 10, and Jeremiah amongst the rest, so they have driven me this day from the inheritance of the Lord i.e. from the revenues of the church that we may liue as we can —god provides—(5) Jeremiah knew at last that this was the word of the Lord v. 8. indeed at first I boggled at it for some reasons and could not tell whether it was my way, but at last I was abundantly satisfyed this was gods will, after I had earnestly by prayer committed the matter to god. (6) the summe paid by weight was 17 shekels wch at 2s 6d a peece, comes to 2li 2s 6d no great summe, but money was rare in those days, they might hauc as much for that sum as we for far more, a shekel or sicle contained half an ounce of silver, on the one side was the effiges of the measure wherin they kept manna in the sanctuary, with this inscription THE SICLE OF ISRAEL, on the other the rod of Aaron flourishing with this, HOLY JERUSALEM : hopefull emblemes, proper to us with the writings were drawn, seeled, the money all paid at once, delievery of possession to me by the man and his wife by a straw,* before witnesses J.P., J.B., J.R., J.B. all subscribing their names and all done as in form according to law and custom, as the writings testify. (7) theres the prophet delivering the evidences of the purchase to Baruck before witnesses to be kept in an earthen vessel as a token that houses, fields, vineyards should be possessed again in that land v. 12—15, oh that we could groundedly say that this my purchase is a type of ministers restauration to and settlement in their respective places ! and that god would make good those further promises to us v. 36 ad fin. god hath already laid us low as Jeremiah was a prisoner, the city was besieged so we are surrounded with dangers and we hauc cause to fear some captivity, the Lord fit us for it, and make good his promises to our posterity if we should not liue to see it tho after a 70 years black day it may be some yonger sort may survive as many in Judah did, however as the prophet fel to prayer for his people after this purchase v. 16 and god answers him v. 26, so o my soul these purchases with spiritual prayers and in due time the Lord wil answer. Amen. this writ March 6, 167½

I was very sollicitous when I resolved upon coming to live in Northourum, so near Halifax, lest Dr H [ook]s

* This is the mode of surrender under Wakefield Manor. J.H.T.

opposition might prejudice our liberty since he hath expressed so much peevishnes agt us, But god hath wonderfully prevented my feares on that behalf for upon May 4th 1672, my license to preach came to my hands with a charge from his majesty to all officers to secure and protect us, the day after being Lords day Dr Hook preacht at Coley chappel tho unknown to any of his friends, by all circumstances we gather he feared my preaching in publick, and thought to prevent it, we were that day at Coley hall made on intermission, appeared very publickly—god helped —On wednesday we removed our habitation, had near 40 neighbours to assist us, god made us to find favour in their eyes, and hath settled us in a convenient habitation : both that morning at Coley hall,* both in my study and family god sweetly inlarged my heart in prayer and also at night at Northourum he graciously assisted beyond my expectation, yet presently after a temptation was prevalent, oh that I might not be highminded but fear, and oh that I might not be secure and imagining a settlement in the world as I am apt to doe for I find by sad experience that then I am next to some sad and strange disaster : but its something strange to me that this declaration for liberty, and my restauration to my ancient habitations (after 12 yeares absence perforce) with a better title should both togather : I am apt to think there is something of god in it more then ordinary, as god continued me in this house almost as long as my publick liberty lasted so the most part of my converting work was done when I lived here, yea and also my work as to discipline, oh that god would restore all the rest with this !

The house I entered into was exceedingly out of repair, within and without, and necessarily required abundance of workmen wch god helpt me in, so that it hath cost me near ten pound this summer in wages and materials besides meat and god hath sent in mony enough to discharge it besides 5li debt I paid to Alice Mellen I borrowed to make the purchase, and 5li paid for my sons tabling abroad and other extraordinary charges, so that still wn god hath more money for me to lay out he sends in proportionably. oh wt abundant cause haue I to trust god for help in order to their supply abroad at learning.

* See *Memoirs of Capt. John Hodgson,* for a history and view of Coley Hall, and Coley Gateway.

Going into Lanc. on thuesday July 14, 74, the day after as my wife and I were riding over Cockey Moor, the way slippery, my horse lost his footing. fell down, I under him, there lay thinking my leg was broken, but I rose and had no hurt, blessed be god.

On Friday being Nov. 13. 74 Mr Copley and White justices kept a private sessions at Wakefield and desired Mr Benson, Sr John Armitage Sr John Kay, to be with them but they understanding the design came not, the only busines of that session was to summon about 40 of Allerthorp meeting before them to convict them of a conventicle myself being in the number for Mr Benson had told them their former convictions were not legal they not having the informers and accused face to face before the justices. accordingly these were summoned by warrants but behold the justices were gone and the court broken up before the accused came there, they sate not half an houre

among Mr. Whites saying those that haue done busines with us the neighbours of this town may come to my house and those of outsides may repair to Mr. Copley of Battley. Mr Dinely, John Kirk—were going to that sessions house being summoned, but met the justices back, speaking courteously to them. its thought the Cause was that the Duke of Buck. at Leeds on Saturday before had rebukt Mr Copley for troubling his neighbours.

I have met with a remarkable providence this day wch is March 4 167⁵ (about this time 45 yeares agoe was I borne) it was this, having been at Ealand to visit J. Brooksbanks wife and intending to come back by Cromwel-bottom, being instructed in the way I went by the mill, they told me to goe in at a gate, through the water, but I offered to goe through a wrong foard, I went past the middle of the river Calder, but finding it deep I went back, yet thinking that the way, I returned into the river, went in to my horses belly, my horse unwilling to goe forward plunged with his feet in the water, I went back and found the right way, wch was an ebbe and safe ford, but am told since that that place was not passable, and that theres a whirle-pit thereabouts, wch might if I had gone little further haue irrecoverably swallowed me up: oh blessed be my god that watcht over me.

Thursday Sept 9 75 coming home from Wakefield, being alone, I set my self to search my heart and life solemnely, and god helpt me to goe through the 10 comts and inquire wherein particularly I had broken them in thought, word, deed. I found I had transgressed them all, some in...ably some in the letter more grossely, god inlarged my heart in judging condemning my self to this righteous law, to mourn for my sins, to flee to Jesus Cht for pardon. oh what a melting journey and duty it was! seldom is my heart in such a frame.   Coming home from York Sept 31 75 upon Winmoor beyond Leeds it being slippery up from a little slack my horse came down in his former feet, I fell off, tho without hurt, got up again al wel lighting, I found my coat torn, a great peece torn almost out, it was a new coat first wearing, Lord teach me good by it, whether it be for humiliation or of some signification.

—::—

Remarkable Providences relating to Others.

1 This morning Jan 23 167¼ being in bed my wife heard a great noyse of running, shouting cracking, at last some body made a great rapping at the gates [of Coley Hall], and told us the Rookes was on fire, we started up, went forth, and by the formidable blaze and terrible noyse we judged it to be the whole housing, house and barnes, Capt Hodgson and I tooke our horses, rid to it, it was only one barn with wheat peas hay &c consuming, 1 horse, 3 oxen, 2 cattell all burnt in it, his man and some others of the family had been at a pig-feaste that night at Widow Sowdens, had left the lanthorn burning in the barn, being drunk—it was an affrighting object, oh but wt. were Londons flame. Nathan Whitley the owner of it, had sometimes sd of our meetings if the house were his he would burn us out, watcht our house often at Norwood green, would have taken me out of Coley chappel, went to a poor widows the morning before, Susan Appleyard, threatened to hurry out all she had for her sons debt wherin she was not concerned. This morning we read in course pro. 3. I thought v. 24—6 were very seasonable—Lord awaken hearts, keep us from rash concerns, Luk. 13 1 to 6 oh that they might study Isa 5 11 12, 24 25 :

2 Mtris Horton the owner of this hall where we liue dyed on thursday night last Feb. 1. and is to be buryed to-morrow at Ealand. a gentlewoman of above 1000 a year, lived sparingly and usually had but ordinary cloaths, she lay from Thuesday till Thursday night speachles, not at all stirred, none were admitted to see her, many things considerable about her, several of the servants were affrighted with a great knocking and variety of musick the night before she dyed—I have been at her funeral this day being thuesday Feb 6 167½ we had a great solemnity, multitudes of people—Dr Hook preacht at Ealand—a fine flourishing flaunting sermon—I pray god it may doe good, these scriptures came fresh in my thoughts psal 49 6 ad fin. pro 41 4

3 Edward Viccars aged 93, dyed last night at Dinah Tetlaws, to be buryed to-morrow feb 6 167½ that hath been a professor a long time, he traded and had lost above 80li by one man and was very sollicitous lest he should never haue enough to maintain him, he made a deed of gift to one Sarah Illingworth, gaue her all, besides funeral expences, she would haue him brought out hansomly —he gave Dinah Tetlaw where he tabled ten pound and two yeares were expired his table amounting to 5li p annum it was gone now he feared went but in the close therof, god hath taken him he was exceedingly cared for and lookt to, and dyed seasonably every way, was at this house to hear me not aboue a fourtnight agoe, lay not aboue 2 days, blessed be god—job 34 19 psal 37 16, 25 ; job 21 22—6

4 Mr Benjaimin Wade at the Grange by Headenly, Justice of peace and alderman of Leeds aged about 80 upon thursday feb 15 167½ being in his own house having several friends at dinner, and as well as he had been of many yeares, after he had sate with them at table rose up, went and sate him down in a chair and immediatly faint away and dyed, drunke, he had an estate of 400 a year and made no will, was buryed on munday following at Leeds. Mr Sam Mitchel was buryed at Halifax on thursday feb 20. it was a very pompous costly funerall, we had great variety and excesse of meat and wines—

5 Upon this day being wednesday Mr John Northend is buryed my son John is gone to the funerall, this is feb. 21. 167½ the circumstances concerning him are wonderful remarkeable—Mary Wright (a precious good woman now in

heaven) had this John only living by a former husband in
whom she took great delight of whom she had extraordinary
care but dying in child bed I think in June 1666 the last
word she spoke to him immediately before her death was
My son if sinners entice thee consent thou not, but he forgetting all his mothers prayers, councels, examples, teares,
tooke strange and sad courses, he going to Oxford I sent for
him, gaue him serious admonitions, at his return, hearing
of his miscarages I sent for him again, discoursed with him
but he gave me no answer. but followed drinking and vain
company, tabled himself at J Scolfields at Thornhil Brigs,
sold some land, kept drinking every day, grew pursey, dis-
eased, resolued to come to his own house in Hipperholm,
drest a room but was intangled in vain company, would goe
to Oxford with yong Scolfield his companion they went
togather to Wakefield there fell a drinking ale, bear, wine
and at last Brandy, in a desperate contest wch should drink
most, he fel down dyed in the place, had 16 li in his pocket,
made yong Scolfield his heir and executor hauing aboue 20
li a year left in land, he was carryed on a board on horse-
back from thence to Thornhill Brigs, and from thence to
Halifax to be buryed, Dr Hook preaching upon 1 cor 4. 5,
about Christmas was 21 yeares agoe I preacht at Halifax at
the funeral of his father, the first funeral sermon that ever
I preacht—my heart is sad upon this yong mans sad death,
its an heavy tragedy, but gods will is done Lev. 10 3; pro
29 1; Eccles 7 17.

6 Abraham Brigge liuing formerly in Holdworth near
Illingworth bestowing much cost in building a fair house,
coming to decay sold it but got no more for house and land
then the building of the house lay him in, having sold it,
came and liued in Halifax, kept ale-house, was a nightly
drinker, usually called amongst them "Prevailed" for a nick-
name, having drunk much, fed excessinely, his wind stopt
by that time they could get him to bed, was buryed Feb. 8,
at Halifax, Dr Hook preacht.

7 Nathaniel Chedwick of Norland formerly was civil and
orderly, of late fallen to excesiue drinking dyed very
suddenly, without sicknes—was buryed yesterday March 14
167¼

8 At Christmas Anno 1671 Mr Taylour, schoolmaster at
Littleborough, who had been a miserable scraper all his

days, now aboue 70 yeares of age, never marryed, had purchased 40 li per annum besides much mony I say when he gaue up schoole at Christmas he came ouer to a tenants house in Norland one Nathan Holroyd, and continuing there a few days begun to like and deal with his daughter who so intangled him that presently they must be marryed, Dr Hook at Halifax put them off one day but they were marryed the second, he lodged with her one night, then went to Littlebrough, fell sick and dyed that day month, could not abide her to come near him, yet left her all he had, deprived his poor kinred of all, she is a braue youg widow gone away with her own cozen to London. thus the covetous old mans monies scatters—

9 Martha Holdworth near Coley sent for me on Saturday morning, being in bed, may 11 1672 she was very sick, likely to die, I prayed with her, &c. that morning she had made her will, left Jeremiah Brooksbank Executor, who tooke away brasse fender, corn and almost all goods, his wife waited on her, her husbands sister was sadly weeping yt she had left her no mony her own sisters children were sore provoked that she left all to a neer stranger. her death was accounted of within a day, but behold she began again to recover, is healthfull again and cannot abide the Brooksbanks and hath called for things taken away &c. see 1 Tim 67-9, 17-18, psal 10 3; psal 49 18; psal 146 3-5.

10 Mr Bowker a minister in Lincolnshire a famous preacher and forward man in the late times but turning conformist, hath been distracted aboue 5 yeares, his place sequestered by reason of his incapacity, lookes on all persons as witches. is fallen out with Is Dimmoks—of Eng. his great patron under whose roof he had made many drunk, then abused them, now will needs kill all about him—

11 Mr Brocklesby a famous conformist in that country hath been long under very great melancholy—Lord sanctify it—Cozen J. C. told me May 25 1672—

12 James King of Willow-hall near Halifax dyed on friday morning, buryed on Lords day May 26 1672, my neighbour saw him well in body, heard him swear desperatly on saturday before was abominably prophane, one told him in jest he must goe to the devil and that shortly; he swore desperatly the devil would haue none of him because his flesh was meazled, the devil loved not mezled flesh, I haue not heard

of his like in all the country yet Dr Hook preaching his funeral sermon yesterday commended him saying wtever his life was he hoped his death was happy, for he repented, desired the prayers of the church, expressed his willingnes to receiue the sacramt but he was not capable, its sd he got a fall off from his horse—he never came to church, Dr. Hook askt him once why he came not to church, he ans: if you will secure me from the bailffs Ile come, he sd a little before he dyed wt a griefe is this that I must dye now when my meanes is newly come to me, he meant by the death of his wiues father Isaac Naylour of Sowerby and he owns he was but a yong man, desperately boisterous: psal 55. 23; Eccl. 7 17; pro 14 32; 29 1; his own father dyed but about two months before left him a great estate—the country rings of his prodigious wickednes Lord open mens eyes by this example, another was buryed the same day that was very near as bad as he, and Nathan Hoile, and several others.

13 one John Naylour near Heptonstall was coming home from Sowerby but was cast off his horse, and a cake of blood was lying by him, he dead, a rich man, some think it was an impostume, buryed yesterday june 7 1672 Dr Hook preaching his funeral sermon at Heptonstall.

14 June 11 72 Susanna Appleyard was buryed at Halifax, her husband Will Ap. was an exacting provident man, had two sons and two daughters, John their eldest son was hopeful forward for good things yet very sparing whom they doted on, confided in, kept always at home. Samuel their second son (a louely young men in person) after he had served an apprenteship was prodigall, at least very generous, they disowned him he went to be a souldier in Scotland long since and dyed. John marryed a woman in Howarth parish, had a son, his father lay long in dotage then dyed, when he was dead they turned their mother out of doores who wandered in the night drazled and amazed, came to haue lodged at her daughter Susan Crowthers, but was disowned, wandred to James Brigs and some friends houses where she was entertained some days, at last her son John tooke her a poore room in Halifax by the church to liue in and there not long after she dyed, she was but poorly kept, though she had brought a great portion, and her husband left a great

estate, it broke her heart that her son should deal so un-
kindly with her, that both her husband and she had so much
confided in, but alas he is fallen to vain company and loving
strong drink and tho he was formerly my intimate companion yet he never owns me : Lord reduce him : Deut 27
16 : Pro 15 20 : 19 26 ; 28 24 : 23 22 : Ezek. 22 27—oh wt
will be the end of these things! the other daughter hath
been marryed 8 times refused to come visit either father or
mother in their sickness, or come to either of their funerals
when dead :

15 Mr Weddal of Bradford, who hath been as great an
atturney as any in the country and was raised to a great
estate of late, had built a sumptuous new house near the
church, had many mens businesses upon his hands, we were
at dinner lately at Mr Milners funeral, speaking of death,
he said complimentally it will surely come &c I advised him
not to goe into his new house too soon, he ans. no not till
towards Micaelmas, he had been exceeding intent upon it,
it must forward, was almost finished, he went up to the
town, came into London on munday june 17 or thuesday
but he dyed on thursday june 20 72, some say he was seized
upon by a palsy, others that he had been at a tavern and
got some hurt with drinking, but he is gone, and his wife
takes on very heavily, they are left in a labyrinth of trouble
not knowing how things stand, he purposed that should be
the last time of his going to London—so it proved, circumst.
sad.

16 When I was last in Lanc : and had preacht at Brother
Cromptons, Grace the daughter of John Crompton of Hacking wife of James Ferniside being there they sent for me
out to her, I discoursed with her, found her exceeding
melancholy, uttered dangerous words, that the devil had got
power of her and she must doe it—I desired them to be
very careful of her—she continued ill,—on May 27 she went
to her mothers to Hacking, a woman carryed her young
child, but in the way had lost some cloath belonging to it,
went back to seek it when she came to the place again Grace
was gone, at last she found her by the water-side, tooke her
home, there she lodged all night, with company in the morning her mother came and lookt at her, here she lay, left her
and they went to prayer in the family, they being fast, she
riseth, goeth up 2 or 3 pairs of staires to the uppermost garret,

and there with a rope that she had brought in her pocket from her husbands house she had hanged herselfe May 28 1672—it was a dreadfull sight, tis hoped she was a good woman, but under prevalency of melancholy, the Lord sanctify it for good, her mother is sorely afflicted with it—Eccl 9 1-4 may be a comfort in this case, its not good to judg persons final state, by outward providences about him.

17 One John Whiteleys son of Halifax being drunk one night and coming by the watch they bade stand, he would not, but (as tis said) fel upon a watchman who recovering his bill struck the watch-bill into his head and tho he dyed not suddenly yet it being falsely healed festered under, only a few days kild him and upon munday July 16 (15) the crowners inquest and a jewry goes upon him—I suppose the watchman is cleared—

11 One Mr Daniel Town minister of Heptonstal, his father was J T minister of Kildwick all of them are accounted anti-nomians. his uncle Robert Town of Ealand—this Mr Daniel Town had lately marryed a widow (being widower also him-self) and lived towards Luddenden, but his wife and he did wofully disagree, her two sons threatened to kill him, did imprison him in Halifax. he got out preached uncles sermon, continued at George Townes house near Kings-crosse [Hali-fax], his wife at last came lovingly to him, desired him to goe home and they would liue lovingly togather, he yielded, went home with her. where were 4 men, they pickt quarrels with him, fell upon him, gave him mortal wounds, cast him out, he was found, carryed to another house. tis said that he was a great horse-racer, was grown loose of later times—its a sad providence: he is yet liuing. the Lord sanctify this sad providence.

19 As I travelled by Hoffe-edg in Lightliff july 22 72 I saw a great number of people togather, some also following the constable Tho Oates, I inquired the cause of that con-course, they told me a man was killed one Toby Medleys son and coroners quest and they went upon him that day, they found him fearfully wounded, and exceeding black and blew, and it seemes they haue sent two men to York and a woman is to appear at the Assises, several concerned in it: I have also heard in this journey of some other murders and deaths by accidents, the particulars wherof I remember not,

wickednes breaks out and blood toucheth blood, they are come off at the assizes :

20 My dear friend and brother Mr Dawson upon a call and the free concent of Mr Broadhead vicar of Burstall did preach several days at Heaton chappel in that parish, but upon Lords day june 24 1672 Mr Broadhead gaue public notice in the forenoon at church, that church-wardens and all officers should take notice of the names of such persons as went from their parish-church and frequented convent-icles, that they might be punished according to law, but immediately after he fell melancholick, raues of a lasse that lived in the house, is sometimes frantick and never preacht to this day wch is Aug 4 and is never likely to preach again.

21 At Hemsworth there is one Mr Mosson the parson who threatened the people if they came not to Sacramt at Easter last, upon which several came, one man a poor ignorant sottish person being there fell distracted that day as soon as he came home had liked to have killed his wife—was never right since that day but goeth up and down in his shirt, cannot work—&c, his name I have forgot but was told it when I was in that town which was July 24 1672.

22 Upon Munday Aug 5 begun the Assizes at York. Dr Spencer preacht before the judges at the minster, but im-mediately after he had taken his text he began to read a story and reading storys about fines for such and such faults was most of his sermon, many cryed shame—there was tryals in open court in plain words about such shameles horrid matters as relating to the secrets of men and women in the filthiest termes in a bruitish manner that exceedingly offended christ. and modest eares—

23 A preacher at Durham of 300 li a year most in-humanely murdered his own wife, the contention arose first about getting him his supper, which increased to grievous words, he shut and locked a door to him, stabbed her then opened it and called for help saying his wife was taken into a swound they came searcht her, found 4 wounds, he was apprehended, denyed the fact tho it was apparent would have entered 1000 li for liberty to preach the day after that being Saturday night, a child being askt what he saw his father doe to his mother answered nothing but I saw my

mother throw a trencher at my fathers head, for they con-
tended at supper—this was (as I suppose) about Aug. 3
1672 : others say it was upon jealousy

24 I being in Bingley parish Aug. 13. 1672 at severall
times they were discoursing of the decay there is of persons
of quality. Mr. Fairbank the minister there said to me
there was a rot among the gentry, and I can say since I
knew that place there is a decay of these houses and familys,
—Mr Savils of Marley, Mr Frank of Cottingley, Mr Bins of
Rushworth Mr Murgatroyd of Riddlesden, Mr Murgatrod of
greenhill, Mr Currow of Nostrop, Mr Johnson—and others
—some are in debt, some imprisond—some rooted out,
title, name—some dead, posterity beggars, oh what un-
thriftines, wickednes, sloth, and gods curse for the same,
this is a good lesson Jno 3 33 : Zech. 5 4.

25 one Abraham Wadsworth, Timothys son, an atturney
is buryed this day at Halifax, he was at the last assizes, yet
distempered, yet his death not suspected, a wild young man,
hath shortened his days by intemperance, immediately before
he dyed, sitting in his chair some company with him, he
begun an health to all Marys (his sweet-heart was Mary
Dean) immediately drawing off his gloue he departed and is
buryed Sep. 2 1672 :

26 I preaching at Howarth June 13 72 at Jonas Fosters
upon that subject of the first resurrection Rev. 20 6 god
helped me to set that home, it being a very ignorant and
prophane place, some were much startled, among wch was
an old man that sate just by me on whom the word had
some operation, so that he could not rest or sleep of several
nights and communicated his thoughts to some neighbours
who advised him to goe to John foster a godly christian at
Denham, to get satisfaction about this work of regeneration,
which he heard was so absolutely necessary to salvation, he
promised a ceartain day to goe but as he went called at an
alehouse, fell to drinking at night was found drunk with
some fidlers and idle company about him, afterwards being
discoursed with he said now he needed not goe for he was
satisfyed, was pretty quiet in his mind and could sleep and
now all is right again : oh dreadful state !

27 Dr Stones one of the Prebends at York minster had a
daughter marryed to Mr Ratcliff born in Wakefield, who had
a tryall at the Assizes, Aug. 20 72 with Mr Shippon about

Kirkheaton parsonage, he stood by the judges, the son at the bar, the cause was called, the jury impanneld, the foreman first named was What-god-will Crosland, living at Almbry, as soon as he was mentioned the jury was excepted agt, another was called, but they lost the suit. Dr Stones rated his lawyer, was very angry, the day after he had a tryall with a quaker about tyths but lost it, grew melancholy and as some say, in his sermon next sabboth railed on judg, jury, lawyers—till they were forced to take him down, he grew wors and worse, is distracted, bound in his bed: Isai 56 11: psal 59 6 14 15:

28 On Lords Day Sept 1 72 a company of children were getting Blackburys about Holbeck, about two a clock in the afternoone or towards three, and there came a terrible thunderclap, and one of the biggest of them was struck dead, his hat-ful of black-berrys were struck close to the tree, towards the bottom of the tree, the grains stuck in, other two children were sore wounded, the rest astonisht, one of them is dead since, he that was found dead was smitten about his back, his cloths burnt, were like raggs—strange—ceartainly true.

29 At Bradford on munday morning a man at the mill cut his own throat yet lived till night, it was Sept 2 72 he confest this was the reason, his master Mr Shuttleworth sent him to take account of the moulter bec. he suspected the honesty of the milner, he sth he had lent some mony out, his master was to come and he could not giue an account of it, he sd dying I haue forfeited my estate to the King, beggared my wife and children—

30 in Manchester parish this summer a youth about 16 yeares of age went into the fields upon a sabboth day and tyed himself to a cow, and struck her, but she run not fast enough, he tyed himself to a wild young heifer, and droue her, she run furiously till she dasht out his brains and killed him, he had used this foolish practice oft upon a sabboth now at last met with his match, it was in june 1672

31 A boy near my brother Hultons in Manchester used to driue the Calendar Horse, had sometimes gone with the horse to the field, but my brother charged him to goe no more being little and lamish with the rickets but John Whitehead my brothers man coming home late at night this boy begged of him to let him ride to the field wch he did

unknown to my brother at ten a clock and when the boy was missing, they went to seek him they found him stifled under the gate that goeth into the field, he was dead, it was an affecting providence, much laid to heart, so that my brother was not well a considerable time after it :

32 about the same time Octob 21 a man went out from his wife and drowned himselfe, he liued in Manchester, he had told his wife the Saturday that he must drown himself wch he effected upon the Munday: the circumstances I know not :

33 My Unkle Mr Nicholas Moseley liuing at Ancoats within a mile of Manchester, Justice of Peace and a great man in those parts, setting forward upon his journey towards London, Octob 18 1672 had his man one Birch, and two of the Dickinsons of Manchester with him, upon the day after being Saturday as they were riding they perceiued his head being down and his hands let hold of the horse goe, they askt him how he did, but he could not speak, they took him off his horse, carryed him into an house, sent for a phisitian, to whom he put out his arme, making signes as tho he desired to be blooded, wch he did and took some blood, but he never spake only opened his eyes twice, liued about 12 houres, then dyed, was brought in a coach to Manchester, he dyed near lichfield, aboue 40 miles from home on Saturday night, was buryed munday sennight after being Oct 28 I came that night to Manchester, went streight to church, heard the warden preach the greatest part of the funeral sermon, its a great blow—its the more observable because he went to London to carry on a suit he had commenced agt his own brother Mr Edward Moseley who was the judg, left executor to Sr Edward Moseleys estate of Hoosted in wch was 7000 li bequeathed as a legacy to Mr Nicholas and tho his brother had offered him land of 850 li a year security till the money was paid, but it was rejected and present money required, wch was impossible he hauing paid 11000 li on one day to Serjeant Maynard with whom he had long sued and whom he had conquered, and as that so this suit is ended—

34 On thursday Octob. 29 72 a man of Heckenwyke hauing been at Hardger [Hartshead,] and coming home full of drink was drowned a little below the town, his hat and staff were quickly found but he was not found of two

days and two nights, when they found him, he smelled strong of drink after so long lying and they found in his pockets severall writs he had got to put in suit some of his neighbours, but god arrested him which stopt the execution— that day he was drowned was a great flood—

35 On thursday Nov 19 72 a yong man and yong woman (that had lived togather severall yeares at Lady Fairfaxes) travelling togather they having been at his friends, going towards his fathers, betwixt Otley and Poole, she (pretending she was cold as he sth) got off horse. walkt a little way, near the water side, cast herself in and before help could come was drowned, the Crowner and Jury sate on Wednesday found it chance medley, but tis vehemently suspected that the young woman was with child, and that they might have some angry words, and that she in a discontent might doe that, yet he will confesse nothing, god knows how things were :

36 about Decemb 12 72 three yong gentlemen were drowned at Cambridg—wch was thus, there was at that time an extraordinary flood by melting of snow and falling of rain, 5 schollers would needs goe recreate themselves in a boat, and swam along the fields hauing none but themselves in it, the wind at last droue them into the channel, the storms tossed the boat, they were afraid, would needs swim out by casting themselves naked into the water, but failed only one got helpe, and another that lay flat in the boat escaped also with the boat—one of these gentlemen was a Knights son in Yorkshire, upon the woulds beyond York, his fathers heir, another a south-country gentlemans son who had sent a horse that night for his son to keep chtmas at home, a third was an Irish Ladys son, an Earles daughter, he was her only child, and she so dear of him that she came purposely to liue in Cambridg where he was, and chargd him not to goe but he out-stole her, and went and was drowned, most of her estate had been spent by her brother, to raise her condition she was marrying a clergyman who was about to be made Bishop, but before that poysoned himself, she left desolate, and this comes in the heeles of the rest to aggravate her sorrows—

37 Sept 8 72 young Scolfeld the schollar and prophaue companion of John Northend dyed and followed his fellow to the graue, and was not much better for his executorship,

only it helpt him to a little mony to spend wch helped him
faster away out of the world, as long as he could speak he
cryed out for more drink, till speech and strength failed him,
and was very stupid about soul-affaires—Lord awake others
by the astonishing examples—

37 the Earl of Darby is lately dead, Lord Charles hauing
endured a long pining disease, his body was opened, and
the phisitian found not one drop of blood in all his body
except a drop or two at his heart, he dyed this Decemb. ult
—1672—it calls to my thoughts his commanding Mr. Christian to be shot to death in the Ile of man upon his mothers
instigation for delivering in the castle there to the Parl.
upon termes many yeares before, in the warres, but this was
upon the Kings coming in, for wch his body frowned on him
—christians blood shed left no blood in noble blood, theres
a losse of him in Lanc. as being the great bulwark agt
papists—

38 a minister in the north formerly ingenious and laborious in his publick work, being a non conformist, and
turned out upon the Act of Uniformity. since wch time
hauing an estate to liue upon hath addicted himself to vain
company and prodigall expences, and now some friends
hauing procured him a licence from his Majesty to preach
he is struck into such terrour and confusion that he cannot,
dare not, preach or make use of it, but is in a lamentable
condition. his case was recommended to our prayers in a
private fast at my house Jan 29 167$\frac{2}{3}$ oh that this may be a
preparation for his future usefulnes—

39 A man buryed at Heptonstal this week feb. 25 7$\frac{2}{3}$ so
fat that 12 men were under the bier at once, had much adoe
to support—50 in all ordered to carry—his name Robt
Thomas—incredible storys.

40 Mr Bins of Rushworth [Hall,] being justice of peace,
dead some 8 or 9 yeares agoe left some three sons and 3
daughters, the eldest son hath been exceeding dissolute, spent
excessiuely, the youngest childrens portions being unpaid
except one, Mr Benson, Clark of the Assize hauing lent him
700 li, seeing all goe so fast feared his mony, demanded it,
put him upon selling his land, demanding also the other
childrens portions, and he hath sold it to Mr Busfield of Leeds,
who pays him 3000li excepting 100li, whereof 700li goeth to
Mr Benson 400 li a piece to two sons, 300 li a piece to two

daughters, the rest to paying his other debts, and yet he is
300li short of discharging debts and hath nothing to liue on,
he is besotted, his brain crackt with drinking and in no
capacity for any imploymt, being unmarryed, &c.

also Mr Tho Murgatroyd hath lyen severall yeares
prisoner in York Castle, making an escape yrons were laid
on him in low jayle, where they haue in processe of time
almost eaten off his leg—that family is the most dreadful
instance in the country, all that know tell strange passages
of them :

41 two men at Deusbury hauing spent Munday and thuesday (March 25 73 at bowles and drinking, on Wednesday
both complained of head ach dyed both on thursday night
in bed none knowing when either of them dyed—Mr Puples
[Peebles ?] in the same town clark of the Sessions about
the same time buryed his son and heir of the small poxe, a
very high man, he being his only son about 10 yeares of age
—he hath built a fine house, made walks, bowling-green &c
—a sad hand of god—

42 one Thomas Welch (whose father was formerly minister at Luddenden) had been at an alehouse near Skircote
got drink, returning home was found dead in a pond of
water, the one side of his head and shoulders being dry,
was churchwarden, had threatened some of his fellows
would not come there bec : they were excommunicated—
boasted all must be brought to the rubrick, &c, another man
a mason about a fourtnight before was found dead on a
moore, had been at the same alehouse. Tho Welch buryed
Saturday April 26 1673

43 on Munday last was buryed at Halifax a woman of
Southowrum whose name was Judith Ramsden, was pretty
ancient but never marryed, she got a bone into her throat
last week, went to Halifax to get help with it out, but it
made an end of her, she dyed at Halifax at the Cock on
friday night and was buryed on monday may 12 73 : she
had been an exceeding covetous penurious woman, and very
rich, hauing scrapt togather 2000li,.... [crossed off] the rest
her relations are gaping and scrambling for—her estate
several thousands. Dr Hook preacht funerall.

44 upon thursday next is to be buryed one Edward
Nickol an old neighbour and formerly a constant hearer of
mine, dyed last night being May 12 73 : just such another

scraper as the former and very rich, but could scarce allow himselfe cloathes for his back, or meat for his belly, was very sick about 6 weeks agoe, and recovered, but relapsed, and since his falling down now by his good will would always be eating and drinking to his end, they could not giue it him fast enough though it ran through him and did him no good, and now his estate, mony and land is likely to goe to a great waster, at least to his children, one Daniel Hemingway who is next a kin who hath sold his own land and made as much [as] he can away.

45 upon Thuesday June 10 73 Mr Holdsworth and I preacht in Rushworth Hall, for wch I procured a licence, providences are strange in so disposing, old Mr Bins that owed it being a justice of peace and a great enemy to such men and meetings, a witty man, left his son in above 2000li debt, the son also prodigal a pace increased it, was an implacable adversary to Joshua Walker, made him pay 8li for breaking up three day work of land contrary to conditions writ tho he had a verbal consent—yet Mr Busfield merchant of Leeds buys it gaue above 3000li for it lets it to Joshua Walker, who hauing a licence makes use of it, and an exceeding convenient place it is and we had a large assembly, blessed be god—his landlord hath now taken off that meeting. [post-scrip.]

46 One J. Pierson born at Lodg in Burstal parish marrying a wife and liuing at Rastrick, had an estate in land of his wife, and drunk excessiuely, he made all away apace, took up 100li of Will Wilton* upon some land in Wyke wn 50li was paid him at once hauing counted it he laid his hands upon it as it lay upon the table saying heres abundance of mony, one would think all this mony would burst me. if it doe not the devil burst me: but it attained that end, for before he had done that mony he killd himself with drinking, and now the land is to be sold, I take part of a field belonging to it this year for hay for my horse, this is June 21 1673:

47 but Henry Northend our near neighbour hath dispatcht his estate before himself—he was an horrible blasphemous swearer, scarce such a one bred in the country, boasted how many whores he had in several places, a prodigious drinker, and sometimes in a condition as tho he

* Of Slead Syke. J.H.T.

was frantick, unruly with all about him, sold his land, got
into much debt—was arrested, was prisonr at Wakefield,
Halifax, and now is in York castle, put in the low jayle for
want of fees, writes lamentable letters to his mother and
grandmother for some relief, being in danger of pining, this
is june 21 1673—dyed shortly.

48 a son of one Matthew Parkers of Morley one Saturday
being july 5 73 being to goe with the horse to the common
took the halter and hanged himself in a tree in the hedg—
one coming towards him seeing him there, casts stones at
him, wondered he stirred not but wn he came to him he was
stark dead—hauing been melancholy, half witted, &c.

49 George the son of Mr Ambrose Spencer of York
(whose father is dead and his mother is marryed again in
York) being tabled with Mr Waterhouse to goe to School at
Bradford to Mr Wood. hauing been there some yeares, about
12 yeares of age, had sold two bookes to buy spice and Mr
Waterhouse hauing spoken roundly to him, took occasion on
wednesday morning july 23 73 to withdraw himself, search
was made for him, notes sent to publick in meeting-places,
Mr Dawson had one but he is not heard of this day july 31,
a report there is that such a boy went up to London with a
carryer from Wakefield—there found.

50 my heart is ready to ake and break with the passages
of two former professours yesterday being july 30 1673 the
one John Lumme the other Sam Wainman both formerly of
Mr Roots church men of great gifts, the former they haue
giuen up as hopeles, they with other base drunken companions sitting at paultry alehouses from day to day, the
storys of both are sad, but this latter in some sort worse for
S. W. he was a souldier professed religion, seemed very
godly, was sick at Swan in Halifax many yeares agoe, sent
for me confessed his rigourousnes, resolved upon more com-
pliance and unity with Presbit—recovered but was as bad
as ever kept distance, my landlord R Best dyed left a widow
with 4000li—this S. W. desired to be tabled there carryed
wonderful soberly, prayed expounded scripture morning and
evening did at last so insinuate himself into the widows
affections that she resolved to marry him, I hope she is
truely good, told me her inducement in marrying him was
religion, that she might be helped heavenwards, and for her
childrens religious education, but presently after they were

marryed he gaue ouer expounding, then had family prayer
but once a day, after a while not at all, and was excessiuely
covetous, would not suffer conveniences to be bought into the
house nor scarce cloths for the children or himself, lockt up
mony from his wife, was miserably penurious—wn John Best
was marryed, sued him for his portion he gaue in his Answer
upon oath that he owned him no more but 8li 7sh 6d and
the third part of...., yet it was proued in particulars, and he
was brought to giue him above 200li and was moderately
dealt with, from that time he is fallen to desperate drinking,
will frequently come home drunk, then cannot sleep but is
like a mad man, and smites on the walls and floor as if he
would strike down the house. she hath a most weary life
dayly his own man and Joseph (Mr Hortons Steward
for...tly thats tabled, yea the apprentice boy all lying out
and drinking sadly, her son Micael who is in great hazzard
to be spoiled, he neuer finds fault with them, if any speak
to him of this sinfull practice, he vindicates it, injoy the
comfort of the creature, hath pickt quarrels with my
preaching will come none to hear me—I fear he is given
up—

51 John Smith of Halifax was buryed Aug 12 1678 he
had been a desperate swearer, drunkard and persecutor, fell
sick on wednesday evening when had been newly jearing Mr
Bentleys hearers, was very dangerously sick but wonderfull
sensative, cared not for my coming at him, then would
speak of death. I went to see him but was not admitted into
his chamber, Mr Dawson went but he would scarce be seen
by him, or speak to him, yea Dr Hook came and went to
prayer with him. he sd wt comes he for, I need none of his
praying, but he recovered a little again, would be carryed
betwixt two men to his brother T. Thorpes to drink and be
merry : expressed abundance of sottishnes, a friend of mine
of his acquaintance came one Saturday into his shop found
him set there, askt him how he did, he answered, indifferent,
said, I think I must march off at this bout, my friend, sd,
it were good then that you prepare yourself, then youl be fit
for life and for death, and fit for heaven, he replyed But I
shall never come there, this he spoke without any reluctancy,
but my honest friend (who told me this passage yesterday)
said he was much troubled at that saying, thus he languished

many moneths without any sense or visible tokens of repentance, on Saturday Aug. 9 he was speechles from ten a clock to eight, then dyed, buryed on thuesday, Dr. Hook preacht upon that text psal. 25 20 commended him much for civil cariage, doing no wrong, waiting on gods ordinances —sent him to heaven, said the most any could object was his speaking agt meetings, but wisht that were the worst of his faults, pressed them not to judge rashly of persons states—told his auditors he had done penance while he had preacht, being indeed sore afflicted with the Emerods, and hauing not preacht some days before, but gain made him strain :

52 On the same day was buryed at Halifax a neighbour of ours one Gyles Tenant living on Northourum Green that had been a covetous scraping man all his days, a great swearer, a very vain talker, but an old hearer of mine, he dyed when I was at York, and I never heard of his sicknes else I should haue visited him. he was a very carnall creature, wedded to the world, he had an 100li of mony in the house lockt up in a chest, but thought it not secure there but took it and hid it in the barn upon an hay-mough, was in danger of breaking his neck as he came down, one came to borrow mony, why he said I haue little mony, but askt if they would bring it again, they sd yes, he went to fetch it but turned and sd, oh man siluer is precious, siluer is as precious as a mans heart-blood—as he lay upon his bed some body came and told him his beasts were got into a neighbours corn, he answered that could not be for they never trespassed, yet before they went he sd fy on them, and bade the devil goe with them for they would never be right : he desired James Brig that as he had been a faithfull friend long so he would be faithfull to the last and see that every one had ate enough cakes at his buryall but not a word of his soul, he was buryed on thuesday, his will proved goods parted divided by wednesday night, thus my old hearers drop into eternity, Robt Crowther (such another) was buryed on thursday, both dyed on munday being neighbours Aug 11 73

53 that Robt Crowther of Lands-head hath been long wearing and decaying, he had 6 children, they workt hard for a poor liuing, went very bare, fared accordingly, bought things upon trust, all their neighbours judged they were ill

set to liue, yet when he dyed he told his wife of abundance of money hid in a wall, his wife sent for her brother Thos Sugden to help to search, they pulled down a wall (found as they acknowledgd) aboue an hundred pound, aboue 20 li of gold, it was molded, rusted and glostened togather, they knew not whether it will be of use at all as coyn, there are some strange ideas his wife knew not of this, but suspected, thought this mony had been hid many generations, yet they haue lived miserably, he was a desperate swearer and curser, a miserable creature, hath not been abroad at chappel this many yeares but his wife and children hath come to hear me—

54 a poor man that hath been a collier 40 yeares having carded wool for his living upon Aug. 14 1673 and got but two pence that day sd nothing is got with this working Ile into the colepit again to-morrow, and Ile never come up again, in the morning he went to the colepit belonging to Mr Rooks at Rhodes-hall, they let him down in a scoop or basket, there being a peece of wood at the other end of the rope to poyse it, when he was near the bottom, the peece of wood slipt out, fell downe upon him and killed him, he was taken up dead, tho no wound appeared on him :

55 One John Holden living by Norwood Green having been in the country a shearing had got some mony wch wn he came home, he gave to his wife, they being very poor, having 3 small children, he went down into Lightcliffe lay in wait for his wife in the fields, he demanded money of her, she gaue him 6d, he not content with that struck her off a stile, laid on her with a great staffe, wch he broke on her, paused her with his feet, set his foot upon her breast, dealt most barbarously with her, left her to goe fetch another staff in the hedge to beat her with, that while she got crept to an house and so was secured from present death, yet had received mortal wounds for this staking her was on Wednesday Aug 27 73 and she dyed the Saturday night following Aug 30 73 : the jury went upon her on munday and they found it manslaughter tho it was clear that he lay in wait for her, but witness were shy in speaking : I spoke with some of the jury, they said she was barbarously and inhumanly dealt with, he had set his foot upon her brest, wch stopt her passage that she could let down no meat—he fled twice, but the former time turned back, the latter was found

in a neigbbour-house, had not power to fly, he is exceeding
sturdy—is sent to York Castle :

56 one Thomas Highley of Clifton was seized on with a
distemper (a feavour as I suppose) coming home from the
field, was distracted all the while he was sick at last dyed
was buryed Dec. 11 73, he was a mighty lusty man marryed
Stephen Ellis daughter, but neither he nor his wife went to
the buryal, having taken some discontent bec. as he sd his
daughter was not preferred to wed as she might have been.

57 John Broadley of Halifax had a cow at Wharlers that
went in that ground giving milk and on friday night Dec.
12 73 when the maid went to milk her she found her killed
and in part flead, and hinder quarter quite taken away, the
thieues had set her up to fetch the rest but tis thought were
frighted : that night the barn doores were part open at
Quarlers and 6 geese stollen : thus people act to keep their
christmas :

58 on Saturday night Dec 20 1673 one Tho. Raundsley
of Clifton and another man were coming from Halifax,
drunk at Brighouse wn they were for going home, it hauing
been much rain the man would be gone the other bide haue
a care for fear of the waters going to passe a brooke,
Raundsley ans : I care neither for god nor the devil, for fire
nor water, accompanied with an oath, so went away, the
other following presently after met the horse back the
master being fallen off and drowned :

59 a woman in Lanc. near Burnley (togather with a man
a wicked filthy confederate with her) killed her husband in
a kiln as he was drying corn, she run to the neighbours
called out come, come, heres thieves come I doubt they will
take something out of the house, and I fear they haue hurt
George (that was her husband) but they spyed blood on her
cloths took her, they are in the gaile—

60 I have been credibly informed of many sad accidents
fallen out of late, one Mr Wood a gentlemans only son near
Chesterfield in Darbishire with another boy riding an horse,
he cast off dragged, had his brains dashed out, lately buryed
sadly mangled—

61 a woman therabouts melancholy had made many
attempts to kill herself, the maid went out having given her
a pen-knife to pare her nailes she being gone cut her throat,

rent it with her finger desperatly, dyed within 24 houres after.

62 this week viz. April 1 1674 two men were drinking at Saddleworth fel out the one took an axe and knockt the other in the head and killed him forthwith, John Hargreaues the Crowner gone from Halifax that day to view him:

63 A man near Doncaster lately being arrested by two bailiffs, his wife stept betwixt to save her husband, the bailiffs kickt her off, paused her with their feet, she being with child, the child fell out of her side—she dyed: oh prodigious wickednes! what will becom of us!

64 a poor man at a little house by Mark Whittakers near Ossit in Wakefield road hangd his own child to death for taking a peece of bread to eat it, another child sd father youl not hang me, I took no bread, the man is gone to the jayle, this was May 11 74:

65 Mr Samuel Sunderland in Bingley parish was robbed May 11 1674 at night, there were nine thieues, they bound all persons in the house, bound him in his bed, went into his chests took 2500 li and went away with it, since I hear 8 of the thieues are taken, Lord sanctify it to him:

66 yesterday being thursday may 14, 1674 there fell out a strange passage wch was this a fine young gentlewoman going a foot and alone by her selfe fell a travelling with child just aboue our meeting house at Quarryhill in the high road by the lane-side, who was discovered by some yong men J Ratliffs servants there she lay groaning as a sad object to all passengers, the child borne, tho still-born, having but one leg and foot, she denyed her name tho well known saying she was one Walkers wife in Burnley parish but she was indeed Capt Hansons daughter having lived at Mr Thur(ton?) with much adoe they got her into our meeting-house sent for her friends 5 sisters, 2 brothers came to her, buryed the child that night at Sowerby, before morning they conveyed her away to Halifax, they made such exclamations of the shame, she was stupid, one landlady told her she might stay there and hear a good sermon, she sd she cared for no sermons, wisht she were gone out of the world, all the neighbourhood came flocking about her she was mad at them, thus god met with them, they intended to hide the shame, god discovered it the more—

67 about July 1 74 there was several gentlemen at Whitley hall, Mr Rich. Beamount of Lassel hall slightly invited
them to his house, they made an appointment among themselves to come, he had laid up 19 gallons of wine agt his
wife lay in being come thither, and besides beer, ale, they
drank all those 19 gallons that night except 4 bottles there
was fearfull blasphemous work—there they lay like swine,
they were but 7 men that drunk all this, T A—N—T—

68 James Stead near Halifax having been at York was
coming homewards (Sept 10 1674) upon a moore beyond
Seacroft fell off his horse, two men came to him, stood over
him, knew him not, a Leeds man came to them they saw he
was alive, knew him not searcht his pockets found his name
in a letter, he desired those countrymen to get him to an
house, they did so but he dyed within 12 houres, it was
supposed he was drunk, he was a great tradesman, had used
strange ways to get mony, marryed a rich widow J. Allisons
wife yet is dead in abundance of debt—oh the vanity of a
wicked world—

69 One DJon Robinson a yong man of Sowerby having got
a yong woman with child her uncle took him with a warrant,
threatened him so as at last he consented to marry her, he
did marry her, on tuesday Sept 15 1674 that day sennight
viz. Sept 22 he had hanged himselfe in a new rope in the
barn belonging to her uncle, where he lived after marriage—
a sad hand of god—he had been often saying to her thou
wilt be a fine widow when I am gone, yet they suspected
him not

70 Many dyed sudden deaths lately, 1, Nathan Crosly
buryed Octob 25 1674, 2, Timothy Wadsworth dyed Octob
23 suddenly in his chair without sickness, 3, Edw Brooks
wife dyed under the cow as she was milking, 4, a woman at
great Horton wel, had a tooth drawn, cryed oh my head laid
her hand on, dyed immediately, 5, one Richard Hodgsons
wife at Bradford on munday Nov. 2, dyed on thuesday the
day after, &c.

71 A dreadful instance of gods justice fell out last night
viz Decemb 17 1674 wch was this one Mr Gilbrend an
atturney in Halifax born in York having been drinking himself drunk very sadly at Mr Anthony Foxcrofts at Woodhouse
a man with a lanthorn was to guide him into the way homewards, he spurs to the horse not knowing what he did, the

horse ran desperatly a clear contrary way down towards the river Calder, near Woodhouse, yet that was not his way to Halifax, run into the river with him, presently came out again without the rider and he is not yet found—This same man was drunk on friday night and lay in the st-cot all night or most of it, one Bensons boys would haue helpt him but could not so left him—called of him on Saturday, sd So you know not me but I would have been your friend last night—now patience with him was expired—his name was Gelibrand, he had been drinking the night before gave un-hansom language to some as he went—wn he was a going down to the water side some of the family where he had been called to him, told him that was not his way, he sd I know wt I doe—he rid on to the waterside amongst the willows in the medow, not in any ford. spurd his horse made him leap in amongst the willows where its likely he fell off, the horse got out they followed him with lanthorns saw him swim down the water but could not reach him, he is not found this is Dec 26, his father came from York on Saturday: they dare not tell his mother how he dyed only that he was dead, hundreds of idle people walkt on Lords day by the waterside to spy if they could find him, they found his handkerchief dropt out of his coat, his office was by the Swan door, nayld up on Thursday. this Mr Gilburn was found under clayhouse, Jan 15 75 by some that cut wood spying brocks about that place—brought into Halifax, his skin whole—breeches gone off, watch gone &c.

72 Joseph Priestleys mother Mtris Brigs of Boystown, bestowed abundance of cost upon repairing yt house, making gardens, orchards, walks, a summer house where she told me once country people might come to her son for councell she having......but he grew fearfull-wild, debaucht indeed nothing but drinking. gaming, exorbitant vanitys yet drinking was his enemy, himself perceived it ruined him, he told S.S one day wn he was drinking I should do well enough if I could keep the black pot from my mouth, but it hath overcome him, he lies a dying, his body is wasted, he hath legs and armes as smal as a childs of 4 years old, flegm thickens, he lies altogether in bed, almost gone, hath Dr Neal and Wastel, they dare give him nothing but lenitines —his estate almost gone for he hath sold much land, mor-gaged more is gone from Boothstown, lyes at Shipley where

he had his wife. Th. Mitchel had been with him yesterday Dec. 25 1674—he is almost gone—yet liued till Jan 19 75, then dyed, was brought from Shipley on mens shoulders under that filthy sign he had set up in the road—buryed at Halifax this day being Jan 22. Dr Hook preacht, gave incouragemt of his salvation, he was buryed in the Quire by Tim Thorp that had also murdered himself by drinking.

73 Sir Francis Cob a great man in the East Riding of Yorkshire travelling to London about Jan 5 1675 lay at a kinsmans house in Lincolnshire one Mr Marwoods in his journey lying long in the morning, his man went to help him up, but he said he was not well, sd intreat my uncle to excuse me for I shall not come to dinner to day, so he left him in his bed, when he was gone Sr francis rose out of his bed fell upon his own sword wch went in at his belly and came out of his back and was fallen dead on the floor, his man sth now that he had askt him to kill him 3 times—the occasion is thought to be the death of one old Mr Kirk of London that had allowed him 500 a year, having little of his own, being in much debt, laid himself in the kings bench—this man was the principall prosecutor of the poor men in the plot-time, having imprisoned several, some wherof dyed by the hands of violence viz. 22, others dyed of feavers and other diseases in York Castle many wherof I knew and could mention

74 Mr George Aislaby the register of the spirituall Court at York did challenge Mr. Jonathan Jennings to a single duel by whom he was slain on Jan. 10 1675 being Lords day, the occasion was this, the Duke of Buckingham living at his own house in York hath several masks, plays, interludes, dancings, at wch a day or two before was amongst the rest Sir John Mallerys daughter living with Mr Aislaby whose wife was her own sister, they stayed at the masquing very late at night, Mr Aislaby and his family went to bed, left a man up to wait for his sisters coming home and open her the gates, the man went to the Dukes house to meet them, but missed of them for Mr. Jon- Jennings (Sr Edmund Jennings brother of Rippon) had taken her into his coach, they coming to the gates in the mans absence, knockt but got not admitted wherupon Mr Jennings takes her to his brother in lawes Dr Watkinsons house where he

lodged, the day after Mr Aislaby and Mr Jennings met to-gather had some words about it, were sharp, Mr Jennings told him it was hard that Sr John Mallerys daughter must wait at George Aislebys gates and not be admitted—it rose so high that Mr. Jennings told him he was the scum of the country—this stuck upon Mr Aislebys big spirit, wherupon after he had been at church in the forenoon, on Sabboth day noon, Jan 10 1675 he sent a challenge to Mr Jennings, charged the servant to deliver it to his own hands, but he being at dinner could not but gaue it to one of the servants, he inquired wt answer he brought, who telling him none, sent again to him, commanding him to bring a positiue answer, hauing delivered the note Mr Jennings sd goe tell your master I will wait upon him presently, the place was called Pin-roes without Boulin [Bootham] Bar, the sign was the tolling of the bel to church, Mr Jennings took a boy with him as tho he would walk, who directed him to that place or near it and sent him back none suspecting the bussines, Mr Aisloby kissed his wife when he went out, she sd loue will you not goe to church, yes sth he but not to the church you goe to, so went out, they met, Mr Aisloby was come first, they fell to't with their swords, Mr Jennings run him up the right arm, his body was untoucht, so many veines being cut he bled excessiuely, Mr Jennings led him back by the arm, then left him, went and told his servants to fetch their master, who made ready his coach got him in it, the last words he was heard speak were, I had him once in my powor, so dyed by that time he was got home, his wife being Sr John Mallerys daughter came to the coach, being big with the 12th child, fell down into a swound, he was searcht by surgeons who find no hurt upon his body, but armes—Mr Jennings was at Dr Watkinsons when he heard it, was ready to tear the flesh off himself wn re-covering he got the Dukes coach went out of town, is gone streight to London, post to beg his pardon, the occasion and beginning of this might be a comedy, but the end is a tragedy: this George Aisleby was servant to one Turbet, Register of the Spiritual Court in the former Bps days, and wn his master dyed he marryed his Mtris, had by her 20000 li and hauing the bookes &c was put into the same office since the Bps governmt was restored and hath made wonder-full improvemt of it for besides the place wch is worth 500li per annm he hath much increased it by buying capiass for excommunicate persons through the country, giving some 80s or 42s for a capias, and if the bailiffs took the persons made them pay 5 li or 6 or 8 or some 10 li a peece or else goe to prison ; this hath been a gainfull trade, doubling yea trebling his mony in a year, so by these shifts he hath gotten two thousand pounds a year, and left it all in an instant, being prodigal of his blood, could not bear an affront, its confidently said that he was ingaged in at least 12 duels formerly in Ireland, wch he could not manage without the guilt of some blood, wch god hath righteously returned upon his own head by such a hand of their own party as god singled out, however this violent persecution of gods people for conscience sake was a sin wch god will seldome suffer to passe unrevenged. I have had suspensions, citations, excommunications agt myself all under his hand. Lord teach this generation something by it : Mr Jennings took two men, went to the high Sheriff, they were bound with him in 500li a peece for his appearance at the Assizes : and got his pardon from the king, and walks up and down York streets with confidence.

75 Dr Anderton (one of the family of Andertons of Lostock-hall in Dean parish in Lancashire) a Doctor of Physick had taken a chamber in Wigan, had been at Bolton on munday feb 1 1674-5, came home at night, they had made him a good fire in his chamber. he being full of drink and turning his back on the fire fell backwards into it, and was wofully burnt before help could come to him, he lived till the Wednesday morning, then dyed, was carryed to his house, and to be buryed in the popish way—

At Ratchdale gods hand is exceedingly out in feavers wch seize on the brain, one told me of one man weak in his bed yet after he had sent his keeper away, got up and would needs kill his own wife—others dye very suddenly, very many, and it was told me that at least 40 lye sick of a feaver in that town, abundance of poor are increased of late, yet much horrible wickednes is committed—drunkennes abounds—

other instances see in my book with rough cover.

On friday Nov 16 1677 and Lords day Nov 18 Prudence Scot (John Scots wife of Lee-bridg was with us at my house both on private fast preparatory to Lords Supper and sate

down with us at that ordinance on Lords day, was well,
went home, slept well that night, eat her breakfast that
morning, about 9 a clock she was struck with a distemper
like the palsey, wch took away her speech, she was sick all
day, and that evening about 6 or 7 a clock she dyed, was
buryed at Halifax on friday Nov. 28 77, it was a solemn
providence, a sudden blow, she was, (I hope) a good woman,
her ancient husband much laments her losse, the night
before going to bed she was speaking of eternity, what a
great thing it was to step out of time into eternity suddenly,
oh sth she when I think of it it can over power my spirits—
before that time the next night she was in eternity—Lord
awaken us—

this night feb 19 167½ the moon was very clearly [seen]
whereas it changed but yesterday 38 minutes after two

Lords day morning Dec 28 73 it thundred and lightened
exceedingly, observed at my house, and in several other
places—

Thursday night viz Jan 1, 73-4 as I was coming home
from Lasselhall at Westercroft brook there was a flash of
lightning apparent to me, tho it was an excessive cold night,
and I scarce saw any clouds in the firmamt, but it being full
of starres—

I haue observed one considerable providence wch is that
since or about the 5 Mile Acts taking place 1666 wherin
ministers were banished from their places god hath given
severall ministers houses of their own in those places from
whence they were banished, as

Mr Nesse bought an house at Hunslet An Dom 1667
Mr Baily bought an house in Morley An Dom 1671
Mr Dawson bought his house at Damhead anno Dom 1667
Myself bought this house in Northourum Anno Dom 1672

As if God Almighty would in his providence crosse and
run counter to mens designs, speaking settlement, wn men
speak a banishment.

Reverend Members of the Assembly: Dr Twisse, pro-
locutor, Mr Charles Herle, assessor, Mr Oliver Bowles, Mr
Matthew Newcomen, Mr Richard Heyrick, Mr Stephen
Marshal, Mr Jeremiah Burroughs, Mr Jerem Whitaker, Mr
Simeon Asle Dr Will. Gouge, Dr Thomas Hill, Dr Anth.
Tuckney, Mr Rich. Vines, Mr Jo White, Mr Will. Strong,

Mr Dern, Dr Will. Spurstow, Mr Edmund Calamy, Mr. Tho. Wilson, Mr Micklethwait:

Decemb 14 1672 Mr Dineley sent me some 30 young trees from Bramhop to set viz. many sicamore-trees, Elmes, Ashes, Apple trees, black-cherry trees, &c, they were set in my lower croft on munday Decemb 16 1672: though I may not liue so long yet future generations may see them flourish: 7 yong saplings set in the upper croft Decemb. 30 —72—by W. S.

October 25 1673 Mr Dinely sent me about a dozen more young plane trees and sycamores bigger then the former, set Oct 27 73:

Novemb 6 1673 Stephen Paulard of Tong brought me 12 appletrees and planted my orchard, god alone knows who reap the fruit of it.

4 view trees set about my house Sept. 1. 1674

5 Ashes set in the croft Dec. 25 74. 8 cherry trees set in the orchard Jan 4 75.

[Completion of " Event-Book."]

Solemne Covenants.

[This little book of COVENANTS and SELF-REFLECTIONS bears
 R. Astley's autograph signature, and the inscriptions in
 Mr. Heywood's writing: "Oliver Heywood bought this
 little book to write Reflections upon yearly, and solemn
 ingagements to be the Lords:" "Bought at Halifax, cost
 6d, by me Oliver Heywood."]

1

On Aug 24 1682 (that which they call Bartholomew day)
20 yeares after our woefull, mournfull separation from the
publick Assemblys, we had a solemne fast at W: Clays, my
heart was very much carryed out for our restouration, there
were extraordinary meltings of soul in most that were
present:

on Aug 30 82 at mine own house, we kept a solemne day
of thanksgiving to god for the publick liberty we haue injoyed in my house without interruption, aboue 10 yeares,
notwithstanding many warrants issued out agt us as well as
others, yet we have been secured through the moderation of
our officers as instrumental, when all the society [s] round
about us haue been sadly broken and scattered, Mr Smith
at Kipping, Mr Dawson at Closes, Mr Jos Holdworth at
Heckmondwyke* meet not in the day, but in the night for
these several months, so at Leeds, Morly, Topliff, Alverthorp,
Mr Whitehurst at Lidiat—all haue been some way hindered
in the places they used to meet in, and the times they had met
on and in Craven they haue been fined, at Sheffield they
were all taken off, some troubled at Sessions, watcht—, at
Jo Armytages they meet in the night at Robt Bins hitherto
obstructed scarce any place in the country free Mr Ward
of York, hunted, fined 40li scattered, scarce any place in
this county free except Hull and yet we, even we at this
poor Northowrum haue been quiet never informed agt,
disturbed, molested only 2 or 3 days we begun a little sooner
then at other times, but god brought full companys, and
that was but wn we knew wt time the officers would come
immediately before the Sessions, and then returned into
our old channel again and haue now vast multitudes that

---

* Corroborated by the numerous entries in the Heckmondwike Church
Book on the purchase of *candles*.

flock to us from all parts of the country, so many meetings being broken : *

This duely considered I lookt on it as our great duty to return god solemne thanks among his people, for these discriminating acts of providence, that our fleece is wet, when others are dry—and accordingly the foresd day we endeavoured to pay our vows, Mr Dawson and Mr Haliday helpt us to praise god and about 30 of my hearers, for whom my wife made a good dinner, and I preacht them a sermon upon Exod 3 3 and being straitened in time, god helpt me that evening in my family, and on the morning following Aug 31 82 in my closet god drew out my heart in thankfulnes, and ingaging my self afresh in a solemne covenant upon my knees, wch now I am desirous to write as followeth : or like in sense :

O Eternall Jehovah, who dwellest between the cherubins, Sweet Jesus who walkest among the golden candlesticks, O holy Ghost who furnishest thy servants with gifts, graces, and dost convince consciences, convert soules, comfort and confirm thy saints : to thee Sacred Trinunity I make my humble addresse, lying under the sense and conviction of my need of all the personal perfections, and hitherto injoying the benefit of the personal operations of this sacred Trinity Thou, O father, hast set forth the soules of sinners in thy profound and free determinations, thou oh Son hast purchased them at a dear rate in thy bloody death and passion, thou Oh Holy ghost takest possession of them, and qualifyest them for glory by grace and sanctification : O, my Lord, thou hast ascended on high given gifts unto men, even Rebellious, which thou hadst first received for them : Thou hast instituted Sabboth and sermons, prayers and Sacraments wherin thou wilt be found : Thou hast magnifyed thy power and grace to me thy worthles servant in accounting me faithfull, putting me into the ministry, converting soules by thy poor servant, finding me out work, people, successe and incouragemt in the worst of times, and greatest spiritual dearth, and now it raines manna about our tents in this small village, thou makest us and the places round about thy hill a blessing and causest showres to come down in due season, there is showres of blessing : and should not those

<hr>

* See my Notes from Sessions' Rolls, in "*Nonconformist Register*, by Heywood and Dickenson," for particulars of these persecutions.

plentifull showres flow back to the sea of thy goodnes through the smaller channels of gratitude ? this is thy due and our duty, this is our debt, and the best we can pay thee : our whole life should be a studying of retribution : yesterday Oh my Lord, thy servants made some solemne testimonys of thankfulnes by frequent songs of praise, repeating thy mercys on our knees, feasting before the Lord : but all this is short the life of praise is in the life of the god-praising soul : new vows must be made upon paying the old : my personall obligations are greater then others, hauing influence upon others : others had helped togather in prayer for us, and so for the gift bestowed upon us by the meanes of many persons, thankes is also given by many on our behalf : and shall I act as a minister, and not as a Christian ? Yea shall I not act as a minister and as a Christian in my private meditations and vows ? Oh my Lord, I am here at thy footstool, a worthles worm, an un-profitable branch, a sinful wretch, fit for nothing but to be cast out as unsavoury salt : but thy kindnes to me hath exceeded thy kindnes to many, (yea any) others, considering my circumstances : and shall not my gratitude be propor-tionable ? and shall I not bind my self to that which my soul doth really intend to doe ? Oh my Lord, thou art my god, thou art the portion of my cup and thou maintainest my Lot : the lines are fallen unto me in pleasant places, I haue a goodly heritage, and thy promises as blessed convey-ances and evidences thereof : ordinances are good, and the best things creatures can injoy, but short of thee they are empty pitchers, wells without water, its thy self, o my Lord, my soul longs for and panteth after, I will goe to the Altar of god, yea unto god my exceeding joy : nothing shall joy me but the injoyment of thee : thou Oh my god art my only choyce, my estate, relations, credit, pleasures, shall not be utmost end or chiefest good, I will not be put off without thee, thou art my only riches, pleasure, and honour : my heart takes content in thee and will seek no further for an happiness : I see so much beauty and excellency in thy self, that other things are base and sordid in comparison of thee : heaven would not be heaven without thee : my soul again, and again chuseth thee, and thee alone, if I may not haue thee, I will haue none for a portion, but goe despairing through the world : if I may have thee to be my god, I will (upon those termes) quit my claim to or comfort in all sublunary injoyments, I lay down all at thy feet, and am content thou take away relations, house, estate bookes, health, life and all, and I see yet no cause to repent of the bargain, for its good for me to draw nigh to god, whatever it cost me: let me haue thee, and let who will haue the world: nor know I any way to the father but by the son, who is the way, truth, life: sweet Jesus I doe here solemnly put my neck under thy easy yoak: by the assistance of that holy spirit that proceeded from father and son, I am resolved from this day forward to take Christ to be my only prophet to guide me in the way of truth, my priest to pay my debts by his death, and to procure my acceptance with the father and to subject myself to his regall scepter, to order my life, conquer my lusts, saue my soul according to his revealed will: my dearest Lord, my soul kisseth thee, and proclaimes war against all thine enemys: my heart is endeared to thee, and adores all thy glorious perfections: my foot shall tread in no other footsteps (by my good will) then what thy self, or thy saints following thee, haue walked in: my soul shall haue no other pardon but what is purchased by thy blood and sealed by thy spirit, no other peace but whats according to truth, no other happines but whats accompanyed with holines: if thou see me rest in the creature or mine own righteousnes, Lord, knock me off by an affliction or a conviction: the life-blood, and purest spirits that supply my soul come most immediatly from thyself, through thy son, by thy spirit: oh my Lord, let me haue thee, and I haue all thou shalt haue me, and my little all: glad I am of oppertunitys of service, not to procure favour, credit or maintenance in the world, but to glorify thee, doe thy will, and promote thy kingdom, in demolishing satans kingdom, converting soules, and bringing them to glory: and since it pleaseth thee to indulge thy sinful servant in the injoyment of priviledges, exemption from sufferings more then others, it may be, because we are weaker, or possibly because greater sufferings are reserved for us: Oh for grace, more grace! my strength is little, I haue had much adoe to goe through my doing work, but if thou wilt strengthen me, my soul shal be more abundant in the work of the Lord, reading, praying, discoursing studying, walking, preaching more affectionatly then ever: and oh for a suffering spirit, if my

dear Lord call me to sufferings for his name! Lord I am
thine, saue me, keep me from the insurrection of the
workers of iniquity, in the shadow of thy wings I will make
my refuge, untill these calamitys be overpast: let thy
strength be perfected in my weaknes: glorify thy self in my
tryals, and welcom; of thine own I haue given thee, of
thine own thou givest me all I haue: make me thy servant:
tye me faster to thee: break the fetters of sin: prevent
wandering into by-paths: prepare me for sufferings: and
carry me safely to glory: Amen:

2

On June 6 1684 I hauing been the day before at Jon:
Priestlys at our usual monthly for publick concerns, and
hauing discoursed on Isaiah 62 6 7 of being the Lords
Remembrancers, and been more then ordinarily inlarged on
the behalf of the church of god and these nations in prayer,
both that day with others, and the morning in my closet, I
am once again moved to renew my covenant with my god
upon these considerations, and with these circumstantial
additions—1 I haue been lately very busy in writing a full
Treatise of personal covenanting. being put on and urged
to such a work, and its fit I should practice the doctrine I
presse on others: 2 I haue had some sharp rebukes of
providence in respect of our liberty, since I writ the last,
Mr O our H C* giuing us some trouble. and I see god in it,
wch calls for self-searching and self-ingaging: 3 yet god
hath in midst of judgmt remembred mercy, and given us
some stollen liberty in mornings and evenings in my own
house and elsewhere, Lords days and week-days, many, very
many fasts we haue had of late wherin god hath in an extraordinary manner appeared in gracious visits: 4 there
are more peculiar ingagemts lying upon then ordinary, in
reference to worldly concerns for tho I haue neither brains
nor any stomack to worldly things, yet upon a solemne
review I find that god hath wonderfully blessed me in
worldly things, far beyond my expectation, so that he hath
made good that word in psal 37 3 which was my support wn
I was turned out from publick imployment now near 22
yeares agoe, wn I owed aboue 30li and knew not where to
get one penny, and wt I had of my own being in my fathers

* High Constable.

hands and being in trouble with the consistory court at York, yet notwithstanding all this god hath raised me up friends, so that god hath wonderfully provided for me this 20 yeares and upwards, so that 1 god hath given me sufficient for family-provision and hospitality. 2 for buying books, storing my house after plundering with goods. 3 buying an house, repairing it, wch hath cost me considerably, 4 to educate my two sons at Mr Fr— and in scotland to provide for them, set them forth. &c wch hath been no smal thing, and yet to keep some considerable mony in my hands, or at my dispose, more then I ever had before in all my life, except when I bought this house, and now these things considered, in token of my gratitude to my dear Lord, I doe devote 40sh a year as long as god continues this bounty that I haue any thing besides the necessary supply of my family, and haue this very morning, after grateful acknowledgments of gods goodnes, and afresh dedicating my soul to god, I say I haue put 40sh into a paper in a purse with this inscription upon it, Money devoted to Charitable uses in this year from June 6 1684 to June 6 1685 and herin I follow Jacobs example gen 28 20 21 22 : and was much satisfyed from Mr Th : Gouge, and Mr Baxters reasons in him that the quotum or proportion fittest to be devoted to god is the 10th penny, and I haue land of my own amounting to 20li a year, and think it my duty while that continues to devote so much to charitable uses togather with my self in such words as these :

O my dear Lord, Thou art Almighty, Alsufficient, omnipresent, and very gracious to me thine unworthy servant, thou hast multiplyed thy mercys upon me, many, O Lord my god, are thy wonderfull works which thou hast done, and thy thoughts to me-ward, they cannot be reckoned up in order unto thee, if I would declare and speak of them, they are more then can be numbered: I will praise thee, for I am fearfully made, and miraculously preserved, graciously redeemed marvellous are thy works and that my soul knoweth right well: my soul-mercys are the very flower and cream of all my mercys, Blessed be the god and father of our Lord Jesus Christ, who hath blessed me with all spiritual blessings in heavenly places in Christ: and as a poor Thank-offering due to my dear Lord, I haue devoted my soul and body and all that I haue to the Lord, many times I haue subscribed my hand to the Lord, and oftener given up my heart and my all to my god, and I doe not repent to this day, and hope I never shall doe may my heart be sincere, Lord make me sound in thy statutes that I may not be ashamed: And now again I am taking a view of thy wonderfull kindnes to me in temporalls, Oh the direction thou hast given thy servant in arduous cases! Oh the protection in dangers! the provision in straits! the satisfaction in doubts! What sweet Relations hath my god provided for me! what health of body, peace in my family, credit to my name, safety in my travells competency of the good things of this life! truely I cannot say, that I lack any thing, though I thought I was sent out without either staff or scrip, yet I haue not been in debt, or in rags or naked, or famishing, or begging my bread, but haue had food, rayment, handsome apparel, my cup running over money in my pocket to giue to such as want, and oh how gracious is my dear Lord herin! when I look back and consider what my dear Lord hath carryed me through, and compare my incomes with some others, I stand astonished, and am ready to conclude surely theres a miracle of multiplication upon what I haue, the oyl runs without staying as long as theres a vessel to receiue it, however the barrel of meale wastes not, nor doth the cruse of oyl faile, the secret blessing of the Lord is upon my tabernacle: And since it is so, and whilest I sensibly perceiue it is so, I am this day, the morning of this day, June 6 1684 determined to giue back, devote dedicate a moity of my yearly incomes to the Lord my god, as a freewill-offering for his use, and for the service of my dear Lord, who hath frankly given me all I haue, and first I will inquire out godly poor that are indigent and diligent, yet their hands are not sufficient for them, also such as are sick lame, impotent, not able to work, or such as are crossed in the world, are in debt, or prisoners for Christ and his cause, or such as are in necessity, I cannot say but I may haue laid out as much as this comes to yearly in acts of Charity, though through grace I can say it, my left hand hath not known what my right hand did, yet upon the cogent reasons I read at Mr R in the forecited book, I took up a Resolution to lay so much by and distribute out of it, as long as it lasts, yet not confineing my self to this summe, but in extraordinary cases to exceed it, upon a just call, and not so much to put pence and smal pence given to beggars on the road, upon this account,—Blessed be god that I haue any thing to giue, and an heart to giue any thing, yea I will draw out my soul to the hungry, as well as bread or money, I will devise liberall things, and cast my bread upon the waters, I will shew mercy and giue, yea in some cases, lend to him that would borrow, not expecting a recompence, for I am sure its a more blessed thing to giue then to receiue: yea in some cases I will giue beyond my power, hauing abundant experience that the liberal soul shall be made fat and he that watereth shall be watered also himself and he that soweth bountifully shall reap bountifully: oh for a truely noble charitable frame to doe good to all, but especially the household of faith! and if my Lord haue occasion for any thing he hath given me, I will as freely return it as I received it in his cause and for his use, even by a whole-sale, in the mean time he shall haue his own with usury, Lord accept of me and it, and mortify my heart to the world, help me to lay up my treasure in heaven, and lay out thy treasure on earth, that making friends of the mammon of unrighteousnes, I may be received into everlasting habitations, Amen, so be it   so sth   O H

3

This day being Jan 28 168⅚ god having graciously helped me, Mr Dawson, and my two sons, John and Eliezer, with some other friends in my house to keep a day of solemne thanksgiving to my dear Lord a second time for my deliverance out of prison, (wherin I was confined to York castle from Jan 26 168⅖ till Decem 19 following, for my preaching the gospel in my own house) and for all the Lords kindnesses to me there, and for his mercy to my sons and family I haue resolved as part of my gratitude to my dear Lord, once more to renew my covenant with him, and to devote three pounds of silver wrapt in a paper, and inscribed —the reason why I inlarge my charity this year is partly because god hath inlarged his bounty to me partly because I lye under deeper obligations—for multiplyed mercys partly because my children are comfortably provided for, my debt to god I thus expresse—

Oh Eternall, infinit, everliving Jehovah, my faithfull defendor and bountifull Benefactor, who gaue me this soul, and preserved my soul in this body and crowned me with

Lovingkindnes and tender mercy: how glorious are thy works and thy thoughts for me are very deep, who layest a foundation of my mercy in misery, and dost me good oft times agt my will, when men took me and carryed me to prison, they carryed me whither I would not (as it was with Peter in his old age) but now I perceiue it hath tended much to my advantage every way, god carryed me to York castle that there he might shew me great and marvellous things that I knew not: to my soul, which he quickened, instructed and comforted more then ever before: he gaue my body health beyond all expectation, increased my credit amongst his people, added to my estate considerably, by trebling my former incomes: thus what men devised for my hurt hath turned to my advantage, yea I now perceiue my sufferings haue tended to the furtherance of the gospel, Let god haue the glory: and now oh my Lord, I will pay thee my vows which my lips haue uttered and my mouth hath spoken when I was in trouble: the anguish and dolours of my heart extortd such promises and professions as these, which now I doe solemnly repeat and renew, 1 that I will more carefully keep gods com[ts], this I haue sworn, and by grace, I will perform, that 1 will keep thy precepts, I can keep none perfectly, but will omit none voluntarily, thy word shall be my canon and rule of my actings, I will study scriptures more inquire more into the meaning of them apply them more to my own soul: 2 I will set my self more to avoid sin, mortify beloved lusts, and crucify the flesh, I am determined to watch my heart, tongue and ways more narrowly, to avoid occasions of sin, I will make a couenant with my eyes eares, hands and feet, that I might not offend god, and where I perceiue the hedg to be lowest and onset hottest, 1 will make the strongest fence: I purpose never to transgresse as I haue done: 3 I will set my self to pray oftener and better in my family, society, and closet, to get my thoughts and my affections more entirely fixed on god: I will meditate, walk close with god and perform every duty with a design to meet with god, and ingage my heart to approach to him and endeavour to get dayly influences from him: 4 I doe purpose, by the assistance of gods grace, that not only I but my house shall serue the Lord: that gods worship may be maintained in my family, and gods work may be effectually wrought in the hearts of my wife, children

servant I will instruct them more carefully, admonish more
faithfully, walk before them more exemplarily, I haue dedicated my sons to the Lord, and god hath accepted them, I
will obserue, what use my Lord will make of them : 5 I vow
this day heart and life as well as lip gratitude : Oh wt shall
I render to the Lord for all his benefits towards me ? I will
loue the Lord, walk before him study to. please him, bring
forth fruit for him, not only the fruit of my lips but my
heart shall more admire his infinit perfections, rejoyce in
him, and take full content in my dear Lord, as the authour
and objéct of all my happines : 6 I doe this day once more
giue my self soul and body to my dear Lord, whose I am,
who hath chosen, purchased, and by his spirit hath taken
possession of me, therefore I doe resolue to glorify god in
my soul and body which are gods : this is my reasonable
sacrifice and service to my Lord, who hath delivered my feet
out of the snare, O that my whole man might be more possessed by him, and acted for him ! 7 more particularly I am
from this time forward resolved to be more active and vigor-
ous in pursuing the great ends of my ministerial function—
to lay out my self more for the glory of god, and the good of
soules, to study more and upon more profitable subjects, to
pray more ardently for, and endeavour in preaching, discourse, and all other meanes the conversion and salvation
of poor sinners : 8 I promise this day to adhere to god, his
ways and truths with full purpose of heart against all opposition, contradiction, my soul desires to forsake relations
estate, life and all for my Lord Jesus and to seal his truth
with my blood. if he call me to it, to resist unto blood in
striving against sin : to follow my dear Lord to Golgotha :
Oh for strength ! 9 I promise to unite and associate with all
the servants of god, in whom I discern sincerity and savour-
ines of spirit, and will maintain charitable thoughts of them.
passing by weaknes, yet endeavouring to inform them, reform whats amisse, edify their soules, and maintain communion with such as fear god, that I may keep the unity of
the spirit in the Bond of peace : 10 I am determined, by the
assistance of gods grace to prepare more for death and
heaven, by drawing my heart off this world, setting my
affections on heavenly objects, examining my conscience,
and conversation, clearing up my evidences for heaven, and
standing dayly on my watch, not knowing wt this year may

bring forth, after confinement in a prison the next news may
be martirdom for Christ: the will of the Lord be done: I
will wait all my appointed time till my change come: come
Lord Jesus, come quickly, amen: these things I haue writ
in the uprightnes of my heart, trusting divine grace for
performance of the same: without Christ I can doe nothing:
but by his strength I shall be able to doe and suffer all
things: out of weaknes I may be made strong: his strength
is perfected in my weaknes: even so be it, my dear Lord to
thy covenanted servant   O H

4

Reflection on the preceding year with further resolutions:
This day, (being munday Jan 24 168⁚) having the oppertunity of being at home which I am very rarely, I haue
reviewed the preceding obligation, the former year under
my hand, and find I haue great cause both of thankfulnes,
and humiliation 1 of thankfulnes, 1 that god hath given me
one year more of liberty and freedom in my own house, wch
I scarce expected, in the beginning of the last year: but
god can doe wt he pleaseth I wonder at it: 2 That god
hath so graciously supported me in my work, and given me
so great liberty of travelling abroad, health of body, and
oppertunitys of service, at home and abroad, for he hath
made me abundant in labours, having travelled aboue 1000
miles, preacht 132 times on week-days besides Lords days,
kept 87 fasts, 15 days of thankfulnes—3 I have been helped
to spend my time profitably studying sermons, writing
severall letter treatises for friends, particularly I writ over
most of my Book of Baptismal-bonds an Epistle—sent it to
London, if it may passe the presse.—haue read over severall
treatises, and kept my times of reading the scriptures: 4 by
divine assistance I haue been helped—freely to distribute
that money I had set apart for charitable uses, and some
more, to fit objects of charity, and god hath drawn out fit
occasions, and yet hath put an end to the weary days of 2
aged men, in my neighbourhood, W B, and J N to whom I
shall giue no more: but blesse god for his mercy to them:
5 god hath the year by-past prevented any breakings out of
corruption in my life, and hath made some discoverys more
of heart-sins then formerly, and helped me some-times by
his grace to bewail them, lye-under the sense of them in the

blood of Jesus Christ: 6 god hath wonderfully drawn out
my heart ordinarily every morning in prayer, wherin my
manner is to turn the hour-glasse, and spend that hour in
reading 2 chapters, and then going to prayer alone, besides
family work, oh wt warm, melting seasons haue I had!
these I can review with comfort, and blesse god for them:
7 1 doe find by the assistance of gods grace, that my heart
is more carryed out to my dear Lord in the duty of thankfulnes, more frequently and more inlargedly: that I haue
oft freely devoted my self to god with more entire resignation: that I haue designed gods glory and the good of
soules, having studyed more seriously, and upon more
profitable subjects: I haue found my heart more confirmed
in the truths, ways, and worship of god, and still more
resolvd to venture all for god: that I haue been this year
more concerned for poor Zion and haue been more carryed
out for the good of the church: and methinks I find my
heart more out of loue with the world, and more desirous to
be at rest with my god: Oh how oft hath my soul longed
that my soul might be snatcht out of my body, and mount
to heaven while my body hath been on its knees or prostrated upon its face! But gods will be done—

Yet 2 As I haue cause of gratitude so of humiliation, 1
that though I have read scriptures, I haue not so carefully
studyed gods mind therein as I ought, reading commenta-
tors, or commenting theron myself, or making application
therof: 2 That I haue not been so watchfull over my lips
as became me, but haue sometimes spoken, lightly or unadvisedly such words as I had afterwards cause to repent of—
3 I haue found my heart working in envy, murmuring or
discontent when I haue perceived my self slighted, and
others preferred or imployed before me, or where I haue not
had cals to places as formerly 4 Though I haue usually
met with my Lord in the morning, yet I haue missed his
gracious presence in the evening, and haue been sometimes
so intent upon my study (if at home) that I haue reserved
little time for secret prayer, or (if Abroad all day) haue
pleaded wearines, or a superseders by other dutys that day,
that I haue been short and cursory, and not so serious
therin as I ought: 5 also I haue not been so serious and
laborious in family-work in discoursing with my wife and
servant about soul-affairs as I ought. in pressing home

truths, dutys and minding eternity, the Lord humble me for
this neglect :

I haue been so much abroad in my travels, that I haue
rarely visited my neighbours, or if I haue, I haue not so
faithfully improved oppertunitys to doe them good in in-
structing admonishing praying with them as I ought : 7 In
days of fasting and prayer I haue oft been drowzy dead-
hearted, distracted, yea sometimes fallen asleep, or haue
been weary, or thinking of other things, when gods servants
haue been sensibly weeping and wrestling with god : alas,
what poor fasts haue I kept with others! and how rarely
haue I got to the duty alone—8 methinks I doe not improue
my travelling-time as I ought, and as I haue sometimes
done, Oh what sweet seasons hath my soul had many a
time, when riding on my old Dick for 15 yeares togather!
but I haue not been so free since I had Guy but its not the
horse, but the heart thats the true cause : I begin a Re-
flexion or meditation on a moor, or solitary lane, but follow
it not to purpose as formerly : Lord, humble me for these
and what other sins I haue found my heart guilty of : Oh
mend the frame of my heart : make me more watchfull :
keep conscience tender : perfect thy work in my soul : increase grace : fit me for glory :

And Now, Lord, here I am, still I find thee good to my
soul, yea every year, every day, every hour better and better,
and see lesse cause to change my Master, still more cause to
cleaue to thee with purpose of heart : if any thing be
amisse not thou, but myself is in the fault I will not blame
thee, but my own soul : Whither can I goe but to thee thou
hast the words of eternall life : thy word is very pure, therfore thy servant loues it : I esteem thy word in all respects
to be right : Oh that my ways were directed to keep thy
commandments! they are holy, just and good : I see more
equity in thy ways, and more evil in sin : oh for an heart
for god Thou art laying new obligations upon my spirit
dayly to love and serue thee better : I am every year drawing
nearer the center, oh that my heart were better! Lord, I
am the beginning of this year tying a new knot on the old
Bond : thou art the same, and changest not : thou hast
grace enough for me for this ensuing year also : if I meet
with difficultys yt I never yet met with, I will trust thee for
new strength I never yet had : god knows what this year

may bring forth : however its birth is, I will hope in thy
mercy that it shal proue fruitful to my soul : I subscribe
the former ingagement, with renewed repentance for failings,
resolutions for more exact obedience, and fresh actings of
faith for gracious assistance : Lord, heal my backslidings
annoint me with fresh oyl, take me by the hand, that I may
run and not be weary, walk and not faint : I giue my self
once more to thee, and as a testimony of my sincerity, I
also giue 3ˡⁱ out of my last yeares incomes to be distributed
to necessitous persons as thy providence shall direct me : I
haue not so much income this last year, as the former : but
I have more then I sometimes expected, and if thou call for
the rest, I freely surrender it with the soul and body of
thy poor servant O H

5

A review of the providences I met with A D 1687 and an
Acknowledgmt of god therin and a covenant subscribed

Jan 13 168⅞ having been abroad 3 days preceding in
preaching work, I fel to review the passages of the preceding
year, and doe find they all doe lay a further and stronger
obligation upon me to be the Lords :

1 This may be called (Annus mirabilis) the wonderful
year, and from this time it may be sd What hath god
wrought, principally in the liberty of the gospel in these
3 nations All persons expected a greater restraint then
formerly, and there was great cause to expect a sudden
desolation or violent persecution from the popish party,
that had long awaited and now at last obtained
a prince of their own Religion : but Behold the contrary,
there comes forth the kings Declaration for liberty
of conscience dated the 4th day of April 1687, wherin he
declares a suspension of all pœnal laws in matters Ecclesiastical, and free liberty to dissenters to preach, wherupon
ministers and people did generally accept this liberty, ad-
drest the king with gratitude, entered into their meeting-
places, preacht the gospel freely, had numerous assemblys,
which liberty hath continued this year out, we haue sacraments, solemne ordination of ministers, conferences, and
Excercises set up on week-days, disciplin and no disturbance
in any thing : Oh what a change ! surely some-body hath
laid hard siege at the throne of grace : and I can truely say

without vanity in this hath my dear Lord answered my importunate prayers, and given me in particular a token for good: 2 Though withal Popish meeting-places haue been set up in many parts of the kingdom, and at first for some novelty did frequent them yet few, yea very few, any where haue turned to them, but some I hear haue turned off from them, since they opened their fopperys more freely: on the other hand, godly dissenters haue gained ground and grown more numerous then ever, so that at Chippin. Wyresdale, Poolton &c in Lanc: meetings are set up, where never any were before even in Popish places, as I haue been informed this week, so that Papists and quakers complain, no body is gainer by this liberty but Presbiterians: blessed be god: 3 god hath raised up a great number of young ministers, I haue had an hand in setting apart 5 very hopeful young men this last year, and six were set apart publickly amongst a great Assembly in the meeting-place at W: and others elsewhere, besides severall young candidates that begun to preach this year, and are in full imployment, that wait for an oppertunity to be set apart regularly for gods work: Aarons rod hath budded blossomes and Almonds: blessed be god: this also is an Answer of prayer: 4 There hath been an Attempt made this year to try who would giue consent for taking of Tests and penal laws, and Nobility, Gentry and commons haue generally declared themselues in the negatiue, from an Universal jeolousy that thats a step to Popery, agt which there is a strang Antipathy among country-people, yea the high church of England men say that the dissenters must either stick to them in this, or they are undone, yea tis verily thought this will be an occasion of a greater union amongst both partys then hath been: this is Digitus dei: 5 In Scotland, yt distressed, peeled nation theres a wonderfull change of affaires, free-liberty granted, meeting-places erected, many built, banished ministers restored out of all parts of the world, meetings wonderfully frequented by persons of all ranks and degrees, so that I haue heard of Earles sitting in meetings among the common people, their classical and provincial meetings celebrated, frequented: so that its like a new world both to them and us, whatever be the meaning of this providence: And these things are the more strange considering the severitys still used agt the protestants in France its sd 1500 fled into England from thence this year: 6 for my own particular god hath carryed me through many vicissitudes this last year, strange haue gods providences been about me, I haue travelled to Nottinghamshire, Westmorland, to York thence into Lanc: my journeys haue been aboue 1400 miles haue preacht aboue 100 times week-days I may say with the Apostle 2 cor 11 26 in journeyings often, in perils —in wearines and painfulnes, in watchings often, in fastings often—I had 5 or 6 desperate falls off my horse, yet not hurt, blessed be god: my dear Lord hath made me of some use in the world, blessed be his name: 7 At last I haue seen something of the fruit of my labours last year, for this year is come forth into the world my Book of Baptismal Bonds or my Treatise of Personal Covenanting which came to my hands, Octob. 10 1687 he let me haue 100 for 10li wch I paid to J T for Mr Parkhurst, 50 he gaue me, besides 12 more, all these I distributed gratis to my hearers about home, my relations and friends abroad in Lanc—at York— &c and doe understand that it is acceptable and likely to proue profitable, blessed be god : and what shall I render to the Lord for all these benefits ? I will ingage myself closer to the Lord in covenant according to the rules I haue given to others in my Book, for shall I bind this burden on others and not touch it my self ? shall I giue instructions and not practice them ? I will therfore subscribe my own name to that blessed bargain, betwixt god and my soul in the words of the Postscript p 321

O Eternal, infinit, omnipotent, omniscient, and glorious Lord God, I thy poor çreature that am fallen from god by Adams Apostacy, and condemned by thy Righteous law for breaking the first covenant made with man in innocency yet understanding by thy word the willingnes of a gracious god, to enter into another covenant with fallen mankind of Reconciliation through Jesus Christ the Mediator, I even I a poor miserable sinner at thy footstool this day, being convinced of my miserable state by nature the necessity I haue of thee, and the equity of the termes of this gospel-covenant, doe here prostrate my self before thee, desiring in the singlenes and sincerity of my heart solemnly and expressely to subscribe to the Articles propounded in thy word, (as the termes upon which thou entertainest a poor sinner), without any let, reserve or evasion: the work is great: my strength small: my heart slippery: but in the name and strength of the Lord Jesus I here set about it: Lord, Assist and accept of me, through the mediator of the new covenant:

First, I humbly desire to accept of god the father, as my only happines in knowledg and injoyment of whom consists my felicity: thou only art the Rest and Refuge, the suitable and satisfying portion of my immortal soul: thou art my utmost and ultimate End: I am resolved to look no where else for an happines, and to design nothing else but thy glory, as my highest End in all my Actions natural, civil, and Religious: and Oh that my soul might glorify and injoy thee as god, and my god! and because god in himself, absolutely considered is a consuming fire to guilty sinners, and theres no approaching to thee but through a mediatour, and thou hast sent thy wel-beloved son, God equall with the father to take upon him humane-nature. and by his actiue and passiue obedience to bring poor souls unto god: I am abundantly satisfyed in this blessed contrivance of free-grace; and humbly desire to take thee, sweet Jesus, as my high-priest, to expiate for my sins, and by thy Blood to reconcile me to God: Angels, men, dutys, graces are not a sufficient price to buy off the guilt of our sin: but I trust in the merits of Christs death and satisfaction only for the pardon of all my sins: I humbly present my person and prayers to god in the name of Christ my Advocate, who intercedes for poor soules at the right hand of god, answering the demands of justice law. Satan, conscience, and rendring our sincere, but defectiue performances, acceptable to god: I take Cht Jesus as the only prophet of his church who revealed gods mind to mortal creatures, personally by his publick ministry on earth, and by his spirit, and Scriptures and ministrys since his ascention to heaven: I am sure he is infallible, and as long as I follow his guidance I shall never erre: I will not follow men any further then they follow Cht:

The Lord Jesus I own as king of his church, my Soveraign Lord, humbly desiring to submit to thy government conquer my stubborn will, subdue my lusts, and rule my heart and life by thy righteous laws and glorious scepter: I humbly own and willingly embrace the Holy Spirit, that proceeds from Father and son, yeelding myself to its convictions, motions and sanctifying operations; depending on its assistance hoping for its quickening, sealing, and comforting impressions; resolving to be led by the holy spirit as long as I liue:

I doe also humbly embrace, and heartily subscribe to all the truths revealed by god in the scriptures, and being satisfied that they are dictated by the infallible god I doe venture my soul and eternall state therupon being assured that the god of truth cannot lye; though many things be aboue my reach or reason: I doe also fully consent and subscribe to the equity of all gods laws and holy commandments, though contrary to my carnall interest, tho difficult and hard to be obeyed, tho hazardous and drawing on trouble and persecution, and will by the Assistance of gods grace addresse my self to comply with the most flesh-displeasing and self-denying dutys prescribed in the word: Lord giue me an obedient heart:

And whatever ordinances thou hast prescribed I will own, I will frequent the assemblys and societys of thy saints hear thy word, honour and improue the seales of thy covenant, Baptism and the Lds supper, and offer up unto thee the dayly sacrifices of prayer and praise, and in all my soul shall presse after communion with thyself, and edification to mine own soul: furthermore I doe purpose by thy grace to submit myself to all thy dispensations, crosse as well as comfortable, I will not chuse my condition in the world, but leaue god to chuse for me, prosperity or adversity, health or sicknes, riches or poverty, liberty or imprisonment, honour or shame, I proclaim liberty to thee, to use me as thou pleasest so thou wilt honour thy self, sanctify it to my good, and saue my soul, Afflictions by Christ I will bear patiently, tribulations for Christ I will bear triumphantly, if thou wilt giue me strength from aboue I will be ordered by thee:

And as I will accept of thee, O Lord, and all that thou proposeth to me, so I will dedicate myself to thee, soul and body and all I am and haue: My soul shall be thine to be reformed, purged and conformed to thine image, from which by sin it is sadly degenerated: my soul shall attend upon thee, for commission from thee for subjection to thee, for assistance of thy grace: my poor soul shall tremble, and never be at rest, till it center upon thee, and get communion with thee, I will dayly put my soul into thy hands, in weldoing, and will commend my expiring soul to thee at death:

hoping thou wilt receiue me : thou hast endowed my noble soul with useful facultys which I desire to devote to thee, and imploy for thee, my mind and understanding is best imployed in conceiving of thee, thinking on thee, fixing upon thee : O that I could meditate on god and spiritual objects day and night ! my conscience shall act for thee, and I resolue to yield to its dictates, and maintain its tendernes, and subject it only to thy authority : I will purge my memory of vain trifles, and stuff it with devine truths, I will remember my sins to be humbled thy mercys to be thankful, my duty to practice it : my will shall chuse thee and thy wayes, cleaue to thee with purpose of heart, and oh that it were kindly melted into thy will ! I wil loue thee, O Lord my Saviour, desire after thee delight in thee, I will fear and stand in awe of thy glorious Majesty : thou shalt be my hope and confidence, I will hate all sin as offensiue to my god, my soul shall rise up in indignation against sinners : and chiefly abhorre my self for my own iniquitys : God forbid that I should rob god of my body, I will imploy it for thee and devote all my members to thee as instruments of righteousnes unto holines : I will breath out my soul to god in prayer and praise : my tongue wch is my glory shall not utter vanity, but speak to gods glory and others edification ; I will restrain my appetite that I may be temperate in all things : I will make a covenant with mine eyes, that they may not be windows to let in vanity, but inlets of light and heavenly objects that may affect my heart ; I will hear gods word and incline mine ear to such discourses as may edify my soul : my hands wil I wash and compasse thine altar, and keeping them from striking, stealing, taking bribes oh that they might act for god ! I will bow my knees dayly to god in prayer, my feet shall carry me to gods ordinances, and godly societys, never to stages or spectacles of sin and vanity : and as I would be the Lords, so all mine shall be his, so far as my power extends, I here dedicate to thee my wife, children, servants, brethren and sisters in the flesh, and all my neighbours, I will use all endeavours in my place to bring all to thee, with whom I haue to doe, by my prayers, example, instructions, admonitions procuring godly ministers to preach to them, that by any means they may be won over to thee, and tho I loue my relations dearly, yet rather then sin against, or forsake thee, I will freely forgoe

them all : That estate in the world, which thou hast given
me shall be freely at thy dispose, to part with for thy sake,
I will distribute frankly for the good of thy church, and
supply of thy saints necessitys, and extremitys of others
(this day I haue put three pounds in a purse to giue my
poor neighbours, wch is the 10th part of my income, statedly,
besides other distributions occasionally, Lord accept this
free-will offering in Cht) my credit shall vail to thy honour,
let my name be trampled on that god may be glorifyed : if
I haue any repute in the world, I will improue it for advancing the interest of my dear Lord : I dedicate my house
to the worship of god, and entertainmt of godly ministers,
pious Christians and strangers, and shall think it wel performed when god is therin Faithfully served : Yea as I
esteem my god aboue all necessary accommadations of life,
so I am willing for thy sake to suffer the losse of all, and
will study that great lesson, in every state therwith to be
content—my self and all that I am and haue is wholly
resigned to thee, to be, doe, endure, and be disposed of
according to thy pleasure : This covenant I subscribe in the
integrity of my heart, hoping for acceptance through the
merits and mediation of my dear Lord Jesus, the mediator
of the covenant, and tho I may fail through infirmity of the
flesh, yet I desire and hope thou wilt cover and cure my
unavoidable infirmitys, recover me out of backslidings,
preserve me, present me blameles before thy Tribunal,
Amen my heart again echoes to my hand and tongue Amen
—thine Oliver Heywood

6

A Solemne Resentment of the Remarkable providences of
god on the year 1688 and some vows to god

This day, which is March 15 168⅞ being the day upon
which I was baptized at Bolton-church in Lancash 59 yeares
agoe, I was much pressed in spirit to spend by my self alone
in solemne prayer and humiliation, and also in the sweet
duty of praise and thankfulnes, for which I am sure no one
breathing hath such abundant cause and so many grounds,
upon personal and publick accounts : 4 times I haue been
upon my knees in the forenoon, wherin my spirit was
abundantly inlarged in thankfulnes for mercys to my own
soul as a Christian, as a minister, to my family, people, and
this year hath not been behind the former, but in some

respects exceeded all that ever went before in gods remarkable appearances in national affaires, the like hath not been heard :

1 for personal, family, and congregational mercys, I may stand wondring and say with holy David, who am I O Lord God, and what is my house, that thou hast brought me hitherto ? 1 It came into my heart, after many debates, and heart-burnings among our neighbours about a meeting-place where we might comfortably improue the foresaid liberty, and whatever was proposed, some were discontented, I say, it pleased god to put it into my heart to build an house for the name of the Lord and my good neighbour William Clay promised to giue me ground to build it on, accordingly I set men on to get stone Jan 25 168$\frac{7}{8}$, they workt hard, they built it, and it was made fit, so that I preacht in it July 8 1688 and haue had 28 lords days comfortably in it, numerous assembly, great priviledges blessed be god, I laid out almost 60ᴸᴵ upon it and doe not repent however things goe for future I must say as David 1 chron 29 14 who am I—that I should be able to offer so willingly after this sort, for I had little help from my people : 2 god helped me to distribute wᵗ I laid by for that end to poor people, and considerably more : Oh that I had been as faithful in performing the rest of my vows : 3 god carryed me safely through my many journeys, into Lanc, Nottinghamshire York &c safely, notwithstanding my old horse fell 9 times with me, yet by the wonderful goodnes of god I was not hurt, except once a stunnying of my foot which was soon well again : 4 god hath graciously helped me through abundance of Work, travelling 1300 miles, preaching 132 week-day sermons, 42 fasts 14 days of thanksgiving, baptized 22 children : oh wt mercy !

Nor were the publick mercys that concern the nation lesse then formerly, but much more, for besides the continued liberty of ordinances there haue been the strangest Revolutions and preventions that ever England saw, a black day grew upon us, a bloody cloud hanged over us, of popery, massacre when all on a sudden a bright sun appeared out of the East, I mean the prince of Orange who landed near Exeter in the West Nov 5 88 with 14000 and Nobility, gentry flock to him, souldiers fell to him this bright sun scattered the clouds, and our feares, K J fled into France

papists fled, or were taken, a pal^t called, sate, chose W P of
O King proclaimed him, day of thanksgiving celebrated
through the kingdom, the whole face of things changed next
to a miracle once in 3 months time, so the managemt of all
things is put into other hands and the scene of things so
altered as if it were a new world, and great hopes of further
mercy, and gracious dispensations both in state and church :
from this time it shall be said what hath god ! my dear
Lord helpt my heart in the afternoon of that day to giue
him the glory of these prodigious acts of providence in these
publick concernes : and my Lord made it a sweet day to my
soul notwithstanding many avocations by several friends :

And now, My dear Lord, thou art my covenanted god, my
sweet and Alsufficient friend, and portion : to thee was I
dedicated by my parents in my infancy in that sacred ordinance of Baptism, how early did my Lord prevent me
with his blessing of goodnes, before I knew god, he knew
and acknowledged me, thou O Lord, didst set thy sheep-
mark upon a poor sprawling infant, my navil was not cut, I
was not washed in water to supple me, nor salted, nor
swadled, I was cast out in the open field to the loathing of
my person, yet thou my dear Lord made that the time of
loue, spread thy skirt over me, entered into covenant with
me, and from that time didst blesse me : for any thing that
I know thou mightest make that ordinance really as wel as
sacramentally the laver of Regeneration, and renewing of
the holy Ghost, and mightest even then convey quickening
grace into my heart, for as my soul had many a bitter pang
in my younger days so I cannot (upon a strict review) make
any probable conjectures when was the time, what the mean
or who the instrument by which my soul was effectually and
initially won over to my dear Lord, howbeit there haue been
such liuely springings of the spirit of grace under some
ordinances, and at some seasons, that I am past doubt the
work of grace is wrought, of wch I haue had some probable
grounds and hopeful conjectures 40 yeares before the Lord
cleared up my condition satisfactorily, which was when I
was prisoner for my Lord in York castle : yet many times
before then did I solemnly renew my covenant with my
dear Lord and pour out my soul to him, and followed on to
know him, tho in the dark, and now I find it is not in vain,
they shall not be ashamed that wait for him—

Blessed, blessed be the name of god, that lookt after me
before I could look after him, that brought me into the
world in so seasonable a time, in so suitable a place, under
such gracious parents, that dropt me into such sweet instructions that prevented such out-breakings of corruption
(tho alas I haue sad cause to bewail the early buddings of
original sin) that gaue me a liberal education, and fixed
many a powerful impression on my heart by his spirit in his
ordinances dispensed by his precious servants blessed be
god, that hath made me a professor, a possessour, yea a
preacher of this gospel-grace, I magnify my office, tho
despised by men, especially under my circumstances, but I
here leaue it upon Record that were I to chuse my calling,
and did I know before-hand all the troubles that would
attend the faithful discharge of the ministerial office, I
would chuse this calling aboue that of the richest merchant
in the Royall exchange or greatest monarch on his throne:
for I tooke on the ministery with another eye then possibly
others doe, the founder of it is the holy god, the gifts belonging to it are the peculiar fruits of Christs glorious
Ascention, the object thereof is the church and immortall
soules, the Ends, the immediate, the converting sinners,
and Edifying the church of god, the ultimate gods glory in a
special manner: and if god blesse an honest ministers upright endeavours with successe I look on it to be more
truely glorious then the conquests of Alexander and
Augustus, however a godly minister shall be glorifyed if
Israel be not gathered: But Oh who am I and what is my
fathers house that god should bring me hitherto! That I
should be so far honoured as to bear gods name and wear
his livery 59 yeares! Oh that such a limb of Satan should
be a member of Christ! an heir of hell be an heir of heaven,
a vessel of wrath to be made a vessel of mercy! grace, free-
grace laid the foundation and hath hitherto raised the building and I humbly hope will lay the top-stone: yea further,
grace called me into the ministry. furnisht me with competent
gifts and graces. grace hath assisted me in all my travels
and labours, grace only hath given me some successe in
converting many soules to god, some wherof are gone to
rest and others are upon their road thither (one of which
visited me the evening of this sweet day to the joy of my
heart) these, these aboue others are my hope, my joy, and

crown of rejoycing, and a brighter crown it is then any princes on earth: this chears my heart in all my tribulations and quiets my spirit in my manifold temptations, and easeth me in my tedious travels in the cold of winter and heat of summer: this is a sufficient recompence for all my layings out, tho the ungrateful world never make reckoning of it, and Christians themselues doe not consider it: peace in my own conscience and acceptance with god is an abundant Recompence: And now, O my Lord I repent of nothing that I haue done or endured for thee, but that I haue done no more and better: my soul is grieved for my omissions and negligent performances, and oh that I could mend my pace in my christian race, and ministerial labours! Thine I am, o Lord, and thee I serue, to thee will I cleaue I will endure all things for the gospel-sake, I will spend and be spent for thee, 38 yeares haue I followed thee in this great work of soul-catching, and soul-saving 12 yeares in the publick temple and 26 and upwards in a private capicity, yet in publick labours, and as I blesse the Lord, I am as fit for studying and preaching this day as ever I was in all my life, so I like my master and work now as well as ever, and hope I shall not abate my diligence while I haue any strength and a call: and if my dear Lord inlarge my liberty (as providence seemes to work that way) my soul resolues by the Assistance of grace, to lay out my strength and utmost endeavours to win soules to Christ: it hath been my meat and my drink to doe the will of him that sent me, and shall be mine endeauour to finish his work: I will chuse and study, and preach on such subjects as haue a direct tendency to convert and edify soules: I will stoop to the meanest capacity, and travel over the poorest creature and greatest sinner, as god giues me oppertunity I will pray more affectionatly for soules, in publick and private, and walk more circumspectly and unblameably before them: I doe, by these presents again subscribe and confirm the foresaid ingagemt of the preceding year, and wherin I haue failed, I will make fresh addresses to the blood of sprinkling for pardon and to the rock of ages for renewed strength: Lord pity my weaknes relieue my necessitys, supply my wants, and thou wilt haue glory thy church profit, and myself the comfort: in humble hopes of Divine grace I enter on the dutys and journeys of this ensuing year not knowing

what a year may bring forth, every year, yea day is big-
bellyed with some burden of crosse or comfort, its welcom
so that god wil be my god, Christ my mediatour and advocate, the spirit my comforter, sanctifyer and supporter : I
will subscribe to every year my Eben-ezer and shall mind
my old Motto By the grace of God I am what I am : I was
delivered out of the mouth of the lion, and the Lord shall
deliver me from every evil work, and will preserue me unto
his heavenly kingdom to whom be glory for ever and ever,
Amen
so subscribes thy humble servant,
hasting to the 60 year, which was   Oliver
the age of Paul the Aged   Heywood

7

A recognition of what hath concerned me in A D 1689
And new obligations : Yet once more it hath pleased the
Lord to spin out my life to the 60th year compleat, this 15th
of March, 16⁵⁹ being the day of my Baptism at Bolton
church 1629, and though I had not the vain ceremony of
the aerial crosse upon my forehead, yet I haue been fighting
under Christs banner, and am not ashamed of the crosse of
Christ, Oh that I may not be a shame to it ! This last year
haue I been also continued in my abundant labours in the
work of my dear Lord hauing upon Jan 14 last reviewed my
last years occurrences, I doe find that I had travelled 1358
miles, preacht 131 times in week-days, kept 34 fasts, 8 days
of thanksgiving, baptized 21 children &c and doe find most
part of my solemn vow performed of distributing to necessitous the 10th part of my yearly income, which is 6ᵘ per
An, for my incom of 60ᵘ a year which I thus distribute, 3ᵘ a
year to my sister Ester Whitehead—for paying her rent, so
much my Cozen W W should pay her out of Bent-hall, but
he hath sold it and is not capable of paying her any thing,
and therfore I think it my duty to help her, especially considering, 1 that my father gaue my sisters but 60ᵘ a piece to
their portions, and he educated us in learning and gaue us
land, (howbeit I have paid for most of both) and they are
children as well as we : 2 my dear brother-in-law W W her
husband prejudiced his estate by his kindnes to My father
and Brother John, paying 50ᵘ at once—so that I think I
am bound in conscience to doe something for his : for the
other 3ᵘ a year I giue it to poor and pious neighbours

2ˢʰ 6ᵈ – or 5ˢʰ or 1ˢʰ a piece as I see cause and haue now
continued it several years and haue elswhere writ down
names and summes distributed, and I think I doe no body
wrong in it, for it is my own, and obtained as the fruit of
my own industry in travelling and preaching 2 yet it is immediatly from God, for I never indent with any wt to haue
but I observe a call, doe my work, take what they give (tho
oft I refuse it as I see cause) god makes my friends able and
willing, and tis of that, I giue : 3 I see many necessitous
in this hard time of bad trading, and a little thing is a
great advantage to help poor people : 4 I haue learned by
experience that my estate therby doth not diminish but increase therby god hath blessed me the more for my liberality,
according to pro 11 24 25 : and besides, 5 since god smiled
upon me in my estate, I doe find my treacherous heart too
much hankering after the world, and think it my duty and
the evidentiall character of saving grace to crosse and contradict those inclinations by contrary motions, Besides 6 my
wife and children will haue a competency to maintain them
when I am gone, and I think it a vain thing to spare and
scrape to leaue superfluitys to surviving relations, I haue
observed the bad effects of it : and 7 lastly, I spend nothing
abroad, all my expences is in hospitality, and liberality, I
doe not spend 2ᵈ in an alehouse for a whole tweluemonth
except travelling yet want nothing, but may well be allowed
to giue to them that are in need, thus I vindicate these acts
of charity, for which no body is worse, and some better
Blessed be god that I haue any thing to giue :

This day then being the Last day of the week, hauing
preacht 7 times, on Lords day twice munday once wednesday twice, thursday and friday, yet blessed be god in perfect
health, set my self this 15th day of march to pray, (for I
was not capable of keeping it, being to travel to Alverthorp
this day) and god helped me with heart-breaking humiliations for my sins hitherto and thankfull adorings of free-
grace for his kindnesses hitherto, about an hour in the
morning in my chamber, and some time in my family to
giue him glory—and then to write down this Reflection and
meditation, and renew my obligations as the year is renewed :

Oh my dear Lord, I am now arrived at the 60th year of
my age, and not one amongst a thousand liue to this age,

and I haue passed many changes and revolutions in the course of my pilgrimage, and must needs say god hath been faithfull, but my heart treacherous, yet I haue often (and doe still) fetch strength from the covenant that was sealed in the ordinance of Baptism to me this day three score yeares, which is as fresh now as it was then, so is the blood that seals it for remission, and so the obligation upon me, and Oh that this day I had an heart to improue the covenant and act over again that sweet ordinance of Baptism! I haue had occasion this week to Baptize 4 children, wch providence hath put into my hands to review and renew my Baptismal-bonds and to bring my own afresh to my Remembrance: I find then there are 4 great Ends, uses, purposes of this seal of the gospel-covenant—

1 It is (sigillum Veritatis) a doctrinall seal to instruct us in many glorious fundamentall truths, as the sign of circumcision was a seal of the rightcousnes of faith to Abraham, Rom 4 11—and therfore the Doctrin of Baptisms, is a foundation-point, Heb 6 2, signifying and confirming all the other Articles, this then is by way of Apposition, confirming the Doctrines of Repentance from dead works, faith towards god, laying on of hands, Resurrection and Eternall judgment: But by my being Baptized I am confirmed in these great truths, taught me in my Baptism, wch I doe firmly belieue, and solemnly professe 1 That there is one only infinit supreme Being, creator of heauen and earth, of a spirituall substance, invisible infinit Eternall, immutable, incomprehensible, yet comprehending all things, the authour and object of the happines of intellectuall and Rationall creatures: 2 That this god, though onely one in Essence, yet I belieue there is three persons, or personal subsistences in the unity of the divine nature, Father, Son, and Holy Ghost, into which I was baptized: that each of these persons hath its distinct personal propertys according to scripture: That this glorious god made all things of nothing by the word of his power, and perfectly good in their kind, and that god created man holy and happy in the state of innocency, in the fruition of all good, communion with himself, Dominion over the creatures, endeared to god by the mutual bond of an amiable covenant: 4 that man by eating the forbidden fruit, lost all his priviledges and perfections, quite violated that covenant, rendered himself and all his

posterity guilty, filthy, obnoxious to wrath, and unable to deliver himself out of this wofull state, but must sink under the curse to all Eternity: 5 That god of his free-grace entred into a new and better covenant, hauing a better mediator, better conditions, and a promise of divine grace to perform them our Lord Jesus reconciling us to god by his death, and purchasing for Elect soules faith and Repentance: 6 I doe belieue that as there is an outward washing with water, so compleat Baptism by the holy Ghost consists in internal Regeneration and being born again by sanctification of the soules facultys, and mortification of the old man, and that these are absolutely necessary to salvation: 7 That in Baptism, pardon of sin, acceptance with god, communion with god, gifts of the holy ghost, an union to Christ, all gospel-privileges and eternall salvation are sealed, to the sincere Believer, together with all the Benefits of Adoption: for we are all the children of god by faith in Jesus Christ, for as many as haue been baptized into Christ, haue put on Christ Gal 3 26 27: had I an eye open, and an heart to conceiue aright of this sacred ordinance of Baptism, Oh how many precious truths might I find therin! how much divine juice and marrow might I suck out thence!

2 Baptism is (signum introductorium) an introductory or initiating sign, by which I am initiated and admitted into the visible church: 1 As the children of Israel were all Baptized into Moses in the cloud and in the sea, i e into the Doctrin of Moses, so am I by baptism admitted into the school of Christ to belieue all devine Revelations: 2 By one spirit we are baptized into one body 1 Cor 12 13, i e into Christ, who is the head, and his church which is the body, not only into a particular society of Christians (for what particular church was the Eunuch baptized into?) But the Catholick church, yea I am joyned to the generall assembly and church of the first-born; part wherof is in heaven part scattered through the earth:

Though Baptism doth not make me a Christian soul, (for by vertue of paternal covenant, and fœderall holines the seed of believers are within the covenant, holy, and members of the church) yet by Baptism I am solemnly entred and entertained amongst believers, and written among the living in Jerusalem, in that sacred Register: 4 By this means I am also joyned to the innumerable company of holy Angels, who doe many good offices : for I may say of these little ones in age, as well as quality, that their angels doe always behold the face of our father, Mat 18 10 : Are they not all ministring spirits (sth the text) sent forth to minister for them, who shall be heires of salvation : I am persuaded the holy Angels are charged with, and doe many good offices for the infants of the church : 5 By Baptism I was interested in the churches prayers, as my own parents groaned out holy Abrahams hearty Ejaculation, Oh that Ishmael may liue in thy sight! so I belieue I haue fared the better for the prayers of those whose faces I never saw, and whose language I understand who conspire in their joynt petitions for all the members of the church militant : 6 And I may plead my paternal covenant and the benefits therof, and say, doubtles, thou art my father, tho Abraham be ignorant of us and Israel acknowledg us not, O Lord thou art our father, our Redeemer : and how often doth god promise to Remember the covenant of parents for posterity ! oh what an incouraging plea is this that god will not cut off this covenant-entail from the posterity of the faithfull ! 7 if the poor infants dye before they arriue to maturity, we haue ground to belieue they shall be saved, not by vertue of their Baptism, but covenant-right for David had good hopes of going to his child in glory though it dyed on the seventh day, before it was to be circumcised : for god saith, I will be thy god and the god of thy seed : Parents and children are wrapt up in the same bond, and sail to heaven in the same bottom of covenant-mercy : god hath brought me through the infancy, child-hood, youth, riper age even to hoar head, Isai 46 34 : Blessed be god :

3 Baptism is (signum distinctium) a distinctiue sign and discriminating Badg, a mark that he sets on his sheep, the abiding character that god imprints on all his, 1 Externally 2 internally : the former is in the outward ministration, the later in spirituall operation of the holy spirit the former is with water, the later with fire : and both are necessary in their kind, John 3 5 verily verily I say unto thee, except a man be born of water, and of the spirit he cannot enter into the kingdom of god : 1 By water and spirit some understand spirit like water, so both one, 2 others think it is water which is (signum visibile) by spirit the invisible grace, as fire is Mat 3 11 : I shall take it in this sense : 1 Theres

the outward sign, it is said, that servants in the Eastern
countreys had in their foreheads the name of their Lord
and master and we know that with us some Noblemen[s] and
gentlemens servants haue a badg on their sleeues, or their
back, for distinguishing them from others: and all the
servants of persons of quality haue their distinct liverys, by
which they are known: now Baptism is the Christians
livery, by which he is distinguisht from heathens, Turks,
Jews, its true its not an abiding impression as circumcision
was, but transient as to the visible token. yet the name, and
Relation remains, and tis as significant and cogent:

1 By submitting my self to Baptisme I doe own gods
authority, and the legislatiue power of Jesus Christ in insti-
tuting ordinances, Mat 28 18 19 all power is given to me—
goe ye therfore—I am satisfyed, that Cht is king of his
church, and fit to rule and govern all the world: this dis-
tinguisheth me from aliens: 2 That I own my self to be a
christian called by his name, Act 11 26 and I am not
ashamed of the crosse of christ, nay I hope to be saved by a
crucifyed Jesus, though to the Jews a stumbling-block, and
to the greeks foolishnes: but tis my greatest honour and
glory: 3 That my name is quite lost, buryed, I am nothing,
greatest of sinners less then the least of all saints let me be
nothing, let Christ be all in all: let me for ever be called by
a new name, all my repute shal be buryed as much as a
wife looseth her first name by her marriage: this is indeed
distinguishing: 4 By this I claim my title to priviledges,
communion of saints, participation of the Lords supper:
as there must be birth before there be external feeding; so a
child may claim his due: none but the circumcised were to
eat the passover and every circumcised Jew was bound to
keep that feast: I am an infant-member by Baptism, and as
an Adult-member may challenge this priviledg if clean, and
duely qualifyd this is a discriminating mark in the churches
account. Thus far (in the outward symbol) an hypocrite
may goe: and if there no more distinction then the outward
badg or our owning it, I may perish for ever: names and
titles goe not far: I may haue a great name to liue and be
really dead: the Jew uncircumcised in heart may fare no
better then uncircumcised in flesh Jer 9 26: my discrimination must be somewhere else:

2 The internal characters graven on the heart, and ex-

ternal course of my life, must be the discriminating Badg
of my Christianity, the spirituall reall effect of Baptism, Oh
that I could feel more liuely fruits of Baptism in my heart,
and life, as 1 Reall implantation into Jesus Christ, this is
true Baptism That I may suck and deriue moisture, sap,
nourishment from him: Rom 11 17: haue I put on Cht
then! I am truely sauingly Baptized: whats a Christian
without Christ? how can I be a member without uniting to
the head? or a branch separated from the vine? or a bride
without espousals to the bridegroom? Lord let me never
please myself with the name without the thing: this indeed
is discriminating: 2 If saving conversion, Regeneration,
as the outward ordinance is the laver of Regeneration, so
this internall is the renewing of the holy ghost, Tit 3 5: Oh
that I could find within me the new creature, the divine
nature, the image of god the renewing in the spirit of my
mind, a blessed stamp upon all my soules facultys: this
transforming by the renewing of my mind would be a discriminating note of true Baptism: a through mortification:
this is an evidence and companion of the former: Oh could
I find that I am buryed with Christ by Baptism into his
death—that my old man may be crucifyed with him, that
the body of sin might be destroyed, and so I may not serue
sin: Rom 6 3-6: Oh if I could find sin more mortifyed,
this would clear my saving Baptism:

4 Resurrection and ascention of soul with Christ, this is
rising-up out of the water, and mounting up to heaven with
glorifyed Jesus: this is a planting in the likenes of Christs
Resurrection: if I be risen with Christ I must and will seek
the things that are aboue, there, there my affections should,
there they shall be, Col 3 1 2: alas, what are these terrene
objects! poor empty nothings, less then nothing vanity: my
home, my rest, my relations my affections are aboue: 5 The
Answer of a good conscience toward god 1 Pet 3 21: alas
what am I better for making a ready Answer to all inter-
rogatorys, unlesse my heart Eccho back therto, and say as
David when thou saist seek my face, my heart answered,
thy face Lord will I seek: if conscience speak for me, and
experience speak within me I may be distinguisht from
others by the fruits of Baptism: 6 The graces and sealings
of the holy spirit this is both a seal and earnest, Eph 1 13-
14: and this clears up my condition, assures me of my

Adoption, and is a pledg of my Eternall salvation : if my conscience thus bear me witnes in the holy ghost what higher discrimination can I have ? 7 Joy in the holy ghost which is one of the great blessings of the kingdom of god Rom 14 17 comforts, refreshment, joy unspeakable, full of glory These are the sweet meats of heaven, the grapes of Canaan, the first-fruits of glory : these indeed discriminate the true Christian from others, this joy of gods salvation antedates those celestial ravishments : May I tast these, and haue the sense of my reconciliation with god Oh what revelations of spirit will it raise in me, what longings to be with god !

4 Yet once more Baptism is (signaculum obligatorium) a strong and binding obligation to the Lord, 1 to parents, 2 to children :

1 To parents, and that in 2 Respects 1 to devote their children to god Oh what an ingagement is this god calls for the fruit of our body betimes, tells us he will haue them to be his, accept them as his and shall we withhold our son our only son from him, he saith all soules are his, but would haue this dedication a free-will-offering yea Lord, take my child as a Nazarite devoted to thee : thus did my parents devote me to thee, thus haue I devoted mine to thee : 2 to Educate their children for god this is the circular motion, the reciprocall acts of god and parents as our Lord Jesus said of his disciples Thine they were, thou gavest them me, I haue given them back to thee thou lendest them back again to me to nurse them for thee, I will bring them up in the nurture and admonition of the Lord, O my Lord, doe thou second my education with thy blessing, that I may again present them to thee with comfort at the great day

2 Its a mighty obligation on children and all Baptized persons to these severall dutys

1 To learn to understand the nature of the ordinance, therfore are we admitted into Chts school not to play but to learn, an heathen said to Rabbi Hillel, (proselytum me fac, ut me doceas) make me a proselite, that thou mayest teach me : you and I must ask our parents, what meaneth this ordinance ? what meaneth this covenant ? this was wont to be one way of Catichizing : Oh for an heart willing to learn !

2 To Belieue the Articles of the Christian faith : Baptism

binds you to giue credit to all divine Revelations without disputation or hesitation : of every divine truth you must say this is a faithfull saying and worthy of all acceptation, shall I be a Christian and not belieue all divine Revelations ? how can I be baptized into the name of the father, son, and Holy Ghost, and not belieue there is such a Trinity of persons in the Unity of Essence ? I am bound to belieue the gospel Mark 1 15 :

3 To consent to all that god requires me to own, yea to take Christ on his own termes, not only assent, but consent as an act of the will as well as mind and intellect : this is receiving Cht John 1 12 : Baptism binds us to take god the father, son, Holy Ghost, one god to be our god, highest End, and chiefest good : Joh 17 3 :

4 To Renounce all spiritual Enemys that fight against the soul, Devil world, flesh, all curious Arts, all pomps, vanitys of the world, grosse sins, and occasions of sin, and a being listed under Christs banner to fight against what opposeth Christ and his interest : Rom 6 11 12 : 13 12 13 : Act 19 19 : 1 pet 2 11

5 To confesse sin, with grief, shame, hatred, and self-loathing, to take a particular account of former miscarriages, and first acknowledg them to god, then to the church wherin we haue given publick scandal or to men we haue wronged, Mat 3 6 Act 19 18 Jam 5 16 : ps 51 : Peccatum non expiatur, usq dum homo oralem edat confessionem : Maim :

6 To dedicate our selues wholly to god in what we are, haue, in doing suffering, the soul with all its facultys the body with all its members, and all that ever we haue, or can doe for god, as volunteers to be at his dispose, and to be no more our own, psal 110 3 : Isai 44 5 : 2 cor 8 5 : Rom 6 16 : 12 1 :

7 To obey the commands of god, this Baptism is a listing our selues under him as our commander, swearing fealty as subjects to their soveraign not that we must promise what we cannot perform, perfectly, to obey, but to endeavour to obey, and apply our hearts to comply psal 119 56, Rom 12 2 :

8 To imitate god and to follow the Example of Jesus Christ : conformity to god is the character of a christian Eph 5 1 : 1 cor 11 1 : 1 pet 1 15 16 not in making, governing the world or working miracles, but in things imitable Mat 11 28 - Joh 13 13 14 1 Pet 4 17

9 To persevere and make progresse in the gifts graces of the spirit, and in the practice of holines abiding in the work and ways of god, and going forward in sanctification Act 11 23 2 cor 3 18 Phi 3 13 14 : 2 Pet 3 18 Mat 4 2 - 10 To make open profession of all this in our lips, liues, this must be in words, deeds, in the sight of men, Rom 10 10—1 Pet 3 15 : Act 8 36 38 : 26 27 : the Jews admitted not proselites till they had asked, and demanded their Answer 1 of the sincerity of their conversion whether it was through fear or loue ? 2 of the Articles of the law whether they believed one god &c 3 of the evil of Idolatry, 4 of the Reward of obedience, punishmt of disobedience, and of a future state in the other world : and upon their Answer they were admitted into the church : that text in 1 Pet 3 21 (of the Answer of a good conscience towards) referres to this :

These things my soul hath duely considered of and been weighted with, and I desire this day to renew my Repentance for my sins of omission, commission, and again to bind my soul to the Lord in renewed actings of faith, and oh that my dear covenanted Lord would confirm this my fresh obligation to him, and vouchsafe some new communications and assistances of divine grace, that my soul may haue clearer evidences of divine loue, clearer discoverys of glorious misterys, nearer communion with god, and may make further and speedier progresse towards perfection, sic Baptizari cupit et Baptizatus Colit,   tibi devotus   sim Oliverus Heywood

8

Some Reflections upon the year 1690 and Resolutions for time following

The providence of god making me prisoner in mine own house, by reason of a sharp frost and deep snow most of this week, part of it I studyed sermons, part of it reviewed the last yeares occurrences, and doe find that I haue travelled 1100 miles, preached 135 times in week-days, kept 40 fasts 17 days of thanksgiving, baptized 29 children—writ my Book of meetnes for heaven in the last years snow— and now this week, on Tuesday Feb 3 169⁷ I was greatly helped all the forenoon to spend some time on my knees and face prostrating my self before the Ld in confessing my sins, supplicating for mercy for my own soul, relations, congregation, nation, church of my god, and to praise him

for his mercys to a poor wretch hitherto : and now on this
5th day of the week and month, I shall once again transcribe
the thoughts of my heart in this paper by such short meditations, reflections, resolutions as then   And god Almighty
ingage my heart in accompanying my hand, that I may
neither dissemble in seeming better then I am, nor contradict these my professions by unsuitable practices in the year
ensuing :

O Eternall Majesty, soveraign disposer of all persons and
things on the face of the Earth, who hast prolonged my life
now through most of my 60th year, and the composednes
of my mind with the health of my body, liberty and oppertunitys of serving thee, blessed be thy holy name, I am got
over the revolution of another year, and will, by the assistance of divine grace look a little both backwards and
forwards, that my heart may be duely affected with, and my
life suitably disposed to both.

In generall, O my Lord, in this lower world of time, we
reckon of succession, by houres. days, months yeares, for
this is suitable to our present state, and time is thus
measured, but the Endles duration of Eternity knows no
such school-boys Arithmetick, but is all infolded in the
grosse summe of (το ννν) oh that Endles, boundles ocean !
how are my thoughts swallowed, and senses confounded in
the contemplation of that I cannot comprehend no nor
duely conceiue of : these short measures will presently be
insignificant termes, Lord, help my heart to dwell only upon
things future and invisible, let me look, not on things that
are seen which are temporall, but on things that are not
seen, which are Eternall : nothing is worth mentioning but
the things that concern Eternity :

2 And how swiftly doth time run on, and hours, days,
weeks, month, yeares, doe pass like a swift river by a city,
and never turn again, all things here below : are upon the
wheel of change, nothing continues in a fixed station,
generations of men and women, enter upon, and passe off
the stage of the world apace, the sun also riseth and the
sun goeth down, the wind whirleth about continually, rivers
doe run into the sea, and thence vapours doe ascend, and
are emptyed out of the clouds upon the Earth, Eccl 1 4-7 :
yea the stage itself must be taken down, this visible world

upon which are acted so many comedys and tragedys, the
two sides of this great globe must be folded together, as an
old vesture they must be changed into another form, but (I
think) not annihilated, psal 102 26, I expect no constancy
in this inconstant world the world passeth away and the
lust therof: heaven and Earth passe away: the glory of
this world fadeth as grasse: it shall not be my center: I
will fix the Anchor of my hope beyond the vail the immutable god shall henceforth be my strength. treasure, refuge
and portion for Ever: farewel transitory transient world,
welcom a city not made with hands, eternall in the heavens
Yea life itself is short, Every day and year added to my life
is so much taken from it: its a flitting shade, a weavers
shuttle, a flying Eagle, a post, a watch by night, we fly
away: how soon are these 60 years of my life past, like
a tale thats told, a dream when one awakes. its but t' other
day that I was an infant, a child, a school boy, and now I
am grown of the older sort, and anon I shall not be here
my place will know me no more: my soul must launch into
the Ocean of Eternity and my body be laid in a bed of dust:
my life is not to be reckoned by yeares, but months, days
houres, hand-breadth, yea its as nothing before the Lord,
Psal 39 4 5: few and evil are my years, its well they are
few since they are so evil: Lord suffer me not to build
tabernacles here: and comforts and crosses doe also fly
away apace, day and night are like two wormes that hourly
gnaw the root of this tree of life and comforts therof, yea
sorrows also passe as the waters that passe away: I will not
be daunted with troubles, nor exalted with injoyments. both
are short-lived: heaven or hell swallow up both: I will look
through clouds and thick mists on a fair day beyond, and I
will despise these glorious gleames that will end in horrid
mists of Eternall darknes:

A little more particularly, I will take a short view of what
hath passed this bypast year, that concerns both my self,
others, and materiall occurrences 1 If I were as rich as
Crœsus, as warlike as Alexander, and as great an Emperour
as Nimrod, and would giue all to retrieue the last year, it
could not be: that was a foolish Request of an expiring lady,
Call time again, alas (post est occasio calva) theres no lock
to get hold of time past by: once gone and ever gone, Esau
found no place of Repentance: if the door be shut, impor-

tunate outcrys cannot open it, if the gulf be fixed theres no passage : no Retrograde motion out of Eternity into time again : no, yesterday cannot be recalled : this morning cannot be fetcht back : a great person cryd out all too late, all too late, A world of wealth for an inch of time : what would damned soules giue for a little time in this world ! Lord, help me to improue oppertunitys, redeem time, work while it is day ; and whatsover my hand finds to doe, doe it with all my might Eccl 9 10, but alas, man knows not his time !

2 I will cast mine eye back again, and review the mercys I haue injoyed this last year : and I may say with David Psal 40 5 many, O Lord my god, are thy wonderful works which thou hast done—they are more then can be numbred : marvellous are thy works and that my soul knoweth right well my many meales of meat, my many nights of Rest, his mercys haue been new every morning, renewed every moment, at home, abroad, on foot and on horseback, alone and in company preventing and priviledging mercys: in spirituals and in temporalls, Oh how many sermons haue I heard and preacht ! how many days and dutys of prayer have I joyned, or be imployed in : what helpes for my soul, what chapters haue I read, what motions of the spirit, rebukes of my own conscience, haue I had ! All these are talents, what haue I done with them ? an account will be called for : what reckoning can I make ? if I cannot make an account to my self, how shall I make account to the righteous judg ? Lord help me to set my accounts streight, and where I am defectiue, act faith in Christs blood for pardon :

3 What sins haue I been guilty of this last year, indeed I may say as David Psal 80 12 innumerable evils compasse me about—they are more then the hairs of my head : Oh how many dutys haue I omitted or negligently performed ! how many vain thoughts haue lodged in me ! what idle words haue I uttered ! how many sinfull actions have escaped me ? if thou Lord shouldest mark iniquity, O Lord who shall stand ? I am cast at the Tribunall of justice, but I flee to the throne of grace : are these my sins repented of, are they pardoned ?

4 What good haue I done this last year, by mouth, pen, purse ? haue I been faithfull to god, to soules ? is this an (Annus impregnatus) a pregnant big-bellied year, as jews call some years ? or hath it been (Annus cavus) an empty

hollow year ? is it filled up with duty in my generall or particular, as a Chtian or as a Minister ? may I not complain, as Titus Vespasian (Amici diem perdidi) who is better by me ? its true I haue been much imployed, but haue I been well imployed : Lord humble me :

5 What deaths haue I heard of this year, what funeralls haue I attended ? Are there not many laid in their graue that were as likely to haue lived as I ? Old, young, rich, poor, strangers Relations, good, bad, are dropt away : many persons are gone of the same age, calling, constitution with me, and why not I ? if god had given death a commission, my soul had left this Body : and whither had I gone ? where had I now been ? doubtles in heaven or in hell : immediatly after death comes judgmt Heb 9 27 : what readines am I now in ?

6 What providences haue I met with this last year, crosse or comfortable ? and how haue I improved them ? what rods of wrath, what cords of loue what sicknesses, recoverys, what losses, dissapointments ? what griefs of heart, and what good improument haue I made of all ? hath not this been an (Annus mirabilis or Miserabilis) upon personal, domestical, or publick accounts ? mayst thou not now set up an, Ebenezer, and say, hitherto the Lord hath helped ? what Elegys or songs of triumph hast thou sung ? what benefit hast thou got by all divine dispensations ?

7 What state is my soul in ? am I the child of god or of the Devil ? in a state of nature or of grace ? Am I a stranger or a fellow-citizen with the saints ? if I haue wandred another year, I am further out of the way, by one years journey : if I be a convert, what progress in holines, increase of grace, knowledg what communion with god ? what clearer Evidences of my state and interest in Christ ? what meetnes for heaven, or preparation for death I doubt I doe not answer my Book writ this Last year : Lord humble and pardon thy sinfull servant :

As for this Ensuing year, I am now Entered upon, I doe purpose by the Assistance of Divine grace

1 Not to make account of long life but get prepared for death : god forbid I should please myself with the hopes of liuing this year to an End, I will not boast myself of to morrow, for who knows what a day or an hour may bring forth Pro 27 1 : I will not Anticipate either my future com-

forts or crosses: sufficient to the day is the Evil therof: I wil liue every day as if it were the last day: my times are in gods hands, not mine own: what sudden deaths haue I seen? why may not I be snatcht away in an instant, oh that I could be always ready:

2 I am resolved not to put off what my conscience is convinced of: but if it be a duty set speedily on the practice of it, if a sin, fall quickly to warre agt it, and mortify it Oh that I could make hast and not delay to keep gods righteous judgments god forbid that I should with Felix adjourn a conviction till a more convenient time: Now only is the accepted time: the wind bloweth where, when how and how long it listeth: it will not always striue: if I put off this day, I shall be lesse fit to morrow: time past is fled away, future is not at my command: O that to day I could hear and obey his voyce!

3 I will be dayly making new vows and renew my covenant with god: as this day I will repent of my broken covenant, so I will tye a new knot, and make additions of new obligations to be the Lords bored servant for ever I haue sworn and will perform that I will keep gods righteous judgmt I will vow and pay, pay and vow this day, this day, my soul write down, what obligation thou hast laid upon thy self, for closer obedience, constant watchfulnes, and dayly intercourse with god:

4 But I doe yet resolve in the strength of god, and would take god along with me: As I would not take my old guilt to a new year, so I am loath to take my old frame into new services, then I shall make bungling work of it: Lord, anoint my soul with fresh oyl: giue me the Assistance of thy holy spirit quicken me, and I shall on thy name create in me a clean heart, renew in me right spirit: stirre up thy grace within me, and bring my soul closer to thee:

5 I will make account of troubles and difficultys this ensuing year: god forbid I should please myself and say I shall have peace, to morrow shall be as this day and much more abundant: I may haue hard service from Satan, world, bad men, good men, my self yea from god Oh that my foot might stand in an even place: I little know whats before me, but whatever it is, if god will be with me and for me, who can be agt me:

6 Therfore I am resolved to put myself into the hands of

god, in doing in suffering: for he is a faithfull creator, a merciful father, a skilfull phisitian, a safe guide: into thy hands O Lord I commend my spirit, and will acknowledg the Lord in all my wayes: he hath delivered, doth deliver in whom I hope he will deliver, and guide me by his councel, and so receiue to his glory:

7 yea once more I desire to be dissolved and to be with Christ, wch is far better then being here: O Lord if it be thy will let this be the last year of my pilgrimage, I haue travelled long enough on this side the mountain: make hast, my beloved and be thou, like to roe or a young hart upon the mountains of spices: come and break this clay-wall, and joyn me to thee in an immediate and Everlasting communion. Oh welcom death that shall come as a messenger to fetch me to my fathers house: I will say with Monica (quid hic facio.) what doe I hear? and with blessed Calvin (usq quo Domine?) how long Lord: not that I am weary of life, or in loue with death through any outward calamitys befalling me, no, I blesse the Lord, I am as free as most men and haue as much comfort and content as ever I haue had in all my life: But oh methinks I am long kept from my dearest Lord, and from that blessed society aboue: I could almost envy the happines of dear and ancient Christian friends, whom I could name, and with whom I haue had sweet communion in private dutys and publick ordinances 20 30 40 yeares agoe, that are now before the throne, and see his blessed face, and god hath wiped all teares from their eyes, whenas my teares are yet on my cheeks: Lord may not this be the blessed Jubile, and year of Release? But as I pray that thy name may be glorifyed, thy Kingdom may come so also that thy will may be done about me and by me, by me here on earth, until I reach to heaven by me here on earth as its done in heaven: and if thou hast any service for a poor worm in thy church militant, I am both willing to it and thankfull for it: only qualify me for it, fortify me agt all oppositions, sanctify to me all dispensations, and giue me a glorious successe in my poor endeavours for thy glory, and thy churches good and the longer I liue and labour for thee, the higher the glory and brighter the crown shall be to   thy aged servant
Feb 5 169⅔   for ever
      Oliver Heywood

9

A review of the year 1691 with new meditations upon renewed occasions

I am arrived at the close of one year more, and haue taken a view of my motions, condition, providences ordinances I haue passed through and upon the whole can truely say as David, Psal 23 6 surely goodnes and mercy haue followed me all the days of my life, I shall dwell in the house of the Lord for ever: the remarkeable Experiments of the year by past speak out both these Attributes powerfully exerted and exercised for and to this poor sinfull worm, god hath dropt goodnes upon me in all my ways, and drawn forth mercy to me, when in misery: there was some Reason why I fell short in travelling and doing work, because my dear Lord thought fit to excercise me some time this year in suffering work: the later was as welcome as the former: for gods rod and his staff haue comforted me: there is oft as much of god in the wildernes as in a Canan, an Eden: he speaks to the heart in the former: then cordials are most sweet, and seasonable This year, I travelled 833 miles about my masters busines, preached 103 week-day sermons, kept 37 fasts 11 days of thanksgiving, baptized 20 children: yet the hand of god was laid upon me in an intermitting feavour, with 6 severe ague-fits, that seized upon my spirits, and kept me 8 lords days from preaching in my chappel, and much longer did my weaknes hinder me from travelling abroad; I had promised to be imployed in 4 places in the beginning, but god discharged me of all my promises by laying his arrest upon me, my distemper begun Oct 1 I went not to chappell till Nov 26: 91: methoughts god sent such a message to me as by Isaiah to Hezekiah, set thy house in order, for thou shalt dye and not liue: But I could not turn my face to the wall, and weep, for my heart was not so tender, yet I was not afraid of death, nay I longed for it, and when many judged me a gone man, I was afraid it was too good news to be true, and was loath to be sent back from the port and haven into the tumultuous sea of a wicked world with a wicked heart for god had immediatly before given me assurance of his loue, and some foretaste of heaven: had I dyed then, I did not question my kind reception into the celestiall paradise but my dear Lord fetcht me back again from the graue: for indeed the people of god

would not let me dye : they kept severall days in severall
places, and many prayd with me and took hold of gods
strength and stayd his hand from falling on me, and god
was willing to be prevailed with for me : it was their kindnes
to me, and gods kindnes to them : and a double mercy to
both that it came as a return of prayer : Phi 2 26 27 : to
god alone be the glory : I had the advice of skilfull phisitians
the care of faithfull attendants, proper medicines, but god
saith I am the Lord that healeth thee : yea the poor heathen
Arabian Doctor, upon long experience, cryed out (solus
sanat languores Deus) I must say it, and adore absolute
soveraignty in it : But Oh that my soul could understand
for what End my Lord did carry me to the graue, and then
countermand that Arrest, and say return ! it may be he
brought me so low, to quicken prayer, awake some conscience, magnify his power, goodnes, and let me see w^t he
could haue done, And possibly my dear Lord did raise me
again, 1 to seek w^t was lost, who knows but I may be sent
into this wildernes to seek a straying : Lord succeed and
speed me herin : 2 to fetch what was forgot, had my soul
forgot god, and the incomes of his grace ? Lord now help
me to remember thee, and fetch in new strength, and inlargements from aboue : or 3 was it to doe that better that
I had marred, alas my conscience tells me how lame my
spirit is, how short my dutys and obedience, Lord make me
more liuely in the practice of godlines : or 4 is it to leaue
behind what I had too much of, alas I haue too much filth,
corruption : Lord help me to mortify the flesh, dye unto sin,
liue unto righteousnes : or 5 was it to strengthen what was
weak was there not some grace in me ready to dye, Oh that
god would perfect what was lacking in my faith, loue, repentance, hope humility Lord that grace may come to its
full pitch, and due proportion : 6 or is it to clear up what
was dark or doubtfull ? was there any flaws in my Evidences, Lord remoue them : Oh that I might arrive from a
dawning to a meridian brightnes ! from good hopes through
grace, to a plerophory : I cannot be too sure upon scripture-
grounds : or 7 is it to leaue some legacys with my surviving
family or people ! Lord tell me what they are, be it truths
or dutys, Lord giue me understanding to know and faithfulnes to presse them home on consciences : 8 Is it to set a
better Example then I haue done ? how defectiue haue I

been herin ? Lord quicken my preaching that my people
may follow me as I follow Christ :—help me herafter to doe
something laudable, imitable 9 Is it to feel or see that evil
I never met with, persecutions, afflictions, publick personall,
outbreakings of corruption in relations ? Lord help me
with faith and patience to goe through all chearfully : 10 or
is it to behold returns of prayer in the churches deliverance,
or injoying personall mercys ? Oh for a frame of spirit,
suited to mercys to rejoyce in a prayer-hearing god ? let
what will come, so my heart and disposition may be suited
to divine dispensations :

And now, oh my soul, what hast thou to doe under the
late providence what is the work that lyes before thee Methinks tis a voyce before thee and behind thee, that Janus-
like thou shouldest haue two faces, one to look backward at
what is past this last year, the other forward at what may
fall out herafter :

1 Then, O my soul, consider and reflect upon wt is past
this last year, thou hast received abundance of mercy, committed much sin, omitted or carelessly performed many
dutys and born some chastisements, and what reason hast
thou to expect all good, and no evil at the Lords hands ? is
not god thy soveraign and can he doe thee any wrong ? is
he not thy father, and will he doe thee any hurt ? thou
hadst injoyed 37 yeares health, and wilt thou be offended
with god for a months sicknes how unreasonable is a quarrel-
som spirit ? no no, I will not dispute with my maker, but
turn my Eyes inward and reflect on my own heart and life,
in these considerations 1 Oh my soul, hadst thou no just
cause to fear that affliction or some other severe dispensation ? haue not thy ways and doings procured these things ?
did not the deadnes hardnes, dulnes, worldlines, unbelief
hypocrisy, formality of thy heart in a sort presage these
things to thee was not this the language of the rod, soul,
what hadst thou been doing ? hast thou not stipt into sin ?
slept in security, been wanton in prosperity ? dost thou not
remember that such a time thou performedst duty sleepily,
formally, distractedly ? and now I come to visit thee for
these things : should not my soul say, yea Lord, I acknowledg thy justice, my offence, and freely accept of the
punishment of mine iniquity :

2 O my soul review thy carriage under the Affliction: how didst thou behaue thy self? what graces were excercised? what meditations of god what dutys performed? Alas, Alas, this affords matter of shame and grief for besides the naturall deadnes, and contracted badnes of my heart, the disease seized upon my brain and spirits, and rendred me uncapable of any devine or even humane excercise it was indeed my great grief and sad complaint that I did chatter like a crane or swallow Isai 38 14 that was my first text, in my own house: and was not this my sin also? I am sure it was a punishment of my former sins: Oh for a repenting heart!

3 O my soul what if god had taken thee out of thy body, and sent thee into Eternity under this disease, where hadst thou been? was thy state safe? were thy Evidences clear? and not blurred? hadst thou not only habituall but an actuall meetnes for heaven? were thy graces in liuely excercise? review it again, o my soul, the matter is weighty, its a solemne thing to launch forth into the ocean of Eternity heaven and hell are momentous cases, it[s] dangerous to be under mistakes it may be god saw thee unready, and may discover more to thee then yet thou wast aware of; be sure thou deal faithfully in this concern:

4 And what good hast thou got, O my soul under this Affliction? it is so far, and no further sanctifyed to thee as thy heart and life is sanctifyed under it: what hast thou learned in this house of correction hath it been a school of instruction to thee? Olevian sd in hoc morbo didici quod sit peccatum, quanta dei majestas? Oh my soul, hast thou found the weight of the guilt of sin upon thy conscience, as wel as the effect of sin in punishment of thy carcasse? hast thou trembled under the sense of gods Majesty and displeasure? hath this fiery furnace melted the metall of thy hard heart? and cleansed away thy drosse? thy Affliction was not joyous, but grievous but hath it brought to thy soul the peaceble fruits of righteousnes? Oh my soul, thou wilt either be better or much worse after this disease: the rod either hardens or softens:

2 Oh my soul, look forward also, and see what my dear Lord calls thee to, under this providence:

1 Be afraid of sin, especially pride and security: pride and self-conceitednes were the sins Hezekiah fell into after

his recovery, 2 kin 20 12—17 : was not my heart apt to be lifted up with multitudes and qualitys of visitors, the Esteem and prayers of gods people ? with the Lords signall appearance for me ? I am afraid I haue been too much tickled with pride and vain-glory : Lord humble me as thou didst Hezekiah for the pride of my heart : 2 chron 32 26 : And now I am recovered, oh my sensuall soul, art thou not apt to please thy self now with hopes of long life, and presume without ground of a longer day, when the date of thy days may be near an End : danger is oft nearest w^n fear is furthest off :

2 O my soul perform thy vows and make new ones : say as David Psal 66 13 14 15 : I will goe into thy house with burnt-offerings, I will pay thee my vows, which my lips haue uttered, and my mouth hath spoken, w^n I was in trouble vow and pay unto the Lord thy God Psal 76 11 : oh my soul, say to god as David, Psal 116 12 - 18 w^t shall I render to the Lord for all his benefits towards me—I will pay my vows to the Lord—and vow again, saying O Lord, truely I am thy servant, I am thy servant, the son of thy handmaid, thou hast loosed my Bonds : I am thine by creation, Redemption, the spirits possession, and self-dedication : thou hast pluckt me out of the hands of Satan, world, flesh : they haue nothing to doe with me, and I will not tamper with them, thou hast laid fresh obligations on me, put new dispositions in me for renewed Acts for thee :

3 I will endeavour by the Assistance of grace to trust god in new straits he hath delivered, doth deliver, in whom we trust that he will deliver is scripturall Ratiocination : its true new straits call for new faith, former actings of faith will not advantage in new tryalls, except by calling up new experiences, which yet are not foundations, but incouragmts to faith, his power, wisdome, mercy, faithfulnes is still the same : he is as able and willing to help me now as formerly why should I distrust him ? in all hazardous adventures I will cast my self at his feet, if I perish, I perish—from this time forth I will call upon god as long as I liue : I will wait for the salvation of my god : and tarry gods time till he help me : for in the mount of the Lord it shall be seen :

4 I will study to regain the thoughts and impressions my soul had, or can desire to haue had in the day of my Affliction : this was the advice of the French kings chaplain, be

and doe that in health, that you wish you had been or done
in a fit of stone, or sickness : Lam 3 19 20, Remembring
mine Affliction and my misery, the wormwood and gall my
soul hath them still in Remembrance and is humbled in me :
I haue smarted for my sins, I will goe away and sin no
more : I was short in my Repentance faith, loue, humility,
new obedience, oh that I could get those defects made up :
now Lord lift up my heart to thee, Oh for clearer evidences,
dearer loue to god, nearer communion with him : my soul
will follow harder after god : Lord, suffer me not to depart
from thee : help me to make up in my health the defects of
my sicknes : to be the more actiue now, as I was sluggish
then : to study to make up what was wanting in the year
bypast And blessed be my dear Lord that hath this day Jan
8 made up a breach betwixt J P and me, that was a gaping
bleeding wound all last year I take it as a pledg and presage
of further and future mercy, this ensuing year : And Oh
that this mercy may be issued in bringing in soules to my
dear Lord : my dear Lord hath directed my thoughts to
pertinent subjects, Oh that the holy Ghost would second
and set home those weighty truths : may I preach as one
raised from the dead, and my people hear me as one risen
from the dead : but my parts are low, my graces lower, my
heart much out of order, Lord, set all right mend whats
amisse, make up whats wanting, accept w^t is thine own and
pardon what is mine : Accomplish thy work in me and by
me : if I liue to the End of this year, let my graces be
stronger, corruptions weaker, my heart better, my life holier,
my assurance firmer, and my soul sensibly nearer to, and
fitter for my heavenly inheritance : if I dye before the close
of this year, Lord take me home to thy self, that where thou
art there I may be also : I haue conversed with gods people
here, I will wish with Augustin and   a german
Divine (ut quem admodum in templo terrene essent coacti,
ita et in Cœlesti illo templo æternum una viorvent)
sic opta !   Jan 9 9½   Ol Heywood
    A gratulatory review of the by past year 1692
    I haue only this day Feb 7 169⅔ at liberty to be at home,
hauing been yesterday at a fast at T H in Horton, must be
if god please at W N, the day after at R R, the day after
that at J L all days of fasting and prayer, upon wch I mostly
preach and therfore I take this day for a Recollection, which

affords me abundant cause of thankfulnes : and oh that my soul were scrued up to the highest rapture of holy admiration for the lovingkindnes of god to me the year by-past ! I may say as David, day unto day utters speech night unto night declareth knowledg : publick mercys, personall mercys, domestical mercys, congregationall mercys, preventing mercys, priviledging mercys, temporal, spirituall mercys, thousands, yea ten thousands that haue escaped my observation : so many so great, so circumstantiated, that I am amazed upon the review of them :

1 I will begin with our publick nationall mercys, in the peace wherof we haue peace : the continuance of the peace of the kingdom when the guilt of our unheard of abominations crys dayly to heaven for vengeance against us : when our civil and Ecclesiasticall dissentions are multiplyed, when multitudes of vipers are in our bosom ready to eat out our bowels : when such a potent enemy as France is so ready to take advantage agt us : and K James is continued aliue hauing his agents and factors among all degrees to open him the door, and bid him welcom. when I think also of the great danger our K William is in at home and abroad, amongst open enemys and fals friend, the plots and treacherys by land and sea, discovered and prevented this last year, the ill-will some grandees bear to our gracious soveraign, and the discord and court-emulation amongst themselues, the generall outcry of the comminalty of oppressions by great taxes and sessements to maintain the warre when I think of these and many more apparent grounds of fear, hitherto superceded by divine providence, I am ready to say, this is the land cared for, from the beginning of the year to the later End of it : god almighty holds the reins in his hands, and stills the raging of the sea and tumults of the people :

2 No lesse is the wonder of publick liberty of the gospel, and spirituall priviledges maintained and increased this year to great admiration : the vast numbers of new meetingplaces erected all over the kingdom, the multitudes of hopefull young men sent out of private schooles yearly to supply them, the vast summes of money distributed through the kingdom from the fund at London for maintenance besides many private well-meaning gentlemen building meetingplaces, and giuing comfortable incouragement to ministers

and all this by Act of Parliamt, King, Lords and commons, in the open face of our Enemys, who gnash their teeth at it, but cannot hinder it, the laws being in force, but penalty taken off, prelacy in power, and many great ones bearing us no good will, and the rabble so much agt us : in consideration of these things I am astonished that the gospel should get so much ground, as it hath done even this last year : and I conclude that either this is break of day, and it will shine brighter and brighter till it come to its meridian splendour, or god is a making hast to gather in his Elect before he remoue the candlestick, which I pray god prevent , But the meaning of these things I doe not understand :

8 My own domesticall mercys haue been strange and very remarkable, that god should spare our lives, so that for this 81 years and upwards no death had broken our little Family, though I haue been apparently under the sentence of death, my wife also, and my two sons at severall times, yet god hath spared and notwithstanding many of our neighbours and naturall relations are laid in the silent dust : god hath preserved the health of our family, and peace in all the members of it : tho sicknesses and contentions are in many other familys : the Lord hath found us out competent supply, though we haue been put to extraordinary charges in hospitality, and my own poll-mony came to 4^{li} , and my own acts of charity haue exceeded, and our constant incomes haue been small, yet I cannot discern that we are run behind, blessed be god : yea although the fire hath consumed many houses wind blown down others, and thieves haue broken into severall houses, and rob'd some of our friends, as thieues broke into Mr. Dawsons house in the night and took plate and goods worth near 8^{li} (as his wife told me yesterday) yet god hath secured our habitation, and given us competent and abundant accomadations, comfort in our neighbourhood, Freedom from phrenzy and distraction, which I know some other familys sorely afflicted with : Oh wonder of mercys : Blessed be our good god :

4 And my personall mercys haue not been short of the former : my Arithmetick here failes me, and falls short in Enumeration they cannot be reckoned up in order unto thee, oh Lord my god, if I would declare them, they are more then can be numbred : I can but touch at the kinds and general heads of them :

1 my outward temporall mercys are indeed innumerable and remarkable such as few injoy, my health hath been continued in great measure, I haue convenient dwelling a lovely companion, hopefull sons, faithfull servant, no sad disaster, or afflictiue accident, kind friends abroad, louing neighbours about home, strifes ceased, great peace in our congregation, when I goe abroad I haue a good strong, chearfull, surefooted horse to ride upon, company usually to attend me, and though old age comes on for I shall be 63 next moneth, and my journeys must lessen, yet this last year 1692 I haue travelled near 1000 miles, preacht near 100 times on weekdays, kept near 50 fasts 14 days of thanksgiuing, baptized aboue 20 children: and in all this I haue not got any dangerous fall, or met with any disappointment, though I haue been twice in Lancashire, once in Nottinghamshire, twice at or as farre as York &c: in all which god still ordered my affairs very mercifully far aboue my expectation, in sending me to relieue a poor kinswoman in debt, to see my dear sister Hilton take her farewell of the world and mounting to heaven, &c: in all which as my mercys were common with others, so they accented to me with a peculiar Emphasis in severall respects:

2 But the soul of my mercys, were the mercys that concern my soul: Oh how many a good hour haue had with my dear Lord in a corner? especially every morning, when my heart hath freely gone out to my dear Lord, and god hath been no niggard in letting out himself to my soul: I haue risen out of my bed fallen down on my knees by my bed-side with my wife, thankt god for that nights mercys, had nothing to doe but goe to my chamber, read my chapter, sometimes a comment theron, (Calvin on Harm. of Luke John, Acts, I read over within the year 1692) fell down on my knees, prayd, went down, made ready, had breakfast, family-prayer, went to my study (except I had some whither to goe) there I studyd read, writ till noon, dined, walkt to some neighbour an hour after dinner, came home took my pipe (in doing which I read in some book, read over many thus doing) went to my study, continued till 4, then read my scripture comment, prayd, went down, we had supper, prayer, went again to my study till 8 or 9 a clock, read some good book to my family till bed-time, then upon our knees put ourselves into the hands of god: ordinarily slept

comfortably: this is my manner of life, none visit me, but christian friends, in w^m is my delight: I goe not to dinners or feasts, nor doe I visit any but such as are sick, or upon spiritual accounts, Lords days are the sweetest days in the week, fast-days are my feast-days, studying and preaching sermons is my recreation, young-mens conferences my delight   god hath also inabled me this year 1692 to write two Treatises, 1 The best Entail, or parents grounds of hope for their surviving children from 2 Sam 23 5 which I finished, sent up to be printed, but because paper was dear, they would not print it but upon unreasonable terms to me, therfore it came back to me and I haue it, 2 the other Family-altar upon gen 35 23 which I haue finisht and sent away Feb 4 9¾ whether it shal haue the same fate or no I know not, but this I can truely say I haue been industrious and spent my time for the good of the church, and chiefly for the glory of my good god: and haue comfort in it: Blessed for ever blessed be my glorious and gracious god that hath helped me hitherto: I will set up the stone Ebenezer: Let all the glory be the Lords, for nothing is due to me: If I haue been or done any thing for god it is grace that helped me, by the grace of god, I am what I am, and if I haue any successe in my labours, praying, preaching, printing the glory therof belongs to the Lord not to me, no not to me, a poore insignificant worm. Alas I am but a tool for god to work by, a pen for god to write with, the meanest of all gods minsters lesse then the least of all saints: let the crown be set on the head of free grace: Oh what rich mercy is that god should single me out to be a vessel of mercy! that god should set me apart to a minister of his glorious gospel, that the great god should open a door for me, and when my sins had shut one door should open another and another successively! who am I that my life should be preserved, and so often restored, when better then I are laid in the silent dust? that the great god should make me so industrious so that I may truely say without a lye or vanity—I haue laboured more abundantly then they all: and blessed be free grace that my labour hath not been in vain: but I am persuaded there are many soules in heaven praising god for his word in my mouth, and more travelling thither-ward: yea some brought to life since god raised me from death: I knew not gods design then, but now

I see it was for gracious Ends: Lord perfect that which concerneth thee: goe on still, second thy word in the mouth of thy poor worm: I doe here afresh giue my self to thee: it is for thee I labour and lay out my strength and time: I desire to liue not one hour longer then to serue thee: and gladly would I dye immediatly to injoy thee
Feb 7 169⅔   even poor Oliver Heywood

Some pleas with god upon a review of the two by-past years 1693 and 1694

Upon my review of my diary, in the year 1693 tho I did not spend the day of my Reflection in solemn humiliation as sometimes, yet upon Jan 3 I writ that I had travelled 841 miles, preacht 109 week-day sermons, kept 35 fasts, 12 days of thanksgiuing, baptized 22 children, and this year, viz 1694 upon my review Jan 2 I find I haue travelled 735 miles, preacht 90 times besides Lords days kept 38 fasts, 17 days of thanksgiuing writ severall treatises:

But this day Jan 8 9⅗ hauing a little leisure and a fair oppertunity in my chamber, I determined to spend some in solemne prayer, I began with reading my usuall chapter in course in greek wch was Mat 27 betwixt 6 and 7 a clock in the morning then down on my knees, spent about an hour in confessing my sins before my dear lord committed the yeares by-past, beginning at my originall corruption, and god did help me with som meltings and relentings then went down to dresse me to family-prayer, betwixt 8 and 9 went up again, determined to spend some time in pleading with god for mercy, I read psal 77 with some tears applyed part of it to my case, prostrated my self before god, was greatly assisted in pleading for mercy, in my personal and publick concerns, as a christian, and as a minister, then I read 1 chron 17 concerning my family, the affairs thereof called me in a peculiar concern to plead with god, which I did for about an hour, being called off to giue something to a poor Irish traveller, I returned to my work, read Isai 37 about nationall affairs, spent som time in pleading with god, was greatly helpt Oh w^t a sweet heart-melting forenoon was it! blessed be god:

Oh my dear Lord, I haue by thy wonderfull hand of providence past another year in mercy haue spent one week in another year, tho a vile cumber-ground, by the interposing mediation of my alsufficient mediator doe now prostrate my self at thy Majestys foot-stool, giuing thee most hearty thanks, setting up an Eben-ezer saying with thy servant David 1 Chron 17 16, Who am I o Lord god and what is my house that thou hast brought me hitherto ? thy kindnes hath contradicted my demerits, and fears, surmounted my hopes and expectations : theres scarce such an instance of divine benignity under the heavens, thou hast regarded me according to the estate of a man of high degree, O Lord god : thou hast made me a member of, yea a minister in thy church, which is indeed an high degree, an office more fit for a prince then a peasant, an Angel then a mortal man, thou hast found me out imployment, publick and private, at home and abroad, hast given me estimation and affections of thy people, hast crowned my labours with abundant successes hast giuen me many visits from heaven, and maintained my lot, and continued me now in some measure of faithfulnes against all oppositions this 44 yeares in this neighbourhood : yea thou hast spoken well of thy servants house for a great while to come : thou hast giuen me two hopefull sons, (a third I hope is in heaven) whom I haue given back to thee, in the ministeriall function My Elder son this last year hath obtained a wife, a prudent companion and therby favour from the Lord : aud hopes of building up my house, thou hast called my son John to pastoral imployment in Pomfret, giuen him an heart concerned for the good of precious soules, and who can tell what spirituall children he may beget in the gospel ? many prayers are filed up in heaven and mounting up to heaven for him : What can thy servant speak more unto thee for the honour of thy servant for thou Lord knowest thy servant : my outward conveniences are not inconsiderable, thou hast giuen me Agurs choyce and lot, neither poverty nor riches, but food convenient for me, hast rather increased then diminished my estate this year : And thou, O my god, hast told thy servant, that thou wilt build me an house, therfore thy servant hath found in his heart to pray before thee :

O my dear Lord, the Eternall everliuing, ever-loving, covenant-keeping, prayer-hearing god, I thy worthles servant, the meanest of my fathers house, and my fathers house the least in our English Israel thou hast taken me, as it were from the sheep-coat, one of the weakest parts and shallowest capacitys of all my fellows, one of the blackest sinners amongst the sons of men, as unlikely and crooked a block as any wretch that ever passed under thy pastorall rod, to bring into the bond of the covenant: yet such is thy transcendent condescending loue, that thou hast been with me whithersoever I haue walked,—and hast made me a name like the name of the great (at least good) men that are in the earth: thou hast lifted me up and thou hast cast me down: in temporalls, in spiritualls, I haue in my day I I haue passed through straits and abundance, liberty, imprisonment, comforts, crosses, honour and dishonour, evil report, and good report, as sorrowfull, yet always rejoycing: my journey to my heavenly Canaan hath been up hill and down I haue met with sweet and bitter, checker-work of black and white hitherto of my days: like sea-faring men, somtimes lifted up to heaven, and presently plunged in the deepest Abysse: but be it so, god is still the same, and changeth not, therfor I am not consumed, whatever disorders or instability there is in my house or heart, I am sure the covenant of grace is ordered in all things and sure, and therin is all my salvation, and all my desire Although he make me not to grow I haue fixt my staff, I haue pitcht my tents under the shadow of thy wings, thou, O Lord, art my rock on which I repose my self, thou hast entertained great sinners propped up weak saints, comforted grieved spirits, relieved released tempted soules, I can set my probatum est to all thy soveraign Receits:

I haue found a belieuing prayer to be as a merchant-ship to fetch good commoditys from a far countrey, a privy key to unlock the treasures of heaven, a channel to convey divine influences: sometimes guilt sets a lock on my lips, and hardnes stupifys my heart, and deadnes benumms my conscience and affections, I am so troubled that I cannot speak, and I am troubled that I cannot speak the agonys of my heart: but presently the tide is turned, and the holy spirit giues free vent to my boiling thoughts: thence flows a torrent of affections, inlarged affections and ebullitions of soul, my heart goes out to god, because god comes in to my soul: he is a free agent, as the wind that comes and goes, moues and blows where and when it listeth: Blessed be god, that my spirituall state and eternal happines depends not on my mutable ebullitions, and out-goings of my heart or

variable motions of his spirit but on his Eternall thoughts
of loue to sinners, Christs death and the infallible promises
of his blessed covenant, there I repose and venture my immortal soul, and tho comforts and inlargements ebbe and
flow yet free-grace, Chts merits, the spirits necessary influences are the support of

thy bored servant O H

A review of some passages in the year 1696 and backwards
upon munday march 15 169⁷ my Baptism day so often
repeated being the 2ᵈ day of the week called munday I resolved to spend the forenoon in secret in my chamber with
god, after morning-devotion both in my chamber and family
I set my self to my work, betwixt 8 and 9 a clock, and continued till about 12—

1 I sought the Lord for a blessing upon my knees, and
he gaue me a token for good

2 I read Rom 6 to direct me in the due improuement of
Baptism, then prayd

3 I read Rom 7 to affect my heart with the corruption of
my nature, then fell on my knees confessed my sins from
my infancy to this day, was helped

4 then read Isai 40 to instruct me in the glorious promises
of the gospel and majesty of Jehovah, then fell down on my
face, was helped to renew my covenant with god, to take
god the father son, Holy ghost for my god and to giue up
my self to him, I hope sincerely

5 then I read Isai 62 to help my soul in pleading for the
church of god and spent some time in prayer, but not so
affectionatly as in the former excercises for which my soul
was afflicted, fearing that prohition in Jer 14 11, yet struggled with my own heart a season, but still was short of what
I desired, and that assistance I perceved in former dutys :

Being called down to dinner, after wᶜʰ returning to my
study I made some Reflections on what past the former
year

1 upon casting up my diary I find I haue travelled last
year 1696 aboue 700 miles, preacht 65 sermons in week
days, kept 34 fasts, 15 days of thanksgiuing baptized 17
children, writ 6 Treatises but none printed, except Jobs
Appeal in 95

2 many sweet experiences I haue had of communion with
god in my chamber and Remarkeable providences about

myself and my little family at home and abroad, though I
haue put in fear often by the distempers on the bodys, both
of my son John and his wife :

3 God hath given me abundant supplys in worldly concerns this year, though many are brought to poverty, are
hard put to't by decay of trade, scarcity of mony, breaking
of chapmen, yet I haue rather laid up then run into debt
blessed be god—

4 I haue had more invitations to considerable places this
year then in many years before, 1 Halifax, where they haue
built a large meeting-place and pitcht on Mr. Nath Priestly
to supply every other day, and Mr Priestly and some others
spoke to me to supply the other vacant day once a fortnight
I had preacht the first sermon in it Nov 11 1696, but durst
not promise to come constantly, only told them I would
help them occasionally at some seasons, which I haue done,
and got supply for Northourum :

2 Oct 14 1696 came two men from Manchester, Mr Wyke
and Mr Matt Pinkerden purposely to giue me a call to Mr.
Newcoms place and supply in joyning with Charlton in their
spacious and famous meeting-place in Manchester they were
so importunate, that I could [not] tell what to say to them, but
put them off that time, they writ again and again but I gaue
them a positiue denyall, that I was resolved to stay where I
was :

3 upon wednesday Febr 17 169: I received a letter from
my son Eliezer at London, giuing me a solemn invitation to
be pastor to Dr Annesleys people there several of his members put him on to write, saying if there was any hopes of
my removall they would giue me a solemn call : But I stopt
it there, and next post writ in the negatiue to my son, gaue
him 7 Reasons why I could not remoue : which satisfys
them, to trouble themselues no further

And who am I, O Lord god, and what is my fathers house
that thou hast brought me hitherto ? I haue continued 67
years in the world, and 46 years in this neighbourhood,
publickly and more privatly, and my old hearers are more
unwilling now to part with me then ever : some of them are
sensible that salary is but small, little aboue 28ll a year,
that I maintain considerable hospitality, that severall are
now gone off from us to Halifax, and some of my friends
inlarge their contributions, without my asking, for I never

stood upon terms with them nay I haue told them, give me
any thing or nothing, I am resolved to stay with them, and
would draw my last breath amongst them : for

1 This was the first and only place that I haue been
settled in : 2 many of them haue adhered to me in difficult
times, and in my imprisonment : 3 god hath given me
many seales of my children born to god in this place whom
I dare not leaue : 4 I cannot but forsee the sad consequences if I should leave them for none will serve them at
the rate that I haue done : 5 god hath giuen me an house of
mine own and I haue been at the charges to build them a
chappel, and let them haue the use of it gratis, and my
habitation is very near it ; 6 I haue somthing of mine own
yearly coming, for necessary supply and I desire not riches,
since my family is small, and my sons are educated. 7 I
haue many Christian friends in the countrey, whom I visit
and to whom I preach, that are kind to me, and some
indigent places for whom I haue procured supplys and I
think if mine own people would let me goe, many others
would not ; And alas how long haue I to liue ? what a bad
example would it be to others and what a reproach would it
raise agt us, that we are covetous, and would remoue for
more means : and I cannot expect that either Manchester or
London would heaven : I might meet with troubles there,
and then call into question my call to remove : besides its
ill transplanting a tree that thrives well in the soyle, as my
father Angier writ to me about my going to Preston, he
added when I sent you without staff or scrip lacked ye any
thing, they said nothing : and I cannot say I haue wanted
conveniencys, nay god hath abundantly blessed me in this
place : Besides I haue seen the sad effects of some persons
remouing to greater places : yea I am sure my poor gifts
are more adapted to a meaner village then a great town or
city and I am sure I haue a numerous assembly constantly
and a society to whom I administer all ordinances as many
as I am able to oversee or discharge my duty : and I think
my genius and constitution suit more to a country then
city-life :

The Eternall god, the Lord Jesus Christ the Holy Ghost
one God, three persons whom I haue chosen as my chiefest
good and utmost End, and haue many times in the uprightnes of my heart giuen up myself unto, this god hath laden

me with mercys, as many as I can well bear for temporall
mercys : 1 god hath giuen me a pious, provident, prudent,
sweet natured wife, whom I love entirely and she loves me
dearly, and is exceeding tender of me, almost to an excesse
with whom I haue liued very peaceably almost 30 yeares : 2
god hath giuen us both our health in a comfortable measure
tho we haue both been under the sentence of death by a
dangerous feaver since we met, which was but for a short
season, but we are free from agues stone, chollick, or any
such acute painfull diseases, or lingring distempers or runnings, which many are sorely afflicted with : 3 god hath
kept death out of our family 36 yeares my dear wife Elizabeth dyed at her Reverend father Angiers at Denton
AD 1661 : and since that time we haue had a continuance
of the same number we were, and the addition of my very
dear wife : 3 I haue two very comfortable sons, that are
exceeding tender of me, beyond compare, both absent and
present, when I was sick, and when well and as their mother
is as affectionate towards them as an own mother can be so
are they as loving and dutifull as to their own mother : 4
god hath added to our family two very louely branches, my
son Johns wife, a very sweet, desirable, and I hope pious
person who took him out of pure loue (not knowing whether
he should have any thing or nothing tho she had aboue 400ᵘ
portion however I haue since giuen him half of my land in
little Leaver) I think I may say she had him upon the
account of Religion, looking on him as a godly minister and
they liue very sweetly togather blessed be god : 5 god hath
added one more, and giuen them the fruits of marriage, a
very louely son, a Timothy, a return of prayer, dedicated
to god in Baptism, so called after Mr Timothy Jolly whom
my daughter in law owned as her spiritual father who was
also my son in the faith as Timothy of old was Pauls, this
yong Timothy my grandson is aboue a year old, comes on
apace, and I hope may bear gods name up in the world as
well as mine in after times : 6 We haue a faithfull, laborious,
conscientious and quiet servant Susanna Tillotson whom we
haue had in our family almost 16 yeares, that kept house
for us carefully and providently that year when we were in
York-castle, indeed a non-such servant with whom we haue
scarce ever had an angry word, however she never answers
again : who naturally cares for family-concerns, and is very

prudent, and I hope feares god : 7 My habitation where I
liue is mine own purchased 25 years agoe, where I haue
liued comfortably, the house, where I first set up house
when first marryed about 40 years agoe, where my 3 sons
were born, where my owne mother ascended to heaven, the
only house I would chuse in all the country a good house,
yet little land that I might not be cumbred with worldly
busines : 8 god gaue me money to build a meeting place
very near my house, that holds many hundreds of people
every Lords day, so that I need but to take a few steps out
of mine house into it, which is a great convenience to me in
mine old age after all my tedious travels : 9 god hath cast
my lot amongst peaceable and louing neighbours in the
village of about 12 or 14 familys so never any difference
hath fallen out among us, and they all generally come to my
chappel, and are seemingly glad of my neighbour-hood : 10
god hath blessed me with a competent estate and tho it
be visibly a smaller income then many haue yet I doe
experience a secret blessing in what I doe injoy so that besides my yearly expences in family, in entertaining friends,
in acts of charity, I doe every year lay up something : 11 I
haue great safety at home freedom from robbers unreasonabe
men and when I travel abroad, amongst the thousands of
miles I haue rid, and many dangerous falls I haue had, I
never broke bone or put out joynt in all my life, wch many
haue met with : 12 the dayly accommadations I haue had,
wholsom meat, hansom cloths, sweet sleep, fire to sit by,
good chamber to sit in, books to read, pen and ink, my
memory, invention, the use of my eyes, ears, hands, feet, all
members in due order what shall I say ? Psal 40 5 many
O Lord my god are thy wonderfull works which thou hast
done—they cannot be reckoned up in order unto thee if I
would declare and speak of them they are more then can be
numbred :

one thing more as an outward mercy (which occasioned
this meditation) is a good esteem among ministers and
Christians, which is no contemptible mercy : 3 Joh 12 De-
metrius hath a good report of all men, and of the truth
itself : this god hath honoured and owned me with as hath
appeared by many demonstrations, particularly this in the
louing invitations I haue had abroad and respect I haue at
home, god forbid this should feed an ambitious humour, yea

it humbles me but I must not bury this in the graue of silence, but adore god in it as an introduction to doing good.

But 2 the best blessings and most sweet and necessary are my soul-mercys, which as they are infinitly of more worth, so they are no fewer: these, these are the soul, life marrow of mercys, god himself, Jesus Christ, the holy spirit, one god, my god, who hath in the covenant of grace made over himself to me, and all his perfections to be imployed for my good: who hath giuen his own and only son, to lay down his life for me, to reconcile me to god, and is becom my prophet, priest, king who hath called me by his grace, put spirituall life into me who was dead in trespasses and sins, inlightened my mind, convinced my conscience, bowed my will renewed and fixed my affections on himself, giuen me an heart to belieue, to repent, to obey the gospel, in-gaged my soul in solemn covenant with god, hath conquered Satan for me, subdued sin in me, loosened my heart from the world helpt me to loue and fear god, to hate sin, and to abstain from appearances of evil, it was only free-grace that hath divorced me from vain company, and brought me into the society of godly christians from my child-hood to this day: O what sweetnes and satisfaction haue I had in com-munion of saints, many of whom are long since landed safe in heauen : O the blessed private fast days of thanksgiuing, and conferences I haue had ! how sweet haue sabboths ser-mons sacraments been to my soul ! many a time haue I sitten under his shadow with great delight, and his fruit hath been sweet to my soul ; he hath cast me down and raised me up by his word and spirit : many sweet refresh-ments and baits in my journey haue I met with in gods sacred institutions : Oh but what out-goings of soul, and incomes of grace hath my soul met with from god in secret ! my dayly communion with god hath been the sweetest seasons in all my life, I haue crept to my dear Lord every morning and other times, and he hath not been a stranger to my soul, there and then hath he giuen me his loues and not disdained my secret groans, sighs and teares : I would not change those exchanges of loue for all the pur-chases on earth : O the kisses of his mouth, the sealings of his spirit, the opening of his treasures of grace to my soul ! though it hath not been always so, yet sometimes my dear Lord hath taken me into his wine-cellar and his banner over me hath been loue : I can truely say that god deales familiarly with man : Oh what multitudes of sins hath god pardoned ! what abundance of prayers hath he answered in kind ! what doubts hath he answered, fears dispelled griefs removed, yea my god hath performed all things for me : these last years I haue been laden with mercys, in my privat and personall capacity, as a Christian, in my publick capacity as a minister, I can look no way but mercy surrounds me, which are past my Arithmetick : O what shall I render to the Lord for all his benefits towards me—I will pay my vows unto the Lord now in the presence of all his people, and make new vows—

A review of the year 1697,

Upon Tuesday March 15 169$\frac{7}{8}$ I was providentially at home, and this was very contrary to my promise, call, inclination, for Tho : Farrand of Bradford came purposely to my house feb 28 to desire me to come to his house to keep a fast with Mr Priestly, Mr Wright, Mr Bairstow and other Christian friends for his wife, near her time, I promised studyed a sermon purposely, they sent Abr firth Clark purposely for me March 14—I got me ready, was booted, spurr'd, but it was a mighty wind and sore rain, my wife declared her utter unwillingnes to let me goe, I durst not venture sent him back alone, undrest me, set myself to study, god helpt, the day following (wch is my Baptism-day wheron I must haue been from home if I had gone for I must haue stayd all night) as god in his providence ordered it, I stayd at home, set my self to spend some time alone in gods work, I was helped in my usuall work, before breakfast and prayers, after that I went up resolving to spend till noon in secret worship, I begun about half hour after 8 designed confession of sin, renewing my Baptismall covenant, read, commented upon Rom 6, god did greatly help me in that work prostrate on my face, pleading with god, about an hour : then rose up purposing next to plead for my wife and children to that purpose I read Gen 48 my heart was much melted in reading it, and in praying for them with warm affections I rose up and designed to spend some time in pleading for my congregation I read 1 Cor 4 did plead both for Coley chappelry and my poor meeting and lastly I read Isai 41 and again fell down on my knees pleaded with god for the church, king, kingdom, I was not so inlarged in this last as in the former continued till near 12 a clock—

this last year viz 1697 I haue but travelled about 500 miles being hindred by old age a severe cold I haue had yet haue preached 82 sermons on week-days kept 40 fasts 15 days of thanksgiuing, baptized 12 children, writ aboue 100 letters writ some treatises, but printed none:

There haue been 2 remarkeable occurrences this year, of composing differences, which had much excercised my thoughts:

one was an old controversy of 10 years standing betwixt old J P* and me about a field he should haue bought for me and bought it for himself: I was silent but JS told him of it, saying he dealt basely with me, the controversy being thus unadvisedly started, grew high, severall meetings in vain, sharp letters, censures past he forsook us, both at sacrament and also fast-days, I tryed all means for accommadation, but all in vain, at last I bethought myself of this expedient, upon Lords day night I called about 12 of our chtian friends Oct 31 1697, told them J P had done me no wrong about the field, I was sorry if I had giuen him any just occasion of offence &c they acquainted him with what I said, he was well satisfyed, sate down with us at the Lords Supper, comes to our private fasts, and hath been at my house severall times, and shews himself very friendly blessed be god for this sweet return of prayer, I must say as Jacob, Gen 33 10

The other was Mr Timothy Ellison, curate at Coley, taught our school, let it goe to naught, I took my 6 lads away, he lockt the school-door, took the key with him which when we demanded, he sent me 2 or 3 angry letters challenging an interest in our school which we had built from the 78 canon I writ him a peaceble letter, desired him to meet me and let us louingly debate things, we did meet he was very high, threatened to enter me into the spirituall court, which I dreaded, he demanded a great summe of money, which he s^d I owed him for teaching I gaue J P† jun the purse with all the money I had in it, wch I had of Ld Whartons Executors, bad him please him out of it, upon condition he would resign up the title he pretended to in the school, accordingly JP gaue him 3^li 12^sh, Mr Ell—gaue a resignation

* Jon^n. Priestley.   † Jon^n. Priestley, junr.

under his hand seal, and discharge wch we haue, and set another master to teach the day after viz Mr John Paul after the school had been vacant near half a year, by which means we had so much money in Bank, and he was the more willing because, he was for going from Coley to Sowerby

Another happy accommadation god made me an instrument of was betwixt old Joseph Wright and his son Joshua, it had been long in sharp debate about a piece of land at Shipden head, I persuaded Joshua to giue his sister Bently 50^{li} (tho by law it fell to him) he yeelded, they were not contented with that, we got him up to 60^{li} accordingly on Jan 12 169⅞ we met at his house sealed writings betwixt them at least 8 writings, and parted friends blessed be god

I haue had abundance of mercy, notwithstanding a severe cold severall times, but cured by gods blessing upon the use of means viz a glasse of sack in the morning with the yolk 'of a new laid egge, drunk down in the morning, and walking upon it to me it was medicinall, for curing my cough, shortnes of breath, 3 severall times let god only haue glory

last night viz March 22 169⅞ I had letters from Mr R S* and Mr R Thorsby of Leeds and some mony to distribute to severall dissenting ministers, and receits to be subscribed, some by my means, viz these were legacys of the Lady Mary Armine deceased, disbursed by her Trustees being part of her legacy or charitable gift bequeathed to poor ministers in the countys of Huntingden, Darby and York part wherof was thus disbursed, viz

1	Mr Joseph Dawson —	02^{li} —	00	—	00
2	Mr Nathan Denton —	01 —	10	—	00
3	Mr William Hawden—	01 —	10	—	00
4	Mr Thomas Johnson—	01 —	00	—	00
5	Mr Mathew Smith —	01 —	10	—	08

this is for the whole year, the rest he sth he sends by Sheffield or York Again he sth I paid to Mr Ludlow 11^{li} 10 to be thus distributed as formerly

1	to Mr Dawson	2 li	—10^{sh} for closes
2	to Mr Denton—	2 li	
3	to Mr Jonson	2 li	
4	to Mr Oates for Hockton	2 li	
5	to Mr Walker for Bingley	2 li	

* Stretton.

for the propagating of the gospel in those places, this is
upon the account of the fund, and thus much is every half-
year, by order of managers of the fund—through England
and Wales.

All this and much more is giuen to other ministers, and
not one peny to me and indeed it is not because they denyed
me, but because I haue not asked any thing, besides 10^{li} a
piece of transmit to Bingley and Bramhup

and yet I am apt to think scarce any of these ministers
but they receiue more of their people then I doe

for Dec 6 1696 the contribution was but 4^{li} 14^{sh}, a quarter,
Octob 14 1696 March was 4^{li} 7^{sh}: June 13 97 it was 4^{li}
14^{sh} 6^{d} Sept 12 97 the contribution at the table was 4^{li} 12:
Dec 12 97—it was 4^{li} 13^{sh} 6 March 13 97 - 4^{li} 8^{sh} which
amounts not to 20^{li} a year:

But I am freely contented with it, tho I think I am put to
more charges then any minister, my house standing near to
my synagogue, theres scarce a Lords day but I haue 6 or 8
or 10 at dinner at my table besides many others in the house
that haue broth and bread, but upon sacrament-days which
is every 8 weekes we haue usually 20 at table and that eat
with us, besides abundance more, thick and threefold that
haue broth and bread and bear, sometimes my maid sth she
hath 50 upon her hands to serue, last Lords day which was
our supper day there was 8 cakes of oat-bread spent, and she
ordinarily buys 2 joynts of meat on the saturday : and a good
part of a barrel especially in summer time is spent : Any
one would think this course will not be endured, its enough
to beggar any body.

To this I must reply, which is matter of wonder to my
self, that notwithstanding this, and the frequent acts of
charity I am called to, yet I sensibly discern that I grow
rich, hauing laid out 140^{li} on a farm in Sowrby, and 150^{li} on
a morgage in Holdworth this last May 1697 and haue 20^{li} —
which I lend to persons in necessity, 10^{sh} I gaue to Nathan
Halsted 10^{sh} to John Butterworth, 5^{sh} to Mr Jollie, 5^{sh} to
Joshua Sonier, a guyney to Cozen Ester Longworth, 50^{sh} to
Cozen James Lomax on my mothers account—besides many
shillings and sixpences last year

Youl say how is it possible all this should be done out of
such small incomes ?

I Ans 1 I have some yearly rents coming in out of Lanc:

tho I haue giuen my son John a farm of 8ⁱⁱ a year, yet I haue about 14ⁱⁱ a year therin, 7ⁱⁱ a year in Sowrby 7ⁱⁱ 15ˢʰ in Holdworth of late

2 my Lady Hewley hath usually giuen me 5ⁱⁱ a year, My Lᵈ Wharton 3ⁱⁱ a year, and somtimes I haue somthing giuen me when I haue travelled abroad, tho age cuts me short in that of late, sometimes funerall sermons and others dropping in, sent by the wise providence of god to excercise faith

3 I haue a notable provident prudent wife, who manageth matters both frugally and hansomly, and makes a little goe far, besides, I spend nothing wastfully, not 2ᵈ in a year, besides what I giue, I goe not to market, or if I goe to Halifax I usually set up my horse at a friends house and drink no shots :

4 But the blessing of god is the main which makes rich and addeth no sorrow this I haue found by abundant experience many years, some that haue had 5 times my incomes haue been put to great straits as Mᵗʳⁱˢ Hide sᵈ to my father Angier, Sir god works miracles at your table for if I set twice as much meat to such a company they would eat it all and think they were pined, its like the womans barrel of meal and cruise of oyl : and indeed tis matter of admiration to think what multitudes of poor people come weekly and dayly to our door, from Halifax and elsewhere besides other mendicants that come with papers, and many of our own society Blessed blessed be god, for this secret and refreshing supply according to psal 37 3 16 : 3 33—I haue not plotted and plodded about worldly matters, yet the Lord hath wonderfully supplyed me—Oh for a thankful heart, and fruitfull life !—

A review of the year 1698

I was to haue gone to Mr Brooksbanks to Ealand upon March 15 9⅗, but desired it might rather be the wednesday before that I might be at home my Baptism-day but in the mean time received a letter from Mr John Faircroft that he would visit me upon busines out of Leistershire that day March 8 which he did, and therfore went to Ealand, kept a fast March 15 and therby was prevented from spending some time alone that day, but wednesday after viz March 22 169⅞ I resolved in the morning to spend that forenoon in meditation, reading and prayer, was much helpt about 7 a clock, immediatly after 8 (when breakfast and family prayer

were over, I set again to my work, craved the Lords assistance, begun with reading psal 94—95 was helped very
sweetly till 9 in pleading the cause of my poor soul, confessing sin, praying for grace, and pardon, successe of my
ministry O how sweet was that hour! then I read a chapter,
prayd for my wife, my two sons, Mr Taylor a dying (as I
had intelligence from my son John the night before) my
servant and some others till 10 a clock, god helpt sweetly in
giuing him the glory of mercys to my wife in recovering her
of her bleeding &c for my two sons, from whom I had letters in these last 8 days, then I read Isai 40 was much
affected in reading ver 12 of gods infinit greatnes, fell down
on my knees and then on my face, pleaded with god for
Zion, conversion of Jews Gentiles destruction of Anticht,
deliverance to the french protestants, was in some measure
helped to plead for England, Scotland and Ireland, particularly for K William for Parlt, made bold to desire of god
this token for good that if the Lord had any mercy for us
by them, that he would incline their hearts to issue out a
proclamation for a fast, to humble our souls for the abominations in the nation, god helpt me to plead for reformation
of Magistracy, ministry, about another hour then my spirits
fainting I desisted, went down to my wife, then set upon
writing this account—Blessed be god

This last year 1698 I travelled for preaching work 410
miles, preacht on week-days besides Lords day work 78
times kept 84 fasts, kept 16 days of thanksgiuing, baptized
11 children been at 6 meetings of ministers, writ 123 letters,
and 4 treatises not printed distributed 38li to ministers
schollers, which I received from the Executors of my Lord
Wharton, reconciled two great differences amongst own
brothers wherin god hath made me successfull beyond my
expectation: received of my hearers 23li and otherways 18 li
spent 80li in house-keeping besides what I haue giuen to
poor: which I am at the tenth peny:

And now, O my soul, what hast thou to boast of? just
nothing let my sins be set anent my dutys they will exceed
them to infinit extent: if I haue done anything thats good
its not I but the grace of god with me: But alas, the good
that I would doe I doe not, but the evil that I would not doe
that I doe: theres abundance of defects in my best dutys: I
dare not stand by the holy performances for justification in

point of commutatiue justice, its well if I be found worthy
in a gospel-sense according to distributiue justice: I haue
carryed a bad heart with me to all I haue donc, I haue
missed it in the manner and End, when I haue done all I
am an unprofitable servant: woe is me, how much pride,
hardnes, deadnes, unbelief, security, distraction cleaues to
me! men see my outward acts, none see my inward paines:
men will scarce belieue what a world of sin lodgeth under a
fair shew: its well if it haue not dominion over me, I am
sure it hath great possession of me: my iniquity preponder-
ates my piety: one sin would be enough to damn me: I
dare not trust to my own righteousnes, Lord forgiue the
sins of my prayers: I must weep over my teares, yet that
weeping will make god no compensation: my omissions are
more then my performances, yea the evil of my performances
is far more then the good therin: I am cast and condemned
if the new-testament Aaron doe not bear the iniquity of my
holy things: I only depend on Christ's sacrifice for satisfaction to justice, and on his intercession for the acceptance of
my person and performances: there I rest, there I center
my soul: I am nothing, I can doe nothing, suffer nothing,
deserve nothing but wrath, if ever god own and saue me its
infinit grace, free grace, I will only set the crown upon the
head of grace running to me through the merits of Jesus
Christ:

Blessed be god that hath brought me hitherto through
varietys of dutys, difficultys, mercys, miserys, companys to
enter upon the 70th year of my life, the age of a man,
whether I shall liue to accomplish that year I know not, nor
am I much concerned, so I may liue to god and finish my
course with joy in his service and to his glory: I said to
my Lord this day, when laid along on the floor now Lord
strike the stroke, and stop my breath and welcom, that this
poor carcasse may never rise, but be carryed to the graue,
so my soul might ascend to heauen: But I am risen, in
health this breath I giue to thee, this carcasse and all its
members shall be for thy use and service, this soul and all
its facultys shall be for thy glory, I am here to comply with
thy mind to be at thy dispose: service or suffering this
ensuing year shall be welcom: make my heart sound in thy
statutes search me to the bottom, discover all the falsehood

and fallacys in my heart let me be weighed in an eaven bal-
lance that god (and myself) may know mine integrity: leaue
me not to myself: hold me by my right hand that my soul
may still follow hard after thee: giue me this year some
more seales of my ministry: set my soul some sensible
steps nearer heaven: let me haue some further attainments
towards perfection : oh that I could bring forth still more
fruit in old age to myself and others, and in both to god :
help me to arise and depart, for this is not my rest : my
soul is aspiring after my Everlasting rest aboue :

This day being the 3ᵈ day in the week called Tuesday Jan
23 16.⅟₀₀ hauing reviewed the last years diary, cast up accounts and keeping house that week for any thing I know, I
designed to spend the forenoon in solemn prayer and seeking
god—and hauing read my chapters below in the house viz
Gen 47 and 48 I went up into my chamber betwixt 6 and 7
a clock, spent some time in my ordinary morning devotion,
wherin god did inlarge my heart, came down, washt me,
took breakfast. my wife read Isai 25 I prayd in the family,
we had Lydia Booth to help Susan in brewing I prayd for
her and her aged mother, then went into my chamber a
quarter after 8, set my self to my work, stood up craved
gods blessing and assistance, I resolved to confesse my sin,
in order to that I read psal 88 a psalm to bring to remembrance, fell down on my knees, but presently was surprized
with sleepines, rouzed my self severall times, was somthing
helped at last, then rose up, read Psal 143 reflected on it,
fell down on my knees, begged pardoning sanctifying grace,
gaue up my self solemnly in covenant to god, accepted Christ
as prophet priest and king. and my heart was much drawn
out, I rose up read Job 33 fell down again, pleaded with god
for my wife children servant, severall Christian friends, and
some relations particularly, was something helped therein
and for my society and all my hearers for converting grace,
then rose up and designed the spending the rest of the time
for publick, read Hosea 13 and 14 fell down on my knees,
confessed the sins of the nation, deprecated gods wrath,
pleaded with god for the land. but alas my heart was much
shut up, yet a little helped for poor protestants, agt Anticht,
—thus continued till towards 12 a clock, blessed be god

A review of the year 1699

This day being March 15 1708 the day wheron I was baptized 70 yeares agoe as I find it in the Register at Bolton in Lanc - where I was born, I hauing preached a preparation-sermon at my chappel this day, when company was gone, I set my self to reflect on some passages of my life-past

1 the day of my Baptism, M^tris Andrew of Little Leaver being the person that held me when I was baptized, when Mr Gregge the vicar there had said those words (I baptize thee in the name of the Father Son and Holy Ghost) she stept back off from the steps and so prevented my being signed with the sign of the crosse, she did it purposely to prevent it which I am glad of since I heard it related that I was not signed with that addition which I look on as not grounded on the word of god, and it may be was a providentiall presage of my prouing a N C Minister :

2 Though I had not that mark yet I own the crosse of Jesus Cht and desire to know nothing saue that and hope I haue not been ashamed to own it in a scripturall sense, yea I haue born the crosse voluntarily near 40 years under the frowns and persecutions of men, censures, and spoiling of my goods, banishment, imprisonment and haue cause to thank god for these marks of honour :

3 I haue by the assistance of divine grace devoted my self soul and body many and many a time to the Lord and accepted the Lord Jesus as my prophet, priest and king in submitting my self to his government as he shall think fit to order me to walk in his ways, fight his battels bear his yoke which I take as the highest honour I can haue on earth, let my Lord doe what he will with me :

4 Though I haue not the aeriall crosse of mens devising, yet I had water sprinkled on of divine institution, wch I account better and more significant O for the blood of Christ sprinkled upon my conscience, to cleanse my soul from the guilt and filth of every sin and to cool my guilty conscience scorched with the sense of guilt, Oh that the Holy Spirit would apply the sufferings of Christ to me !

5 I am ingaged by my Baptism to our god the father, god the son, god the Holy Ghost as our god, one name, one nature, I doe own god the father as my chiefest good and ultimate End, to whom I come by faith through the mediation of the son and by the assistance of the Holy Ghost thus I worship god, thus I rely upon him expect all from

him, return my gratitude to him: Oh that I were incor-
porated into his family, may receive the blessings of the
covenant from him

6 My busines now is not only a participation of water-
baptism, but the Baptism of the spirit Alas what will the
outward Baptism of water advantage me without inward
Baptism by the Holy Ghost? What am I better for being
ingrafted into the visible church the society of those that
professe the name of Christ, unlesse my soul be by faith
ingrafted into the mysticall body of Christ to be joyned to
the Lord that I may be one spirit with him according to 1
Cor 12 12 13 : Joh 3 5

7 My soul dreads to be under the old covenant, the
covenant of works O that I may be brought within the
covenant of grace, the badg and seal wherof I am under : I
am undone if I be still in the old Adam, involved in the
guilt of the breach of the law of innocency for I can haue
no life by personall perpetuall obedience, but Oh for an
interest in the second Adam, who hath fulfilled all righteousnes and purchased pardon and life for poor sinners,
according to the freenes of his grace and riches of his
mercy in Christ.

8 Yet further my soul pants and breathes after the conditions and dispositions to which these promises of the
covenant belong : that is faith and repentance without
which graces the Devils haue as good a right as I : these
are solemn and necessary graces Oh for an heart to accept
of Christ upon his own termes, to mourn evangelically for
my sins, hate them, remoue sin, self, and all thats incon-
sistent with the grace of the gospel :

9 It becomes me solemnly to reflect on my course of life
how I haue kept my Baptismall vow Alas childhood and
youth are vanity Lord Remember not the sins of my youth,
and multitudes of backslidings since my soul owned this
covenant in truth, how many are mine offences but I trust
in my dear Redeemer for pardon according to Tit 3 4 5 6 7 :

10 Yet once more I am solemnly bound publickly and
perpetually to own this Baptism I received in infancy Lord
assist me in so doing, not only inwardly but outwardly, with
my tongue, and hand, subscribing to it, professing to whom
I belong in the midst of persecution, to ingage me to all

dutys to god and man, and mortifying corruption, Resisting temptations &c

A Review of 1700

Upon March 12 17$\frac{00}{01}$ I stayd at home, set my self solemnly to spend all that forenoon in secret prayer in my chamber—because my Baptism-day lights on the last day of the week, according after I had performed usuall chamber-work, and family-duty, at 9 a clock I went into my chamber—set upon my work, read psal 51—fell on my knees humbled my soul for sin, pleaded for pardon, grace, about an hour, god greatly helped, then read Isai 64 prayd for the church and nation god helpt then read psal 102 prayd again—for the interest of Cht abroad in the world was helped—then read 1 tim 4—set upon a pleading for my sons—congregation, Relations—till 12 a clock—it was a sweet forenoon blessed be god—after dinner I walkt to Ab Whitwams prayd with his wife Grace—Tho Bentleys prayd with his daughter Mary in small pox, called of Will Clay—talkt with his son John—returned found old Jon Priestly who told me the good news of a fast, other good news—which was an Answer to my poor prayers that morning—

O what abundant cause haue I to admire the gracious providences of god to me this last year upon many accounts which this day March 15 17$\frac{00}{01}$ I desire to contemplate, wch is the 71st year of my life, longer by far then I made account to haue liued, longer then my mother, brothers or sisters haue liued, or most of my Relations except my own father, who was aboue 80 years of age—o what haue I been doing? what doth the Lord spare my life for, from year to year?

this year by-past 1700 I haue had these signall Experiments

1 I cannot but admire that I should be kept aliue when so many of my age and under of this year are laid in the silent dust, of whom I haue a catalogue it hath been a year of great mortality:

2 This time twelue-months I was taken very ill, when both my sons and their wiues came to see me in a great fright, and I was lookt upon in great hazzard, but am better now then I was then

3 my wind hath been exceeding short so that it hath been great difficulty to goe up into my chamber, yea when I haue

laid me down in my bed I haue panted, and cought as if I should not haue ever returned, haue had much adoe to get my breath, was scarce able to walk to my chappel—or any neighbours house,—yet when I haue got settled in my pulpit, I haue prayd and preached administred Baptism, Lords supper with as strong a voyce as formerly, which many people haue wondred at—

4 Though I haue been confined for severall weeks and months to mine own house, and durst not ride, yet god found me out suitable work for I writ 7 severall Treatises, had a call to write them, some pretty large which some young men transcribed and possibly may be printed—god kept me in good measure of health and at ease in my body, tho my wind is still short, yet I haue not stone nor strangury tho I am forced to sit much, almost altogather though many of my brethren, and some much younger then I are wofully torn and tortured with such acute diseases blessed, blessed be the name of my god he is the god of my life, health, soul and authour of all my comforts—

A review of the year 1701

Upon Febr 4 170$\frac{1}{2}$ in the morning I desired to spend the forenoon in prayer which I attempted to doe, and begun about 9 a clock, read Psal 142 143—set about humbling my soul for personall sins, begging grace and mercy in gods sight, but alas for a considerable time I was so distracted and confused I could make nothing of it, yet in a little time divine assistance came in then I read another scripture prayed and praised god for my wife, children, Relations, congregation rose again read Isai 62 set my self to plead with god for the church conversion of Jews fulnesse of Gentiles, the Destruction of Antichrist, and ordering the present warres betwixt the Emperour of Germany and the King of France and Spain and Italy to his glory, then I set my self to pray for England, but alas my heart fell, I was daunted, whatever the issue will be, yea it hath been frequently so with me, yet I dare not but goe on in pleading for the interest of Christ in these poor kingdomes—While I was thus puzzling my wife called me down to speak with John Bently about the Baptizing of his child—I went a little to my study again but could doe little—W Clay came after dinner I studyed in the afternoon—god helpt in my work—the morning after I heard that Susanna Baxter was delivered that night of a son, for whom I had prayd, blessed be god.—

I haue had multiplyed mercys this year

1 my life is still prolonged notwithstanding my many infirmitys, especially my sore affliction of the Asthma or short-breathing which hath so increased upon me that I could not walk to my chappel on foot but my friends haue provided me a chair in which two men carry me they begun Dec 7 1701 by Joshua Stocks and John Craven—whom I pay :

2 Yet was enabled when I got into the pulpit to preach audibly—baptized 8 children, kept 8 conferences, preacht on week-days 23 times. writ 7 treatises 4 short for Warly-people, 104 letters observed 14 fasts, 3 days of thanksgiuing 2 Books printed viz the two worlds and Christs intercession —my dear Lord was with me all along—

3 my dear wife had a long and dangerous feaver in July which kept her ill 8 or 9 weeks—she would haue been gone desired me not to pray for her life I gaue her into gods hands beg'd her again—yet with submission to gods will and he answered my desire—but is weak and tender still hath not yet been at the chappel, this is Feb 5 170½ yet is very helpfull to me and to others tho she be coming towards 70 years of age

4 tho there be many deaths about us yet death hath not broken in upon me or mine aboue 40 yeares except a little son of my son Eliezers which they called Oliver, that was about 7 days old, though my son Johns two children Timothy and Elizabeth haue had chin-caugh small-pox and other sore diseases this last year, yea my son John hath had dangerous distempers upon him but hitherto the Lord hath spared them blessed be god,—but who knows w^t the next year shall bring forth ?

I haue capacity for studying sermons writing much—sleep well and eat my meat well have a good digestion have much ease only fits of caughing but are quickly over—blessed be god—

[The good man lived three months after this date.]

Self-reflections*

1 Novemb 1 1677 in the evening I set my self to the practice of much-neglected duty of self-examination, and my soul issued itself in such thoughts as these which for some reasons I am willing to write down:

My soul, thou and I haue been long strangers, I goe on in the profession of religion, and preaching, studying, performing of religious excercises, alone and in company, but dost thou not read of considering, searching a man's way? doth not god command persons to commune with their own hearts hast not thou in thy publick ministry lately prest this duty? doth not the Apostle call for all Christians examining themselues whether they be in the faith? proue your owne work as the best remedy agt-self deceit? are not trying times coming on? is not self-judging in the petty sessions a good help to prevent or prepare for the great assizes? hath not god indued thee with a soul and self-reflecting faculty for this end? and shall this be in vain? is not the matter of very great importance? are salvation and damnation inconsiderable in thine eyes? art thou content to goe hood-wink't and liue in a confused unceartainty? would not a through self-tryal pay for the trouble of it and the issue bear its charges in the advantages of it? art thou so earnest that others doe it and wilt not thou doe it thyself? wilt thou bind burdens on others back and not touch them with one of thy fingers? surely my soul this is a profitable duty, it is so difficult, it is most likely to be necessary because a subtile devil and a wicked heart doe so much oppose it, and is this indeed so hard? is it such a long journey for a man to travel into his owne heart? shall the difficulty of it discourage thee? nay shall it not rather quicken thy endeavours considering its necessity: oh my soul how oft hast thou beene bungling at the work, sometimes in thy closet, sometimes on the road as thou hast

The marginal scripture references alongside the above paragraph read: Ps 44; 2 Cor 13 5; Gal 6 3 4.

* In the same book as the foregoing " Covenants and Reflections." On the fly-leaf:—*Bought at Halifax, cost 6d., by me Oliver Heywood.*

travelled in ordinary, and extraordinary cases, under a heart-rending affliction, or before thy participation of the Lord's supper, but thou hast done it but by halues, thou hast ask't the question, but what answer hast thou returned? or hast thou proved the answer? hast thou weighed thy self in scripture-ballances? and doth thy tryed, proved, approved state, and the proofs therof stand upon record, its true I find in a little book with clasps 20 evidences of my state gathered and registered aboue 20 yeares agoe, but is it enough to doe it once? is it not time to renew thy self-reflection, as god hath helped thee by grace frequently to renew thy covenant? Art thou approaching towards the 50 year of thy life? and is not that the afternoon of thy day? will not death shortly cause thy sun to set? and will it not then be of singular use to haue thy evidences fair written? who knows what violent assaults satan may make upon thee? or how thy Lord may withdraw from thee, and leaue thee in the dark, and then thy case wel stated, resolved, confirmed upon scripture grounds may stand thee in some stead, thou mayst be put to it:

Come then, my soul, and let me take thee to task, and ask thee some important questions; but doe not (as thou art wont) shuffle and trifle, and put me off with good words and moods, and hopeful flourishes, but goe to the bottome way, lay the axe to the root of the tree, be faithful to god and thine own conscience in this great affair, self-flattery is the high-road to inevitable eternall misery:

1 My soul, dost thou beleeue that when thou art separated from this body in wch now thou lodgest, that thou shalt be annihilated? or that thou dyest as the beasts, and have no existence? Ans: No, I am assured both from scripture and reason that I must haue an existence Mat in a separate state, for Cht sth man may kill the 10 20 body, but god can cast the soul into hell, when the body is laid in the graue and that there shall be a resurrection when the body must follow the state of the soul, and I find that I can act (as in dreames and exstacys) without the help of or dependance upon the body therfore I am sure I shall live when the body is left a dead carcasse, Christianity and reason teach me this lesson:

2 But what a life must thou liue, when thou must depart

out of this tabernacle of flesh and bones ? Ans: I doe
verily beleeue, that I (as well as other mens soules) must
     goe into an unchangeable state of joy or misery : com-
Ecc   fort or torment in heaven or hell : and that when
12 7 the body returnes to dust as it was, the soul shall
Heb   return to god who gaue it, to receiue from him a
9 4   sentence of absolution or condemnation, for as it is
     appointed to all men once to dye so after that is the
judgment, *i e* a personal judgmt that prepares for that
generall and solemne day of judgment to all the world :
and I am as confident that when the soul departs out of
the body it enters either joy or woe, as I doe beleeue it
must depart, wch dayly experience assures me of (while I
was writing these things word came to the door under my
study that a young woman was departing Ester Wilson,
who had been sick of a feaver 21 days, with w^m I had
taken some paines and prayed often, she dyed at 8 a clock
Nov 1677 :. this was an affecting consideration and did
quicken my meditations :)

   3 My soul, what eternity dost thou think thou must
enter upon immediately after thy soul and body are separated? Ans: I know not, nor am I much concerned at what
time this body will molder to dust, or by what meanes this
breath must be stopt, whether I shall dye a natural or
violent death, by a sudden accident, or the hands of perse-
cutors, but this I now beleeve with some measure of con-
     fidence (though I was long under many discouraging
2 Cor doubts and feares) that whenever the earthly house
5 1   of this my fleshy tabernacle is dissolved, I haue a
     house not made with hands eternall in the heavens,
it hath indeed cost me many griefs, groanes, many prayers,
teares, temptations, conflicts and desertions before I arrived
     at this comfortable assurance, it is not the work of a
2Tim day or two, but of many yeares, and now I know
1 12 whom I haue beleeved and am persuaded he is able
     to keep that wch I haue committed to him (even this
Ps 73 immortal soul) till that day, the day of death and
23   judgment, he will guide me by his councel and after-
     wards receiue me to glory, the same gracious and
faithfull god that tooke me from my mothers wombe, and
was the support of my childhood, and staff of my youth,
will also be the crown and comfort of my gray head, the god

that hath kept me hitherto and provided for me all my life long, will not leaue me in old age, I dare trust him and say with old Polycarp, when tempted by the consul to forsake Cht 86 years hath the Lord kept me and shall I now forsake him in my old age, I can say aboue 40 years hath god sensibly enticed, and drawn out my heart after himself, and shall I now forsake him, will he now forsake me? indeed I was ready to sink and faint many a time, many yeares agoe, and thought I should not stand one day longer, or move one step further, but through grace I haue set up many an Eben-ezer, for a monument, saying hitherto the Lord hath helped. and still having obtained help of God I continue to this day as a monument of divine mercy to posterity what god hath done for a silly wretch, and a perpetuall occasion of admiration of divine grace to s[ain]ts and angels in heaven to all eternity

4 But, o my soul, thou seemest to be very confident, is not this presumption, and an hope, built upon the sands? how dost thou think to be saved? art not thou a sinner doth not god threaten death to sinners the soul that sinneth, it shal dye? is he a man that he should repent? will he reverse this sentence for thee, is not hell prepared for sinners? are not the fallen angels reserved in chains? are not thousands of rational creatures (just like thee by natural and moral conception and birth) now roaming in hell? and what ground hast thou to hope for immunity or expect felicity?

Ans: my case is indeed the same by nature with
Eph 2 3   vessels of wrath for I am a child of wrath by nature as well as others, and god might haue thrown me into hell the first moment of my breathing this aire and haue done me no wrong. for I was a
Psal 58 2   transgressour from the womb, and he might justly haue dealt with me as men deale with young snakes, toads, spiders, for no better was I in gods sight then such, but it was his good pleasure to spare my life to yeares of discretion, and then I heard upon what termes god and man stand each to other, by divine revelation in the scripture, and the promulgation of the gospel in preaching the word by the ministry of men, now so far as I
Gen 2 7   conceiue, the case stands thus, when god had formed mans body of the dust of the earth, and breathed into his nostrils the breath of life, so

that man became a living soul, he designed to govern man
by a law, that he might know. loue, serue, and obey his
creator, not only by a naturall law of instinct that necessi-
tates their motions according to their natures, but as he had
endowed man with a more noble soul, so with more excellent
and elevated facultys of understanding to conceiue of god as
his first agent and ultimate end, and an actiue will, free in
its choyce and operations, to embrace god, and doe all for
him, god had also ingrauen his own image upon mans soule
and had written a law of righteousnes in his heart, in
obedience wherto he might injoy him for ever but that god
might manifest his soueraignty, and mans subjection, his
own authority. and mans dependence on him, besides that
he gaue him a positiue law, prohibiting his eating of the
fruit of one tree, but man violating that command through
Satans subtilty and his own instability fell off from god,
lost his image. communion with him, became subject to gods
wrath, curse, death, temporal spirituall eternall, according
to the sanction of that divine law, in the day thou eatest
therof thou shalt dye the death, nor was this the case of the
first man only but of all his posterity, because he was the
root, spring, and common head, representing all his offspring,
but god out of his infinit loue and grace, pittying lapsed
mankind when there was none in heaven or earth of sufficient power to rescue foloru wretches sent his owne son, out
of his own bosom, the second person of the sacred trinity,
who thought it no robbery to be equall with god, being very
god, to take upon him mans nature, liue a life of sorrows,
dye a cursed death upon the cross, to satisfy wronged justice,
and appease the offended deity, and make
1 Tim 1 15   reconciliation between god and man, and this
is a faithful saying, worthy of all acceptation
that Jesus Christ came into the world to saue sinners and
is ascended into heaven, there sitting at gods right hand, to
pursue the same soul-saving design as prophet to teach, as
priest to intercede, as king to gather and rule his purchased
flock, and at last to bring them to heaven, where their soules
(with this of mine I hope) shall everlastingly injoy god, with
the glorious angels, and glorifyed spirits of just men made
perfect :

5 And dost thou imagine, Oh my soul, that all the men
and women in the world shal be saved by Christs merits and

undertakings? what ground hast thou to beleeue that thou shalt haue benefit by Christs redeeming loue more then others who notwithstanding Christs death shall eternally perish, though many may be within the sound of the gospel, and may as confidently hope for salvation as thou? Ans: God hath in his infinite wisdom and goodnes made a new and second covenant, wherin he hath declared his good pleasure upon what termes he will deale with sinners about life and salvation, and though the conditions of this covenant on mans part be wrought by his sanctifying spirit, yet he hath peremptorily determined that none shal be everlastingly saued but such in whose hearts and liues are found those saving conditions dispositions and qualifications and if I can find that god hath by his grace wrought these in me, I haue good reason to hope that I also shal be saved, because a saving faith, sound repentance &c are things that accompany salvation and though there be no merit or worthines in me to deserue it yet god is faithful to his promises and tis as impossible that a truly penitent, beleeving, and sanctifyed soul shall goe to hell, as for an impenitent, unbeleeving, unsanctifyed soul shall goe to heaven. I find that

Col 1 12   god makes sinners meet for heaven here, and works
2 Cor 5 5   them for it, and giues them the earnest of his
Eph 1 13   spirit in their hearts, and seals them up to the day
of redemption, and giues them an inheritance that are sanctifyed, and whom he calleth, he also glorifyed, its true the bottom, middle, and topstone of this building are of grace, pure grace, meer grace, but when free grace will magnify itself in giving these gracious habits and drawing them out in liuely exercise, nothing shall hinder the eternall salvation of that soule, for he that hath begun a
Phi 1 6   good work in my soul he will also perform it to the
day of Christ, and this I may be confident of, because faithful is he that hath promised who also will do it and though I be a weak worm of my self, and
1 Pet 1 5   easily overturned, yet I shall be kept by the
power of god through faith unto salvation
6 Yea, my soul, this is a truth according to scripture, that those that are sanctifyed are also justifyed and
Rom 8 30   shall be saved, but art thou sanctifyed? in whom
lodgeth such a multitude of vile lusts? art thou
Col 1 12   made meet for heaven that art not meet for any

Eph 4 30   good work here? art thou sealed by the holy
                spirit of promise, that art dayly grieving the
Spirit by sinning against god? is there any good work
wrought in thy heart that canst not but be conscious of so
much evil? and canst not at some times perceiue in thyself
                the motions of any good? is this likely or any
Rom 7 18   way consistent? Souls Ans: I must confess that
                in me (that is my flesh) dwels no good thing, I
am as vile a wretch and as filthy a beast as inhabits this
earth, yea I am apt to think sometimes that there is not a
                worse sinner in hell then I am, to me belongs
Eph 3 8   nothing but confusion of face, I am the least of
1 tim 1 11 saints if a saint, the chiefest of sinners, when I
                look into my heart I find a cage of unclean and
noysom lusts, severe abominations, and such a sea and sink
of sin, that I am ready to say, surely no dram or spark of
saving grace can lodg in such an heart: can grace and sin
dwell togather? what agreemt betwixt Christ and belial,
god and satan? can they share so narrow a compasse as an
humane soul? will not our Lord be supreme King and
sovcraign, where he comes to take possession? and is it
imaginable he should rule there where the devils interest is
so strong and prevalent? surely this very consideration may
                damp my hopes and discourage my heart, wheras
Mat 5 8   my Lord often makes heart-purity a necessary
Psal 32 2   property of them that shall see god and are in a
Psal 73 1   justifyed state and to whom god will be god,
Rom 2 29   thats indeed the circumcision thats in the heart
                and spirit, whose praise is not of men but of god
when I read these scriptures methinks I am much cast down
in mine owne eyes, especially reflecting upon the badnes of
a wicked heart, and the swarms of vain thoughts that lodg in
me and issue from me, this makes me oft to think and say
can such a proud, vain, hard, unbeleeving, distracted, hypo-
critical heart as this is be a renewed sanctifyed, and spirituall
heart? these thoughts make me think all my workings
within, and worship outwardly is but painted and fine-spun
hypocrisy, wch will be swept away as the spiders web with
all the hope that shrouds itself under these specious fig-
leaues, surely the goodly house is built upon the sand, and
will fall w^tever shew it now makes, and great will be the
fall therof:

But stay, my soul, be not too peremptory, condemne not all the generation of the just, and thy self with them, learne to distinguish of a christian state in point of sanctification, betwixt a perfection of parts and of degrees, a state of sin, and the stirrings of sin, hauing hypocrisy, and being an hypocrite, the indwellings of corruption, and the dominion of it, a state of imperfection in grace, and a state of perfection of grace in glory, hauing sin, and loving sin, distinguish well of these and then descend into thy heart:

Oh my soul, though thou canst not say my heart is clean, yet canst thou not say having these promises thou art cleaning thy self from all filthines of flesh and spirit; hauing this hope, thou art purifying thy self? canst thou not truely say thou hatest every false way and regardest not iniquity in thy heart? dost thou not study to keep thy self from thine own iniquity? darest thou not appeal to god to search and try thee and see if there be any way of iniquity in thee? wouldest thou not willingly be delivered from the body of death? dost thou not groan under this heavy taskmaster as thy greatest enemy? wouldst thou not be holy as he is holy in all manner of meditations and conversation? dost thou not say concerning such a sin, how shall I doe this wickednes and sin agt god? dost thou not hide the word in thy heart that thou mayst not sin agt god? art thou not content, oh my soul, to pluck out a right eye and cut off a right hand? doth sin reign in thy mortall body or immortal soul to fulfill the lusts therof? doth not the spirit within thee lust agt the flesh? canst thou not truely say thou art dead to sin, and that the Spirit of life in Christ Jesus hath made thee free from the law of sin and death?

I hope this soul of mine can comfortably answer these characteristical interrogations: its true I haue a troublesom inmate a body of death hangs upon me there is a sin that doth easily beset me, and too much prevails, but I can call god for a record upon my soul, how many prayers and teares, groanings and moanings my corruptions haue cost me, I look

on them as my deadliest foes that haue done me most mischief
Oh the bitter agonys of spirit, for breakings out of corruption !
Oh the breathings and pantings for a perfect sanctification !
what would I giue that I might be perfectly rid of sin ? Oh
it would be the best news and blessedst day that ever I heard
or saw, if god would set me at liberty from these cursed
tyrants, my base lusts, I hope I could more rejoyce therin
then in the gain of the world, how oft am I weary of my self,
and of being in the world because of sin ? God knows and
this conscience can witnesse, and some roomes where I haue
been can bear this testimony. that no affliction that ever
befell me in all my life hath lyen so sadly on my spirit as my
sins haue done : and rather then commit them again agt
my louing Lord I thought I could be content to be upon a
rack, yea to endure hellish torments, Oh my broken bones,
my weeping eyes, my confessing mouth, and perplexed
spirit ! hath not my god found me many a time upon my
face blubbering out my sad complaints for those sins that
the world hath known nothing of, and for spiritual wicked-
nesses ? haue I not inquired into the scripturall ways of
mortifying beloved lusts ? haue I not watched agt occasions
beat down this body, fasted and turned to spiritual acts of a
contrary nature ? hath not my soul been striking at the root
of sin, and made fresh applications by faith to the death of
Christ for crucifying the flesh with the affections and lusts ?
and hath my spiritual combats been altogether without some
blessed conquests ? hath not my heavenly Joshua sometimes
caused me to set my feet upon the necks of these Cananitish
Kings ? haue I not seen these Ægiptian hosts dead upon the
shore ? surely my soul can say thanks be to god that hath
giuen me the victory through Jesus Cht my Lord :

Well then, this soul of mine can truely answer without a
lye, that though I haue a corrupt heart, much sin, Yet I doe
not willingly allow myself in any guilt, that sin reigns not,
that there is a sincere opposition to it, that integrity and
uprightnes shall preserue me, that though I be not a
glorifyed saint in heaven Yet I am an upright saint on
earth—that although sin be stirring in me, yet I am not in
a state of sin, though I haue too much hypocrisy, yet I am
            not an hypocrite, yea I hate and abhorre lying,
Job 10 7   this soul of mine can say with Job, thou knowest

Psal 18 24   that I am not wicked, and with David, that I
haue not wickedly departed from my god:

7 Yea, my soul, thou mayst be upright in avoiding sin
and not willingly allow any lust, but whats all this to the
purpose since thou confessest that thou art dayly

Jam 2 10   sinning? and doth not the scripture say that

Gal 3 10   whosoever shall keep the whole law, yet offend in
one point he is guilty of all, and cursed is every
one that continueth not in all things that are written in the
book of the law to doe them? and what art thou then better
for thy fighting agt and mourning for sin, seeing thou art
dayly overtaken with it? will this make god amends, that
thou dost sin unwillingly? nay canst thou say truely thou
commitest any sin agt thy will? but however what will that
advantage thee before the pure and holy god? will thy
honest mind giue him satisfaction for violating his laws?
will thy purpose to sin no more procure a dispensation to
sin again, or absolution for by-past offences? will all these
repentings, conflictings. and sometimes conquests appease
gods wrath, justify thy person, or saue thy soul?

Soules Ans: Oh no, it will not doe it, I know it, and am
sure of it, when I haue done all, (if that were

Luk 17 10   possible) I am still an unprofitable servant, its
but duty, and doing duty will pay no debt:
whatever I can doe or suffer can bear no valuable proportion
to infinite justice wronged by my sinning: what I doe or
however I resist sin, the strength wherby I act

1 Cor 15 10   is not mine own but my Lords, by the grace
of god I am what I am, and doe what I doe,
yea my best actings and strivings are but faint, weak,
defectiue, imperfect, my righteousnes is but as filthy raggs,
my workings for god or agt Satan are mixed with abundance
of slightnes and vanity, yea the very graces of the spirit as
acted by me, are too short a garment to cover my naked
soul, yea as filthy rags and need cleansing them-

Isai 6 5   selves, and therfore cannot possibly cleanse me:

Isai 64 6   woe is me I am a person of unclean lips, and of
uncircumcised heart! I am an unclean thing,
nothing that I doe is free from pollution as proceeding from
me, for who can bring a clean thing out of an

Job 9 20   unclean? and if I justify my self mine own

1 Cor 4 4   mouth shall condemne me : yea if I knew nothing
           thats evil by my self, yet am I not herby justifyed
if my goodnes had all the demensions that might denominate
it perfect yet it were but finite, and could bear no proportion
to infinit justice the righteousnes by wch a sinner is justifyed
           must be adequate to the infinite holines and
Jer 23 6   justice of the great god. and this god hath
Act 13 38 39 provided in his gospel, for Cht is become
           (Jehovah Zidkenn) the Lord our Righteousnes,
through this man is preacht to us the forgiuenes of sins, and
by him all that beleeue are justifyed from all things from
           wch they could not be justifyed by the law of
2 Cor 5 21 Moses. yea god hath made him to be sin for us
           that knew no sin that we might be [made the
righteousnes of god in him.]

8 on March 15 1693 in the morning I set my self to spend
some time in prayer being that day 65 years before wherin I
was baptized, I begun with reading my ordinary chapter, 1
Cor 3 set my self about 7 a clock to confesse the sins of
nature, heart, life in the course of my pilgrimage about an
hour, came down to family duty, went up again read a ch—
Isai 40 then set my self a pleading with god for the nation
congregation but was straitened discouraged rose off my
knees, considered a little, had thoughts of desisting but resolved to try once more read Psal 115 resolved on the duty
of thankfulnes, and Oh what a field of matter, wt a flood of
teares, what meltings of heart had I for about an hour,
blessed be god for that little corner of heaven, I must write
it down, and set a star upon it as one of the days of heaven,
an anticipation of that glory I am hasting to, and not far off.

Oh my dear Lord, who or what was I or what was my
fathers house that thou hast brought me hitherto ? and is this
the manner of man, O Lord God : Thy poor servant knows
not the day of my birth, but I am assured, both by my
fathers writing and the Register at Bolton that this is the
day of my Baptizing, which was as I suppose not long after
my birth, old Adam Hilton my grandmother Heywoods
brother was my goff or godfather (as then used) Mtris Andrews of little Leaver-hall was my godmother so called she
held me at the font, when the minister (I suppose Mr William
Gregge, that marryed my present wiues sister) had sd the
words, in the name of the father, Son, and holy ghost she

stept back off the stone and suffered him not to crosse me with the sign of the crosse from whence and that solemnity arose these meditations.

1 my dear parents presented me to the Lord in the ordinance of Baptism. devoted me then and therby doubtles prayed for me and offered me a pious and liberal education, 2 yet little did they or such as presented me imagin that the stepping down and preventing that ceremonious rite of the crosse that it was a presage of my being a N C minister to bear my testimony agt those superstitious usages, and preaching and suffering so much for the good old cause of puritanism and Nonconformity, and as little could it be thought that I should liue aboue 60 years to see such changes in Civils and Ecclesiasticks, as I haue done since 1640, Bps up, then down, then up again, that I should be a publick preacher aboue 44 yeares, haue such measure of health, liberty, oppertunitys. more then most of my brethren, some good successe and fruit of my poor labours, marry famous Mr Angiers daughter, print so many bookes, injoy so many comforts of life, bring up two sons to be ministers build a chappel, help so many poor ministers and Christians in their necessitys by my self and others and yet haue a competency for my self and wife to liue upon nothing more improbable then these things and many more experiments I might produce, wch I record not for ostentation but to set off the riches of grace, and that I and my posterity in future generations may learn to trust god, and glorify his Alsufficiency: Oh my soul, reflect upon thy self, thy life hath been a life of wonders, my Lord hath shewn himself marvellous upon me, this life of nature hath been attended with a better life of grace, and Oh the liuely influences of grace! many a sweet hour hath my god and my soul had together this hath been, condimentum vitæ, the seasoning of my life, I could not haue liued or carryed on without my god. this is the Antidote agt the poyson of sin, the pledge and presage of a better life! and hath my dear Lord not only put me into a posture for injoying him in the life to come. but made me instrumental to propagate this life to others ? Oh blessed be his holy name : and who knows but those sons of my own and others that I haue been instrumentall to train up for the ministry may be instruments to convert others ? this, this is better to me then crowns or kingdoms, or thousands a year :

my soul, praise the Lord, speak well of him, act more rigorously for him, keep closer to him, liue always as in his sight, loug to be with him, and make thy self ready for his immediate presence :

9 On Feb 2 169⅗ morning I had a design to spend some time in prayer, as sometimes I haue doue with some good success after I had read my chapters in Ezra 3 4 in the house, I went up to my chamber, hauing a fire it being darkish, I fell on my knees, was assisted about half an hour, confessing sin, pleading for mercy, god was with me till about 8 a clock, then I went down, washt me, ate my break-fast, went to family-prayer came up again at 9 a clock, set my self to my work, read psal 73 meditated on it, then fell on my knees pleaded with god was moved to fall down on my face, so continued till 10, was greatly inlarged in con-fession supplication : then rose up read psal 72, fell on my knees again, pleaded for my wife, my son John, his wife, children, god helpt me then for my son El and for his settle-ment otherways after almost 20 years continuance as chaplain in Mr Taylors family then 1 pleaded for my servant S T for a saving work of graces then for my neighbours and people many of them by name, particularly for William Clay with whom I had some busines of moment about his daughter that day then about 11 a clock I rose up read the 74th psalm, descanted upon it, with reference to the church, fell down again upon my knees, begun to plead for Zion which I did a season, but was a little straitened for both affection and words, I rose up, leaned upon my table, fell to reading psal 74 again, turned it into prayer and plea, was something more inlarged, quickened, thought the words were suitable, and lift up my heart to god, in making application of them to the state of the nation and church of god now, 1 in generall (o god why hast thou cast us off—Remember thy congrega-tion which thou hast purchased of old) this I applyed to the godly people, who formerly were called puritans then Round-heads, whom Christ Redeemed with his blood, god Redeemed by remarkeable providences, deliverances and the blood of his precious servants : 2 (lift up thy foot unto the perpetuall desolations) this scattering and silencing hath continued near 36 years, and designed for ever 3 (wt the Enemy hath done wickedly in the sanctuary) not in civils but in spirituals to the famishing of themselves of soules (4 thine enemys roar

in the midst of the congregation) they hector it out, in a
roaring noise in threats and singing) 5 (they set up three
Ensigns for signs) they place their superstitions inventions
in roome of divine institutions: Ensignes of pride and war:
6 (a man was famous according as he had lifted up axes upon the thick trees) godly reformers made laws agt superstitious usages and for rectifying what was amisse according to
gods word: 7 (But now they break down the carved work
therof with axes and hammers) they make contrary laws,
yea doubling those laws against things and persons to knock
them in the head and kill them that were dead: 8 (they
haue cast fire into thy sanctuary) bones of bitter contention
about the administration of holy things never such a fire,
that hath set us all in a flame 9 (they haue defiled) mens
inventions haue polluted gods worship and render it odious
to god and good men: 10 (they sd in their hearts, let us
destroy them together) we'l cut them off all at once, 2000
ministers in one day, we will never be troubled with N C
more: 11 (we see not our signes) alas hundreds of congregations are left desolate, and many dumb dogs set up in the
room of faithfull prophets, 12 (how long shall the Enemy
blaspheme thy name?) if it were our persons or names it
would signify nothing, but the name of god is wofully re-
proached this s'rikes us to the heart 13 (why withdrawest
thou thy hand) god himself seems to forsake us in his
providence, giuing no means of escape: 14 but (god is our
King of old) we hope still in the King of heaven, there is
still a relation betwixt thee and us, as low as our condition
is: 15 (thou didst divide the sea by thy strength) our god
did work Reformation from popery, prelacey, brake Levia-
thans head, and is still as strong now as ever he was: 16
(thou driedst up mighty rivers) removing mighty obstructions
making Jordan in its overflowing its banks to turn back, and
canst doe so again: 17 (the day is thine, the night also is
thine) thou orderest national motions, and canst cause a
succession of light and sun to the night: a day-break may
yet appear to us: 18 (oh deliver not the soul of thy turtle-
doue unto the multitude of the wicked) alas we are helples
things and haue no relief but groaning, our enemys are
many: 19 (haue respect unto thy covenant) the covenant of
gospel-grace, that also of Reformation 20 (O let not the

oppressed return ashamed) thou dost not use to turn any poor despised supplicants from thy door with shame:

Thus this sinful creature kept pleading these scripture argumts till 12 a clock—Lord hear and answer—Act 9 19:

10 on wednesday July 5 1699 in the morning. hauing dispatcht my usuall course of closet-prayer and family-prayer I set myself to spend some time in solemn work that forenoon, I begun at 8 a clock. read psal 86, reflected on it, applyed wt was pertinent to my own case, fell down on my knees, then on my face, confessed my sins god brought many to my remembrance that I had forgot, spent about an hour in that work with some brokennes of heart.

about 4 a clock I read psal 57 set my self to pray for pardon of my sins. for sanctifying assisting grace—then read another scripture prayd for my wife, sons relations, then read Isai 49 pleaded with god for my congregation and hearers then read Isai 50 - and sought the Lord for the church in generall. protestant interest, these nations, it was a sweet time till towards 12 a clock, blessed be god—Lord shew a token for good—

Sept 21 1699 my two sons came unexpectedly to visit me, my son El had a weighty busines to impart to me. to ask my advice and consent concerning a marriage betwixt him and Mr Rotherhams daughter of Dranfield in Darbishire, an hopefull young woman Madam Taylor driues on the match I consented freely, writ a letter to M Taylor of my willingnes —told her what I would give my son at present viz 7li 10sh a year of Rent-charge and divide the rest of my estate betwixt them when I and my wife dye—I look't upon this as an Answer of my prayer. he hauing been aboue 20 years chaplain at Wallin-wels, and being 42 years of age I extremely desired his settlemt in a family of his own, and this is a fair prospect towards it—

the morning after which was Sept 22 1699 I designed us three, my self and two sons to spend the forenoon in prayer and praise (as we are wont to doe) so we begun in my chamber about 9 a clock after family-prayer, my son Eliezer begun, prayed understandingly and affectionatly, then my son John, but he exceeded both in expressions and affection, with floods of teares, then I concluded and oh how my heart was warmed and melted! such a frame is very rare, and I tooke speciall notice what a mighty alteration there was in the spirit of my son John, from this time it shall be sd what hath god wrought! I thought surely god is now fitting him for some signall service or for death, Lord prepare for thy whole pleasure :

In the afternoon of the same day we had appointed a meeting at my house concerning making and sealing some writings for that land I bought of the Executors for James Halsteds children in Ovenden John Sugden and his son Joshua made the writings, Anthony Naylor, and Abm: Bolton were Executors, Jon. Priestly jun entred bond with them, Tim Bancroft present as witnesse, and my sons,—I paid them 50li that day, and 30li before, in all paid already 80li - 30li behind to be paid in March when Martha Halsted comes to her age and seales, the rest (4 more) to seal as they come to age, I give 110li for it and haue Ant Naylor, Abr Bolton, Jon Priestly and Josiah Stansfield bound in a double summe to bring the children to seal at age, or I shall haue my money again—Lord I look up to thee.

December 4 1699 I reflected a little on my bodily health and my condition—the case is thus with me—My wind grows exceeding short, any little motion puts me out of order —my chappel is near me, but when I walk to it (as yesterday) my wind so failes that I am forced to stand and get new breath, before I goe into my pulpit when I goe up to my chamber, my breath cuts, that I am forced to sit a season in my chair to breath me, when I lay me down in my bed I pant a considerable time and caugh and oftimes my water comes from me with motion—yet for all this

1 I have not any disease, runnings, or acute pain of stone, strangury gout—as many of my brethren have and as my dear brother had

2 I sleep well most of the night and haue not caughing wheezing and am refreshed and haue ease all the day and study comfortably

3 I can pray and preach as long and as loud as ever, that I feel nothing of ailing to myself and no body can discern any thing I ail—

4 I haue not the oppertunitys of travelling abroad as formerly, but when I doe travel little journeys I ride with much ease and safety blessed be god

5 I haue a sweet comfortable wife that takes great care of

me, provides sack, and yoke of egge every morning and all other conveniences

6 I haue a competence of worldly yearly incomes more then ever I expected deserved or so much as desired, when many better then I are in want—

7 Aboue all I humbly hope god hath given me an interest in himself and doth help me morning and evening in secret to pour out my soul to him

Jan 21 16.⅗ being Lords day morning Aut Lea told me he was at Leeds the Tuesday before, and it was confidently reported there that I was dead, severall came to inquire of him, and Joe Baxter they said it was reported there that I was seized with an Apoplexy at Mr Sharps the thursday before, 5 or 6 letters were writ up to London to signify it, they assured them of the contrary—and blessed be god I am in my usuall health—they were glad it was not so—The thoughts of this report reflect these meditations in my heart—

1 Alas what a lying world is this ! some raise a groundles report, others tell it confidently without examining the grounds therof—as in this so in many other cases of greater consequence

2 what cause haue I to admire the good hand of providence that hath kept me alive thus long whatever his design is thereby when I dayly hear of many others younger then I that are pluckt away by death—

3 O that this may quicken and rouze up my spirit to be the more actiue for god, as one raised up from the graue that henceforth more good may be done by me than ever, and it may appear god had glorious Ends in sparing my life for more then I yet see

4 And such a report as this tho false should leaue a reall impression upon my spirit, to mortify my corruptions wean my heart from this world work in my soul to heavenly objects prepare for death, for one of these days it will be a true report, he s dead—

[With this remarkable soliloquy ends another of Mr. Heywood's volumes,—a volume that reveals the religious inner life of the writer more vividly than any of his Biographies. His views on the Trinity are particularly worthy of note, in the light of the discussions of the present century. Lady Hewley's Trustees may apply this touchstone.]

Experiments with Reflections*

* This small book bears the inscription "Bought at Halifax, cost 6d., 1679;" also R. Astley's autograph signature.

EXPERIMENT 1.   As I was riding, upon a speciall occasion on Feb 2 1680, I had a sin brought to my remembrance committed many yeares agoe, and set myself to mourn for it, but instead of griefe, hatred and shame which my soul desired and designed, my heart began to be tickled with delight and pleasure in speculation, and base imagination, it run to my heart and struck me with astonishment when I perceived a solace rather then sorrow, and so a fresh commission, rather than reformation.   Immediately after, discoursing with a precious experienced chtian, who (not knowing wt I had lately felt) told me that wn she had a promise before her pat and pertinent for her support and consolation, being ready to apply and improve it, Satan foisted in more hideous and blasphemous suggestions then at any other time, this I laid up and thought of as a paralel case—

REFLECTION   Oh, strange instance of a deceitful heart! what shall I say? where shall I appear? are my repentings my returnings to sin? is my detestation of sin become a licking up my vomit with delight? do I aggravate sin when I set myself to lessen it? woe is me am not I like Israel of old, of wm god sth, "when I would haue healed Israel, then the Iniquity of Ephraim was discovered," or as Aholibah that multiplied her whoredoms in calling to remembrance the days of her youth, wherein she played the harlot in the land of Egipt.   alas, alas, how unlikely is my repentance to satisfy justice, that provokes wrath! that man is in ill taking whose phisick poysons him, and whose remedy is his disease, I need a pardon of my repenting, as wel as sinning, the fountain set open for Judah must wash my teares as wel as sins away, yea the sins of my teares: Christ is a perfect Saviour, but my best dutys are imperfect, my wine is mixed with water, yea with the gall and wormwood of sin and corruption;

Hos 7 1

Ezek 23 19

Zec 13 1

Psal 130 3   David sth "if thou Lord shouldest mark iniquity,
               o Lord who shall stand?" but I may say, if the
Lord should mark graces or dutys, who can stand? but is
this strange frame consistent with sincerity? and whence
may this proceed? truth it is, Satan (that grand master of
misrules) rageth most when any good is on foot, when the
gospel is likely to be most propogated in hearts, or church,
               that infernall fiend raiseth greatest storms of
Mat 13 21 25   opposition, the enemy sows tares when our
               Lord sows good seed: Satan stands at
Zec 3 1   Joshua's right hand to be a Satan to him
               when he would act and pray as a saint; cor-
rupt nature also breaks out most when grace would correct
it, as a disease wrestleth with a contrary cure, or as a
distracted person doth most rage and storm when he is
               bound in chains; Sin (sth blessed Paul in
Rom 7 8 9 10   his experiment) taking occasion by the com-
               mandment wrought in me all manner of
concupiscence: the seemingly dead snake reviues and hisseth
outrageously when approaching the fire; Alas! the best man
is two men, the flesh is tickled with that wch turns the spirits
stomack agt it, and on the contrary, theres an utter aversa-
tion in the flesh to that wch the better part approues, these
will never be reconciled, the antipathy is bred in their natures,
the one must utterly be abolished: I hope grace shal not, it
is the seed of god, and shall never dye: Oh my soul, dost
thou not obserue the workings of both? canst thou not
discern the meetings of these counterworking streams and
champions? which side dost thou take? doe not thy sinful
pleasures in sin cost thee pain in repentance? the more
delight in sin hast thou not the more grief for it? dost thou
not consent to the law that its good when it pricks and
pincheth flesh most? doth not thy heart hate the sweetest
sin, and loue the severest duty? canst thou not truly say
that thou delightest in the law of god after the inward man
dost thou not bind thy soul with stricter bonds and scourge
thy unruly flesh with sharper lashes. Lord apply thy grace,
defeat Satan, pardon my failings and fallings short accept
my good will to repent, and giue me a repentance not to be
repented of. And oh succour thy tempted handmaid, that
is haunted with such furious fiends that disturb her rest
though they cannot damne her soule, that obscure her

comfort though they shal not obstruct her communion with
thyself, clap the healing salue of Christs blood spread upon
the plaister of promises warm to her bleeding wound and
stop that issue that runs out in so many despairing thoughts,
let not Satan haue advantage in this his hour
Rom 16 20 and power of darkness "thou that hast trod
him under thy feet" let him be trodden under
hers and that shortly, impute not his sin to her charge, prevent her wound by his stings, and let her sail safely through
these rocks, storms, sands and way-laying pirates, by thy
steerage and land seasonably and triumphantly in that
blessed haven of heaven. the sweet and safe harbour of poor
weather-beaten soules, that she and I and all the ransomed
of the Lord looking back from that blessed shore on this
tempestuous sea may eccho forth thy glorious praises to all
eternity for thy safe conduct into those quiet and everlasting
mansions whither Satan shall never shoot a dart, nor shall
this rotten flesh within or a tempting world ever disturb the
glorifyed soules serenity or perfect exercise of suitable graces
for evermore. Amen.

EXPERIMENT 2 Upon July 20 1680 being alone in my
house I set myself to spend some time in prayer, meditation,
self-examination, and my dear Lord was near to my heart,
and gaue my soul some tokens and tastes of his gracious
presence but that night I was guilty of an omission of secret
prayer, and in the morning my heart was dead and much
shut up, both in family and closet, and thus it hath been
frequently with me, that after an inlargement comes a
straitnes, after a quickening comes a deadnes.

REFLECTION And whats the reason of this oh my soul?
what must be the remedy? what is the meaning of my dear
Lord in this sudden change? Surely he sees my soul cannot
bear a succession of inlargements, I must not dayly feed on
daintys and delicates, tasting is as good for me as feeding,
to quicken my appetite and let me see who is master of the
feast. An overflowing tide and spring flood of injoyments is
not for every day, winter blasts and barrennes are as usefull
as spring and summer plenty and pleasures, bitter gall and
wormwood are as wholsom as sweetest honey and
2 Cor 12 sugar, Paul will be lifted up with abundance of

Psal 30   revelations, David will imagin his mountain is
           impregnable wn the sun of gods favour shines
upon it,—vicissitudes of tempers are most proper for us in
this lower region : god will not always smile nor always
frown, to let us see we are neither in heaven nor in hell, but
on earth ; they in heaven are always in their zenith of an
uninterrupted communion with god, soules in hel are in the
uttermost hopeless point of distance from god, gods poor
children on earth must be glad of a glimpse of god now and
then through those lattices of ordinances, and then he steps
behind our wall that our sin reares. O, my soul, mayst thou
not thank thyself for this sudden and sad change ? wast not
thou the cause ? hast not thou given occasion ? didst thou
not give way to security, pride, vain glory, carnal confidence ?
wast not thou ready to think and say, " so, now thou hast
done wel, soul take thine ease, goe to bed and take thy rest,
put off thy shoes, thou hast travelled farre enough for this
day, put off thy cloaths of grace exercised, god will indulge
thee a little respite for this tucking up thy garments and
wrestling." thus thy careles soul hath sate down after sweat
and catcht a dangerous surfeit, sudden coolings after violent
heats are prejudiciall : oh, my sinful soul, what shal I say ?
thou hast by heedlesnes lost that in an instant thou tookst
some pains to get thou has provoked the Lord to withdraw
by thy slinking away so hastily from him. God is just I am
vile my sitting loose from god hath robbed me of my treasure,
my turning my back upon god hath hid his face from me :
oh how long hath it been thus, and when shall it be otherwise, oh when shall gods candle still shine upon my head ?
when shall I haue a perpetuall harvest, a spring without a
fall, a summer without winter, a day without night, sweet
outgoings of heart to god, incomes of grace to my soule,
without such ecclipses and intermissions ? oh, what would I
giue that my beloved would lodg all night betwixt my breasts ?
oh, that I could hold him and not let him goe, that this King
of heaven might still be held in the gallerys ; surely did I
not disturbe this quiet repose I should haue more of his
company, were I more louely in princes shoes of holy life,
and the rare qualifications according to the word, and in the
timely exercise of faith, loue, repentance, humility, self-
denyal, my soul might haue more constant settled intercourse
with my god ; but oh this dodging, toyish, frisking heart kills

me, its like a deceitfull bow, backsliding heifer, it will not abide bent for god, nor be steady in motion godwards : Lord establish my soul with thy grace, giue me a more constant spirit, unite my heart to fear thy name, come Lord and knit my spirit to thee, pardon my instability, endear my soul unto thee, afford me thine assistance, annoint me with fresh oyl, supply me with dayly influence. I see yesterdays inlargements will not advantage me this day, no more then last weeks meat hath Actuall efficacy for strengthening my body this day : however let me thus goe from strength to strength till at last my soul shall appear perfect before my god in Sion, where I shal never haue returns of deadnes, hardnes, distraction for ever but a perpetual acting of grace, and al my facultys in full vigour upon god, and feeling a living illapses upon my heart to all eternity :   Amen :

Expt 3 I was extraordinarily imployed in Lancashire preaching almost every day for almost a fortnight in several places about Manch., Bolton, Ratchdal, had laid out my self in weeping, wrestling, beating my braines, lungs, but had no incouragment concerning the successe of my labours on consciences, the last day, viz Sep 30 1689 returning homewards I preached near Heywood chappel to a numerous assembly there I heard a passage wch exceedingly cheared me, which was that one Mr Chaderton now a serious christian and famous preacher (though liuing obscurely with Mr Sarjeant at Stand) was wrought upon by a sermon that I preacht at Underwood near Ratchdall many yeares agoe, wch I never heard of till that day, the like I heard from Mr Timothy Hodgson himself owning me as an instrument of good to his soul :

Reflection And is this so ? oh my soule, is any soul wrought upon by the word, yea by the word in thy mouth ? yea hath god owned thy labours for good to any, yea so many, yea, and to such of such a quality and tendency towards the sacred office of the ministry. Oh adore, admire free-grace in it, give god the glory of it, speak, liue, walk in his praise, whose the work alone is, from first to last. Oh ! who or what was I that god should single me out for that high function, " the least in my fathers house, and my fathers house the meanest in Israel" one of the most blackish, sottish, wicked, worthles creatures in all the school I learned

in, amongst all the companions I convers'd with unlikely to
make anything of, incapable of being a vessel of honour, or
yet of mercy I haue thought sometimes if my Lord had rak'd
up all the scum in the countrey, the like to me could not
have been found, grace is more magnifyed in me than in
any other but god wil doe what he pleaseth, a skilful workman can make a Mercury out of any block, and pour his
gifts into the emptyest cask, or giue success to unlikely
instruments, the silly asse shal forbid the madnes of a prophet
and the household cock shall convince a fallen Apostle if a
divine power accompany them, the walls of
Josh 6 8   Jericho shall fall at sounding the rams hornes,
Judg 7 22   Gideons 300 shall defeat the Midianites, yea the
breaking of the pitchers, shining of the lamps
and sounding of the trumpets shall destroy the enemys, the
Apostle alluding to this sth " we have this trea-
2 Cor 4 7   sure in earthern vessels that the excellency of the
power may be of god and not of us."   Oh, that
ever free-grace (wch had great choyce among the sons of
men) would single out such a silly worm as poor me, making
and accounting me faithfull, putting me into the ministry,
bringing me in through the scripturall door, making me
laborious in my studys, faithful to sound principles, conscientious in practise compassionate to sinners, in labours
abundant, in troubles constant in my calling, in
2 Cor 11   journeyings often, and some of those 30 things
paul speaks of himself, poor I may assert without
a lye before my dear Lord : Who am I that god should ingage
my heart to the suffering side, to trust god when so many
turn aside to worldly preferments ? yea that god should find
me out fit and full employment when so many choyce
ministers would gladly work and cannot, none calls them to
labour in the vineyard, but they stand idle in the open
market all the day or this night of persecution and banishment from publick assemblys, yea lastly that god should
giue me this blessed success, when many better then I labour
all the day and yet catch nothing :
Oh wonder of distinguishing grace, I cannot say I haue
laboured altogether in vain or spent my strength for naught,
some of Israel is gained, some souls gathered to Cht by me,
even by me, the unworthyst and weakest of all my brethren,
yea some are gained that may gain others, Oh! free-grace.

Luke 22 31

1 John 1 1 2

Aarons rod doth blossome and brings forth Almonds; when peter is converted he will seek to convert and strengthen his brethren; when David had a right spirit renewed in him, he will teach transgressors gods ways and sinners shall be converted to him: oh that these may also feel what they speak. and speak what they feel that "those wch haue handled of the word of life" may bear witnes and show to others eternall life: may these lights be set upon an hill to giue light to all the house, may these springs be opened to refresh the city of our god; oh, that the same divine power that begets saints, appoints his ministers, may at last bring you into sweet communion in ordinances.

EXPERIMENT 4 Upon Friday night, Dec 3 1680 after a day of solemn fasting and prayer purposely for the church and nation wherin god did extraordinarily assist, expecting my son John out of Nottinghamshire, he came not, but Mr Tho. Colton came to supply for me on Lords day, he brought me great and good tidings of the Parliaments undertakings for the good of the kingdom and ease of dissenters, which was gratefull, and a quick return of prayer but withall had no tidings of my son John at wch I was troubled (however he came to Denby that night).

REFLECTION Oh Deceitfull heart! what wild work art thou making? what unparaleld contradictions art thou guilty of? didst thou not that very day tell the Lord (as at many other times) that if the Lord would but take care of his owne interest and the concernes of his son, let him doe what seemes good to him with thy person and family thou couldst posthabit thy own interest as inconsiderable compared with Zions. And behold god puts thee to it suddenly to see how thoult bear it and behaue thyself and alas thou faintest and succumbest under thy feares about domesticall concernes, and art not erected with the hopes of public immunitys: one would haue thought that to a person of thy pretensions publick safety would haue counterpoised particular hazzards, but alas its otherwise, a bad heart can bury many great mercys of common influence in the grave of personal troubles, yea, in the imaginary pit of self-made troubles, poor soul thou couldst fret and vex thyself and disturb thy sleep because thy son returned not home at the appointed time, wch was yet præfixed by thy self not promised by him. Ah wicked carnall, unbelieving heart! how opposite art thou to lip-profession wt wilt thou make of it when thou comest to harder tryals ? thou often tellest thy Lord what thou couldst be content to doe or endure for him, but ex ungue bonem its easy to guesse by smaller what thourt likely to make of it in greater exercises, Jer 12 5 "if thou run with footmen and they wearyed thee how shalt thou contend with horses ?" I may more truely say of thee than Jobs friends of him "Behold thou hast instructed many, and thou Job 4 3 6 hast strengthened weak hands—but now it is come upon thee and thou fainted it toucheth thee and thou art troubled." is not this thy fear and thy confidence, the uprightnes of thy ways and thy hope ? alas, alas, my soul darest thou not trust a child with god, that pretendest to trust church, soul and all concernes with god ? is he needs sick or dead when he comes not in thy time ? its wel if thy faith be not harder put to it : But alas what are we when god leaves us ? and wt can we not doe if god assist at some times a small tryal shal overturn us nay the very shadow and conceit of a tryal shal bear us down, wn at other times the soul shall brauely mount over the proudest waues : received grace is one thing assisting grace is another : this is clear in Abraham the renowned father of the faithfull, who yet through unbelief did twice deny his wife : But thy affliction was in groundless imaginations so was Jacobs of Joseph, "without doubt he is torn in pieces." But my soul was jeolous of his sinning and being led away by some temptation ; tis true but hadst thou not by faith committed him to god, and by thy prayers laid him at gods feet, "Oh thou of little faith wherefore didst thou doubt " ? the worst was that thou wast more taken up with personal than public concernes, Lord humble, pardon, assist to a more public spirit.

Experiment 5   On Tuesday Feb 8 168⁷⁄₈ being called to spend a day of fasting and prayer at N. Tilsons at Sowerby Bridg for his afflicted wife Mr Dawson should haue gone with me, I sent him word I would not goe because a great quantity of snow had fallen the night before and made it hazardous going, so we went not, but afterwards was troubled yt I went not, not knowing wt use such people might make of our breach of promise ; the same week Friday Feb 11 I had ingaged to go to baptize a child, preach and keep a day of thanksgiving at Isaac Balmes, but that morning coming it was farre more terrible then the former, very stormy, much snow,—so I was discouraged and did not goe imagining we wld not get through, thus I stayed at home all that week, but that night I lay waking a good part of the night, tossed these things in my mind, was exceedingly perplexed and this morning Feb 12 utter my troubles in such reflections as these

REFLECTION   O my poor soul whence comes this to passe, that thou eschewest thy work through some danger and difficulty, why beginn'st thou now to be afraid ? hast thou not had abundant experience of gods protection ? sufficient to silence unbelief for ever ; how many times hast thou gone out and come in in safety according to gods promise ? and dost thou now begin to distrust god ? was thy call clear and didst thou not obey it ? did people expect thy pains and didst thou, durst thou thus disappoint them ? was this thy zeal for god, and loue to soules ? had these been working and flaming they would haue melted or made a way through mountains of snow. how canst thou tell but thou mightst haue won a soul wch would haue countervaild'd thy pains ? how knowest thou that ever thou shalt haue such another oppertunity of doing good in that place ? who knowest but some or other may take offence and censure thee for breach of promise yea possibly some sinners may be hardened against the ways of god condemning thee of levity as some did Paul in a like case : and what art thou grown so delicate and tender of late that a little sharp weather or outward danger daunts thee ? shouldst not thou endure hardnes as a good souldier of Jesus Christ ? alas, alas, how wilt thou endure to be turned out of house and harbour in cold & frosty nights to make thy bed in snow drifts ? yea dost thou not deserve to be thus dealt with in suffering that would not venture for god in doing work ? how easy is it to take a good horse, hap thee warm, haue the assistance of good company, and ride a few miles in comparison of being turned out to wander naked and barefoot in danger of thy life, none

daring to entertain thee ? thou hast known something of a
weary wandring life but that may be but small compared to
wts behind ; what if thy dear and affectionate companion
had been troubled, could not god haue born up her heart ?
and is not thy Lords work and soules good dearer then
gratifying nearest relation ? and what if thou hadst lost thy
limbs or life in this adventure (as thou hearest some haue
done in this snow) could not god haue made up that abundantly or recompenced thee by a quick passage into glory,
nay, nay, my soul I fear thou coolest in thy zeal for god, tis
well if thy faith doe not begin to fail, and thy loue languish ;
time hath been that thou hast taken more pains, been at
more hazzards for god and soules then these would haue in
all probability amounted to. Besides will not the men of
the world venture further to their markets in pursuit of
worldly gain ? oh shame thyself for this timerous flesh
pleasing discouragement : Lord humble me thoroughly for
my sloth and slight what pains doe many others take to
travel further to this house in bad weather as far as this ?
and must thou haue it pleasant way and weather, or thou
wilt not goe to them ? for shame mend this fault and doe so
no more : the god of heaven pardon this fault and folly and
inable me to double my diligence for future in my Lords
work : Lord strengthen my inward and outward man in thy
work at home and abroad, let me spare no pains or cost for
thy glory and the good of soules that I may spend and be
spent for god and giue me good successe in my next undertakings :

Notwithstanding my perplexity I was not expected in
either place nor was it passable, as since I understand

EXPERIMENT 6 On Munday morning February 21 168⅞
setting my self to spend an hour in secret prayer principally
for the church and nation, beginning with personal and
family concernes my heart was dull at first but afterwards
sweetly melted. but proceeding to the publick I was much
daunted and damped, and god directed me to read 102
psalm, wch quickened me, but I could not return to the
work of prayer, and I haue oft found my heart straitened
in my pleadings for Zion : that same day discoursing with
a gracious experienced christian of a public spirit, without
my communicating this told me of the like discouragement

alledging two daunting texts cast in in prayers for the nation, the one Isai 3 " A wt could haue been done to my vineyard "? the other Levit 26 23 " I will bring a sword upon you that shall avenge the quarel of my covenant "

REFLECTION And now, oh my soul, what shall I say to this multiplyed Experiment thou hast had, and the harmony of another witnessing to the same? must the thing be doubted to manifest certainty, as Pharaoh's dream? will god withdraw as an omen and sad prognostick of future woe? whats the meaning of this astonishing shutting up the spirit of prayer? hast thou not found it many, yea

Psal 10 17   many a time, that god hath prepared the heart when he hath bowed his ear to hear? and now our Lord is saying to his servants as once to Moses " speak no more to me of this matter," or as to Jeremiah " pray not thou for this people": its true we hear him not audibly declaring his will to us, but interpretatingly he seems thus to say in withdrawing the spirit of prayer would to god it were only our experiment? oft hath my heart been inlarged for assisting grace in approaching tryals, sometimes for hiding and exemption from common calamitys in a personal way, and as oft puzzled and much left in pleading for national exemption, yet I cannot deny but at some seasons god hath carryed out my soul in mighty wrestlings for the church of god: tis not fit for me to make conjectures. but it will not off my heart, yt god will not be intreated for sparing of the nation, but yet that he will condescend to a carefull provision for his church, it may fall on us according to the prophecy, "two parts therein shall be cut off and dye. but

Zech 13 8 9   the third shall be left therein, and I will bring the third part through the fire and refine them as silver is refined and try them as gold is tryed": and must it be so, O Lord and is there no remedy? wilt thou be so angry that thou wilt not hear thy people pray? and therefore will not help thy people in prayer? where oh where is the Lord god of Elijah yea where is Elijahs spirit, where are those groanings and pleadings, those strong crys and teares that gods children haue been wont to pour out in such a day as this? Lord hast thou forsaken the hearts of thy people, and must this be a token of ensuing wrath to the nation? Alas its sad and dolefull to wrestle and try at the oars and not to get forward, the ship still tossed, no instruments raised, the hearts of some hardened, the Lords work hindred, popish plots detected yet incouraged, and will god haue it thus ? his will be done, theres no remedy, he will punish formal professors, and take away the wicked as drosse, only Lord do not withdraw from the hearts of thy people thy quickening and thy comforting presence assist in personal concernes, prepare for sufferings, credit thy gospel by them and perform that good word to thy children, as to Jeremiah, "the Lord sd verily it shall be well with thy remnant, very I will cause thy enemy to intreat thee wel in the time of evil, and in the time of Affliction.

Jer 15 11

EXPERIMENT 7   On March 15 168⅞, the same day I was baptized 51 yeares ago god helped me in the morning to confesse my sins before the Lord and towards noon god graciously inlarged my heart in thankfulnes to god for his mercys, and reading a portion of Scripture withall, reading the life of John Hesse in Mechior Adams book vit: germ: theol: in pag 188 I found a pithy and pertinent passage in an Epistle of Luthers to him wch so fully suiting me I cannot but transcribe, its this " Adscendisti in navem cum Christo, quid expectabis, serenum. imo ventum et procellas, et fluctus navem operientes, ut mergi incipiat, sed hoc Baptismo baptizandus prius es : tum sequetur serenum excitato et implorato Christo, qui saltem dormiet aliquando"; this passage had strong impression on my spirit and I was ready to think it was spoken to me more especially under our present circumstances

REFLECTION   And now, oh my soul what canst thou say in this case ? god hath continued thee long in this vale of teares, and thou art past the zenith and meridian of thy days, thy sun is turned in the firmament and beginneth to decline few and evil haue been the days of the years of my life and I haue not attained to the days of the years of the life of my fathers, my grandfather and father attained to about 80 yet I haue survived my brothers and many of my kindred and how long I may liue god only knows, or by what death I must dye, natural or violent by the hands of men, cruel men, or some other way I am not solicitous, so

that I may dye in the Lord, and it will be my honour to dye
for my Lord, poor creature, this day 51 yeares ago thou
didst ascend into the ship with Christ, the ark of Noah, the
ship of the church, and hast been sailing with thy Lord
upon the fluctuating sea of this weary world and though
there haue been storms and tempests, rocks and sands, yea
pirates without and leaks within yet through the care and
skill of the pilate, thou hast not been split or sunk or
suffered shipwreck, blessed be grace; what couldst thou
expect? a serene sea by the indulgence of our Lord it hath
been a great calm hitherto: a halcyon day thou hast had,
possibly to victual, and rigge, and lay in for a sharper time,
clouds haue hitherto blown over, it hath but hitherto been
threats and not a full execution, once the Sectarys molested
now the prelatists haue playd their game, and turned thee
out of publick work, and shot sundry sharp arrows at thee,
but though they haue caused some smart yet haue not
fetched blood.   But behold I see a cloud arising, a storm is
approaching, another sort of men are now entering upon
the stage, to whom our Lord seemes to giue a commission
wch are more fierce by farre then former opposers, the Anti-
christian party, how doe papists plot and rage and gnash
their teeth, what winds and storms from that quarter now
more then ever threaten the ship of the church; how doe
waues seem to couer her, what a flood is vomited out of the
mouth of that red dragon to swallow up the poor woman
that had been long in the wildernes; either damnable here-
sys are corrupting her vitals, or else wounding persecutions
to murder her members: my fear is more that this ship of
the church should be stuck fast in the former quicksands
then dashed by the violence of the latter, but blessed be
god her skilful pilot was never yet baffled nor never will be,
the gates of hell shall never prevail agt her, the ark will
mount above all impetuous waues; Oh but particular soules
may be lost, not if they be in the ark, in the ship, the
master hath charged himself with every passenger; but
many haue a name to liue and are dead, some are listed
under Christs banner in baptism that will be found in the
enemys camp fighting agt god: thou wast baptized with
water, art thou baptized with the holy ghost
1 Cor 10 25   and fire ? Israel were all baptized unto Moses
in the cloud and in the sea, which was an

extraordinary baptisme, yet with many of them god was not
well pleased : but, oh my soul, hast thou not many a time
devoted thyself afresh to god ? and hath not thy Lord taken
possession of thee by his Spirit ? and now if thou be baptized in thine own blood its welcom, it is nothing but what
thou didst make account of heaven cannot be bought too
dear : a calm will come after a storm, after a dark night
comes a bright morning and peace is always sweetest after
warre : the great danger is that our Lord is not in the ship,
and if he haue forsaken us we sink, we perish, must drown,
but it cannot be, surely he hath not left his church on earth,
he that sd " Loe I am with you to the end of the world, and
I will not leave you comfortless, but will come to you " cear-
                    tainly is not quite gone, he is in the ship, only
Mat 8 24 25   he is asleep, oh that the disciples of Christ
                    might by prayers and teares awake him, and
cry out Lord saue, we perish ; and ceartainly he will awake
and rouze himself as a mighty man and shew he is the
mighty god by rebuking the stormes and causing a calm.
Happy ship that carrys such a passenger, happy soul that is
in such a ship where the interest of Christ is in the same
bottome with him, this is my comfort, though I sleep, yet
my Lord is never asleep he hath a watchfull eye and powerfull hand for his churches good ; And o my soul how art
thou priviledged to haue such a pilate such companions,
such a haven, fear not, hold up faith and patience, tho the
ship and thy own soul be in a storm fix the anchor of hope
beyond the vail and thou shall come at last safe to shore.

EXPERIMENT 8   My son Eliezer hauing lyen under various
infirmitys of body, temptations of Satan, desertions of spirit,
exceeding despondencys, writ to me from Wallinwels, complained sadly came over, hoped for some help in Craven and
found none, was much discouraged, went to god much in
secret prayers, and in other dutys lamented a hard heart,
gods withdrawings. at last we had a solemne day of fasting
and prayer at James Greaues, where he sadly bewailed his
case Sep 7 81 I was much troubled for him and concluding
the day god helped my heart much in pleading for him, the
day after as we rode togather he told me god came in to his
heart and gaue him some token for good in that duty, and
the evening after going to prayer with me in the family he

was carryed out much in thankfulnes to god for the smiles
of his face, and incouragemt in Secret desiring to giue up
himself to the ministry in the meanest place, blessed, blessed
be my god—

We designed a day of thankfulnes to god Sept 13 1681
and in the interim on the day before. Sep 12 our dear Lord
gaue us in another mercy to his body for having directions
from Dr Cart at Manchester to help him agt his quartan
ague that had hanged on him 8 months the Lord blessed
the medicine he took so that he missed his fit that day
and again on thursday Sep 15 and we haue good hopes of
his recovery so we spent tuesday Sep 13 in thanksgiving,
our god made it a sweet heart melting day, helped Jo. Learoyd, W Naylor Tim Holt in giving praise, Eli. prayd and
praised god affectionately, but John exceeded, my heart was
wonderfully drawn out, I haue seldom met with the like in
company ; O what a day was it for about 6 houres, surely
gods presence was with us, let him alone haue the glory !

REFLECTION And now what shall I say, my dear Lord
hath out done my thoughts, prevented us with his blessings,
contradicted our feares and desires, he hath magnifyed his
word aboue all his name, how many mercys come thronging
in upon us, health of body, peace of conscience, actings of
grace, and hopes of glory so well doth our Lord tune a
thankfull heart that he lays in new matters of gratitude
when he sees us aiming at it, the very design of paying our
vows pleaseth him, and brings in fresh mercys, yea in the
day of our gratitude we had new grounds of gratitude,
healing to body is sweet especially coming as a return of
prayer, comfort to a drooping spirit is very desirable as
a performance of promise, but oh the workings of the spirit
of adoption in the hearts and lips of my children is transcendent loue as it is the fruit of Christs purchase, an
evidence of grace and a forerunner of glory, but especially
when this comes as light after darknes as resurrection
after death: Oh that ever my Lord should deal thus well
with me, god hath known my feares and cares, teares
and prayers for these very mercys, he saw in secret and
rewards openly. oh that ever god should giue me children,
spare their liues, make them capable of learning, train
them up hitherto, sanctify them by his grace, employ

them in his work, set one of them apart in his way, make the other at last willing and desirous of that office agt all discouragements within and without, make them chuse the persecuted way of nonconformity in such a day as this is, not consulting flesh and blood, but opposing all argts fetcht from thence with the glorious genuine ends of the ministry, begging of the Lord that he would betrust them with an oppertunity to travel over poor sinners tho in the most mean and contemptible places : this, this is to my greater satisfaction then if they were preferred to the highest dignity in the church : My soul magnify the Lord, my spirit, rejoice thou in god my saviour, for he hath regarded the low estate of his servant, he that is mighty hath done to me great things and holy is his name, his mercy is unto them that fear him from generation to generation, Lord thou hast given me more comfort in giving me and mine covenant grace then if thou hadst made us earthly princes. Oh for a thankful heart ! oh for an obedient life, what shal I render to the Lord for all his benefits towards me, I will take the cup of Salvation and call on the name of the Lord, I will pay my vows to the Lord now in the presence of all his people. O Lord, truely I am thy servant, I am thy servant, the son of thy handmaid, thou hast loosed my bonds ; now, even now god begins to hear the prayers of ancestours, now the graces that flourished in mother and grandmother spring up in young Timothys ; may the blessings of their father prevail aboue the blessings of my progenitors. who knows what a reserve my Lord hath for his church by these my sons and their companions. Lord haue respect to the rising generation, let thy Urim and Thummim (light and perfection) be in the minds and hearts of these consecrated to thee

EXPERIMENT 9 Having taken a review of the last yeares providences concerning my state and actings, I found that the speciall hand of my dear Lord had been upon me for good in my Lords work, wherein he had helped me to be abundant. for in the year 1681 he helped me in preaching on week days at home and abroad (besides Lords day work) 108 times, in keeping 30 fasts, 9 days of thanksgiving, and travelling 1400 miles about my masters work, having made this review, I set myself upon tuesday forenoon Jan 10 1681 to spend some time with my dear Lord in my closet and was from about 9 to 12 in that work first I fel down on my knees and face, giving god the glory of the preceding yeares mercys, about an hour, oh what a sweet melting duty was it, then spent another hour in confessing and bewailing my sins and slips that year, begging pardon and power, and lastly as it fel providentially in my course of reading I read and commented on Ezek 34 pleading promises in latter part of it for the church, and had some comfortable impressions of approaching deliverance.

REFLECTION Oh my soul mayst thou not sing of mercy and judgment, mercy first afterwards of judgment, yet sing of both, mercy to soul, body, work, family, judgment in the afflictions met with, sing of both, for god allays the sweet of mercy with a dash of wholesome wormwood in thy cup, and thy Lord remembers mercy in the midst of judgment, and stays the rough wind in the day of the East wind, sharply afflicting, sweetly supporting and making all tend to good, blessed be god.

Oh what a year of mercy hath the preceding year been I have ridden many hundred miles, got no dangerous falls however, no hurt, all my bones doe speake and say, " Lord who is like to thee"? how many sad Examples of great troubles in others short journeys have I heard of haue fallen out this year? god hath delivered my soul from death, mine eyes from tears, my feet from falling, this year also he hath spared me, another year is added to, yet also taken from my life, what art thou better oh my soul in the end then thou wast in the beginning of this year? what increase of grace, progresse in holines power agt corruption oh what good hast thou got or done to soules? what additions hast thou made to stock of knowledge, loue to god, faith, repentance, god hath been kind to thee, hast thou been dutifull to him or faithfull to thy trust, or faithful in thy generation? surely thy mercys haue been new every morning, every moment, great in his faithfulness: haue thy acts of gratitude and obedience been dayly renewed? canst thou reflect on thy spending this year with comfort? thou hast been much imployed, hast thou been well imployed? canst thou reflect with comfort on the manner as wel as the number of thy works for god? haue thy principles, management and thy designes in all been according to the word of god? thou hast

preached oft, hast thou preached well? thou hast put up
many prayers, canst thou say they were sincere, believing
and fervent? thou hast kept many fasts, were they such
fasts as god hath chose? what a frame of spirit hast thou
carryed with thee in thy journeys? what edifying discourse
hast thou uttered in all the companys thou hast conversed
with? alas, alas, I may take chance to myself; the sins of
the last year have been many and multiplyed, its well if all
scores be cleared betwixt god and thy soul, now the former
year is expired and a new year begun; if the Lord should
mark iniquity who could stand? I cannot answer him one
of a thousand upon casting up my accounts I find my Arithmetick far short of recounting either my mercys or iniquitys,
David accounts both innumerable, so may I; many O Lord
my god are thy wonderfull works—" they cannot be reckoned up in order unto thee "— *(psal 40 5)*
more then can be numbered: and with all
innumerable evils haue compassed me about— *(ver 12)*
Oh what a load of mercys! Blessed be the
Lord who dayly loadeth us with his benefits: *(psal 68 9)*
woe to me that haue dayly laden him with my
iniquitys, yea as a cart pressed with sheaues, *(Amos 2 13)*
this (dayly) is not every day a mercy, that it
should only be 365 as many as there are days in a year, but
mercy hath filled up every hour of the day, every moment
of the hour. and so haue my sins: their numbers are vast
and unmeasurable, alas my thanksgiving days have been
short of my fasting days but how much more short of my
mercys? my repentings short of my solemne professions
of humiliations but infinitely short of proportion to my sins:
oh how may I sit down wondering that god hath not shak'd
mee off the hand of his providence as a viper into the fire
of hell. Lord take thou the glory of the last yeares providences and patience, pardon my last yeares offences and
provocations; wash away all scores in the blood of Jesus;
giue my soul the comfort, and thy people the benefit of my
dayly labours in the gospel; giue me a stock of grace for
the services and sufferings of the ensuing year maintain
the like liberty one year more; if not fit me for dayly
crosses and if this year produce more notable revolutions of
providence then many preceding in mercy or judgmt oh lead
me safe through all to thy glory and my comfort—

Experiment 10—On Munday night Jan 23 168½ being in my study busy at my book, reading and writing, and delaying to goe to god by secret prayer, I was shifting my wax candle and accidentally put it out, besides my purpose, seeing it was so and I could not follow my study, I judged that to be providence of god calling me to another work then I was upon, so I set myself to the duty of secret prayer, and god made it a sweet melting duty, and did my soul good in my addresses to the throne of grace, and this Experiment I haue met with many times, blessed be my good god.

Reflection Oh my soul how loath art thou to goe to thy father and friend in heaven, theres thy sloth and sin, but god doth thee good in a sort against thy will theres his kindnes and loue. Oh how bad and backward art thou, god almighty must hire thee or driue thee to himself yea he hath hired thee many a time by the incomes of his spirit, and returnes of prayer but that would not doe; he hath driven thee by a rod of affliction upon thy back of severall sorts, still thou hast loytered, it will not be some excuse or evasion thou hast made to shift and shuffle off duty, and now darkness comes upon thee providentially that thou canst doe nothing else but pray, its well thou hast that duty left for a reserue, no thanks to thee in a sort, for thou art forced to it, so god hedgeth up sinners way from their vain vagarys, Joh 12 35 thus night puts an end to some kinds of work, oh that I could walk while I haue the light lest darknes come upon me but blessed be god that in darkest night, and closest prison or lowest dungeon soules haue accesse to god by prayer, so Jeremiah in his dungeon, Daniel in the lions den, Jonah in the belly of hell, psal 139 11 12 can pray to god, darknes hides not from him the night becomes light about me, my Lord can discern wickednes though committed in greatest darknes and obscurity, the same Lord can discover singleness of heart though wrapt up under the thickest vaile of secrecy; yea the greater darknes the clearer evidence of grace and freedom from distraction. Our Lord that bids us pray in a closet, will hear when theres no candle; a soule may oft see gods face most clearly when its Col 1 12   darkest both in a natural and metaphorical Rev 21 23   sense; heaven is the inheritance of saints in

U

Rev 22 8   light, yet theres no need of either sun or
             candle, thers no night there; where the king
             is theres the court; god is light, in him theres
1 Joh 1-8   no darknes at all, and they that injoy him are
             in the light; blessed be my Lord, that hath
given me the light of life, that hath rescued me from the
power of darknes and notwithstanding the prince of darknes
hath secured my soul from his rage, yea made darknes to
shine as the light about him, by the shine of his face upon
me, Blessed be my god for the works of light in place of
             darknes, his light shineth in a dark place; the
2 Pet 1 19   word of god is a light to my feet and a lan-
             thorn to my paths, the spirit inlightens my
understanding, oh let the light of thy countenance shine on
my soul, let the sun of righteousness rise upon me with
healing under his wings, my spirit is oft in the dark about
my state, may I get clearnes from thee in such a dark dis-
             consolate frame though I work it out in the
2 Cor 46   dark. god caused light at first to shine out of
             darknes, oh for the light of the knowledg of
the way of god in my soul; well, through grace diuine help
comes in, my heart is inlarged, god is not limited, solitari-
ness may hauc the best company attending it, darkness the
sweetest light, restraint the best inlargment, let guilty consciences tremble to be in the dark, my soul, my soul will
affect it, so that I may haue the father of lights with me,
the son of god to shine upon me, and the spirit of god thus
to inlighten and inliven me, Lord, evermore lead me through
the dark entry of this wicked world to the Land of light
and life, Amen.

EXPERIMENT 11   On friday, feb 17 168½ in the morning I
had a design to spend that forenoon in that sweet and
solemne work of seeking the Lord by secret prayer in my
study, and god did further me in that work, keeping away
visitors and other distractions, before family prayer I begged
his assistance and presence, then we read a chapter and
went to prayer in the family, but I gaue no hint of my purpose, about 9 o'clock I set on my work, my course in reading
was Mal 2 which god helped me to improue and comment
upon for my humiliation for personal and ministerial sins so
I fell on my knees, then on my face in bitterness of spirit

confessing all the sins of my heart and life, that I could
remember, and begging pardon, grace, familiarity with god,
for about an hour, then I rose up and read part of the 89th
psal. god helpt me to act faith on the promises that concern
my own soul and my seed all along, then fell on my knees
and face and pleaded it with my dear Lord with some
measure of warmth, about another hour in that work, then
rose up and read with some sensiblenes and application the
rest of that psal and then fell down before my Lord and
though I cannot say my heart was in such a melting frame
that last hour for the church and nation yet my Lord was
not altogether a stranger, particularly he helpt me to plead
affectionately for Dr Hook and some conformists who had
cast much dirt upon us of late, and particularly on the
kings day Jan 30 8½ wherein he charged the murder of Old
king Charles on Non-conformists by name, it troubled me,
and god helped me to spread it before the Lord, and his late
book also, as Hezekiah did Rabshakehs letter, it was an
heart melting season, god will hear, howbeit on the day
after (being Saturday) my heart was much shut up alone,
tho I confesse I had meltings in praying with my wife.

REFLECTION And now, oh my soul, what dost thou say
concerning these strange and various dealings of thy Lord
with thee, O what mercy is it that I haue an house to serue
god in, yea a corner of that house, a little hole where I can
be retired, a heart to creep to my heavenly father, a father,
such a father and friend to make my moan to, such a
mediator and master of requests to present my suit to him,
such a spirit to assist me with sighs and groans, such promises, presidents, experiences for my incouragement; oh
what kindnesse is this, my dear Lord doth not altogather
absent himself, nor hide his face, let him haue the glory of
these his discoverys, for alas, though I doe fast and pray
with others and alone I haue nothing to boast of, its but
duty though a free-will-offering, yea I doe short of duty in
all, yea I sin in all, I haue need to pray for a pardon of my
prayers, mourn over my mournings, fast for my fastings,
and get my teares washt in that pure fountain of Christs
precious blood, Lord take away the iniquity of my holy
things; teach me O my Lord so to be thankfull for inlargements as not to trust in my performances, to magnify free

grace is to vilify my self, so to doe what thou dost inable me as to deny my own righteousness and to expect accesse to god and acceptance mcerly upon the account of the satisfaction and intercession of my Lord Jesus Christ, thou that hast helpt me in duty help me also above duty to thy self, and to goe out of my self in all, and oh my Lord, hear the groanings of thy poor dejected servant that haue eased my heart to thee and haue laid my Load on thee, casting my care on thee, according to thy command, thou hast promised to care for me, yea to sustain not only my

Psal 83 8   burden, but me under my burden ; I will hark what the Lord my God will say, for he will speak peace to his saints, but oh that I might

1 Chron 29   never return to folly, Lord god of Abraham,

18   Isaac and Jacob, keep this for ever in the imagination of the thoughts of the heart of thy

servant, and prepare my heart unto thee ; god is good to the soul that seeks him, to my soul that waits on him, and for he giues present mercy, he bestows after mercys in return of prayer, before the revolution of a week my Lord giues me the very mercys in kind I begged of him ;

Isai 65 24   before I call he answers, and whilst I am speaking the Lord heares, divine providence

brings home my son in mercy for whom I prayed a few days before, oh for a thankfull heart, yet as yesterdays grace will not serve to days necessitys, and I find yesterdays inlargements afar off to-day, so my injoyment of mercys yesterday will not keep me from wants or prevent new afflictions to morrow, oh for a thankfull heart for wts past and a prepared heart for wt is to come.

EXPERIMENT 12   On Lords day, March 5, 168¼ I was wonderfully carryed out to god in prayer in publick, and for god in preaching pertinently and with much affection and had laid out my strength to the full, yet was well, eat my supper went to my study, stayd a little too long, it was cold, thinking to goe to prayer I omitted, thought I would inlarge below in my family, which sinful evasion my wicked heart hath made many times, and sometimes god hath accordingly assisted in my family work, but that night he withdrew, as it was righteous he should, tho I struggled before I went to bed I begun to be ill with chollick, thought a stool might ease me, but it did not, I lay waking, tossing in pain al night, my wife rose and maid to help me, but all did no good, I rose about 2 or 3 o'clock, sate by the fire, went to bed, got no ease, vomited much, gods hand was on me in the morning I thought it would be death, but god gaue ease next day, and so recovery shortly, blessed be god.

REFLECTION Reflect, oh my soul on that providence and the circumstances attending the same, surely

Job 6 v 8 affliction cometh not forth of the dust, neither doth trouble spring out of the ground, god

Job 8 11 alone maketh sore and bindeth up; can the rush grow up without mire? can the flag grow without water? is there not some sin in the subject afflicted? doe not shoures proceed from ascending vapours? didst not thou o my soul, first provoke god, and so draw a rod on thy oun back? god had not scourged thee but that he saw something amisse in thee, wast thou not proud and highly conceited of thy Lords days inlargement, was not this a prick to that bladder? as thirst was to victorious and vapouring Sampson, didst thou study and act things that evening proper and suitable to that days work? didst thou not put off prayer till thou wast unfit and then totally omit? alas thus, thus it was, god saw thy spirit backward to return and give him the tribute of thanks, its well if thou didst not set the crown on thine oun head and then no wonder if he cast not thy crown to the ground, well, thus it was, god afflicted, pain came suddenly like one wt travelleth, and unavoidably, like an armed man; and what didst thou under it, O my soul, Alas nothing but tosse and tumble about, a clear emblem of thy restles fancy, and unsettled mind, be ashamed, O my tumultuous spirit that when gods rod was on thy back, thou didst not mend thy face heavenwards, nay thou couldst doe just nothing but lye tossing like a wild bull in a net full of the fury of the Lord, not a thought fixed on god, not a grace in exercise, not a duty spiritually performed; oh soul, herein thou mayst discern thy sin and punishment to suit, yea thy antecedent sinning of oun distractions to be punished in this subsequent sin of discomposed thoughts from bodily pain; alas, how unfit is the sympathizing soul with a pained body to mind spiritual objects; had I been then to haue

lookt after the initial life of god, or work of grace, how for-
lorn had my case been, what fooles are they that put off this
great affair to sick-bed; yet I will not excuse myself from
gods work by bodily distresse, no, no, it was my sin, and
fault which I have cause to bewail, for former diligence is
no supersedes from sick-bed duty however divine indulgence
graciously spares weak children. But the lesse thou couldst
doe then, O my soul, the more active be thou now, redeem
that lost time, make more speed in thy christian course;
pray more, mortify lust, watch thy heart, exercise grace,
                    clear up thy evidences, make ready for glory
Mark 13 39   lest coming suddenly he find thee sleeping;
                    what a quick dispatch can our Lord make, he
oft takes from pulpit to bed, from bed to graue; oh, pray,
next time, as if the last time; preach as if it were thine oun
funerall sermon, as ready to giue an account to him that
shal judg the quick and dead.   Lord let me so liue as I dare
dye, so act as ceasing to act, so dye as to liue with god for
ever, prepare my soul for the next encounter, and when
death comes, receiue me to glory.

EXPERIMENT 13   Upon wednesday morning June 28 168¼
came Ralph Leeming (one that had been my servant) to
invite me to his fathers funeral, (old Joseph Blamire) at
Bradford, but I told him I was for Lancashire that day; I
hear Ralph (said I) you are turned preacher, he sd there are
few preachers now adays, but readers, expounders, I askt
him wt call he had, he sd he had a call from god, I told him
he must haue either an ordinary call, and then he must be
tryed by such as had discerning or extraordinary and then
let him shew it by extraordinary gifts and miracles; he sd a
man is fittest to judg of his call, &c, I told him wt the
Apostle sd, 1 Cor 7 20 let every man abide in the calling—I
told him of his calling to be a cloth-miller, then he presumed
to be a phisitian, and now a preacher, which I knew he was
not fit for, he sd I was not his judg, and that Paul was a
tent maker and preacher, so might he follow all these call-
ings, I told him paul was an apostle, not of men nor by
men, an extraordinary person, nor for to be imitated thus he
and I talkt a considerable time at the gates, god put me into
an unusual heat, 1 to protest against that course he was
taking, and told him he sinned in it, and god would not

blesse him in presuming upon such a mighty work without a call, 2 I minded him of his former profession, aboue 20 yeares agoe when he lived with me and indeed I fear he hath lost that Religion he seemed once to haue ; alas for him

REFLECTION What art thou to learn, oh my soul, from this unexpected affair, surely theres something of god in it, Alas, alls not gold that glistrs, many hopefull convictions prayers, affections haue been blasted, and come to nothing, this young man came from Grindleton or Downham in Lanc. many yeares agoe under my ministry in publick, had strange impressions, hopeful workings, anxious to some knowledg, performed dutys got into christian society, was always proud and conceited, which I utterly dislikt in him, and now corruption breakes out, and whilst he act an Empireck upon mens bodys, patience bore with him, but now that he usurpes the tremendous calling of the ministry, I am afraid of him, and haue faithfully discharged my duty to him, though god knows not without some passion and unskilfulnes, Lord pardon that and accept of my good will to bear my testimony for god, set in with what I haue said, and accomplish thy work on his heart, prevent his offering his strange fire, lest fire come from heaven to devour him, whatever his pretended good meaning be let him not touch the Ark, or bring sacrifice lest he meet with Uzzahs or Uzziahs dismal catastrophe ; Lord what madness and phrenzy are some raw heads seized on by that can scarce read a chapter true in English and yet pretend abilities for this sacred function ; a poor worm trained up from my infancy to it, exercised in it aboue thirty yeares see more insufficiency for it than ever, and well I may when such a one as Paul crys out *Tisikaros;* I see all short, they see nothing wanting in themselves ; Alas, what dreadful consequences haue been produced of such conceited fooles intruding into that sacred office, that are fitter to learn than to teach, that understand neither what they say nor whereof they affirm that pervert the soules of sinners and have brought in damnable doctrines ; Lord haue mercy on thy poor church that is seduced and rent in pieces betwixt prophane, formal, superstitious wretches that hate the power of godliness on the one hand, and such unlearned conceited dunces that pretend to it on the other, my heart within me is broken, because of the prophets all my bones shake—

Jer 23 9   because of the Lord, and because of the words
of his holiness, such a word as that I haue

v 21   not sent these prophets yet they ran, I haue
not spoken to them yet they prophecyed, woe

to the Lord, woe to these preachers both wch are like to
proue the   pest of the church, I haue seen the dreadfull
effects of such things and discern its dissonancy to the
scripture-rule and order, and they shall not profit

ver 32   this people at all: Lord help me to be more thankful for mission, commission, qualification, successe

and to be more abounding in the work of the Lord, since
men are heaping up such vain teachers, Lord amend them

Experiment 14   Although in my journey in Lanc. and
at home for a considerable time my heart hath been in a
good sensible frame in mornings in closet-prayer, oh wt a
presence of grace haue I felt, yet the morning after I came
home being July 6 1682 in family prayer my spirit was not
so liuely, but dul, though I had met with god in my closet
that morning, yet a friend coming to whom I paid some
mony to return for L H and hauing severall reckonings, one
business I had forgot, but in family prayer it came glancing
into my mind, which I told them after, and upon it we
discoursed whether such a thing foysted into ones mind at
duty came from Satan, or from a mans own trifling vain
heart, I judged it came from the devil, who is that bad spirit
that brings evil or impertinent things to our remembrance,
as the good spirit brings good things into our minds, however closing with them is from our base hearts, they are
ordinarily from Satan.

Reflection   Oh my soul, consider this sad evil wherewith
thou art so often overtaken, and bewail it before the Lord
oh subtile devil, who snatcheth and catcheth the oppertunity
of setting on a soul presently after it hath been with god,
how like is Satan to sharking companions that haunt a
young heire, or theeues that set upon a person when he hath
received his rents, or pirates that set upon a wel-fraught
ship, it is the devil's hellish policy, to try to win the soul
from its dearest Lord after sweetest embraces, oh then how
he insults, when a gracious heart hath come off wel in

spiritual conflicts, then satan comes unexpectly on the blind side, and giues them the foyl he seeks to win the fort royal of the heart from god; oh how he waylays the traveller especially after a good bait; but as bad as the devil is we may wrong him, our bad hearts are the setters and under-mine us, doing us more mischief then the devil himself; yea every man is a satan to himself and if gods word did not record it, theres a proof within us James 1 14 that every man is tempted "when he is drawn away of his own lust and enticed;" oh wicked heart that bandyeth with Satan and keeps secret correspon-dence with that open enemy, no sooner doth satan tempt but we consent, if he be fire we are pouches, if his sparks fly into our flax, als afire suddenly; satan can present ob-jects, but cannot compel us to entertain them; we cannot hinder birds from lighting on our heads, but we may keep them from making nests in our haire; hence our Lord lays the blame of evil thoughts upon an evil heart and the worst of vain thoughts is their lodging in us; and if we will reform and be saved, we must wash our hearts, Jer 4 14, "Oh, Jerusalem, wash thy heart from wickedness, that thou mayst be saved, how long shall thy vain thoughts lodg within thee." its not their stepping into thee oh my soul but lying and abiding within thee thats likely to be thy ruine; oh that I could hate vain thoughts, oh, that my heart were more furnished and filled with graces and gracious meditations especially. oh my god let nothing in-terpose betwixt god and my soul in religious worship, unite my heart to thee, make my heart one with thy sacred majesty.

EXPERIMENT 15 Upon Tuesday July 25 1682 rising before 5 a clock, going to my study, reading my chapters, and going to prayer, god drew out my heart graciously for my sons at London near an hour, coming down towards 7 and expecting a letter from them (hauing been 2 or 3 weeks without) I fell into a chaffe agt them for not writing to me, I found my spirit disordered, writ an angry letter to them, then set myself according to purpose after family prayer, to spend that forenoon in solemne closet-work, first I examined my self about my souls state, and work of grace and so went to prayer, god helpt, then I read part of 52 and 53

of Isaiah in order to the Lords supper approaching and
commented, applyed, oh how sweet was it, so prayd again,
and in confessing of sin that morning, god brought many
sins to my remembrance I had not thought of before humbled my heart, gaue me repentance, and I hope sealed a
pardon in the blood of Christ, then I set myself to plead for
Zion, read Isai 54 which was suitable and god made affecting, but in prayer my heart was something shut up, I struggled a season with my untoward heart, then my wife cald
me off about 11 a clock, I yielded and went not to the work
again yt day, and the evening of that day heard a piece of
bad news as to public affaires.

REFLECTION   Oh my soul, what hast thou been doing this
day? this day (at least part of it) thou designest to spend
in prayer, and thy Lord did not deny either oppertunity or
assistance some houres about personal work, but denyed
both as to public concernes. doth not this seem to say, that
god will hear thee for thine own soul, but
Ezek 14 14   not for the nation as god saith of Noah,
Daniel, Job if they stand before him they
shall deliver their own soules by their righteousnes; well
blessed be god for that, personal returnes of prayer are
worth observing and very comfortable : But how dost thou
know after what manner prayer shall be answered? Be it
as god thinks fit, an answer is a kindnes to
psal 65 5   gracious soules tho it be by terrible things in
righteousnes, for still he is the god of our salvation, and I am indifferent whether my Lord saue me from
troubles or by troubles whether his providence shal secure
me, or his influence assist me, his will be done, if my Lord
will hide me in his chamber Ile thank him, if he will send
me to bed Ile thank him better though the graue doe not
praise him, yet the soul (the better part glorifyed shal sound
the Lords praises at a better rate than in this thick lower
region, only my Lord hear my prayer for furnishing my soul
for better for worse. I am thine saue me, this day haue I
made new vows, I haue signed another deed of gift to be the
Lords in life in death : my dear Lord, help me to perform,
second my ingagements with assistance, and let it appear
openly the fruit of what hath passed betwixt thy majesty
and my soul in a corner when I shall be called forth to bear

my publick testimony for thee : But I cannot forgoe or cease
my suit for Zion, this night thou didst giue me a loose, that
I might giue Zion a lift, Lord hear, thou art much concerned therin, nor doth the churches welfare depend on the
inlargemts of such a silly worm, god may awake though he
be asleep Amen, and Amen—

EXPERIMENT 16   On thursday Nov 23 1682 in the morning
I rose early at Mr I Disons went to prayer, god sweetly assisted my heart in recommending my self and the work of
that day to him, he brought me safely through very slippery
and dangerous ways to Sowrby, there god graciously helpt
me in praying preaching to a full assembly, affected their
hearts, preserved our liberty, so I returned home in the
evening, as I came home at godley brook I rode through a
deep place to wash my horse, hauing passed safely through
once, I would ride through again, the horse was loath to goe
in, I forc'd him, and (whether it was by a sudden turn or a
stumbling on a stone I know not, but) my horse came down
not hauing fast hold on him, and I fell into the water, was
sore wet in my lower parts, got out, got on rid home fast,
shifted me, I could not but reflect on my old Schoolfellow
Mr Th : Isherwood, vicar of Eccles, yt had been drinking
with some gentlemen, returning home fell off his horse, was
drowned in a ditch that scarce covered all his head

REFLECTION   Oh my Lord, thou art my god, my guard,
my safety, and protection, thou leadest me in the way wher-
                    in I should goe, to thee I committed my soul,
psal 121 8 :   body, and all my concerns, thou dost preserve
                    my goings out and my comings in according
to thy gracious promise, thou giuest thy angels charge to
                    keep me in all my ways : he sd when thou
Isai 43 2   passest through the waters I will be with thee,
                    or through the rivers they shall not overflow
thee : how suddenly could my Lord haue cast me, and kept
me under my horse in that deep hole, till I had been choakt
and stifled ! and there haue lyen all that night, and been
found with astonishment dead in the morning, as unlikely
an occasion hath been the death of as great a man, but my
Lord got my feet quickly out of the stirrups, which else
might haue been fastened there, and being a lusty and

young horse might haue dragg'd me and dasht me in peeces, without remedy or help, it being in the night nor could my many kind friends or applause from men, or estate or worldly advantages or accommadations haue secured me, and oh what a rumour would haue gone of it all the country over, some would haue been grieved, others haue rejoyced at my fall, and who knows what reports would haue been spread or constructions made of such a providence, Lidia Priestly was drowned in that same brook Dec 17 1681 about that time twenty months, but god pluckt me out sent me home, gaue me incouragemt, that I am not any worse for it, though a frosty night Blessed, blessed be my god, that delivered mine eyes from teares, my soul from death, and my feet from falling, to god the lord belong the issues from death, he that is my god is the god of salvations : He keepeth all my bones, so that none of them is broken : and now all my bones shall speak and say, Lord who is like unto thee ? alas I deserved not this mercy, yea I forfeited this safety : how many deliverances haue I forgot ? how many preventing mercys did I slight ? I had but a little before (viz Lords day Nov 5 82) a very narrow escape out of the hands of mine enemys that sought to apprehend me, but god preserved me and disappointed them, but alas, I was not duely affected with that mercifull deliverance : yea this very day I had escaped many falls in slippery ways, but did not duely acknowledg god in all my ways, did not meditate on the Lord in my solitary journeys could not get my heart to close with god in contemplation, nor with my self in self-examination : Lord humble me, Let my soul be serious in committing all my concerns to god, and more thankfull for dayly preservation Oh my Lord, what is thy design hast thou in this ? what dost thou preserue me for ? dost thou spare me for service or for suffering ? if for the former, shew me my work, and help me to doe it, inlarge my heart in studying, conversing praying, preaching, bring in soules by me to thy self, giue me tokens of acceptances, and blessed successe : or is it for suffering greater things yet for thy names sake, as that Martyr sd in a storm, thou carryest a Bp that must be burnt, not drowned : Lord, thy will be done, fire, racks, prison, banishment, death, any thing so I may injoy my Lord Christ mortify sin, quicken grace, raise my affections, prepare me for the worst, assist me to bear my burden, to passe a fiery tryall with comfort and courage, and deal with me as thou pleasest : Let not me escape the flames of Sodom to becom a pillar of salt by looking back to the world ; but as thou hast by thy grace hitherto kept thy worthles servant so secure me still, and keep me by thy power through faith to salvation Amen, Amen :

EXPERIMENT 17   On munday March 12 168$\frac{3}{4}$ in the morning god drew out my heart graciously, so that I seemed to be so much concerned for the church, that I told my Lord I would set aside any concernes of my wife and family that I might mend Zion oh wt a good breakfast had I. then I attended the funeral of Sam : Halidays child at Halifax, thence went at 2 a clock to James Scolfie [1] ds in Southowram, it was a day of thankfulnes, I spent an hour in discoursing Extempore on psal 116 12 what shal I render —god did help graciously, tho in prayer I had not that wonted inlargement, I came homewards, on Halifax Bank-top my horse stumbled on the rough causey fell clear down, threw me off the cawsey, fell on me, I lay in the mire, he lay upon me, I could not get up, nor my horse, lying with his feet upwards to the cawsey, I knew not wt to doe, it was dark, no body near me, I wriggled and struggled to get my leg and thigh from under him, I was afraid of his rising before me, lest he had trod on me, at last I got my leg from under him, then he rose, I stood up, my hat, cap, hood were scattered, then Sam Sharp came to me, helpt, dresst me, led down my horse, I got up, rid home, told my family the wonderful work of god and as I was able, gaue god thanks

REFLECTION   And now, Oh my soul, since my dear Lord hath done these great things for such an unworthy ungrate-full wretch ; Reflect on this mercy, and consider the aggravations therof, thy danger was great, therfore the mercy could not be small, had the horse cast thee on the stones, it had shattered thy bones, or in all probability broken thy neck, but god gaue thee thy life for a prey, as he hath done many a time, not only in apparent, but unseen dangers he sent his angel to guard thee he came himself and gaue order to the horse thus to fall, not to hurt, but durty thee, to stain thy pride, and lay thine honour in the dirt, his armes were under thee, and his goodnes did reach and surround

thee, blessed be the Lord, may be god saw thee guilty of
some sin, that day search thy heart, mourn for sin beg a
pardon, prepare for new troubles of another nature :

EXPERIMENT 18 On munday morning April 2 1683 according to my usuall course I set my self in my study to
plead with god for his church, this nation and our congregations, god did wonderfully draw out my heart, and my
soul was warm and working busily at it, my wife called me
down upon a slight occasion, I came down, chid her, and
gaue her sharp words, tho alas she was ignorant of what I
was doing, she took it sadly, fell a weeping was disconsolate
all that day, Satan got hold, foysted vain imaginations into
her mind, helpt her to make bad constructions of it, that
day we had little conference, but the morning after we dis-
courst it, I confessed my fault and folly in my passionate
finding fault with her, and vain-glory in discovering wt I
was doing, we knelt down by the bed-side, I prayd we both
wept, were comfortably closed : this workt kindly on my
heart through grace, I got to my study, fell to my reading
my chapters, praying god sweetly helpt, so in the family,
then I resolved to spend the remainder of that fore-noon in
that sweet work. so I designed to confesse my own sins before that reading and commenting on psal 38 then prostrating my self, reckoning with grief wt sins I could call to
mind : rose up, read psal 51, then fell down, pleaded for
pardon, grace, for my self, wiue : then was taken off,
returned, read psal 69, fell down, pleaded with god for
church, nation, king, yet was not so large and inlarged as in
the former

REFLECTION Oh my Lord, prayer is good, passion is bad,
and its pitty two things so opposite should be such near
neighbours, its hard indeed to goe off the knees, and be
                   angry on the feet, surely the wrath of man
Jam 1 20   works not the righteousnes of god : wrath is the
                   wind wch the bad spirit raiseth : and why should
these fumes be in heavenly breasts ! should not the water of
prayer quench that flame ? Oh how sad a thing is with
Jonah to be angry on our knees, or to rise up with wrath !
but a wrestling Jacob must halt on his thigh : imperfections
and passions must shew we are but men : yet even praying

prevailing Elijah was subject to like passions
Jam 5 17   as we are : yet his sinfull passions hindred not
the fruit of his prayers : god doth not hear us
for the perfection of our prayers, but for the intercession of
his son : nor can it be expected our dutys should be sinles,
but our soules believing in, and improving Jesus our advocate at gods right hand, who doth mingle his much incense
with our defectiue prayers, and takes away the iniquitys of
our holy things : yea such a good Chimist is our dear Lord,
that he can extract a wholsom medicine out of poyson and
make use of a passion of anger to stirre up godly sorrow :
tho sin must be hated, and is no way good, yet free-grace
can bring good out of evil : yet oh my soul venture not on
sin, be sure to watch thy heart, and with most care after the
sweetest inlargements : take of pride and vain-glory, which
is a worm that breeds soonest in the finest and sweetest
flowr : obserue, when thou art strongest, thou becomes the
weakest, and when weakest in thy self thou art strongest in
thy Lord : god resists the proud, but giues grace to humble,
never put off thy garments or armour, mind where the hedg
is lowest and there fence best, yea where thou thinkest it
highest make a double Barricade : walk close with god in
duty and out of duty : blessed is he that feareth always :

EXPERIMENT 19   Coming to London Dec 29 1682 and immediatly after going to Mr Tho : Parkhurst, my Bookseller
to whom I had sent a Manuscript several months before,
called Israels Lamentatious after the Lord, on 1 Sam 72
wch I made account had been printed, but he had not begun
it tho he designed the printing of it, being incouraged by
some ministers in London, he resolved presently to set
about it, and print it before I went out of town wch he did,
only in reading the Epistle he found some smart reflections
wch (hauing sent for me) he communicated to me, thinking
it was not safe to print them, being then a very hazardous
time, upon reading them I thought so too, so expunged
them, which I am heartily glad I did, for when it came
down into the country, Dr H [ook] sent for it and greedily,
(and I fear captiously) read it over, sd it was a seditious
piece, another sd it was full of faction, consulting with his
clergy they all censured it deeply, yea Justice H [orton ?]
had it and Sir J K [aye] and a confident story was brought

me from Halifax that on Munday April 16 1683 the justices
met at Huthersfield to consider of my Book, I was also
summoned to the sessions that week, tho not on that account, my feares were great my trouble surprising, and the
rather 1 Because in so writing I had brought my self into
trouble, and begun to question my call to write : 2 bec : my
adversarys seemed to haue got the advantage agt me they
had long been seeking, 3 some of my friends censured me,
and some at M. sd I had laid my self open, another gaue
hints, as tho I had not done wisely, 4 a godly eminent
Minister, to wm I shewed the passage they excepted agt,
shakt the head, and sd it was true that I writ (viz that a
law was made to thrust out 2000 ministers Aug 24 1662—)
but sth he they will interpret it a complaining of the laws,
but (sth he) you must stand by it, upon this I was still more
troubled, dejected, could not tell what to say this was Apr
18 1683,—but after a while god helped me to humble my
soul before god, beg pardon of wt I had done amisse agt
god and men, committing my self and my all to god, comforting my self that what I had writ was in the uprightnes
of my heart to doe good, and yt I had no seditious design in
it, and notwithstanding all that talk I haue reasons to think
there was no such thing, for to this day wch is May 28 1683
I hear no more of it, blessed be god—I mean I hear of
nothing further of the justices concerning themselues about
it, and question whether it was so or no, nor any thing else

REFLECTION   Oh my soul, return home again consider thy
state, thy god, thy main work, what answer canst thou make
to these questions ? didst thou not vain-gloriously affect
applause in being seen and admired in print ? didst thou
discard and renounce self in appearing thus on the stage of
the world ? didst thou mind thy call to the work, and purely
seek the glory of god and good of the church rather than
thy credit ? (for profit thou hast had none, but worldly losse,
nor didst thou expect gain) didst thou send forth thy books
with prayers and teares, that god might haue the glory and
his church the advantage by thy labours ? didst thou take
that paines about it in revising, correcting, taking out whatever might be offensiue to men ? didst thou write so humbly,
charitably, candidly of thy superiours in church or state as
became thee ? didst thou take shame to thyself and giue

glory to god under this long dispensation of 20 yeares suspension ? hast thou practiced the duty thou teachest others
in thy book ? hast thou not been a keeper of the vineyards,
but not kept thine own vineyard ? alas, my soul, I fear
thou hast not taken that paines with thine own heart, as a
christian that thou hast imposed on others as a Minister I
feel my heart is growing loose, mindles of mine own concernes, sin gaines, grace looseth ground : theres much of
earth, little of heaven in my heart, Lord humble me, pardon,
purge me, giue me an heart to repent, reform, and practice
the rules I haue prescribed in that book : and let gods will
be done with it or me : how different are the apprehensions
of men, our high-church-men say these are glorious times,
alls right, order, ordinances in great purity, solemnity : and
theres no hinderance of our compleat felicity but factious
nonconformists that obscure their glory, however they are
sure they haue both the Ark and gods presence, and are in
no danger of losing either : I say as Jeremiah said, Amen,
Jer 28 6 : and may converting influencing presence of grace
be in and with the ordinances, let gods will be done concerning our publick libertys, let Cht liue though we dye :

EXPERIMENT 20   On Lords day morning July 15 1683
hauing preacht in the morning at 4 a clock in my own
house, because of danger, and going to chappel that forenoon, with a design to go thence to D T [Dinah Tetley,] at
noon, and preach there in the intermission-time, and did so,
but withal I found some guilt on my conscience in these
cases, 1 I had promised D T [etley] on friday that I would
come to her on Lords-day morning and spend forenoon with
her, but was afraid of danger, so sent back-word that I
would come at noon, 2 in the morning M W askt me whether
I would preach anywhere at noon, I put her off with little
lesse then a lie or æquivocation, and so another at noon,
not daring to tell them, 3 when I came thither, had dined,
several people came, I prayd, preacht, they would haue had
me to stay all the afternoon I had a fair oppertunity to doe
good but neglected, broke off, 4 Mr E told me Dr H [ook]
would be at chappel I had a mind to please him, loath to
offend him, by absence, tho he was not there, so I missed
my end—I sensibly found god withdrew his wonted presence

from me, both in point of councel, leauing me to act indis-
creetly and in prayer, 1 at D my heart was shut up, 2 at
W C at night, 3 in my family, 4 the morning after, at wch
season I am wont to haue much of gods gracious assistance
in pleading with him for the nation, but alas stroue almost
an hour in vain : therfore this morning July 16 god brought
these sins to my remembrance, and made me take shame to
my self, giue glory to god, by confessing, and then, oh then
he gaue me a loose, and drew out my heart affectionately
for Zion, and made it a good season :

REFLECTION Oh my soul, what hast thou done ? where
hast thou been ? art thou not wont to be otherwise imployed
on the Lords-days ? art thou affrighted with mens threats ?
where is thy wonted zeal ? doe not men insult over thee and
laugh thee to scorn, that had stood out so long and now
yieldest ? who ever would haue thought that so small a push
would haue overthrown such a champion ? Lord humble me
if there be sin and weaknes in me : but if thou hast judged
it lawfull to goe hear an honest conformist yet why wouldst
thou turn thy back on thy work to doe it ? doth not our
Lord say its more blessed to giue then to receive, yea, why
didst thou deny to acquaint such as longed to hear the
word ? yea why didst thou dissemble or deny ? why wast
thou so afraid of man ? or desiredst so much to please
men ? Alas this carriage did little becom such a one as thou
art or pretendest to be : Lord, what are we when thou withdrawest from us ? how doe we adde one sin to another ? oh
my soul hadst thou not by some antecedent sin provoked
god to withdraw ? alas my spending so little time in secret
prayer, meditation, self-tryal, the day before, I fear had provoked god to leaue me so much to my self, and oh how
heartles was I in the worship of god that day, notwithstanding my pretended zeal and fervour alas it was but
forced and affected my spirit came not off freely to god or
for god : how easily may we deceiue others in maintaining
the husk and shell of worship, wn the kernel and marrow is
gone, David might offer sacrifice, pray sing &c all that 10
mouths under his guilt, and not be detected by others but
oh its one thing to doe the work, another to doe it kindly
and evangelically, oh methought, I worshipt afar off, god
stood at a distance, the spring was stopt my heart was dead,

distracted, I stroue but it would not be, no grace was excercised, the Lord stood even afar off from me, oh it was a
gloomy day, I visited sick and discoursed and prayd but alas
not as I was wont, my strength was departed from me, I
thought to shake my self, and goe forth as at other times,
but I wist not that god was gone, wondered wt was the
matter, at last, upon the 3d god opened my eyes, shewed
me the cause, laid sin, such particular sins with their aggravations upon my heart and conscience then I said I
would confesse my sin, and god forgaue the iniquity of
my sin, I hope so, my heart was broken, I was helped to lay
the stresse of my soul on Christ, reaching forth for his
blood, righteousnes for my justification, acceptance, and Oh
then god drew out my heart for his church, my body was
prostrate at his feet, my soul in bitternes god helpt my
heart in pleading for king, city, kingdom, congregations,
Lord hear help, pardon, and oh for a heart to be more
watchfull carefull, faithful for the future, oh that I might
know gods way and keep close to god in it, oh Lord prevent
my turning aside to the right hand or left, kill in me the
fear of man, kindle in me loue to soules, make me faithfull
to death, heal backslidings and prevent for future—

Experiment 21   On munday Nov 19 1683 I was at Halifax at the funeral of John Ingham, and when we were
sitting at dinner at Cock, Dr Hook spoke to Mr Wiltar of
Sowrby and Mr Sam : Maud, I am glad to see you two sit
so quietly togather that are such great Antagonists saying,
Mr Maud denys originall sin, Mr Maud sd he did so, the Dr
opposed him, and Mr Wiltar, and Mr Sunderland of Luddenden, and sometimes Mr Wood of Rippenden they all at
him grievously, the Dr called him an heretick (yet drunk to
him) askt him why he baptized his children, he sd to wash
away naturall pollution, Mr Sund— called him Quaker, there
was very high words, they played one upon another, broke
jests, I sate by and sd not one word, they were all in a heat,
the Dr told Mr Maud he would make an excellent Pres-
biterian preacher he was so full of zeal, he answered, some
Presb preachers are honest men, Mr H R replyed, how can
they be honest men that obey not the kings laws, I had set
a lock on my lips, and answered not a word, thinking of
David, psal 39 123 many absurd things were spoken and

some things, as I thought weakly about original sin, free-will, saving faith, and historical faith, yet I judged it then my duty to keep silence, and let them manage it that were so hasty to begin it, in such an inconvenient place and time: But since then I haue had many sad temptations that I haue betrayed the truth of god by my sinful silence, and these two last nights, I haue lyen waking, poring on that lost oppertunity of clearing the poor censured man, and the run-down truth, when as I had some distinctions that might haue helpt both, and I might haue sd I hope Mr Maud doth not dispute de re, but de modo, how original sin becomes ours, as to the thing, there is 1 peccatum originaus, in Adam, that I hope he denys not, but that Adam fell, 2 peccatum originatum, as conveyed some way to his posterity but how conveyed is the dispute whether 1 only by propaga-tion, or communication, as we are in the same nature, and so haue the same defects that he had as hereditary diseases, or 2 by imputation, and so the guilt of Adams first sin be-comes ours, as he had our stock in his hands, and was our representatiue which I conceiue is a truth, but I perceiue Mr Maud denys—I say had I mentioned these things, pos-sibly it might haue driven the controversy to some head, but I did not, but sate by as unconcerned:

REFLECTION   Lord, what a wretch am I! oh base creature that I am that had nothing to say for god and his truths! what was my tongue null for? where was my zeal for god? what was the reason, was it base cowardice or was it sullen-nes, because I was not in the company I loved? or was it inconsideratenes? for I confesse god brought not these things to my thoughts at that time till afterwards, and I thought I had better hold my peace then speak imperti-nently as some of them did, I cannot tell what was the reason but I haue deeply censured myself for it, Lord humble my heart, for vain speaking and sinfull silence, make me more serious considerate and zealous for truth for the future, giue thy servant the tongue of the Learned to know when to speak a word in season: awake my conscience that it may smite me for sins of omission, as well as com-mission, and let my reines instruct me in the night-season:

EXPERIMENT 22   Upon Tuesday Nov 27 83 I went a con-siderable journey about my Lords work, upon a call, up into a Wildernes-place, amongst the people of Crosse-stone, beyond Heptonstall, A. N. went along with me, the place we were ordered to goe to is called Stiperden, a vale amongst the moores in the road to Lanc— where there are but two houses, the one a poor house where I was to preach, one Nathaniel Sutliff, living alone, without wife or child or any but himself, when we came thither he bad us kindly welcome, saying, what would become of me if I should shut my doores agt Christ or his gospel? but he had little to entertain us with, only a woman had sent for two penyworth of ale, he made a tost of oat-bread, brought us butter on a trencher but had not another trencher, but wt had butter on, but we made a shift, I desired a blessing, we eat heartily of bread and butter, tost and ale, gaue god thanks, me-thoughts it was a savoury, satisfying supper, then I preacht on Jer 13 17 god sent abundance of people many miles, tho it was in the night and very dark and slippery, it did me good to see such willingnes, god affected my heart with poor ignorant soules sad condition in the want of powerfull preaching, I struggled with them in my Lords name 3 houres that night, till I was tired and very hoarse: the in-keeper there (one Will Foster, a Smith) took me and my companion to his house, made us a fire, lodged us lovingly, would take nothing for our selues or horses, were much affected, we took leaue, I prayd with them at parting, who can tell what good may be done? that shall be my pay, it pleaseth me that I had not one penny amongst them all but gaue the poor man a shilling, where I preacht, nor had I a farthing in Warley the night after where I also preacht, nor haue I had any collections at home these two quarters as formerly, god thinking good to excercise my faith with ordering the officers to come both times on the days of warning or collection:

REFLECTION. Oh my soul, what saist thou to this dispensation? dost thou make it kindly welcom? not an hair falls from thy head or a sparrow to the ground without a divine providence: dost thou willingly deny thyself in worldly things so thou mayst doe thy master some service? wt sayst thou? now thy dear Lord seems to put thee to't whether thou wilt be and act according to thy former vows and covenants that if the Lord will but make use of thee, and doe good by thee, thou dost not care what fare thou hast, or whether thou haue any reward from men, oh how often hath thy soul breathed out these and such like workings of heart to god, and now god will try thee whether thou be in good earnest: oh my soul, what dost thou say? art thou freely content to want as well as expound? hast thou learned Pauls lesson? lay thy hand upon thy heart, the heart-searching god knows whether thou hast done these things willingly or grudgingly, dost thou repent that thou didst not conform, when such fair offers were made thee at St Martins in York many yeares agoe when thou wast under violent prosecutions by the spiritual court? dost thou not envy them that liue in pomp and prosperity? and wish thy self in their condition? my soul shall answer, and upon good advise-ment write down this 3d of December 1683 aboue 21 yeares after our dolefull turning out of our publick station: that I am so well satisfyed in my refusing subscription and con-formity to the termes injoyned by law for the exercise of my publick ministry that notwithstanding all the taunts rebukes, and affronts I haue had from men, the weary travels many thousand miles, the hazardous meetings, plunderings, im-prisonings, exercises of faith and patience, about worldly subsistence, banishings from my own house, coming home with fear in the night &c which are the least part of my affliction under this dispensation, for banishing from my people, stopping my mouth, which hath occasioned many sad temptations, discouragements, lest god should be angry with me, lay me aside and make no use of me, which haue caused many sad thoughts, griefes, and searchings of heart: Notwithstanding all this, I am so fully satisfied in my conscience that my nonconformity as a minister, is the way of god, and I hauc so much peace in my spirit, that what I doe for the main is according to the word, that if I knew of all these troubles before-hand and were to begin again I would persist in this course to my dying day, and if god call me to it seal it with my blood, for to me conformity would be sinfull, and we must resist to death, striving agt sin:

EXPERIMENT 23   upon Thursday morning March 13 168¾ hauing promised to goe to preach at Jo: Armitages in Kirk-burton parish, on the Lords day before wn it was fair weather (hauing not been there of some years, nor such a

journey of several months) in the interim it fell a considerable snow, and was some frost, but yet because of my
promise I resolved to goe, and god helped me to commit my
self into his hands, I set out, found it very dangerous way
for it snow-balled on my horses feet, I resolved to call of Mr
Thorp at Hopton-hall, going towards his house, on the hill-
side northwards, being yielding ground, my horses feet being
balled, in a bare-place, all his feet slipt from under him,
and he came down on his side, and I lay along, I know not
how, the horse lying still, till I was got up, and when I
recollected my self, I perceived no hurt, only my thigh a
little stunn'd, but is now well: but the same day I had a
more wonderfull deliverance for going in the snow from Mr
Lockwoods of Blakehouse to J Armitages going down the
hill from Thurstiland to Lidiat, hauing no tract in the new
snow, I mist my way, and went down too soon, and so got
intangled in a wood, among bogs, and very dangerous pre-
cipices, I made towards the end of the wood where I knew
my way lay, but toyled hard, one while riding where I durst,
another while struggling and sweating a foot, till my breath
was spent, I stood still, and breathed and at it again, my
horse followed me, tho with great difficulty, it was moon-
light, at last I got to J A when I told him where I had been
he was much astonished, and wondred how I ever got quit,
and sd I did not know my danger, for that place is full of
pits, so that its called Sinking-hills,* by the inhabitants, he
sd that while I was in that hazzard he thought on me and
trembled in fear for me, and had met me, but that he despaired of my coming, because of the badnes of the weather,
I was still on a sweat, but got hot drink, fell to praying,
preaching to about 40 persons, on mat 6 88, went out after
half a mile near 12 a clock lodged at J R that night the
people gaue me 3sh—6d for my paines some 6d some 3d—I
was well content, blesse god for it:

And now, o my soul, what improuement dost thou make
of these various and gracious providences? our adversarys
envy us this paines, toyl, travel, this hazzard and danger
for our dear Lord and the good of sinners, they injoy their
fat Benefices, fair parsonages, and fruitfull glebe, they step
out of their houses into their churches and read their easy
service, and say their eloquent orations, and eat the fat and

* Still known as Sinking Wood.—J.H.T.

drink the sweet, are companions with Nobles, and gentlemen, peeres of the Realm, haue 1000 s [thousands] a year,
make laws for us, and yet think much at us for a poor liue-
lihood, and a little house-work, weeping and wrestling with
god and sinners to doe good, yet they call us makebaits,
schismatics, seditious and what not? exasperate magistrates
against us, punish, banish, imprison us, confiscate our goods,
excommunicate, censure us, and think and say we are not
worthy to liue, while we liue peacebly, pray for them, and
dare challenge them, if ever they found any fault in us saue
in the matters of our god, O Lord judge betwixt them and
us and plead the cause of thy servants and let the Lord be
with the good: In the mean time, o my soule, thou hast
great reason to admire the gracious providences of god, preventing and priviledging, in this especially, how desolate
and uninhabited were these places, both of them, especially
the latter! how long might I haue lyen, being alone, before
any had passed those ways, if I had been hurt I might haue
perisht before I had been found, and haue been a grief to
my friends and laughing-stock to mine enemys but my god
had mercy on me, sent his angels to bear me up in their
hands from hurts and sinking, let god haue the glory: may
but sinners be gained to god, I haue the reward of all my
travels, god will haue glory and I shall haue comfort, whatever becom of my body: in the mean time methinks I haue
satisfaction in the review of my paines—in the gospel, and
think this will afford me more comfort in after-times, then
all our church-mens worldly wealth, ease, honour, revenues
and grandure: let them take these, since they are their
choyce, I have my choyce, and though it be grievous to the
flesh yet the ease I haue in my owne conscience abundantly
countervailes it, and methinks our condition is somthing
like the Apostles, 1 cor 4 10 13: 1 6 9: 2 Cor 4 8—12: 6
8—10: 11 23 ad finem:

EXPERIMENT 24 Upon Tuesday night July 8 1684 J P[riest-
ley] brought me a post-letter, as soon as I saw it, I saw
that it was not my sons hand, I was struck with trembling
fearing bad news, opening it, I found it was from Mr
Streaton giuing me a long and sad account of my son Jo:
going away from the Lady Hatten, and the reason of it, viz
going with her to her son in law Stuarts (a great drinker)

near Cambr— he was made drunk, with severall aggravating circumstances— Oh how my heart trembled and my bones quivered! I could rest no where, but tossed to and fro, being overwhelmed with grief, but could not shed one tear, I went to my study and thought to ease my heart to god in prayer, but I could not pray, god withdrew, and I was full of confusion, distractions, there I tugged, struggled for aboue half an hour, yet was heartles, could not pray to any purpose in my family, oh what a condition was I in! at last I went to bed but slept not one wink of all night, but tossed and tumbled up and down, being weary I got up by 4 a clock, went to my study, read my chapters then prostrated my self on my face, god then graciously drew out my heart in justifying god, condemning my self, confessing my sin, accepting the punishmt of my sin, and taking delight in god, as my god, pleading with him for my poor prodigal son, and sion at severall times near 2 houres, oh what a morning was it! then I thought I was eased, went to family-prayer my study —and was pretty quiet, tho I had returns of sadnes:

REFLECTION Oh my soul, how comes it to passe that thou must haue such a sharp purge? alas, I fear my heart was filling! why hast thou such a loud alarums? alas thou wast in a dead sleep: nothing else would doe, or accomplish the end: nay this stupendous tidings did not work kindly, alas it amazed and amused my spirit, the blow did affright but not affect me, its sad very sad, that stupendous providences rather overwhelm my spirit then tender my heart, I may say of my self as Eliphaz to Job, behold thou hast instructed many, thou hast strengthened the weak hands thy words haue upholden him that was falling, thou hast strengthened the feeble knees, but now it is come upon thee, and thou faintest it approacheth thee and thou art troubled, is not this thy fear thy confidence, the uprightnes of thy ways and thy hope, Job 4 3 4 5 6—this is just my case: O my soul, how canst thou boast of thy grace, when thou canst not use it a pinch? nay how canst thou evidence the truth of thy grace when thou porest on thy troubles as though thou hadst neither god to take hold of, nor faith to lay hold of him by to stay thee from sinking? but this is my comfort, that in sudden, amazing surprizals grace may be there in the habit that yet is not drawn forth into act: in a swoon life seemes gone, but blessed be god, theres a rising again : the fire breakes out from under the ashes, when the spring comes the root buds forth, blessed be god, though a sudden blow stounded thee, yet divine grace helps to a recollection of spirits, though sorrow made sullen, and astonished me in the evening, yet gospel-sorrow the foundation of true joy came in the morning, after a tossing-night, god helpt me to cast anchor on himself in the day, the waters of Marah were bitter, the teares of repentance were sweet, oh how it eased my heart when I could freely pour out my soul to my dear Lord in a corner, I poured out my complaint before him, I shewed before him my trouble, when my spirit was overwhelmed within me, then thou knewest my path, thou knowest the way that I take, I cannot cast off my burden, it sticks on me and follows me, but I cast my burden on the Lord and he doth sustain me : blessed be free grace, I haue gone about my masters work with composednes that day, and laid me down at night and slept quietly for thou Lord makest me dwell in safety : But still I cannot but be troubled for the dishonour done to the name of my dear Lord, scandal to the gospel, opening the mouths of the wicked, saddening the hearts of gods children, and all by the son of my vows and hopes : alas what is his discredit or losse of prefermt, my grief or disappointment to this ? this is my daily excercise and returns upon me with an intollerable load, but since my dear Lord helps me to take his way for relief, I am not without hopes even this also shall turn to some good, who can tell but it may proue the further awaking of his conscience, deeper humbling of his soul, giuing him experience of the abominable treachery of his own heart, provoking him to more accurate search and diligent watchfulnes, and then making more use of him in his church, whereby my Lord can secure and advance his glory —Amen god hath answered

EXPERIMENT 25   At this time Dec 29 1684 I am under the heaviest circumstances as to my liberty of doing god service and good to soules that ever I was in, in all my life : men haue broken in upon us, and scattered our meeting,* indited me for a riot at the sessions I am bound in 100 li to

* The years 1683-5 were the years of severest trials and persecutions. I met with the record of Mr. Heywood's trial some years ago when searching the West Riding Sessions Rolls.

traverse, and to be of the good behaviour, my adversarys are watching me narrowly to find me breaking my bond, they have catcht W N, charged him to be witnes agt me, are laying wait for others, few dare own me, providences seem to make agt me, and that wch is the heaviest of all, it is an occasion of some difference betwixt me and my dear wife, for she being naturally timerous wn we are at any time aboue the number of 4 she is perplexed exceedingly tho it be not purposely but providentially, and wn I am to goe to preach abroad she is under great affrightments, particularly last night wn I went to W H, lest we should be too many and be discovered and truely my zeal for gods glory, and loue to soules, and desire to doe my masters work on one side, and endeared loue to my wife, feares of being censured for rashnes and indiscretion by prudent men, and making myself a prey to knaues on the other side, doe so rack and torture my spirit that it almost makes me weary of my life, and I am hard put to't am oft forced to contradict my wiues mind, to perform my promise, sometimes god helps me by prayer to roll myself on god, and then I am easy, but oh how oft am I at a losse!

REFLECTION Oh my soul, this is a strait a very great strait that providence hath cast me into, the hand of the Lord is gone out agt me in this thou o Lord hast proved me, thou hast tryed me as silver is tryed thou broughtest me into the net thou laidest affliction upon my loynes, thou hast caused men to ride over our heads, we haue gone through fire and water oh that I could also say, thou wilt bring us out into a wealthy (or spacious) place, that I may goe to thy house with burnt-offerings and pay thee my vows, wch my lips haue uttered in this my great trouble, how long shall thy church be thus sadly confused? Oh how long wilt thou hide thy face from me? how long shall I take councel in my soule hauing sorrow in my heart dayly? how long shall mine enemy be exalted over me? Oh how long shall these humane inuentions thrust out divine institutions? how long shall the hand of the Magistrate be stretched out agt thy poor ministers? how long shall beggarly wicked villaines be incouraged in their plotting and informing agt thy poor servants for their worshipping of thee? Oh my dear Lord, dost thou approue of these malicious and covetous practices of lewd men? art not thou of purer eyes than to behold iniquity? wherfore lookest thou upon them that deal treacherously and holdest thy tongue when the wicked devoureth the man that is more righteous than he? Lord hast thou no respect to thy servants? would not thy ministers gladly preach thy word and travel over poor sinners? and doe not our dear people long to haue their ancient pastours? doe not the nurses brests ake to be giuing suck, and the children cry for sincere milk of the word? doth it not run to the heart of this poor worm to hear poor creatures say when shall we come and hear you? they are desirous to come by day or by night and prudence or danger forbids us to entertain them, mine eyes doe fail with teares, my bowels are troubled, because the children swoon in the streets, and say to their mother where is corn? alas we goe to publick but get no good, some beat and abuse us, others haue such filthy hands as makes our stomacks rise agt that wch is otherwise good doctrin, wholsom meat, others deliver it so dryly, formally, that we are ready to fall asleep under ordinances: Alas our own shepherds pitty us not, and whither shall we goe for suitable and soul-nourishing pasture? and alas, our hearts ake to consider the perishing condition of thousands of precious soules, and the pining state of gracious hearts that are forced to liue upon old store the harvest truely is plenteous, and the labourers few, o thou Lord of the harvest, thrust in labourers, wm men haue thrust out this 22 yeares, Lord take away these troublous days or take us from them, if thou haue no more work for us to doe in this world, give thy servants a quietus est, by removing us to heaven, hide us in the graue untill thy wrath be past,—turn us unto thee, o Lord, and we shal be turned, Renew our days as of old

EXPERIMENT 26 Hauing made a long intervall of my Observing experiments I now return to them again: On Wednesday March 23 9½ my son Eliezer came home at   a clock afternoon that day we had a solemn work in hand of fasting and prayer, at my house, Joseph Lister was at prayer, pleaded with god warmly and familiarly an hour and half, then I put my son on the work, preacht &c when all was done, and we could talk freely, he told me the tragi-comedy of both their ilnes and recovery: my son El: had been in a feaver at Wallin-wels, yet had been blooded, had taken a vomit, purge, was recovered in a fortnights time, I never knew one syllable of it, till himself told me : my son John going with the High Sheriff to York Assizes, fell desperatly ill of Collick or griping, wch was very violent, but got ease by a 2d blister H L told me he was better, before I knew of his distemper : and his brother brings me word he had preacht the day before at Redford : O blessed be god for preventing mercy : that promise is verifyed to me Isai 65 24 before they call I will answer—my Lord provides a remedy before I know my malady : as he did for Adam : and claps on the plaister as soon as wound is made, blessed be the name of my prayer-hearing god :

EXPERIMENT 27   March 28 1692 I rode upon a call to preach at John Rhodes house in Howarth-town, god greatly helped my heart in weeping wrestling with god for the conversion of sinners, and in preaching on Isai 55 7—there was a great crowd of people they were very attentiue, who knows wt good may be done? the same day (being Easter-munday) the vicar of Bradford sat all day in an Ale house, gathering his dues in Howarth perish, theres wont always to be a Sermon in the church that day, but Mr Pemberton hath laid yt aside, many flockt to him to pay him Easter-reckonings, which come to about 10li, many of them came to hear me, I had nothing for my pains but yt 4 or 5 thrust me 6d a piece into my hand, I rid 14 miles forward and backward, was greatly comforted in my days work, thought it was far better then his : though my worldly gaine were short, yet may I but gain one soul to Christ by my hard labour, I haue the better of him : my soul rejoyceth in the god of my mercy : that hath set me upon the high imployment of moving sinners for Christ, made me faithfull, in some measure successfull, giues me oppertunity and an heart to be laying out my self for good : made me to chuse the laborious, painfull part of the ministry with persecution : rather then the honourable, easy, gainful part :

EXPERIMENT 28   I bethought myself of a method in praying, which the servants of god used in Longworth many yeares agoe, before I was born, it was my uncles, Nathan, Francis, Hugh, Ralph Critchlaw, my mothers brothers that with severall others spent evenings in prayer, my dear friend

Luke Hoyl was with them, it was this, one took the part of prayer of confession of sin, another took petition for mercys, a third thanksgiving, and thus they spent their hour or therabouts, I resolved to take the same method in my morning and evening devotions in my chamber, and begun Nov 1 1699 with confession, then with supplication, on Friday night Nov 3 my heart was wonderfully drawn out in thanksgiving in reckoning up my many mercys, personall, domesticall, congregationall, nationall, oh it was a sweet savoury time, a corner of heaven I find this way very beneficiall to contract my thoughts to one sort of subject wheras my thoughts otherwise were roving and scattered, this ingageth my heart to be more intent and solemn in prayer, Nov 6 I set my self adorning to mention in my thoughts the nature and transcendent excellency, and perfections of god, that I might be weighted with a due sense of the object I worshipt and give him glory—

—::—

On Prayer.

["An Essay in the handwriting of Oliver Heywood, R. Slate." This short MS. was lent me by G. H. Adshead, Esq., J.H.T.]

My soul hauing been so often helped to pray and seek god with some more then ordinary importunity in several cases and haue received such remarkeable returns of Answers to my poor prayers, both as to personal, domestical, Ecclesiastical, and national accounts, this morning, Jan 7 168¾ I am moved to consider, and answer this case of conscience for my own satisfaction and promoting of thankfulnes, viz :

When doth god Answer his peoples prayers! or how shall I know that the mercys in this book or elsewhere enumerated doe come in as an Answer to my prayers! The answer to this case, I shall rank under these 4 heads

    1   The state and disposition of the person praying.

    2   The meanes and manner of bringing about the mercy prayed for.

3 The season and time wherein the mercy is bestowed.

4 The effects and fruits which the mercy leaues upon the heart, life:

1 I know or may scripturally guesse that such and such a mercy comes in Answer to prayer, by the state and disposition of the person praying: and that either 1 habitually or 2 actually.

1 habitually, if I be not a convert, a child of god, a reall saint in a state of grace I cannot expect that god should in mercy and in a covenant way hear my prayer, the poor blind man cured could say Joh. 9. 31. now we know that god heareth not sinners: but if any man be a worshipper of god [a god-fearing person   ] and doth his will, him heareth pro. 29. the Lord is far from the wicked, but heareth the prayer of the righteous. so v. 8 if I can clear it to mine conscience that I haue a relation to Christ that I am within the covenant, that I haue the holy spirit of god to be a spirit of adoption to help me to cry Abba, father, I think I can also evidence that god heares my prayer for the Lord takes speciall notice of and Christ doth graciously intercede for every child in his family Rom. 8. 26. 27: this for the main I haue elsewhere and otherways cleared up to mine own soul and can, through grace comfortably say, that I am one of god's children:

2 for Actuall, dispositions for hearing prayer I doe verily beleeue that god puts his children into a praying frame, and a receiving disposition when he intends them a mercy. psal. 10 17 Lord thou hast heard the desire of the humble thou wilt prepare their heart (or establish) thou wilt cause thine ear to hear, and when I haue found these actual dispositions working within me they haue been presages of Answers and I haue observed there hath seldom been a failure of return.

1 When god hath furnished me with strong pleas, motiues, Arguments in prayer, and withal hath giuen me the spirit of grace and supplication to manage and make use of them: Zech. 12 10: not to moue god but affect mine own heart as that disposition to which the promises belong, thus god bids us take with you words Hos. 14. 2. Job will order his cause—fill his mouth with Arguments ch 23. 4. David had found it in his heart to pray a prayer, 2 Sam. 7. 27. Oh how oft hath god given me materials for prayer,

and I am not ashamed to own it though in this ridiculing day, men scorn it, when I knew not what to pray for as I ought, the spirit hath suggested matter and words in prayer, and manner composing my spirit, and putting it into a praying frame, bowing my will, inlightening my mind quickening my affections, inlarged my desires after the mercy caused a restlesnes of spirit till I haue poured out my soul to god. Rom. 8. 26.

2 When god hath knit my heart to himself in the duty and raised my soul to high expectations from him : not only of the injoyment of the mercy desired but of god himself as better then the mercy the very marrow and quintescence of the good thing desired to delight myself in the Lord and then I haue my desires psal. 37. 4. I haue sometimes been drawn out with greater importunitys from discouraging hinderances wch. I take as a sure token of good successe Luk 11 5-9 18·1—8 Mat 15 . 22——28 when though I would submit to god for manner, time and other circumstances, yet could not giue over the suit for the thing however for God his spirit grace lovingkindnes : methinks my heart hath run with Davids psal 69 13—18.

3 When my heart is quieted and satisfyed upon performance of the duty This hath been oft my case when I haue come and laid my load and burden of cares and feares on god and been eased much refreshed as Hanna 1 Sam. 1. 18. my anxiousnes and sollicitude of spirit hath been removed, my mind pacifyed, and my soul secretly persuaded that god will giue me the mercy or something as good, and quiet my heart in the want of it which is all one—For I had my errand for the main god had welcomed me into his presence, for when I cryed he said here I am, Isai. 58. 9. and hauing found god I had my end, and referred it to him, what he would doe with me further for I said with David psal 6. 9. the Lord hath heard my supplication the Lord will receiue my prayer, and therefore charged my heart cheerfully to wait on god psal. 27- 14 for he had done much in easing my heart and bearing up my fainting spirit. psal. 55. 22. phi. 4. 6. however I had got well by him already and something in hand for a pawn.

4 When upon the performance of the duty, god hath immediately directed to, assisted and succeeded in the use of lawfull meanes for the obtaining of the mercy thus god

directed Jacob, and vouchsafed his blessing to the meanes:
Gen. 32 9—13 24: c 33 2—13 thus Hezekiah, 2 Kin 20
2—7: praying without probable meanes used is but a
tempting of god, council from heaven, and successe of
meanes is a token for good of god's answers especially when
prayers help against sinfull shifts and the soul desires no
other answers but such as are consistent with god's faithfulnes in the performance of promises psal 143. 1. when I can
truely say I haue discarded all sin and regard not iniquity
in my heart, I may groundedly say god heares my prayers.
psal 66. 18. 19 as sin allowed enervates my prayers. so
desires after holines is a pledg of gods audience and acceptance: Job. 27. 8. 9: 11. 13. 14. 15.   Neh. 1. 11.   When
my heart is as cordiall in pleading with god for holines and
against sin as for deliverance and agt. judgments, I think
its a return of prayer:

2. The next sign and token of return of prayer is in some
characters ingraven visibly upon the mercy granted or in
the manner of its coming to us: these are 4

1   When the mercy prayed for is brought to our hands
through many difficultys and oppositions: so when god
gaue Abraham a son aboue the power of nature, gen 15. 2.
17. 17. Rom 4. 17. thus it was in David's case psal 18 6—
16 and Peter's Act. 12. 5. 10 sometimes it appears that
none but god could bring about such things: as in Esther's
days ch 4. 3—16: ch. 5. 2. 3: 8. 11. 50: Ezra 8. 21. 23:
Neh. 4. 9. 6. 16.

2   When god facilitates the means of affecting it when
there is such a blessed conjunction and concurrence of all
circumstances falling in unexpectedly as appears to proceed
from a peculiar hand of providence thus in Israels deliverance out of Egypt they cryed Exod. 2. 23 god sent Moses,
Aaron, at last inclined pharaoh & the people to thrust them
out ch. 12. 39. god gaue them favour ch. 11. 3. yea not a
dog moved his tongue, ver. 7 though in the dead of the
night: so in Neh. 2. 4. 6: thus it was with Eliezer Abraham's servant, there was a remarkable conspiring of circumstances to further the return of his prayer, just as he
prayed as if he prescribed to god how it must be brought
about: Gen. 24. 12. 15. 27. 42 3.   When theres more put
into the Answer, then was in the prayer: its a ceartain sign
prayer is well answered when god giues in additionall

mercys beyond what we could ask or think, according to Eph. 3. 20. thus Solomon asked wisdom god gaue him more even riches and honour 1 Kin. 3. 9—13 the mercy prayed for comes not alone but bearing double god puts in a Moreover a furthermore 1 chron. 17. 10 : god always giues good measure he asked life of thee and thou gavst it him, even length of days for ever and ever thou preventest him with thy blessings of goodnes : psal. 21. 3. 4.

4 When god dips the mercy in covenant-loue, and thereby giues it a delicate rellish and also makes that mercy the first-fruits of a further harvest psal. 86. 17 : shew me a token for good, sometimes one mercy proues preparatory and introductory to more that hang, as it were, upon the same string of covenant, loue, as Rom. 8. 32. he that spareth not his own son— how shall he not with him also freely giue all things : thus if he giue to faith and repentance, he will also giue pardon and heaven : yea sometimes even in outward things, he that gaue Hanna a Samuel asked of god, gaue her also more children : 1 Sam. 1. 27 : 2. 20. 21 :

3. The third thing whereby I am secretly supported and comfortably satisfied that such and such mercys are returns of prayer is from the circumstance of time : the timing of mercy carries a great emphasis with it as :

1 When the mercy comes unexpectedly,—when persons haue been long praying and were almost hopeles, yet the mercy comes, then they are as persons in a dream psal. 126. 1. 2 and thus both the first and second coming of the son of man was sudden when scarce faith of it was found on earth Mat. 3. 1 : Luk. 18. 8 : yet its never out of season but in an acceptable time haue I heard thee sth. god, Isa 49. 8 :

2 When gods children are brought to the greatest pinch and extremity, as a woman in pangs, can hold out no longer, in the mount of the Lord, it shall be seen gen. 22. 14. so it was with the Jews in Ægipt and in Esther's days : just at the nick of time psal. 142. 3. so Jonah 2. 4—10 gods children are lost before they are found, Valley of Achor is a door of hope Hos. 2. 15.

3. When their hearts are carryed out to god with greatest importunity, when zeal transports their hearts in vehement wrestlings and god giues in the mercy just at that time they

may be sure it comes as a return of prayer, Isai. 65 24. while they are yet speaking I will hear : so Dan. 9. 20 : and those for peter Act. 12 5—12.

4. When the hearts of gods children are laid low under the sense of their own unworthines : look on themselves as dust, ashes, gen. 18. 27 : lesse than least mercy gen. 32. 10 : when they justify god in all the evils they feel, fear Ezra. 9. 6. 13 : take shame to themselues giue glory to god when gods servants lye in Zions dust. She is raised out of the dust psal. 102. 13. 14. god waits for such a time when he shall be most exalted Isai. 30. 18. that is, when men are most humbled Isai. 2. 11. 17: 5. 15. 16: god stays purposely for such a day and frame as that is, for then lusts are mortifyed grace excercised and the heart subdued to be at gods disposal.

4. I haue some comfortable guesse that these mercys are in Answer to my poor prayers by the effects they haue upon my heart when gods grace doth work kindly therwith its a good sign in these respects 1 When they draw the heart nearer to god, endear the thoughts of god to the soul makes us loue him more : yea ingage our hearts to approaches to him psal. 116 1 2—7 : 18 . 1 . 3 . 6 : psal. 4. 1.

2. When they ingage the heart to rejoyce more in god then in the mercy the giver then in the gift, and by the stream the soul is led up to the fountain, so did Hanna 1 Sam 21. my heart rejoyceth in the Lord my soul doth magnify the Lord Luk. 1. 46. 47.

3. When the soul is more set at a distance from sin sinful companys, ways, psal. 6. 8. Depart from me all ye workers of iniquity for the Lord hath heard the voyce of my weeping I haue better company then you god heares me. see psal. 85. 7. 8

4. When the soul pays its vows to god Job. 22. 27. thou shalt make thy prayer he shall hear thee thou shalt pay thy vows thus did Jacob gen. 35. 3 David psal. 66. 13. 14. psal. 116. 14. 18:

5. When the soul makes a new deed of gift in dedicating itself to god in token of thankfulnes psal. 116. 16 studys to be suitable in lip, life, frame of spirit c. 12. 17. ingaging the soul in reckoning up mercys, blessing god psal. 103. 1. 2. 3.

6 When the Christian is quite taken off all conceits of his own merit or worthines and puts all upon the score of free-grace and the intercession of Jesus Christ. psal. 115. 1. not unto us, O Lord, not unto us—our righteousnesses are as filthy rags Isai. 64. 1—6: our advocate only prevailed 1 Joh. 2. 1. 2.

7. When the soul desires to perpetuate gods praises, and thereby to propagate Religion, prayer, and piety, therefore tells what great things god hath done psal. 66. 16: sets up a memorial 1 Sam 7. 12 : psal 34. 2—6 oh that others would doe as I haue done that they may speed as I haue sped psal. 32. 6.

8. When the soul is strengthened in its faith for future answers of prayer so David psal 86. 5—7, thou wilt answer me psal. 27. 9. 14. David can sing the same song of confidence in the caue and upon the throne psal. 57. compared with psal. 108. see both see psal. 6. 9.

9 When togather with the mercy god giues composednes of heart, and assurance of his loue to the Christian psal. 3. 4. 5. he heard me out of his holy hill—I laid me down and slept—this return of prayer carries its own evidence along with it Joh. 16. 24. ask—that your joy may be full.

10. When fire comes along with the answer of prayer, as it was wont to doe of old in token of acceptance, as to Elijah 1 Kin. 18. 37. 38. to Solomon, David, 1 Chron. 21. 26. and such a blessed descent of the Holy Ghost was on the apostles Acts 2. 1. 2. so when the quickening influences of the spirit animate soules and raise them aboue themselues in an holy flame for god and zeal for his glory and promoting of his own ends, its a good evidence of mercys coming in mercy and as returns of prayer psal. 80. 18. 19.

Something through grace my soul can say to all these, in some measure of sincerity aiming at an higher degree in all and haue great cause to bewail my short-comings.

obj. 1 but how can such unworthy creatures expect, or imagin that when a mercy comes, it comes as answer of prayer? who are we? what can we doe to procure it?

Ans just nothing in strictnes of justice psal. 143. 1. 2: But there is a gospel way opened to the throne of grace, through cht the mediator, wherein god hath promised to sincere petitioners a gracious answer, in many scriptures:

and though we must deny ourselves, yet we must own gods faithfulnes in performing his promises see Lam. 3 55—58

obj. 2. How can such a guilty sinner as I am think that god heares my prayers, that haue so much pride passion, distraction deadnes to marre my prayers!

Ans. Elias was a man subject to like passions, as we are, yet he prayed, and prevailed Jam. 5. 17. 18. his passions did not totally invalidate his prayers for these sins bewailed, hated, resisted, and the soul-acting faith on clit. shall be pardon'd psal. 65. 2. 3. o thou that hearest prayer. Alas saith the church or soul, whats that to me a sinning wretch, Mark the answer, As for our transgressions thou shalt purge them away.

obj. 3. But doth not god require faith in order to his answering of prayers, and doth not want of faith exclude hearing Jam. 1. 6. 7. and didst thou not in some cases want faith ?

Ans. theres a two-fold faith. 1. a persuasion of gods power and faithfulnes, that he is able to answer and will also answer me if I pray aright, and the thing be for my good, it is this faith James speaks of: and this is a fundamental article of our Religion and qualification in prayer Heb. 11. 6. without this I can expect no audience, but through grace, I hope god hath helpt me to this faith : 2. a particular persuasion that god will doe this thing for me or bestow this mercy on me. This I confesse I haue sometimes wanted yet in this god hath oft out-done my faith and hopes, and given me the answer of my prayers, notwithstanding my defects in faith yea contrary to my hopes thus I find he did with David psal. 31. 22. I said in my hast I am cut off. Nevertheles thou heardest psal 116. 2. 11 : thus god doth beyond our askings, Eph. 3. 22 :

obj. 4. But haue not others with thee begg'd for the same mercy that thou hast begg'd what reason hast thou then to think that its a return of thy prayer.

Ans. I know through divine grace, my prayers haue been answered tho' others haue joyned by those good tokens

1. When god hath stirred up in my heart the excercise of those heavenly graces, and holy affections, that others haue or to which the mercy is promised when theres a sympathy in motions harmony in designs when I agree with them, Mat. 18. 19. the same spirit unites affections makes the

musick, Lot and Abraham prayed but god heard Abr. gen. 19. 29.

2 When god fills my heart with joy in the accomplishmt. of the mercy prayed for and can truely be thankful for the mercy tho it concern others, or the publick so did the church praying for the King. psal. 20. 1—5: so did old Simeon Luk. 2. 29: so did paul for them 1 Thes. 3. 6. 7. 9.

3. When my own concern is swallowed up in the publick and I can almost forget my personal affairs to remember Zion then I espouse it aboue my chiefest joy psal. 137. 6. yea when I am heartily glad of and pray for others joy as if it were mine own psal. 35. 27.

4. When if it be mine owne concern thus comes a peculiar accent and Emphasis to myself in speciall upon the receit of the mercy and its a prevention of the wickeds insulting over me psal 88. 16. this I know god is for me psal. 56. 9. there a banner to them that loue him psal. 60. 4. 5: a peculiar heritage as to such as fear god. psal. 61. 5. more fresh peculiar discoverys of interest in god psal. 28. 6. 7. 8. see phi. 1. 19 see a difficult text psal. 81. 7.

But may not a child of god pray and scarce ever know that god doth answer prayer? and what shall a soul doe in that case?

Ans. 1. Yes but most ordinarily it may be so that the poor soul takes not notice of gods answers, either through negligence in advertency we lose many observable returns for want of observation or through bitternes of soul when gods hand lyes very heavy still on us this was their case Exod 6. 9. Job. 16: or through mean conceits of ourselues, and services. &c,

2. god may really deny to answer the prayers of his people psal. 80. 4. Lam. 3. 8. either when they ask things hurtful and he sees its not for their good, or when they have offended him, and turns away his ear as their punishment pro. 1. 24. 28. Jer. 7. 16: 11. 24: zech. 7. 13. what must a soul doe in that case.

1 Examine our faults, the sins that thus provoke god to shut out our prayers 1 Sam. 14. 37:

2 Examin our prayers, whether they were put up right or no, Jam. 4. 1. 2. Zech 7. 1. 5. doe as the fisher with his angle, take it up, examine the bait, and hook.

3. pray more fervantly, fall to it with greater importunity, possibly thou wast too slack Isai. 64. 7. adde crys to
your prayers:—yea fasting. judg. 20. 26:

4. Reform whats amisse take away the matter of provo-
cation, stone the Achan Josh. 7. 10. 11: so did they judg.
10. 14. 16.

5. Justify god and condemne thyself if he deny thee,
take heed of challenging god: tell god you deserue to be
denyed, Dan. 9. 7. 9. 13.

6. Use all meanes for the obtaining of the mercy prayed
for, thus the church in Cant. 3. 1. 3. 4. else we doe but
tempt god.

7. Rightly interpret gods answers we are apt to mistake
them gods denyals in one thing, may be made up in a better
as in David's child. 2 Sam. 12. 16. 24. 25: study psal. 65. 5:
99. 8: gen 17. 18. 19.

8. Take thankfully any beginnings of Answer though we
may not haue all, god goes far in yielding to satisfy saints
desires, when he doth not all as to Abraham, gen. 18. 24.
32, oh make much of any thing.

9. Beleeue and be persuaded god heares tho' we caunot
at present feel it, yet if it be according to gods will we may
be sure the prayer is filed up and shall be accepted and
answered in due time 1 Joh 5. 14. 15.

10. Wait on god psal 40. 1. its fit we should tarry god's
time, tho he come not in ours, Hab. 2. 3. Heb. 10. 36. 37.
its not in vain to wait on him Lam. 3. 25. 26. 27. he will
pay for waiting Isai. 30. 18.

11. pray still faint not in the work Luk. 18. 1. 7. god
loues to be honoured, with due attendance psal. 130. 5. 6. 7:
let nothing daunt, as that poor woman, Mat. 22. 28. Heb.
12. 12. Isai 62. 1. 7: Rom. 12. 12.

12. Acquiesce fully in gods disposeal, let the Lord use
his pleasure, and doe as he sees good, 2 Sam. 15. 29. let us
quiet our hearts in gods good pleasure, so David and Christ
psal 22. 2. 3. take answers tho in the negatiue freely,
quietly, not sturdily—

It becomes gods children, not to be too peremptory   in
temporals but still conditionall if god see it good,—petulant
froward children must be crossed in their desires till
they be bowed to a due subjection to gods pleasure: Thus
much I think a gracious soul may truely say that he never

found his heart kindly drawn out for a mercy but god gaue it him, or somthing æquivalent which made a good woman say, she never askt anything of god, but he gaue it her : it was objected that such a child dyed, yea sd. she, but I never found my heart carryed out so for that childs life as in many other cases :

and obserue it if god put us to't to wait long under many repulses for a mercy its usually a double mercy when it comes as Isaac to Abraham, Joseph to Rachel, Samuel to Hanna, a Sampson to Manoah, John to Elizabeth, and many others :—

study these scriptures, Isai. 45. 19: psal 73. 28: 2 chron 30. 27: Act. 10. 4:

—::—

Mr. Heywood's Imprisonment.

I discovered the following some years ago (page 346*n*,) amongst the Sessions Rolls :—

At the Wakefield Sessions, January, 1684.

"Whereas Oliver Heywood of North Owram stands Indicted for a ryott, rout and an unlawful assemblie upon wch there is judgmt agt him & a fine of 50 li is imposed upon him wch sd sum being demanded upon him in open Cort hee hath refused to pay ye same These are therefore in his Majties name to will and require you to receive into yor Goale ye body of ye said Oliver Heywood and him safely keepe untill hee shall pay ye fine aboue sd And bee from thence delivered by due course of law, fail not as you will answer ye contrary, dated at ye sd sessions as above." See *Nonconformity in Idle and History of Airedale College, p.* 23.

—::—

Biblical Note Book.

This little pocket-book bears the autograph of " R. Astley," and, in Mr. Heywood's writing—

" Bought at Halifax of francis Bently stationer there Jan. 15. 1676, cost 6d.

    begun March 1, 7⁵ gathered scriptures.
    begun March 1677 gathering threatenings
    begun March 1, 1678 gathering promises
    begun to write the texts March 1. 1679.

Directions how to read the bible over in a year by dayly proportions :

    March 1.   Genesis 1. 2. 3.
     ,,   2.   ,,   4. 5. 6. 7."

and so on.

This book contains thousands of texts, mostly copied in full, classified under hundreds of minor heads.

One head runs—Scriptures that in reading I found hard to be understood, and would gladly be resolved in the meaning therof :

Gen. 4. 13. 14. 15 to Rev. 14. 20, nearly one hundred texts.

" Scriptures that shew me how I must behave myself towards the church of god, reall saints, in ordinances, conferences :

" Miscellanys, not reduced to any particular head, but worthy to be read oft and remembered "

    " Threatenings against Hypocrites "

    " Threatenings against Drunkards "

An index to Subjects is given.

In this volume is a tolerably complete textual analysis, and discovers the vast biblical learning and industry of Mr. Oliver Heywood. The last page gives a list of " Texts presented to me "—

    A. N. ps. 50. 15.
    J. W. act. 5. 31
    For Schollers at N. [atland ?] 2 chron. 29. 11.
    M. R. Heb. 4. 15.

Conventicle Notice.

The following is a copy of the folio fly sheet, issued to all Constables in the West Riding, announcing the suppression of Conventicles. An original sheet is in my possession.— J. H. T.

West Rid. } _ff._   _Ad General Sessionem pac'. Domini Regis tent'._
Com. Ebor }   _apud_ Doncaster, _per Adjournum in & pro_ _Le_ Westrid'. _Com predict._ Decimo Septimo _die_ January, _Anno Regni Domini Nostri_ Caroli _Secundi dei gratia_ Angliæ, Scotiæ, Franciæ, & Hibarniæ, _Regis fidei Defensor &c._ Tricesimo Tertio, _Coram_ Joh: Boynton _Mil'._, Thoma Yarbrough & Jasper Blythman, _Aris. Justir paces ibm._

WHEREAS His Majesty hath been pleased to express his resolution that the Justices of the Peace, of the severall Countyes within this His Kingdom of _England_ should use their utmost indeavours to suppress all Conventicles, and unlawfull meetings under Colour or Pretence, of any exercize of Religion in other manner, then according to the Liturgy and practice of the Church of _England_. It is this day ordered by this Court, in obedience to His Majesties said Resolution. That the Laws for the suppressing such meetings and Conventicles be put in due Execution and that the Justices of Peace use their vtmost indeavours to suppress all Conventicles, and unlawfull meetings, upon pretence of such Religious worship within this County. And to the end this good work may be effectually performed. It is further Ordered that a Warrant be made, and directed to the Constables, Headboroughs, Church wardings, and Overseers of the Poor, of every Parish and precinct within this Ryding, Comanding them, and every of them within their Parishes, Divissions and Limitts, that they and every of them do make a diligent enquiry of all such Conventicles, and unlawfull meetings in their several Parishes and Precincts. And that they do

take the Christian-name, Sir-name, and place of abode of
every person, that hath Preached, or Teached in any such
meeting within a month last past, or shall Preach, or Teach,
in any such meeting, at any time before the next quarter
Sessions of the Peace, to be holden for this Ryding, and
also the Christian-name and Sir-name, with the addicions
of the most considerable persons that frequent such Conventicles or meetings, and of such as wittingly, or willingly,
suffer any such Conventicles, meeting or unlawfull assembly
in his, or her house, out house, or Barne, and on the first
day of the said Sessions they do make a true Returne in
writeing of the Preachers, or Teachers in such Conventicles
and meetings, and of the most considerable persons that
wittingly or willingly suffer any such Conventicle in his, or
her house. Together with the day of the Month when and
the place where such Conventicles, or Meetings were held,
and that the respective Officers or some of them do prove
the same upon oath, to the end every such Preacher in such
Conventicles and unlawfull meetings, and such other persons as aforesaid may be convicted, according to Law.
And to the Intent this Order may be put in effectuall Execution. Its further Ordered that the respective high
Constables, do personally deliver the said warrant to the
person of some, or one of those Officers, to whom it is
directed, that he may make Oath of the personall delivery
thereof, and that he attend the first day of the said Sessions,
to give an Accompt thereof.

Pro Curiam.

INDEX OF SURNAMES.

Ratcliffe, 138, 194, 206
Rathband, 68
Raundsley, 205
Rawson, 162
Rawden, 67
Ray, 54
Reiner, 75, 102
Richardson, 69, 119 pass, 121, 123, 138, 161, 174 bis
Riddlesden, 69
Rich, 55, 57, 71
Rigg, 75
Rhodes, Rodes, 55, 56, 66, 68, 69, 70, 71, 72, 76 bis, 128, 138, 157, 180, 349
Rimer, 76
Roberts, 6, 16, 53, 54, 67, 72
Robinson, 51, 52, 53, 54, 65, 66, 68, 69, 71 bis, 72, 75 pass, 168, 207
Roebuck, 51, 54, 57, 66 bis, 70, 120
Rookby, 56, 57, 95
Rooks, 204
Root, 52, 70, 72, 109, 118, 130, 131, 179, 201
Roscoe, 67 pass
Rostorn, 89
Rothwell, 17, 56
Rotherham, 300
Rushworth, 51, 54, 56, 66, 69, 70, 88, 166, 171, 179
Russel, 52, 67, 70, 75, 93
Ryland, 9
Ryley, 75
S. J., 274
S. S., 208
S. W., 213
Sagar, 66, 76
Sale, 67, 75, 76
Saltonstall, 72
Sandel, 102
Savil, 100, 170, 194
Sawry, 96
Saxton, 56
Shackston, 57
Scarborough, 55
Scolefield, 54, 56, 68, 72, 188 bis, 197, 333
Scill, 165
Scolecroft, 17, 76
Scott, 55, 67, 76, 211
Scurr, 70

Seddon, 67
Seargeant, 55, 76, 307
Sharp, 52, 55, 56, 67, 68, 69, 75, 77, 93, 94, 106, 122, 145, 153, 173, 302, 333
Shaw, 57, 75
Shippon, 194
Shrigley, 95
Shelmenden, 98
Shuttleworth, 195
Simpson, 66, 71, 75, 147, 159
Slate, 9, 16, 350
Slater, 73, 170
Skelton, 69
Smallwood, 17
Smith, 51 bis, 52, 57 pass, 66 pass, 68 pass, 69 pass, 70 bis, 71 pass, 72 pass, 89, 102, 131 bis, 135, 136, 145, 151, 174, 177, 202, 214, 275
Sowden, 186
Sotwel, 51, 71
Sonier, Soynier, 53, 54, 57, 66, 174, 276
Spencer, 51, 54, 55, 56, 69, 193, 201
Spurstow, 213
Squire, 56
Stanhope, 76
Stanford, 51, 67
Standen, 10
Stancliffe, 52, 65, 70, 73, 132, 163, 166, 174
Stanley, 52, 67, 70
Stansfield, 53, 55, 57, 72, 73, 75, 76, 137, 146, 301
Starkey, 170
Stead, 55, 76 bis, 147, 207
Stephenson, 52, 139
Stocks, 54, 57 bis, 76, 285
Stot, 53, 54, 57 bis, 150
Stoppart, 98
Stones, 194, 195
Strong, 212
Strangeways, 67
Stretton, 56, 176, 275, 344
Stuart, 344
Sutcliffe, 131, 341
Sugden, 204, 301
Sunderland, 206, 339
Swain, 53, 72, 75
Swyft, 75

INDEX LOCORUM.

THREE WEEKS' TRIP TO FRANCE AND
   SWITZERLAND.   Post 8vo., 100 pp.   Published
   1864.   (F. Pitman.)..............................*(Out of Print.)*

   Do.   Do.   *Second Edition.*   Crown 8vo.
   Published 1865.   (W. H. Smith & Son.)..............   Do.

A YORKSHIREMAN'S TRIP TO ROME.   Post 8vo.
   200 pp.   Published 1866.   (Longmans.)..............   Do.

RAMBLES ABOUT MORLEY.   Crown 8vo.   Illustrated.
   200 pp.   Published 1886.   (J. R. Smith.)..............   Do.

HISTORY AND ANTIQUITIES OF MORLEY.   Demy
   8vo.   Illustrated.   300 pp.   Published 1876.   (Longmans.)...   Do.

OLD YORKSHIRE.   Vols. I., II., III., and IV., 1881-3.
   Demy 8vo.   Profusely Illustrated.   320 pp. each.   Pub-   s.   d.
   lished Yearly in October.   (Longmans)   Per Vol.   7   6

   Do.   Do.   Demy 4to. ....   ,, ...   15   0

Sold to Subscribers at the following Prices :—

   Demy 8vo. ....   ,, ...   5   0

   Demy 4to. ....   ,, ...   10   6

. Complete Sets of "OLD YORKSHIRE," Vols. I. to
   IV., Carriage Free, for.............................   25   0

———— o ————

MR. WM. SMITH,

  Osborne House,

    Morley, near Leeds.

Local Books,

By J. HORSFALL TURNER.

HAWORTH, PAST AND PRESENT: A History of Haworth, Stanbury, and Oxenhope. 20 Illustrations. 3s.

> "Mr. J. Horsfall Turner has here given us a delightful little history of a place which will always have an interest for the student of English literature. We have not space to deal with it as lengthily as it deserves, but we can say that all should read it who care to know anything of the little village made memorable by the Brontës' fame. It may be obtained of the author, Idel, Bradford, and is ridiculously cheap."—*Graphic*, Jan. 31, 1880.

NONCONFORMIST REGISTER of Births, Marriages, and Deaths, 1644-1750, by the Revs. O. Heywood and T. Dickenson, from the MS. in the Congregational Memorial Hall, London, comprehending numerous notices of Puritans and Anti-Puritans in Yorkshire, Lancashire, Cheshire, London, &c., with Lists of Popish Recusants, Quakers, &c. Five Illustrations, 380 pages, 6s.

THE REV. O. HEYWOOD, B.A., 1630-1702: His Autobiography, Diaries, Anecdote and Event Books, illustrating the General and Family History of Yorkshire and Lancashire. Four volumes, 380 pages each, illustrated, bound in cloth, 6s. each.

> A partial idea of their genealogical and historical interest may be formed from the "Lives" of Heywood, by Dr. Fawcett, Rev. R. Slate, and Rev Joseph Hunter, F.S.A.

INDEPENDENCY AT BRIGHOUSE: Pastors and People, 4 Illustrations. 3s.

NONCONFORMITY IN IDEL, AND HISTORY OF AIREDALE COLLEGE, 10 Illustrations, (autotype portraits of Rev. J. Dawson, Founder of Low Moor Ironworks; Rev. W. Vint S.T.P.), &c. 3s.

WITH CHAPTERS ON

PREHISTORIC REMAINS, By JOHN HOLMES,

GEOLOGY, - - - By J. W. DAVIS, F.G.S., F.S.A., F.L.S., ETC.

BOTANY, - - - By F. ARNOLD LEES, F.L.S., ETC., and

FAUNA, - - - By W. EAGLE CLARKE, W. DENISON ROEBUCK, and J. W. TAYLOR.

BY kind permission of W. MYDDELTON, Esq., the vast and hitherto unexplored Muniments at Myddelton Lodge have been laid under contribution, as also the Parish Registers, by leave of the Vicar.

The stories are told of the British LLECAN, Roman OLICANA, Teutonic Ilkley, Austby, Nessfield, Stubham, Middleton. and Wheatley; the Dapifers and De Kymes, Percies and Plumptons, Myddeltons and Fairfaxes, Hebers and Longfellows; the Church and its Vicars, the Castle and Halls, Grammar School and Bridge; the Doles, Customs, and Folk Lore; the palatial Ben Rhydding and Ilkley Hydropathic Establishment, with the Modern History, mainly narrated in Dr. Collyer's unique style, and illustrated by beautiful engravings, by Mr. Sabin, of New York, and others.

The names of the writers of the special chapters are sufficient guarantee to ensure a full, original, and sparkling history of a place rich in Archæological remains, and a favourite field of the Naturalist.

MAPS, PLANS, STEEL AND OTHER ENGRAVINGS.

Biographia Halifaxiensis: A Biographical and Genealogical History for Halifax Parish. Two volumes, 880 pages, with Portraits, 6s. each.

> Vol. I. is a reprint of half of Mr. Watson's "Halifax," that is, such chapters as the Halifax Worthies, Vicars, Benefactors, &c. This volume thus serves a double purpose, as it is a literatim reprint.

> Vol. II. will be an original compilation, noting the Families and Worthies for six hundred years.

Life of Captain John Hodgson, 1640-88. Illustrated, 1s. 3d.

> This is a reprint of the 1806 publication, said to have been edited by Sir Walter Scott. The Captain narrates his exploits in the Wars at Bradford, Leeds, Lancashire, Isle of Man, Scotland, &c., and the troubles that followed on his settlement at Coley Hall, near Halifax, his imprisonment in York Castle, &c.

The Antiquities of Halifax: By the Rev. Thomas Wright, A Literatim Reprint. 1s. 6d.

> I have no sympathy with that form of Bibliomania that hoards up a book because it is scarce. Wright's "Halifax" is here offered for one-twelfth the selling price of the 1738 volume.

Ready for the press :—

The Bridges of W. R. Yorkshire: Their Histories and Mysteries. By the late Fairless Barber, Esq., F.S.A., and J. Horsfall Turner.

*** P.O. Orders payable at Idel, near Bradford.